Love Me Through the Grief

A White River Romance (Book One)

J.S. Tazwell

Love Me Through the Grief © 2025 J.S. Tazwell

Published by J.S. Tazwell Books

Edited by Derek Moreland

ISBN (Paperback): 979-8-9991468-1-6

ISBN (Hardcover): 979-8-9991468-0-9

LCCN: 2025911736

ASIN: B0D2NRWNCK

Printed in the United States of America.

Cover and interior design by Jessica Senesac

Typeset and formatted using Atticus

www.jstazwell.com

For rights or media inquiries: j.s.tazwell@gmail.com

Trigger Warnings

Love Me Through the Grief contains themes and depictions that may be distressing to some readers. This novel explores grief, complex family dynamics, emotional trauma, and the aftermath of sexual assault (S.A.), including manipulation, gaslighting, and the long-term impact of abuse. It also includes references to remembered homophobic hate crimes, alcohol use, PTSD, and emotionally intense situations involving loss and mourning.

While this story is ultimately about healing, love, and reclaiming one's voice, readers are encouraged to prioritize their mental and emotional well-being. If you are in a vulnerable place, please proceed with care or seek support as needed.

You are not alone. You are worthy of love and healing—always.

With warmth,

J.S. Tazwell

If you or someone you love is struggling, here are a few resources you can reach out to:

RAINN (Rape, Abuse & Incest National Network) – 24/7 Confidential Support 1-800-656-HOPE (4673) | www.rainn.org

GriefShare – Support groups and resources for grief www.griefshare.org

The Trevor Project – Crisis support for LGBTQ+ youth 1-866-488-7386 | Text START to 678-678 | www.thetrevorproject.org

Dedication

For my father, Tracy. I can hear you laughing already at how embarrassed I'd be if you ever read the steamy parts of this love story. Thanking you for shining down on me throughout the entire process of writing this story. Grieving you has been one of the hardest things I've ever had to do. I love and miss you, my "Favorite Dad".

CHAPTER ONE

Never Alone

LUCY

D eath.

It's the part of life I'd like to pretend only exists in movies, books, the news… You know, the whole "it won't happen to me, not my family" mentality. But it's hard as hell to avoid when you get that one phone call that changes everything. The kind of call that leaves you breathless, blood pounding in your ears—

The moment you realize—

It *happened*.

To you.

To your family.

The plane braked hard as it touched down, jolting me forward in my seat. Anxiety had gnawed at me throughout the draining ten-hour flight—so much that I hadn't even realized we were about to land. The moment the cabin lights flickered on, I switched my phone off airplane mode and checked for a Lyft.

A voicemail from my Aunt Diane lit up my lock screen.

Then—

Everything went black.

My chest tightened as I gripped my shirt. A silent sob tore through me. Thankfully, no one seemed to notice. And thank God I was sitting alone in my own row.

"I'm so sorry."

Those were the last words that registered before a high-pitched ringing filled my ears, drowning out the voicemail.

Yes.

A *fucking* voicemail.

That was how I learned I was too late to say goodbye.

As the plane taxied toward the gate, I was only vaguely aware of the Highwood Mountains standing silhouetted in the distance. I clasped a hand over my mouth, squeezing my eyes shut. I was alone, surrounded by strangers, and my father—my dad—was dead.

Emptiness washed over me, raw and unrelenting. I couldn't feel him anymore. His spirit didn't wrap around me in comfort. I reached out with my heart, my mind—

But there was *nothing*.

My hands trembled as my jaw quivered uncontrollably. The seatbelt sign dinged off, and passengers shot to their feet, rushing to deplane as if each had somewhere critical to be.

I had *nowhere* to be.

I hadn't even gotten to say *goodbye*.

I shoved the thought down, forcing myself into stoic stillness. I waved others ahead of me, unable to focus on what came next. What was I even doing here instead of in my flat in London?

It was pointless.

All. Fucking. *Pointless*.

I buried the rage bubbling inside. Swallowed the ceaseless thoughts of *if only...* I had to keep it together. I didn't want the attention. Especially not from a stranger.

Besides, saying it aloud would make it real.

And this *couldn't* be real.

I grabbed my carry-on from the overhead compartment and shuffled down the aisle. Forcing a smile at the flight attendant, I barely registered her cheerful goodbye.

My feet moved on autopilot.

I needed a minute to gather myself.

But where?

I found the nearest restroom.

Splashing icy water on my face, I whispered, "Get it together. You can break down once you're safe at home." I paused, gripping the sink.

"Home? Really, Lucy?" My voice cracked as I swallowed the lump forming in my throat.

I hadn't been *home* in over six years. The word felt foreign. *Hollow.*

I took a slow, steadying breath.

You've survived worse. A few hours in baggage claim won't kill you.

The cold water stung my face as I splashed it over my skin again, grounding myself in the sensation. I gripped the edge of the sink, meeting my own reflection in the mirror.

"Okay. Grab your suitcase, get a Lyft, and then you can lose it behind closed doors."

My chest tightened at the thought of going to the ranch—

To *his* house.

Where every inch of space carried a memory.

My voice came out hoarse. "A hotel," I decided. "You can get a hotel."

Squaring my shoulders, I turned and headed for baggage claim.

Bing. Ping. Bing.

Buzz. Buzz. Buzz.

Notifications flooded my phone. Scrolling to silence them, I froze. My name was tagged in a post—

Two hours old.

"Fuck," I gasped, dread tightening my chest.

Everyone knew.

My dad had passed away while I clung to hope at 35,000 feet, thinking I'd see him...

One. Last. Time.

Panic set in.

My breaths came in short, shallow bursts—too fast, too loud.

Heat flushed my face as I gasped for air.

My vision blurred as the edges of the terminal seemed to close in. The world spun around me, my legs trembling beneath the weight of grief and shock.

Then—

Warm arms wrapped around me, pulling me into a broad chest. I froze. My body tensed on instinct.

But then, a familiar scent hit me: fresh hay, sweat, warm earth, and a hint of masculine cologne.

Something old.

Something safe.

A low, honeyed voice broke through the noise. "I'm so sorry, Lucy. I'm here. I've got you."

My breath caught.

No. It couldn't be.

I turned, easing back just enough to see him.

Bright blue eyes.

A cowboy hat.

Five o'clock shadow.

My heart stopped.

"Connor?"

He nodded, his voice richer, deeper than I remembered. "Yeah, it's me."

Seeing him again knocked the air from my lungs in a way I wasn't prepared for. But this wasn't the same boy I pined over six years ago. He wasn't just my best friend's older brother anymore. No. That boy was gone. In his place stood a *man*—taller, broader, with a jawline sharpened by time and a quiet intensity in his eyes that hadn't been there when I'd left. His worn jeans and plaid shirt were dusted with the grit of ranch life, and the brim of his hat cast a shadow over a gaze that still somehow felt like home.

He looked like everything I'd run from and everything I didn't know I still missed.

"How—why are you here?" I took a step back, crossing my arms like a shield.

"Your Aunt Diane sent me your itinerary." His voice sounded calm, matter-of-fact.

I scoffed, brows furrowing. "Oh God. Why would she think this was your responsibility? I'm so sorry."

He swallowed hard. "I manage the ranch. She didn't send me, exactly—just passed along your flight info. I thought... if you landed and found out alone—"

Tears welled in his eyes. The sight nearly undid me.

My chest burned, heart racing with something old and too tangled to name. "You came for me?"

His grip on me tightened. "Of course I did. Lucy, we've known each other most of our lives. I thought—hell, I thought I might have to tell you myself, but—"

"The whole fucking world already knows," I bit out.

"I'm so sorry, Luce." His voice cracked, rough with restrained grief.

My shoulders shook, sobs breaking free. For the first time since landing, I didn't care who saw. Connor's large hand stroked my back as he pulled me close again.

I closed my eyes, sinking into his embrace. The unfamiliar warmth of safety enveloped me, and I allowed the feeling to wash over me.

I wasn't alone.

Thank *God*, I wasn't alone.

CHAPTER TWO

Where He's Not

LUCY

I didn't know how I'd ended up in his truck, but I was buckled into the passenger seat of *Connor Lochland's* pickup. The cab smelled of stale coffee, soil, and a long day's work. His hand rested over mine, pulling me back into awareness. The glow of headlights momentarily illuminated us in pale, white light before casting us back into the inky blackness of a winding country road.

"Diane left me a voicemail." My voice cracked through the silence, brittle and raw.

Connor's thumb brushed over my knuckles, unwavering and patient, waiting for me to continue.

"Why? So I'd know the second I landed?" My voice shook, my breath coming in uneven gasps. "She couldn't wait a few hours to tell me in person? Or—I don't know—at least hold off on posting his death all over social media?"

I ran a hand through my hair, my pulse hammering. "Jesus." My throat tightened, the pressure unbearable. "Sorry. It's just so..."

"Fucked up?" he offered gently, his grip on my hand steady.

I nodded, tears welling up again. "Exactly."

The knot in my chest eased slightly at his validation. His quiet understanding filled the cab, cushioning my anger and grief.

"I can't imagine finding out like that," he murmured, the sorrow and empathy lacing his words too much for me to unravel.

I stared out the window into the passing darkness, unable to absorb the star-lit Montana night, my thoughts tangled in grief too raw to appreciate its beauty.

"You know the worst part? I tried to get here sooner. Diane booked me this stupid flight because it was *cheaper*. I was buying my own ticket—with my *own* money—and I would've been here last week. But no, she heard I was booking a flight and stopped me mid-checkout."

Connor winced, his jaw tightening.

"I missed him every day, you know," I whispered. "He video chatted with me three times a week, even though he was so awful at it. I spent half the time looking at his chin, the other half up his nose."

A choked laugh escaped me.

"I should have come back sooner. It's just... I got into a good college, and things felt—*harder...*"

My voice trailed off. When I spoke again, it was steadier, quieter.

"Oh God, so many excuses." I let out another bitter laugh, but it sounded hollow even to me. "At least he visited me a couple times—*twice.*"

My throat tightened. "Maybe it was hard to get away from the ranch... or maybe he just didn't want to be so close to my mother. I don't know..."

A sob ripped through me before I could stop it.

"God, I hate everyone." My jaw quivered as another wave of emotion threatened to pull me under.

I exhaled sharply, trying to rein myself in. "Well, not you. And not *everyone*, I guess."

"Why *did* your mom take you to London that summer?" Connor's brow furrowed, his focus on the winding road ahead. "I always wondered. Your dad never would say. Sam was radio silent."

Sam.

His name left a pang of longing in my chest. While Sam was Connor's brother, he was also *my* best friend. And I missed him. More than I missed White River itself.

"Honestly? I've been trying to figure that out myself." My jaw tightened. "If you ask her, she claims a 'close friend' of mine told her I thought I *might* be pregnant. Which is ridiculous. I only have one close friend, and Sam sure as hell wouldn't lie about me like that."

But deep down, I had a sneaking suspicion I knew who would. Amanda Johnson. Head cheerleader. Mayor's daughter. My worst enemy. My fingers curled into fists.

"Whatever my mother was told, it gave her the perfect excuse to take me away. And no matter how many times I told her it wasn't true, she never believed me."

Connor exhaled sharply, massaging the crease between his brows before gripping the wheel again. "Christ, Lucy. I'm so sorry."

"It's fine. It is what it is." I let my head fall back against the seat, exhaustion creeping in.

After a few minutes, I breathed, "Thank you."

"What for?" he mused, his voice low and smooth—like smoky whiskey.

"For coming for me," I whispered.

"Of course." He cleared his throat, shifting in his seat, then added, "Always."

"I'm serious." A sad smile tugged at my lips. "We haven't spoken to or seen each other in six years. I'm no one at this point. You didn't have to come, but you did. So... *thank you.*"

"Lucy," Connor growled, his tone carrying an edge of frustration. "You've *never* been 'no one' to me. Not ever."

His words slammed into the very center of my soul, cutting straight through to old wounds that haven't healed. I struggled to hold back fresh tears. I focused on breathing, counting slowly.

It didn't work.

The ache in my chest deepened.

For six years, I'd felt like no one. And maybe, in some ways, I'd made sure of that. I was broken when I moved to London, and when most of my friends and family in White River didn't reach out... I acted out, made all the wrong choices, and fell into a pattern of letting in all the wrong people.

Connor reached for my hand again, his firm grip pulling me from my thoughts. "Listen to me. This pain... it doesn't go away. But it does get easier to bear. Eventually, you'll let yourself feel happiness again. Until then, I'm here. I've got you."

My eyes flew open, startled by the certainty in his voice—the weight of his words, the quiet understanding beneath them.

He'd lost someone.

And I'd been gone so long, hiding myself away from updates back home, that I hadn't even known.

"What happened?" I asked, my heart thumping wildly.

He hesitated, his gaze fixed ahead on the road.

"I lost a friend a couple of years ago. Drunk driver. You never met him, but he was a good man."

I squeezed his hand, my chest tightening. "I'm so sorry."

"Me too."

The weight of his words settled over us, thick and heavy.

Then we pulled onto the long dirt driveway leading up to the ranch, the surrounding trees casting shadows in the moonlight. My stomach churned as my old home came into view.

I straightened in my seat. "You brought me to the ranch."

"Yeah, is something wrong?"

I shook my head, forcing a small smile. "No, it's nothing."

I swallowed, taking in the house. The light fixture beside the front door cast a warm glow over the wraparound porch of the single-story home. Details were hard to see in the darkness, but it almost felt... frozen in time.

"It looks exactly how I remember it." I exhaled, my words barely a whisper.

"It's one of my favorite places in the whole world," he said, a soft smile playing at his lips as he threw the truck into park.

I fumbled around, searching for my carry-on when the truck door opened.

"Thanks," I breathed as Connor held out a hand to help me down. His grip was steady, and for a moment, his unwavering touch anchored me to the earth.

Every step up the porch stairs became heavier than the last. My grip on Connor's arm tightened, as if bracing for a fall as he unlocked the front door.

I closed my eyes as a rush of frigid air hit my face. A soft, single laugh escaped me—somewhere between elation and devastation. My dad had always loved keeping the house at freezing temperatures.

Before my thoughts could linger too long and the pain too unbearable, the sound of scrambling paws on hardwood greeted us. My heart twisted as I dropped to my knees.

"Buddy!" I cried.

The yellow lab bounded toward me, tail wagging furiously.

"It's so good to see you too! I missed you so much." Tears pricked my eyes as I buried my face in his fur.

Connor's warm voice lifted, touched by the sight. "Where do you want these?" He nodded toward the luggage.

Buddy, now recognizing Connor's presence, circled his legs, tail wagging furiously, like a wind-up toy finally set loose.

"I can get them," I replied, wiping my face.

"Nope. I've got it. Your old room it is," he insisted.

Some things never changed. Connor Lochland, king of quiet stubbornness.

I sighed but let him go, taking in the familiar room around me. It looked the same, yet without my dad's booming voice filling the space, it all felt so... *different*.

To the right was the living room, still furnished with early 2000s décor. A wooden bar sat behind the back of the worn leather couch, and a sliding glass door opened out to the back of the house.

To the left, the dining area was dominated by the eight-foot solid wood table my father had built by hand, complete with matching chairs. Parallel to it sat the kitchen, separated by a breakfast bar lined with rustic stools.

I sank onto the sofa, Buddy never leaving my side as he settled beside me.

The house smelled like him—like Dad. Leather, wood, and the faintest trace of coffee and bourbon.

It was comforting and suffocating all at once.

Connor lingered near the door. "If you need anything, I'll be just across the driveway in the trailer."

"Could you stay?" My voice cracked. "I don't think I can be alone in here. Without him, it's... it's too much."

His expression softened, and he nodded.

"Can I get you a drink?" He offered a faint smile. "I could use one myself."

Relief flooded through me. "Please."

Connor moved behind me to the bar, pouring two generous glasses of whiskey. He returned, handing me one before settling on the opposite end of the couch.

"To Robert," I said, raising my glass. My voice broke on his name. "The best dad a girl could ask for."

"To Bob," Connor echoed, his voice low and reverent. "A great man, mentor, and friend."

The clink of our glasses was soft, almost sacred. The smoky burn of the whiskey spread warmth through my chest, easing some of the tightness that had taken root there. I prayed it would carry me away, even if only for a little while.

We sat in silence for a moment, the whiskey working its way through the edges of my grief. Connor's presence was solid, his quiet strength filling the space without pushing.

"You know," I began, my voice hoarse, "I was planning on getting a hotel tonight."

Connor turned his head slightly, the warm glow of the lamp casting soft shadows across his face. His blue eyes met mine. "I can still take you, if you want."

"No, no." I waved him off. "Being here—with Buddy, with you—it feels... right. Like I'm where I'm supposed to be."

My throat tightened. "As much as it hurts, it's still home."

A small smile tugged at the corner of his mouth. "Well, I'm glad you're here. I don't particularly want to be alone tonight either."

My chest tightened at his words, and I took another sip of whiskey, letting the burn chase away the ache.

Connor leaned back against the couch, his posture relaxed, but his gaze thoughtful.

"You know, your dad used to talk about you all the time. He'd always find a way to bring you up. I lost count of how many times he told me about the time you won first place in that statewide riding competition."

I let out a small laugh, the memory bittersweet. "Oh my gosh—honestly, I only won because the girl who always got first place had a sprained ankle that day."

Connor chuckled, the sound low and warm. "He said you practiced every day for weeks leading up to that competition. He was proud of you, Lucy."

I blinked back tears, biting my lip to keep my emotions in check. "Yeah... I guess he was. Even over the little stuff. I swear he thought I could do no wrong."

Connor smirked. "Sounds about right."

"It was nice, but also a lot of pressure. I hated the thought of disappointing him. Still do."

I knocked back the rest of my drink, the whiskey going down smoother now.

"There's so much he doesn't—*didn't* know about me..." My throat tightened as I swallowed, guilt and self-loathing knotting in my core.

Connor leaned forward, his gaze locking onto mine. "There's nothing you could do to change his opinion of you, Lucy. *Nothing.*"

Warmth spread through my cheeks, the edges of my sorrow blurring. "Thanks."

"It's true," Connor leaned forward, resting his elbows over his knees. "You know... he was like a second father to me."

I smiled and nodded weakly, setting my empty glass on the coffee table.

Connor watched me for a moment, emotions I couldn't place flickering in his gaze. Then he stood, turning to look down at me with impossible gentleness. "How about some water before bed? You've had a long day, and that whiskey's not exactly hydrating."

I nodded, my eyelids feeling heavier now. "Yeah, that's probably a good idea."

He disappeared into the kitchen and returned with a glass of water, handing it to me before settling back on the couch.

"Do you remember when we were kids, and Sam dared you to climb the hayloft?" I asked suddenly, the memory bubbling up through the haze of grief and alcohol.

Connor laughed, his eyes crinkling at the corners. "Yeah, and you were the one who ended up climbing it because I chickened out."

I grinned, the memory warming me. "You were so scared of heights, and Sam gave you so much crap I thought you were going to throw a hay bale at him."

"I should've," Connor said with mock indignation.

We both laughed, the sound filling the quiet house.

For a moment, it felt like old times—like we weren't two adults navigating grief and responsibility but kids sharing stories in the barn.

Connor stood, setting his glass on the counter. "Come on, Luce. Let's get you to bed."

I yawned, letting him pull me to my feet. "I'm not tired," I mumbled, even as I leaned into him for balance.

"No, you're not. You're exhausted," he countered, guiding me down the hall to my old room.

The moment we stepped inside, the scent of aged wood and faded lavender hit me, and I froze. The room was exactly as I'd left it—horse posters on the walls, ribbons from riding competitions hanging neatly by the vanity, and the quilt my grandmother crocheted for me draped over the bed.

Connor's hand was gentle as he ran soothing strokes down my arm. "You okay?"

I swallowed hard, nodding. "Yeah. It's just... being here is like stepping back in time."

He gave me a small smile. "Love the One Direction poster you have over there."

"Shut it." I turned and swatted him.

The rumbling of his laughter in his chest made my breath hitch.

"Connor... thank you. For all of this."

"Luce, you don't have to keep thanking me," he said, his voice cracking with grief and exhaustion. "Now, get some rest, okay?"

He turned to leave, but I caught his hand, holding him back as panic settled in my chest. "Would you mind staying—just until I fall asleep?"

His blue eyes searched mine for a moment before he nodded. "Of course."

Connor sat on the edge of the bed as I curled up under the quilt. Buddy hopped up beside me and curled up on the corner of the bed.

Connor's presence was comforting, the weight of his hand resting lightly on mine. It was the permission I needed to let sleep pull me under.

CHAPTER THREE

Tangled Roots

LUCY

The morning sun stabbed through the thin curtains, illuminating the dust motes swirling in the air. My eyes cracked open, wincing at the brightness. My head throbbed, a dull, persistent reminder of the whiskey Connor and I had shared the night before.

I groaned, kicking the quilt off and sitting up slowly.

Buddy bounded onto the bed, tail wagging. He nuzzled into me, his warm, familiar presence easing some of the weight pressing on me.

"Okay, okay, I'm up," I muttered, scratching behind his ears. "You're lucky you're cute."

Sliding out of bed, I shuffled to the bathroom, every step heavy with exhaustion from a long night of tossing and turning. The mirror reflected a face I barely recognized—puffy, hazel-green eyes rimmed with dark shadows, and dyed auburn hair that looked as chaotic as I felt. A modern shag haircut had seemed like a fun idea at the time, but with my naturally straight hair in the front and wavy curls in the back, my hair was the visual embodiment of my disheveled state.

I splashed cold water onto my face, the icy shock sending goosebumps prickling over my skin. But even that sharp sensation wasn't enough to shake the grief and restlessness that clung to me, heavy and unyielding, like a second skin.

Anxiety twisted in my chest as flashes of last night's nightmares played in my mind—scenes I couldn't escape. My brain, cruel and obsessive, had started filling in the gaps about the hospital—the things I wasn't there to see.

What did my father look like on the ventilator? Who was in the room when his heart stopped? Did they even try to save him, or was it already too late?

These questions swirled on, relentless, their weight pressing on me even in sleep.

My dreams had taken those intrusive thoughts and twisted them into something grotesque... turning my father into a figure I barely recognized. Swollen features, skin bloated and unnaturally soft. It wasn't him, not really, but my mind told me it was.

Those images wouldn't leave me, their ugliness etched into my memory like a scar.

Maybe it was the alcohol. God, I hoped it was the alcohol. Because if it wasn't, I didn't know how I'd survive another night of it.

I wasn't sure *anyone* could.

As I brushed my teeth, I blinked away the painful images and allowed comforting ones to take their place.

Memories of the previous night drifted back—Connor sitting on the edge of the bed, his hand resting on mine, his quiet presence offering a support and solace I hadn't realized I needed.

Out of nowhere, a faint flutter of old, familiar butterflies stirred in my chest. I frowned, shaking off the wildly inappropriate sensation.

This had to be my grief talking, searching for any escape from the heartbreak sitting like a bag of bricks on my chest. Or maybe it was nothing more than the lingering remnants of a childhood crush.

Dressed in a pair of well-worn jeans and a baby-powder-pink sweater with an elastic hem that hugged my thighs, I headed to the kitchen. The rich aroma of coffee and sizzling bacon wrapped around me, coaxing my stomach to rumble in anticipation. Connor stood at the stove, flipping pancakes with an easy confidence. In the soft morning light, his broad shoulders and relaxed posture struck a comforting contrast to the heavy ache that lingered in my chest.

"Morning," I said, my voice still scratchy from sleep.

A glance at my phone showed three missed calls from Mom. I swiped the notifications away without hesitation—whatever she wanted, I wasn't ready to hear it.

He turned, a warm smile lighting up his face. "Morning, sunshine. Coffee's on the counter. You sleep okay?"

I poured myself a cup, letting the warmth seep into my hands before taking a cautious sip. The bitterness calmed me. "I think so, all things considered." My voice softened as I added, "You can cook?"

"Of course," he said simply, turning back to the stove. "I figured you could use a good breakfast. Hope you're hungry."

I nodded, sliding onto a stool at the breakfast bar. "Starving, thanks."

He set a plate in front of me, piled high with pancakes, bacon, and scrambled eggs. I dug in, the warm buttery flavors comforting in a way I hadn't expected.

"This is amazing," I said between bites.

He chuckled, his blue eyes crinkling at the corners. "Thanks. Glad you like it."

"Who knew." I started to laugh, but the moment was interrupted by the buzz of my phone on the counter.

A notification lit the screen, and my eyes rolled.

"What is it?" Connor asked, a hint of wary anxiety creeping into his tone.

I scoffed. "Nothing. My mother commented on Diane's post from yesterday. It's just... ridiculous. She ignored his existence while he was alive, and now she's so devastated and sorry he's gone."

A fresh wave of pain swept over me, squeezing my chest.

Connor's hand was on my back in an instant, his touch inviting and steady. "I'm sorry, Lucy. Is she doing okay otherwise?"

I let out a bitter laugh. "Oh yeah. She's living her best life. My dad's child support gave her the boost she needed to start her own business. Now she's running one of the hottest fashion lines in London. It's *gross*, how *good* she's doing."

Connor tilted his head, curiosity and concern etched into his features. "Gross?" he asked gently.

I sighed, the sound heavy with years of resentment. "I guess I just mean she got what she wanted—money and fame. Everyone loves her, but no one knows how she really got her start."

"Maybe she just wanted to create an even better life for you?" Connor suggested. His voice carrying a heartbreaking innocence that tugged at my defenses.

I shook my head, the ache of old wounds surfacing. "I wish that were true. I barely saw her. To her, I was just a paycheck."

A sharp pang hit my chest. I winced. "Sorry. Too early in the morning for all that. Let's talk about something else."

"No worries," he said, the corners of his mouth lifting in an easy grin. "Let's see what the weather's like this week."

He chuckled at his own attempt to change the subject, the sound pulling me back from the edge of my darker thoughts.

We ate in companionable silence for a while, the clinking of utensils and Buddy's occasional tail thumps filling the space between us. As the plates emptied, my thoughts drifted back to my father and the long day that lay ahead.

"So, what's the plan for today?" I asked, pushing my plate aside.

Connor leaned back against the counter, crossing his arms. "I thought we'd start with the animals. They'll need feeding and checking. After that, we can take a look around the property, see what needs done."

I nodded. "Sounds good. Just one problem."

His brow furrowed. "What's that?"

"I don't have boots," I admitted, heat creeping up my neck. "I didn't exactly pack for ranch work."

Connor's lips twitched into a grin. "Figures. You've gone full London on me."

"Hey!" I protested, but he raised a hand to stop me.

"Kidding!" He glanced toward the hallway. "Check your old room. Maybe you left a pair behind."

I hurried back to my closet, sliding the door open to reveal a dusty pair of brown boots. A wave of relief washed over me as I pulled them out and slipped them on. They still fit, though they felt stiff from years of neglect.

"Found some!" I called, bouncing back into the kitchen.

Connor's grin widened. "Good. Let's get to work, then."

The morning passed in a blur of activity. We started at the stables, adding fresh hay to the stalls and checking the horses. Daisy, my old palomino show horse, greeted me with a soft whinny, nuzzling my neck like we'd never spent a day apart. Tears pricked my eyes as I stroked her mane, the familiar rhythm of her breaths grounding me.

"She's missed you," Connor said, his voice gentle.

"I've missed her too," I whispered, pressing my forehead to Daisy's.

After finishing with the horses, we moved on to the goats, chickens, and finally cattle. The physical work was a welcome distraction, the ache in my heart easing with every task completed. By the time we returned to the house for lunch, I was covered in dirt and sweat. But at least I felt lighter than I had in days.

Lunch was simple: sandwiches and iced tea on the porch. The sun was warm on my face, the breeze carrying the familiar scents of hay and earth. Connor leaned back in his chair, his hat tipped low over his eyes.

"You're good at this," he said, breaking the silence.

"At what?"

"Ranch work. It's like you never left."

I smiled, picking at the crust of my sandwich. "It feels good to be back. *Hard*, but good."

He nodded, his gaze thoughtful. "Your dad would be proud."

The words hit me harder than I expected, and I blinked quickly to keep the tears at bay. "Thanks, Connor. That means a lot."

We sat in comfortable silence, the weight of grief a little less heavy in the warmth of the afternoon sun.

A soft breeze ruffled my hair as I sipped the last of my tea. For a brief moment, I felt... okay. Not whole. Not healed. But like maybe I could breathe again.

I glanced sideways at Connor, who leaned back in his chair, his hat low over his eyes. A slow comfort had settled between us—unspoken and easy. I smiled at the sight.

Suddenly, I was sixteen again, staring at the boy whose lopsided grin gave me butterflies. The boy who stood up for me, always held open the door when I was near, and was annoyingly right all the time.

But good moments like this? They never last.

My head whipped toward the crunch of tires on gravel as a sleek white SUV pulled into the driveway. My stomach twisted as the driver's door opened, revealing a pair of long, tanned legs... followed by the all-too-familiar figure of Amanda Johnson.

Shock. Pure, unadulterated shock.

My chest tightened, a slow burn igniting in my ribcage. I hadn't seen her in years, yet here she was, sauntering up my father's driveway like she *belonged* here. My jaw locked.

What the hell is she doing here?

She wore tight jean shorts, cowboy boots that looked brand new, and a white blouse that probably cost more than my monthly rent in London. Her honey-blonde hair fell in perfectly styled waves over her shoulders. She adjusted her oversized sunglasses as she swept her gaze over me like she was appraising a long-forgotten relic.

"Lucy," she called, her voice syrupy sweet. "Welcome home. We've missed you around here."

I blinked, unable to formulate a response.

Connor stiffened beside me, his easy demeanor replaced by a wary edge. "Amanda. What brings you by?"

I stood, forcing a polite smile, holding my breath and waiting for her toxic reply.

"I heard Lucy was back in town," she said, ascending the porch steps with practiced grace. Her tone was warm, her movements methodical.

Too methodical.

"I wanted to stop by and offer my condolences." Amanda turned to me, her expression the picture of concern. "Your father was such a wonderful man."

My throat tightened. "Thank you."

Amanda and *sincerity* had never been close friends.

Her gaze drifted to Connor, lingering just long enough that something in my gut twisted.

Her smile widened as she stepped closer, trailing a manicured fingernail down his arm. Slow. Purposeful.

"Connor," she purred. The way she said his name made my stomach churn. "It's good to see you again."

Connor stiffened. His shoulders squared, but he didn't immediately pull away. "You too."

His response sent ice coursing through my veins.

She bit her lip, giving him a seductive, knowing wink. "I miss you."

He swallowed. Paused. His expression unreadable. "Right. Was there anything else you wanted to say? We've got to get back to work."

Amanda arched a brow. She was testing him. And she knew I knew it.

After a beat, she turned back to me, flashing a saccharine-sweet smile. "If there's anything you need, Lucy, don't hesitate to ask. I'd love to help out in any way I can."

I forced my lips into a smile that didn't reach my eyes. "Oh, I'm sure."

Her eyes gleamed—she was enjoying this.

"Well," she said, feigning innocence. "I'll let you get back to your day. I'm sure we'll be seeing more of each other."

"Hopefully not," I replied flatly.

Amanda gave a light, airy laugh, as if I'd just said something adorable. "Oh, Lucy. Don't be like that. We're all adults now."

Right.

My fists tightened at my sides as she turned and sauntered away, each step deliberate, controlled. She didn't look back. She didn't have to.

My stomach churned. I stood frozen, the phantom weight of her presence still pressing down on me. All the years of humiliation, the whispered lies, the way she turned people against me—it rose like bile in my throat.

I should've said more. I should've told her off. But I was too stunned, too angry, too afraid I'd unravel in front of Connor if I did.

The second her SUV disappeared from view, I exhaled. Sharp. Shaky. "How dare she come here. After everything she's done."

Connor turned to me, his brow furrowed. "What do you mean?"

I let out a bitter laugh. "Seriously?" I searched his face and found only confusion. My anger wavered for half a second, giving way to something colder. "Wait... Sam never told you?"

His frown deepened. "No..."

The knot in my stomach tightened. "She tormented us our whole lives," I said, my voice low, measured. "There were so many times she pitted our friends against us. She made our lives hell. And now she just shows up to 'offer her condolences'?" I let out a sharp breath. "This is a power play, and I can't stand her for it."

Connor's expression shifted, his brows pulling together. "That... doesn't add up."

I stiffened. "What?"

His voice was careful. Too careful. "There must be some misunderstanding. She was... *devastated* after you left."

My mind blanked.

I shook my head, a sharp, disbelieving laugh escaping me. "Misunderstanding?" My voice wavered between incredulity and something closer to betrayal. "Connor, just call Sam. Ask *him* about Amanda."

I stepped back, the sudden weight of the conversation pressing against my ribs. "I don't have the energy to explain, and it's not worth my sanity to relive it."

He opened his mouth, hesitated.

I turned away before I could see his expression change.

Maybe I was overreacting. But I couldn't control it. Not today. Not after she had the nerve to show up the day after my father...

I turned on my heel, my voice sharper than I intended. "I'll see you at dinner."

"Lucy, wait—" Connor sprang to his feet after me.

I took off down the dirt path and, on instinct, stomped my way to a lightly wooded section of the property. I sighed and sat down at the base of a tree, leaning back against the rough bark. Memories of Amanda's cruel smirk and the endless humiliation flooded me, tightening the knot in my stomach.

Buddy padded up a few minutes later, flopping down beside me with a soft whine. I buried my fingers in his fur, grateful for his quiet presence.

"What the hell is he talking about?" I whispered. "Amanda, *devastated*? It's bullshit."

The woods around me were still, offering no answers—only the soft rustling of leaves in the wind. I tipped my head back, closing my eyes. *God, I hate this so much.*

Buddy licked my hand, his warm, steady presence soothing me. I pressed a kiss to the top of his head. "Thanks, Buddy." My voice was hoarse. "It's just—every toxic relationship I've ever had—Diane, my mother, Amanda—they've all been thrown in my face since... since I found out—"

The words caught in my throat, a tight, aching knot forming in my chest.

My father died.

But I couldn't say it. Not even to Buddy.

The familiar ache pressed against my ribs, creeping higher, threatening to break me open. But I swallowed hard, pushing it back down. *Again.*

A deep breath. A slow exhale. One foot in front of the other.

The scent of hay and warm earth pulled me forward. I needed to move, to do something, anything, before grief swallowed me whole.

The rustling of hay and the low grunts of effort drew me in.

Connor stood, the late afternoon light casting sharp lines over his broad, sweat-slicked shoulders. His plaid shirt was tied around his waist, his white undershirt damp, streaked with dirt. His muscles flexed as he lifted another bale of hay, the motion easy, familiar.

He paused when he saw me, wiping his forehead with the back of his arm.

"Hey," he greeted, setting the bundle down and meeting my tentative smile with a lopsided grin.

"Hey," I replied, my voice soft. "Sorry about earlier. I just needed a minute. Apparently, I have some personal issues I need to work through." I let out a nervous chuckle, keeping my gaze fixed on the ground.

Connor's lips shifted into a small frown. "I took your advice and called Sam." My eyebrows raised at his admission. "You're right, Amanda should have known better than to show up unannounced. I'll talk to her."

"No. Please, just let me handle it. I'll talk to her—*eventually*. But right now, there are more important things going on."

Connor furrowed his brow but nodded. "That's true. Have you talked to Diane yet?"

I shook my head. "Not yet. I'll text her now. I need to find out what I'm supposed to be doing to help with..." My voice trailed off, the weight of unspoken words hanging between us.

"Here." Connor pulled out his phone, his tone gentle. "I'll message her real quick, then I need to put you back to work. You're too good at this rancher life, and these hay bales won't stack themselves."

His grin was so infectious that I couldn't help but crack a smile as he typed quickly into his phone. When he finished, he turned on some music and put me to work.

Connor sang along, hilariously off-key, but with such unrestrained enthusiasm that I couldn't resist joining in.

My face split into a wide grin as we belted out lyrics. Even Buddy howled along, either joining in or begging us to *stop*.

We doubled over in shared laughter, the sound echoing through the barn—warm, wild, and full of everything I hadn't realized I'd missed.

When I looked up, Connor was already watching me. His blue eyes crinkled at the corners, his grin easy and unguarded. Something fluttered in my chest.

My breath caught, just a little, and I couldn't tell if it was from the laughter or the way he looked at me like nothing else existed outside this moment.

Then he reached for me.

His fingers wrapped around my wrist. Warm, firm, familiar.

A jolt of electricity pulsed through me, my heart kicking up. I didn't have time to overthink it.

He spun me, and a breathless laugh burst out of me as I stumbled, caught, and found my footing again—his hand steady in mine.

For the first time all day, I wasn't weighed down by grief or unwelcome thoughts.

The six years apart faded into nothing.

CHAPTER FOUR

The Cost of Closure

LUCY

The sun cast a golden glow over the garden as I knelt among the neatly arranged rows of vegetables, gathering fresh produce for dinner. I smiled absently, still thinking about Connor's awful singing, while my muscles ached pleasantly from a hard day's work.

The scent of sun-warmed earth and basil lingered in the air, and bees hummed lazily around the flowering herbs at the edge of the patch. Vibrant green zucchini leaves stretched wide, their vines curling along the soil, while bright red tomatoes hung heavy on their stems, ripe for picking. Everything felt peaceful—simple, centering.

Just as I reached for another tomato, my phone buzzed.

My aunt's name flashed across the screen, and my stomach tightened.

"Hi, Aunt Diane," I answered, straining to sound cheerful and polite.

Diane laced her greeting with a sad moan. "Hi, honey. How are you?" Her voice trembled with feigned emotion.

I stiffened. Last night's voicemail echoed in my mind—cold, impersonal, delivering life-shattering news like it was nothing.

Aunt Diane was *that* family member. The one you tolerated because, well, she was family. But trust? Vulnerability? She had never earned those things. And after the complete disregard she'd shown for my emotional well-being, my walls shot up instantly.

"I'm fine," I said, my tone carefully neutral. "You?"

"Oh God, I just can't stop crying. My baby brother—he's *gone*," she choked out, her voice dissolving into a full-on sob.

"I'm so sorry," I said, my lips tightening together.

A loud sniffle and heavy sigh went off like a shotgun in my ear, forcing me to turn down the call volume.

"No. I'm sorry, hun. I'm just a mess."

"I understand," I sighed. Though I didn't. Not really. I was a mess too, but my resentment toward her made sympathy impossible.

"Listen, honey, we need to start making arrangements for your father's funeral and memorial service." Diane's voice clipped into a business-like tone, as if we were planning a dinner party and not laying my father to rest. "Do you want to meet me at the funeral home tomorrow so we can start getting everything in order? And don't worry, I found a *great deal* online for a headstone."

The blood drained from my face. "Uh, sure." The words came out flat, automatic. I blinked, struggling to process what she was saying.

A headstone. A *deal*. Like she was buying a used car.

I took a breath, forcing my thoughts to catch up. This wasn't just an errand. It was my last chance to honor him—a final gift, one I had to get right, no matter how hard it would be.

Even if it meant working alongside Diane.

Then, her words truly registered, and my jaw clenched.

I exhaled slowly, gathering every ounce of patience I had left. "Hold off on ordering anything just yet. Let's talk to the funeral director first."

"But Lucy—"

"*Please.*" My voice was firmer now. Steadier. "Just wait. We'll look at it together."

A pause. Then a begrudging sigh. "Alright, if you insist."

I closed my eyes, inhaling through my nose. "I do."

A loud cough erupted before Diane's hoarse voice continued. "I wrote up the obituary today. I'd like you to take a look and let me know if it's good. They need it by five to run it in tomorrow's paper. But don't add too much, we pay by the letter."

I fumed for a moment before answering with edged syrupy sweetness, "Yeah, just email it to me. And whatever I want to add, I'll pay for myself."

"But you don't know how much—"

"Send me the price sheet and the contact information for the paper. I'll take care of it," I said, biting my cheek to stop myself from saying more. If there was one thing I was good at, it was managing my money. The idea of arguing over finances for something as important as my father's obituary was absurd—almost laughable.

My mind screamed with unspoken words: *How dare you not wait until I knew my dad was gone before posting about it on social media? And worse—how could you think it was acceptable to leave a voicemail to tell me he'd died? You disrespectful, selfish...* I clenched my fists, struggling to keep my composure.

"Oh. Okay. I'll do that," she replied, her voice small and pitiful—so obviously manipulative it made my fists clench.

I exhaled through my nose, forcing myself to keep my temper in check. "Thanks."

A tense beat passed, and despite everything, I heard my father's voice in my head, reminding me to be *civil*.

I worked my jaw, then forced out, "And... I'm sorry you lost your brother." The words felt more like an obligation than genuine sympathy, but at least I'd said them.

Her quiet cries answered a moment later until she forced herself to speak. "I'm so sorry you lost your dad. Oh God... What does that make you? An orphan?"

What. The. Actual. *Hell?!*

I blinked, stunned. Of all the selfish, tone-deaf—

"Nope, Aunt Diane. Not an orphan," I said through gritted teeth. "I'll see you tomorrow. I need to go cook dinner now."

"Of course, sweetie. I'll send you the details for the obituary now."

"Thanks. Bye." I said, hanging up before my aunt could say *anything* else.

I collapsed back onto the dirt as exhaustion washed over me. I sat in the garden, staring absently at the bell peppers in my hands. I felt trapped in this God-awful moment, stretching endlessly, as if time itself refused to let me escape.

A sudden voice sounded beside me.

"Lucy, you okay?"

Connor's question suddenly pulled me back from wherever I'd gone.

I blinked up at him. "Sorry—what?"

"You've been grabbing vegetables out here for a while now. You okay?" Connor asked, casting a long shadow over me.

I hesitated, thinking through what had just happened. "Um... yeah. Sorry. Diane called, and I guess I just needed a minute."

Panic shot through me, and I gasped, fumbling for my phone to check the time. My shoulders tensed. I had half an hour to handle the obituary.

"Hey, could you take these veggies and get started on dinner? I have to read this and make any changes I want for my dad's obituary within the next thirty minutes." My words shot out in rapid-fire as I handed Connor the basket and jumped to my feet.

"Why don't you read it to me while we walk back to the house? Maybe I can help make it go faster?"

I nodded as I scrolled to the email from Diane. "Okay, here it is: 'Campbell, Robert M., 61, of White River, passed May 15, 2025, at White River Medical Center.'" I paused, clasping a hand over my mouth to stifle the sobs threatening to escape. The pain piercing through my chest was almost unbearable, like a physical wound. Fighting through the mounting grief that paralyzed me, I forced myself to regain control. "Sorry," I whispered hoarsely.

"It's okay. Do you want me to read it?" Connor offered, his voice low and calm, grounding me once again with his presence.

"No, I've got it," I insisted, my voice trembling but determined. I took another breath and continued, "He was a rancher, father, son, brother, and pillar of the community. He is survived by his daughter, Lucy—" My words caught as a fresh, slicing wave of grief left my cheeks numb and tingling. Gritting my teeth, I forced myself to finish the last line. "—and his sister, Diane. Funeral and Memorial TBD." I inhaled shakily, feeling the dizzying weight of my new reality.

We fell into silence, my thoughts circling the same impossible question:

How is any of this real?

"I guess that sums it up," I murmured, my lips pressing into a thin line as we climbed the stairs to the back porch.

Connor's voice was hard, low. "No. No, it doesn't. He deserves so much more than that."

His words cut through the stillness, stealing my breath.

"You're right." My chest tightened, and for an agonizing moment, I fought to keep my composure. "He deserves more than a few sterile lines in a newspaper."

Connor nodded, his voice rough with conviction. "He deserves a story—one that captures the light he brought to this world, the countless ways he made life better for everyone around him."

"Yeah," I whispered, my throat tightening. "I just... I've never written one of these before."

"I learned a lot last year when I helped Alex's family with his. Let's sit down and get this done together. Dinner can wait."

I frowned. "Alex. That was your friend?"

"Yeah," Connor answered with sudden, unexpected sharpness.

I put a hand on Connor's arm and gave it a gentle squeeze. His warmth, even through the fabric of his shirt, sent a surprising jolt through me. My lips parted. A soft gasp escaped me.

Swallowing hard, I forced my voice to come out steady. "Thank you for this."

"Of course, Luce, but I want to do this—for *him*." His blue eyes bore into mine, unwavering. "Thank *you* for letting me help. Now, let's get to work."

We jumped right in. I squinted through the glare of the fan light bouncing off the laptop screen as Connor dove into his thoughts, asking all the right questions to get mine flowing.

"How would you like to celebrate him?"

That lit the spark. Everything else fell into place from there.

By the time we finished the final line, Connor was already on the phone with Eddie, his former football teammate who worked at the paper.

"We're sending it now. Yeah, it's got to be in tomorrow's paper—I don't give a damn what the deadline was. You and I both know you can make it happen. This is Robert we're talking about."

A pause.

"Thanks, man. I owe you one. Yeah, talk soon. Bye."

He hung up just as the email finally changed from "Sending..." to "Sent."

I leaned back in the dining room chair, exhaling. "We did it." A slow, relieved smile pulled at my lips.

Without thinking, I jumped up and wrapped my arms around Connor's neck, squeezing him tight.

"We did it," he echoed, his arms slipping around my waist.

Then—

The air shifted.

The solid warmth of him anchored me in place. I closed my eyes, letting myself sink into it.

I let out a breath, my cheek grazing his. His stubble scraped lightly against my skin, sending a shiver down my spine. His breath was warm at my temple, too close, too familiar. An unspoken charge sparked between us, humming beneath my skin.

I should step back.

But I didn't.

His hands rested at my waist, firm but hesitant, like he wasn't sure if he should pull me closer or let go. My palms slid down to his chest, his body heat burning through his shirt beneath my fingertips. My gaze flickered to his parted lips, and warmth spread beneath my collarbone, pooling into something deeper—an ache I didn't know what to do with.

The moment stretched.

I felt it shift—felt him pause, felt the weight of something unspoken settle between us. The awareness tightened, like a drawn wire.

Then, just as quickly, Connor exhaled and stepped back, his grip loosening. I let my hands fall away.

I swallowed hard, settling myself. *It's just Connor.*

Only, it didn't feel like *just* anything anymore.

Heat rose to my cheeks, and I took a sudden step back. "Thanks for your help." I shoved my hands into my pockets, hoping to hide the way they still tingled beneath the surface. "The obituary is perfect—thanks to you."

Connor scratched the back of his neck, his throat bobbing. "Yeah, my pleasure. I—uh, you did great. Everyone's going to love the invitation you made."

I lowered my gaze to the floor, willing my pulse to steady. "I hope so."

Connor's fingers brushed along my jaw, tilting my chin up until our eyes met. "They will."

My breath hitched.

I froze, caught in the pull of his gaze, unsure of his next move. The space between us felt charged, every breath thick with anticipation.

And then—

His hand slipped away.

Connor cleared his throat, the muscle in his jaw flexing as he stepped back, his attempt at casualness betrayed by the hesitation in his movements. "Dinner?"

"Oh. Right." I forced a laugh, the sound rushing out breathier than I intended.

His lips twitched like he noticed, but instead of calling me on it, he turned toward the basket of vegetables on the counter. "Hope you're hungry," he said, his voice light, too easy—except for the way his fingers lingered for half a second longer than necessary before picking up a tomato.

The wind rushed out of me as I took a moment to gather myself. "Yeah, I'll start slicing the vegetables."

"Perfect. I'll make the fajita seasoning."

We cooked and ate in near silence, a stillness settling between us, charged and impossible to ignore. Every glance, every pause carried an undeniable tension, a current I wasn't ready to confront.

When dinner was done, we cleaned up together in an easy, practiced rhythm. Yet, the air between us remained taut with unspoken words and an undercurrent of something dangerously close to crossing a line.

"Good night, Lucy." Connor's voice was low, rough at the edges. He gave me a short wave before striding toward the front door.

"Night." My voice was quieter than I intended, my stomach twisting with something I didn't want to name.

Stop him. Say something. Just—

But I didn't.

The door shut, and I collapsed onto the couch, exhaustion pressing into my bones. I wasn't just drained—I was unraveling. The fine line between raw grief and the slow, undeniable pull toward Connor was getting harder to ignore.

"Oh God, Buddy." I groaned into the quiet, dragging a hand over my face. "What am I going to do?"

CHAPTER FIVE

Before the Knock

LUCY

The next morning, a copy of the *White River Gazette* waited for me on the kitchen counter. My heart skipped. I nearly collapsed at the sight of the front page.

There he was.

My dad.

His strong, weathered face—lined from years of sun and hard work—beamed beside his pickup truck, the ranch stretching out behind him. His once-dark hair had faded to silver, with traces of its original shade beneath, and a salt-and-pepper mustache framed his easy smile—the same one that had made him so well-loved throughout the town.

The headline read, "White River Mourns Loss of Beloved Local Philanthropist." The poignant article by Eddie Jones detailed the many ways my father had given back to the community.

Reading Eddie's words—his personal reflections on what my father had meant to him—brought tears to my eyes. The piece ended with a note on where to find the obituary we'd submitted, both in the newspaper and online.

I flipped through the pages and began reading:

It is with heavy hearts that we announce the passing of one of White River's finest. Robert M. Campbell passed away on May 15, 2025, at WRMC. He was a loving father, a devoted brother, and a cherished friend.

Robert always had a kind word or a funny anecdote to share with the people of White River, whom he loved dearly. We will miss his charm, wit, and generous spirit.

As we grieve this tremendous loss, we invite you to Campbell Ranch for a Celebration of Life this Friday at 5 p.m. Please bring a favorite story to share in his honor.

If you'd like, you may also bring a dish, a beverage, or a game Robert would have loved for everyone to enjoy.

Robert was all about community and bringing people together. It is our honor to host an event that reflects everything he loved about this town—coming together not just as a community, but as a chosen family.

The date of the funeral will be announced later this week.

"It's perfect," I whispered, grinning as I bit the corner of my lower lip. A stray tear rolled down my cheek, and I let it fall, unashamed.

I lifted my steaming cup of coffee to my lips, the scent comforting even as the tight knot of grief refused to loosen. Setting the morning paper aside, I scrolled through my notifications.

A text from my mother sat unread beneath the news alerts:

Call me.

I exhaled slowly, staring at it for a beat before locking my phone. Not today.

Outside, Connor was already back to his usual routine with the other ranch hands. With breakfast finished, it was high time I joined him. I made my way down the long dirt driveway, passing a patch of wildflowers that tugged a small smile from the heavy corners of my lips. I found him across from the storage barn, helping a few ranch hands mend a section of fencing in the pasture.

"Hey, what can I do to help?" I offered, eager to dive back into the physical labor that had soothed my nerves yesterday.

Connor swiped his forearm across his brow. "We've got things handled here."

"Are you sure?" My gaze swept over the men hard at work.

Johnny, one of the newer ranch hands, called over his shoulder, "Yeah, you've got enough on your plate. Let us handle the ranch."

My throat bobbed. Guilt gnawed at me, but he was right. Diane would be here soon to carpool to the funeral home.

I exhaled, forcing myself to let go. "Alright."

My phone belted out a funky ringtone, vibrating in the tight grip of my hand. *Sam Bestie.*

A sudden, uncontrollable burst of relief rushed through me. I waved goodbye to the guys and snatched up the phone.

"Hey, Sam," I answered, my voice lighter.

"Luce, how are you holding up?" His smooth, familiar tone wrapped around me like a hug.

I sighed, his question sobering me as I made my way back to the house. "Okay. Could be worse."

"Connor better be taking care of you until I'm there," Sam warned.

"Wait—" I gasped, excitement bubbling in my voice. "You're coming here?!"

"I wouldn't miss Papa Bob's celebration of life for anything," Sam said, his voice warm but edged with emotion. Then, he brightened. "Besides, I need to see you, bitch."

I grinned, opening the front door and letting myself inside. "Oh my God, that's amazing! How did you find out about the celebration?"

"Connor texted me last night," Sam said offhandedly. Then his voice bubbled with excitement. "But, I'll be there tonight! Can I stay at your place?"

A smile spread across my face. "Yeah, absolutely."

Sam let out an exaggerated sigh. "I can't believe Amanda showed up yesterday, especially knowing Connor was there."

I stilled. "What do you mean?"

"They just broke up like a few weeks ago," he spat.

My stomach dropped. A sharp pang of something bitter curled in my chest—unbidden, unearned.

"Connor and... *Amanda*? Wow. I guess that explains why he seemed so uncomfortable around her."

Frowning, I switched Sam to speakerphone, grabbing frozen waffles from the freezer and popping them into the toaster.

"They've been on and off since... well, not long after you moved to London," Sam said. "You know Amanda—she always has to have the best. And if you ask around, local gossip still says Connor's the most eligible bachelor in White River. Apparently people think my brother's... *hot*." He made a dramatic gagging sound, then shuddered.

But the thought of Amanda with Connor made me sick for an entirely different reason. "Seriously, Sam, how could you forget to mention your brother was dating *the literal enemy*?"

"First off, I like to pretend their relationship never existed. Second, you forbade me from sharing any White River gossip. And third, you *know* I only enjoy stories where I'm the star," Sam said, his voice laced with theatrical flair and a playful lilt.

I groaned. "Fine. But still—you didn't warn him? After what she did? After telling everyone—"

"That was a long time ago," he cut in, his voice sharpening. "It wasn't my place to tell him she's a raging bitch. Boundaries, Luce. I don't tell him who to date, and he doesn't tell me who to date."

"You're deflecting."

"Lucy..."

I sighed as I took a bite of my waffle. "*Sam.*" I rolled my eyes, relenting, "I'm sorry, it's just really shocking. I get the boundaries thing, but this is *Amanda.*"

"Ahem." Connor cleared his throat beside the breakfast bar.

I jumped, my attention snapping to him. Our eyes met, and his intense gaze sent a rush of heat flooding my cheeks.

"Look, I know Amanda's a complete psycho but—"

I snatched my phone off the counter, turning off speakerphone. "Sam," I rasped, my voice low, "I have to call you back."

"Okay, see you tonight!" he sang, happy to end the subject.

"Can't wait. Bye." I clipped, hanging up.

My heart thumped hard in my chest, the flush in my cheeks deepening. "Oh my God, Connor, I'm so sorry. How much did you hear?"

Connor chuckled, shaking his head. "Enough to know you must think I'm a complete idiot—"

"Oh no." I groaned.

"It's fine. Lucy, I started dating her in high school because—" He stopped abruptly, rubbing his chin as his gaze dropped to his feet. His posture shifted.

I swallowed hard. "You really don't have to explain yourself—or your love life. Especially not to me."

He shook his head, his eyes narrowing slightly. "What do you mean?"

"I mean... it's me," I stammered, moving out of the kitchen to close the distance between us, searching for the right words to fix this. "I've been gone for how long? Who am I to judge? I've probably dated guys *way* worse than Amanda." I let out a short, self-deprecating laugh. "Besides, I'm your little brother's best friend, which makes us like family, right? It's not like I..."

My words trailed off as I met his darkening gaze.

Connor stepped forward, and my breath hitched at the sudden closeness. He cupped my face in his hands, and my lips parted as I drew in an unsteady breath.

"We are not family," he insisted, his low rumble sending shockwaves of desire through me.

"Connor..." his name fell from my lips like a plea, barely above a whisper.

He shook his head, words tumbling out in a low, urgent growl. "The day you left, Lucy, it wrecked me."

I bit the corner of my lip, and his heated gaze locked onto the movement, setting every nerve in my body on fire.

"Last night, I couldn't sleep. I can't stop thinking about you. It's like I'm in fucking high school again. Maybe this is wrong, maybe the timing's shit, but..."

His gaze dropped to my lips, hunger tightening his jaw. "Lucy... you have no idea what you're doing to me. Every time you bite that damned lip..."

He swallowed hard, his hands sliding to my waist, fingers digging in. His whisper was hot against my ear as our cheeks brushed. "The things I've imagined doing to you... what I want right now—it's not innocent. And it sure as hell isn't something you do with someone you see as family, Lucy."

The way he said my name sent a shiver down my spine.

His lips brushed my jaw, and I gasped.

"When you laugh, I forget how to breathe," he murmured. "When you walk away, all I want is to pull you back in."

His hands moved deliberately up my sides, giving me every chance to say no.

I couldn't.

I didn't want to.

"I wanted you for two years before I finally asked you to homecoming. And lost my shot."

Our lips hovered—so close.

"Now that you're back... I can't make the same mistake."

"Connor..." I breathed.

"Lucy, as much as I've tried... nothing's changed for me."

His confession broke something loose in me.

I pulled him in and our lips collided in a heated, unspoken understanding.

Connor's hands tangled in my dark auburn hair, catching my lower lip gently between his teeth before grazing it with his tongue. My eager response matched his deep longing, my hands roaming over the taut muscles of his chest. His touch was both wild and controlled, igniting a blaze of fire under my skin.

His hands trailed down my back and snaked around my waist. With one effortless shift, he lifted me onto the breakfast bar. My knees parted instinctively, cradling his hips as he stepped between them.

His mouth found mine again, urgent, devouring me with a hunger that stole my breath. My fingers tangled in his thick, unruly hair as I pressed myself harder against him, needing to erase every last millimeter of space between us.

I clutched his shirt, trembling at the thought of pulling it off. His hands grasped mine. The kiss softened, slowing into something painfully tender.

Connor broke away, trailing soft kisses along my jawline. His voice dropped to a whisper, hot and breathless against my ear.

"Tell me to stop, Lucy... and I will. Even if it destroys me."

His words sent a shiver down my spine.

"If you stop, I'll never forgive you," I gasped, my breath uneven.

He pressed his mouth against my neck, his tongue swirling over my skin as he sucked gently. A moan escaped my lips, my nails raking down his back.

Connor's deep growl rippled through me, his hands gripping my waist tighter, pulling me impossibly close. Heat coiled low in my stomach, my pulse hammering as his lips trailed lower, teeth grazing against my collarbone.

God, this was happening. *Finally.*

His breath was hot against my skin, his voice a rough whisper. "Lucy..."

A deep, aching need surged through me as my fingers raked against the hard plains of his back, scratching just enough to pull a sharp inhale from him. His hands roamed—up my sides, cupping my face before sliding back to grasp my hair, then skimming the sensitive strip of skin just beneath the hem of my shirt. My stomach clenched as his thumbs brushed just beneath my ribs, and heat surged through me.

"Connor—" I gasped his name against his lips, my hands fisting in the fabric of his shirt as if I could anchor myself there, as if letting go would shatter me.

He groaned low in his throat as he ground his hardness into me, the sound vibrating against my mouth, and it nearly undid me.

His lips left mine only to trail soft, open-mouthed kisses down my jaw, along my neck, across my collarbone.

I gasped as he bent his knees, moving lower... lower. His breath was hot against the sliver of skin exposed just above my waistband.

My head tipped back, pulse thrumming in my ears, as his fingers reached the button on my jeans—

Then—

BANG. BANG. BANG.

"Hello... LUCY?! I'm here!"

We froze, every muscle locking tight as reality came crashing back in.

Connor's forehead dropped to my shoulder, his breath ragged. "You have got to be kidding me."

I swallowed hard, my body still humming with electricity, heart pounding against my ribs begging me to pull him back in and keep going.

Another knock. Louder this time.

"Lucy?" Diane's voice carried through the door, sing-song and expectant.

Connor exhaled sharply, stepping back as if he'd been burned, running a hand over his face.

"Unbelievable." I squeezed my eyes shut, taking a shaky breath before forcing myself to move. My legs wobbled, heat still simmering beneath my skin.

Of course. It had to be *Diane*.

I shot Connor a look, my voice hushed but urgent. "Do I look like I was just... making terrible life choices?"

His smirk was instant and smug, blue eyes dark with lingering heat. "Oh, sweetheart, you look exactly like you were making terrible life choices."

My jaw dropped. "Not helpful."

He chuckled under his breath, rubbing the back of his neck as he took a deep, steadying breath. "Okay. Show no weakness. Deep breath. You got this."

One more knock.

I groaned, my lips swollen and tingling. Smoothing my shirt, I ran my fingers through my hair, praying I looked somewhat decent before reaching for the door.

When I swung it open, Diane burst into tears and collided into me with a sloppy hug. I grimaced, patting her back awkwardly, praying the moment would end soon. Her floral perfume did little to mask her sweat.

Pulling away, she slumped slightly, and I found myself studying her. She seemed shorter than I remembered, her stout frame accentuated by wide shoulders that looked almost cartoonish against her disproportionately thin legs. I vaguely recalled my father mentioning her MS diagnosis, a detail I was surprised she hadn't broadcast all over social media. Her square face was framed by thinning, dyed-brown hair, and her jawline sagged with loose skin. Yet, her dark brown eyes—usually guarded—were filled with grief, an emotion that appeared foreign on her.

"Oh, I'm so sorry. I'm just a mess!" Diane apologized, swiping at her eyes as she handed me a large white plastic bag. I took it without thinking.

"I get it," I sighed, patting her back once more.

She pulled away slowly, her gaze locking onto mine. "He was my only baby brother. I'm all alone now. Our parents are gone, he's gone..."

I stiffened.

"You understand. You've lost them too." She wiped her nose with a tissue pulled from her pocket, then nodded toward the bag in my hands. "These are your father's things from the hospital. I thought you'd like to have them."

The words barely registered before the weight of the bag hit me.

My breath caught. My fingers curled tighter around the plastic, as if the objects inside could keep me upright, but the world had already tilted.

My father's things. The last pieces of him.

The realization crashed over me like an avalanche, sudden and crushing. My chest tightened, my throat closing around a lump too big to swallow.

Connor's calloused hands slid over mine, his warmth soothing me as he gently pried the bag from my grasp. "I'll put this on his bed. When you're ready, you can go through it."

I exhaled shakily, barely nodding as he stepped away.

Diane, pulling herself together so fast it gave me emotional whiplash, smoothed her hair and squared her shoulders. "Are you ready to head to the funeral home?"

The shift was jarring, but maybe that was her way of coping—*keep moving, keep planning*.

I forced myself to answer, though my voice felt distant. "Yeah. Let's go. I'll drive."

"Oh, that would be nice," she said with a long sigh, her tone hovering between gratitude and something more calculated.

Connor returned then beside me, his tone casual but deliberate. "I could drive you both over. I was heading into town anyway. I got a call that I need to grab some supplies from the hardware store to fix my fence."

"That's right. Lucy, have you heard? Connor has the second-best ranch in White River." My aunt boasted beside me, resentment barely concealed beneath the surface.

Connor flushed. "I wouldn't go that far. Should we head over now?"

I nodded, swallowing my surprise. "No, that's fine. You focus on getting your fence repaired, and I'll meet up with you later. Thanks for taking care of my animals this morning—I seriously appreciate everything you're doing to help out around here."

Connor shook off the compliment. "Don't worry about it. It's my job. Are you sure you don't want a ride? It's really no problem."

"I'm sure. Who knows how long this will take."

I was so consumed by learning Connor not only worked on my father's ranch, but had his own to care for, that I hadn't noticed Diane fuming beside me.

"*Your* animals?" she seethed.

The words were a trap, and I walked right into it.

"I—I mean, they are, aren't they?" My voice wavered, uncertainty curling in my gut. I'd called them mine since I was little. It'd been a force of habit more than a proclamation.

Buddy padded up beside me, pressing his warm weight against my leg. I let my fingers curl into his fur for emotional support.

Diane's laughter was sharp, laced with acidity. "*Bold*, isn't it?" She crossed her arms, her smile cutting like a blade. "Honey, when was the last time you even rode a horse? Do you *really* think my brother would give someone so inexperienced his ranch?"

I stiffened, my pulse thrumming in my ears.

"I was the one here, taking care of things while he was sick." She scoffed, shifting her weight, planting one aggressive hand on her hip. "Have you even *seen* Robert's will?"

Her words slammed into me, one gut punch after another.

My mouth opened, but no words came out.

"Lucy's already proven herself around here," Connor's voice cut through the tension, even and sharp as a knife. "When's the last time *you* worked the ranch?"

Diane paled, her eyes flicking to him, assessing, calculating.

Then, like a switch flipping, she burst into tears.

"I'm just so overwhelmed!" Her voice cracked as she pressed a trembling hand to her chest. "I lost my brother! And now you're treating me like a *villain*!"

We stood in stunned silence, watching her unravel.

I swallowed hard, searching for something—*anything*—to say. "I'll... look for the will when I get back today."

Diane sniffled, blinking up at me through watery eyes, her expression just a little too controlled.

Before she could sink her claws in further, Connor stepped forward. His voice was firm. Final. "That's a great idea," he said smoothly. "Now, you two better get going—don't wanna be late."

Diane's lips pressed into a thin line, her eyes flicking between us. A forced retreat.

He leaned in for a quick hug and whispered in my ear, "Don't let her get to you. I can't wait to see you tonight."

He pulled back, his eyes softening just for me as he gave my hand a reassuring squeeze.

Warmth spread through me, and I couldn't help but smile. "Me too. Are you picking Sam up from the airport tonight, or am I?"

He shrugged. "We could go together?"

"I think he'd love that," I said, a grin spreading across my face. But what I really meant was, *I'd* love that. A drive alone with him in his Dodge Ram was *exactly* what I needed.

Diane chimed in, "Just don't forget to find that paperwork."

I bit back a retort, forcing a calm nod. "I will." Then, turning toward the door, I added, "Let's go."

CHAPTER SIX

The Town That Loved Him

LUCY

A blast of cold air rushed out as Diane and I stepped through the heavy oak doors of the funeral home, carrying the faint scent of polished wood and lavender. Todd, a six-foot-tall, third-generation funeral director with slicked back blonde hair, greeted us with practiced yet genuine warmth.

"Good afternoon, ladies. Please come in," he said. "I'm so sorry for your loss. Your father was a remarkable man."

I swallowed hard and nodded, shaking his outstretched hand. "Thank you, Todd. That means a lot. I—"

Diane stepped forward, her voice tinged with authority. "Thank you, Todd. We're here to make sure everything is absolutely perfect. My brother deserves nothing less."

"Of course." Todd gestured toward a cozy seating area bathed in soft light, with stunning floral arrangements strategically placed to soften the morbidity of the space. "Let's sit down and go over the arrangements."

The room exuded a somber kind of comfort, though I couldn't bring myself to appreciate it. I sank into the chair, my mind buzzing, lifting out of my body as if I were hovering above the scene. The tension from the drive over faded, replaced by the numbing reality of why I was here.

Todd opened a pristine leather binder, his voice calm and reassuring. "Your father pre-arranged and prepaid for everything. He was very thorough—he wanted to make this process as easy as possible for you both. There's very little left to—"

The rush of relief hit me, cutting through the numbness and nearly knocking the air out of me. Todd's voice faded into the background as the sharp contrast of emotions left me lightheaded.

Then a catalog of prayer cards appeared in my hands.

"What's this for?" I asked, the question slipping out before I could think.

Diane's lips pressed into a tight line, her expression hardening. "Lucy, pay attention."

Todd placed a gentle hand on mine, ignoring Diane's sharp tone. "It's normal to feel a little out of focus right now," he said softly. "Your father wanted you to choose the prayer cards for the service, but only if you feel up to it."

Diane leaned forward, her voice cracking just a little. "No, Lucy, you'll regret it if you don't pick one. Go on, take a look."

I glanced up at her, finally seeing genuine grief beneath her stern exterior. Her squared features softened, and her dark eyes glistened faintly.

For the first time, I had a twinge of sympathy for her.

"Aunt Diane," I said gently, reaching out to touch her arm. "Would you like to help me choose?"

Her shoulders relaxed as she let out the breath she'd been holding. "Thank you, Lucy," she said, her voice unsteady but grateful.

We worked together, flipping through the catalog until we agreed on printing two designs my father would have loved. It felt right, and for the first time that day, I felt like I had accomplished something meaningful.

"Now, I just need a date and time," Todd said, his voice pulling my attention back to him.

Diane was quick to respond, slipping effortlessly back into her usual commanding persona. "The celebration of life is this Friday. We should hold the funeral that afternoon."

Funny how one sentence could completely unravel me.

One moment, I felt relief—like I had finally done something for my father that he would have appreciated. The next, a wave of detachment washed over me, dulling everything.

Overwhelmed, I asked absently, "Will that give people enough time to make arrangements?"

Diane brushed off my concern. "We'll post it to the town's community page, both online and on social media. That gives everyone a few days. I think—"

"Friday it is," I interrupted, turning to Todd, my gaze unfocused, seeing him but not truly seeing. "Can you make that happen?"

"Absolutely," he said with a nod. "One last thing. Your father prepaid for his floral arrangements. Head over to *White River Blooms* just a few doors down. Jenna's expecting you."

"Jenna?" I blinked at him. "Jenna Waverly?"

"That's the one. She's the new owner," Todd explained, a gentle smile lifting his lips.

A soft lift found its way to mine, matching his gaze. "She used to babysit me."

"Yes, that's nice, Lucy, but we'd better get going." Diane tapped my thigh, her tone clipped with impatience.

The dull ache of muddied fog gripped me again. I stood as if on autopilot and allowed Diane to lead the way.

The chilling rush of air washed over me once more as the oak doors opened. Diane looped her arm through mine as we stepped outside. The crisp Montana breeze cooled my cheeks, while the golden warmth of the sun pulled me fully into the present.

Downtown White River stretched out like a picture-perfect postcard. Brick-lined sidewalks framed the historic storefronts, and the snow-dusted mountains stood tall in the distance.

My eyes widened as we passed *The Rustic Roast*, a new coffee shop. "Didn't that used to be *R&J Games*?" I asked, glancing at Diane.

She waved me off dismissively. "That went out of business years ago."

My phone buzzed in my pocket. I glanced at the screen—Mom, again. With a sigh, I silenced it and slipped my phone back into my jacket.

At least *Frontier Tools & Supply* still stood next door, unchanged, to my relief. We continued on to the florist.

White River Blooms was impossible to miss, its large windows overflowing with colorful displays. Above the bright yellow door was a hand-painted sign in cheerful, vine-like script.

Diane stepped inside first, and the sweet aroma of fresh flowers enveloped us.

Jenna looked up from her notebook and burst into tears at the sight of me. Her curly black hair bounced as she rushed around the counter, her caramel skin glowing softly in the sunlight streaming through the windows.

Jenna had always been stunning, with her high cheekbones, long face, and a knack for transforming even the simplest outfit into a stylish ensemble. Today was no different—her floral-print dress was cinched at the waist with a braided leather belt, and an open button-up plaid tee draped effortlessly over her shoulders, adding a casual charm to her polished look.

"Lucy!" she cried, pulling me into a tight hug.

"I'm so sorry," she breathed, taking a much-needed moment to gather her words. "Your father was such a wonderful man. He lit up the room wherever he went."

Her grief broke something inside me. I hugged her back, tears streaming silently down my face. "Thank you," I whispered. "Thank you for saying that."

Jenna walked me through the shop, showing me concept books and suggesting arrangements, her kindness a stark contrast to Diane's overbearing input beside us. Whenever I had the chance, I found myself subtly turning my back on my aunt to focus on Jenna's warmth instead.

Word of my presence spread quickly. Soon, townspeople began filing in, each with their own story about my father. Mr. Richards, owner of *Frontier Tools & Supply*, practically boomed, "Lucy, your dad was one of the best," while eighty-year-old Agnes Mayweather shuffled up with her cane, her sharp eyes narrowing as she glanced at Diane. "The nerve of some people," she muttered loud enough for everyone to hear, "putting family business on the internet before the poor girl even landed."

The comment sent ripples of laughter through the shop, but it didn't sit well with me. If the remark had been private, I may have felt differently. I glanced at Diane, her face turned beet red. Her lips pressed into a thin line, and for the first time since my arrival, she seemed... deflated. The sharp retort I expected never came, and that silence spoke louder than any words could have.

Straightening, I cleared my throat. "We're all doing the best we can. That's all anyone can ask."

Agnes huffed, her expression softening as she turned to me, patting my cheek with her cool, soft hand. "You've always been so thoughtful, my dear. I'm sure your father is looking down on you right now, just beaming with pride."

The care in her words comforted me, and for a fleeting moment, I felt something else... something I couldn't explain.

Goosebumps prickled my arms as a subtle warmth spread across my back, like invisible arms wrapping around me.

My eyes fluttered shut, and a whisper of a thought crossed my mind: *Dad*?

The sensation lingered for only a heartbeat before logic pushed it away. It couldn't be. Could it?

I shook myself, dismissing the idea. The warmth faded, replaced by a lingering chill as my shoulders dropped.

By the time we left the florist, I was emotionally drained.

My father had left a mark on so many people, and hearing their words filled me with a bittersweet mix of pride and loss.

After parking the old Ford F-250 in my dad's usual spot, I turned to Diane. She sat quietly beside me, her earlier bravado settled into an uneasy stillness.

Her hands clasped tightly in her lap, her expression unreadable. Diane's uncharacteristic silence unnerved me.

"I'll see you tomorrow," I murmured, breaking the tension.

She nodded, her voice subdued. "Thank you, Lucy."

Her words lingered in the air before she climbed out of my father's truck and into her beat-up sedan, driving off without a trace of her usual toxic dramatics.

Once inside, I collapsed onto the couch, exhaustion washing over me in waves.

Buddy padded over and curled up beside me, resting his head on my lap. I stroked his fur absently, my thoughts churning through the day's events until, *slowly*, they began to settle.

As Buddy's soft snores filled the room, a quiet comfort wrapped around me—one I hadn't realized I needed.

I closed my eyes for a moment.

Before I could resist, sleep pulled me under.

CHAPTER SEVEN

Besties and Baggage

LUCY

A sharp knock rattled the door, Buddy's furious barking echoing through the house. I jolted upright, my heart hammering.

Clutching my chest, I blinked, swiped drool from my chin, and stumbled toward the door. "Coming!"

The moment I swung it open, a squeal of pure joy escaped me.

Sam stood in the doorway, arms spread wide like he was making his Broadway debut. His jet-black-to-blue ombre hair was styled to perfection, and he was every bit the NYC-chic vision in skinny jeans, a billowy button-up, and a chiffon scarf that screamed, *I'm an absolute vibe.*

The faint scent of expensive cologne wafted in as he struck a pose, basking in his well-deserved moment of glory. Seeing him standing there, radiating main-character energy, sent a wave of comfort and pure joy through me.

I pounced on him, wrapping my arms around him in a tight squeeze. "Oh my God, you're here!"

"Surprise! *Apparently*, Sleeping Beauty couldn't be bothered to pick up a filthy peasant like me from the airport," he teased, throwing me an exaggerated pout.

My gaze shot over to Connor, who leaned casually against the doorframe, watching us with relaxed amusement.

"I tried calling," Connor explained with a shrug. "When I dropped by and saw you and Buddy curled up on the couch, I didn't have the heart to wake you."

My heart melted, a small smile tugging at my lips. But Sam—ever the attention-stealer—pulled me away from my lovesick gaze.

"Okay, where do I drop my bags, and where's the liquor? No way we're looking through your dad's stuff without proper emotional support in a glass."

Shit. Dad's will. I winced at the reminder.

Grabbing one of Sam's bags from the porch, I wheeled it inside. "I'm so glad you're here."

"You have no idea, sis. I made Connor stop at the store so I can make us some Old Fashioneds," Sam sang as he strutted inside.

"You're amazing. You can put all of that on the kitchen counter."

His eyes darted around the room. "Wow, this place hasn't changed a bit."

"I know." I frowned, but only for a moment, because Sam was already whisking me toward the kitchen, forcing me to drop the luggage handles.

"We have to make quesadillas. It's tradition."

I laughed. "You're right! Ham and cheese?"

"Duh!" he exclaimed.

The memory flashed through my mind—us ransacking the fridge and finding nothing but ham, cheese, tortillas, and ranch. That day, we decided it was our special meal. Because best friends needed traditions, of *course.*

It was the same weekend we declared our signature friendship drink to be a virgin strawberry daiquiri—served in a fancy glass lined with chocolate syrup.

"I'll start cooking while you whip us up some drinks. Connor, can you take Sam's bags to the guest room?"

"I guess." Connor's playful baritone made my heart skip a beat.

I forced a scowl and he chuckled, grabbing all four of Sam's suitcases.

"I'm going, I'm going!" Connor exclaimed in mock defense, hoisting the suitcases with a loud grunt and wobbling away.

Sam rolled his eyes. "Stop it, Connor. I didn't pack *that* much."

Connor called back over his shoulder, "Oh, my back! I think I pulled something..."

Sam scrunched up his face. "God, he's annoying."

I bent over, giggling. "I've missed seeing you two together."

As soon as Connor was out of earshot, Sam turned to me, his eyes narrowing with suspicion. "Is there something going on between you two?"

I froze. "What? No! Why would you even—"

"You're blushing. Ew. You two didn't..." He thrust his hips suggestively at a nearby barstool.

I squeaked, mortified. "No!"

Sam's jaw dropped. "Oh. My. God! But you *want* to!"

"Sam!" I swatted at his arm, my face blazing. "Stop. It was just one kiss!"

"Excuse me! Lucy, you have a boyfriend waiting for you back in London." Sam's voice was tinged with judgment.

Connor's voice cut through the room, startling me. "You have a boyfriend?"

My heart thudded as I spun around to see him standing in the doorway. Panic surged, and I shook my head frantically. "No. I don't."

"Really?" Sam's tone dripped with skepticism.

"Yes, really! We broke up before I left," I snapped, my glare cutting into Sam. Even now, the memory of my ex sent a fresh jolt of rage through me.

"What?! Why didn't you tell me?" Sam clutched his chest as if injured. "He was a duke, Lucy! How could you?"

I sighed, exasperated. "He was also self-absorbed, Sam. The guy never listened. He never even cared enough to ask how my dad was doing or if I was okay. Not once." I cut my eyes to Connor's, my cheeks heated under his burning gaze.

"But... *royalty*, Lucy," Sam whined.

I snapped my eyes back to Sam. "He was an ass—just like every other guy I dated in London."

My voice was sure, but the bitterness in my chest lingered. "You're the one who made me see I need to start doing better for myself, remember?" I closed my eyes, inhaling sharply, forcing every unwanted memory that surfaced back into the box where they belonged.

"Yeah, but I didn't think this one was so bad..."

"Let's just say, when I broke things off, he already had another woman waiting to take my place. Literally swapped us out at dinner, like I was disposable." I let out a humorless laugh, shaking my head. "I think we can both agree I deserve better."

Sam hesitated, then nodded solemnly.

"I never liked him," Sam growled dutifully.

"Good." I forced a laugh, but the edge in my voice lingered. "Because my days of settling are over. No more assholes. No more lowering the bar just to make things work."

The words had barely left my mouth before I caught Connor's stare.

His gaze locked onto mine—heated, unreadable, charged with something I couldn't name. A shiver ghosted over my skin.

"I hope I never meet him," Connor said, every word laced with quiet restraint and a darkness I'd never seen before. "If I do, he'll regret ever taking you for granted."

I inhaled sharply.

Sam groaned. "Holy crap, you two, get a room! You're grossing me out."

Connor laughed, rich and deep.

Sam clutched his chest theatrically. "Connor, as I told you in high school, if things go south, I'm keeping Lucy in the divorce. She's my favorite. So if you're willing to risk losing me, go for it—because that kind of gamble must mean it's true love." He ended the last two words in a sing-song sigh.

I gaped. "Wait, what?"

Sam smirked, that same careless half-grin he and Connor had inherited from their father. "Relax, Luce. I'm just teasing. But for the record, I've always wanted a sister."

Heat rushed to my face. "Okay, that's enough. Sam, make my drink a double—we need to talk."

Sam set to work, all business. "Connor, go away. Make yourself busy."

Connor shook his head, crossing his arms. "I'm good."

Sam rolled his eyes. "Ugh, no you don't. Now shoo!"

Connor sighed, calling for Buddy as he headed to the door. "Guess we're going for a walk."

He shot me a wink over his shoulder just before the back door slid shut.

My breath hitched. Why did he have to be so damn good looking?

Shaking off the rush of heat, I turned to Sam. "Okay. Spill. You knew Connor had a thing for me and didn't tell me?"

"It was too tragic." Sam threw up his hands. "I found out right before homecoming. He swore me to secrecy. Then you were gone before he could tell you himself."

I frowned. "Still, you should've said something. We don't keep secrets."

Sam winced. "I thought it was for the best."

"Really?"

Sam raised two dark brows at me. "*Yes.*"

I swallowed, my mind drifting back. "Do you think that's why I never heard from him after I left?"

Sam sighed. "That's something you'll have to ask him. I have no idea what goes on inside the mind of a straight man." He pursed his lips in false disdain.

"I always thought he must have believed the rumors—that I was the kind of girl who..." My throat tightened. "You know how small towns are. A lie like that ruins people."

Sam placed his hand on my forearm and gave it a gentle, knowing squeeze.

My voice cracked. "Even my mom insisted I was lying—Sam, you know I'd never..."

His expression darkened. "Luce." He pulled me into a hug. "No one ever really believed that rumor. Especially not Connor."

I hesitated. "How do you know?"

Sam's gaze didn't waver. "I just do."

I took a long sip of my drink. "You know, I still think Amanda started those rumors."

Sam frowned. "Didn't your mom say it wasn't her?"

"She did, but my mother isn't exactly a reliable source. Besides, we both know Amanda could've had one of her minions do it."

"Fair," Sam conceded, then smoothly shifted gears. "Anyway, that's all in the past. What I want to know is—are you *actually* into my brother?"

My stomach fluttered. Then guilt crept in. "Yes... but until now, I was so caught up in him—and all the grief—that I almost forgot he ghosted me after I left."

Sam scoffed, a little too dismissive for my taste, as he strummed the countertop. "So what? You ghosted literally everyone but me and your dad."

"Actually, I didn't." My voice sharpened, the need to defend myself rising. "I sent Connor letters, Christmas cards, emails..." the words cut like shards of glass. "But I never heard from him."

My admission reignited the countless restless nights I'd spent wondering if he thought the worst of me.

Sam shook his head. "I don't know, Luce. But dragging up the past won't do you any favors."

I exhaled. "But—"

"Let it go," Sam said, waving me off.

Doubt crawled into my gut. I had a history of picking the wrong guys. And if Connor cared *so much*, why hadn't he called me *once* in six years?

I sighed. "I haven't been thinking straight since I got here."

"With good reason," Sam said.

"Maybe I need to step back before jumping into anything. I have to finish school—I can't just start something and leave a couple of weeks later. That'd be crazy, right?"

Sam shrugged. "Well... yeah."

I nodded. "So, you think I should keep things... in the friend zone?"

Sam hesitated.

Just a fraction of a second too long.

I narrowed my eyes. "Tell me."

"It's nothing," he said, too quickly. "Connor's great. Thoughtful, generous..."

The way he trailed off made my stomach tighten.

"Sam. Just say it."

His face crumpled, and he sighed. "Fine. Connor has a reputation for sleeping around."

I sank back, relief washing over me. "Well, that's not so bad."

After all, I'd done the same—tried to forget him, to forget everything. Not that it did me much good. I'd spent the past year trying to relearn how to love myself after the fallout of those toxic choices.

I closed my eyes, forcing away the memories I refused to touch. "Sam, he's a good guy though, right?"

His features tensed.

The pause stretched, just a beat too long.

Then, finally, he nodded. "Yeah. He really is." A flicker of something unreadable passed through his expression. "I wish I was half as good a person as him."

I exhaled sharply. "I hate that I can't trust my instincts. For a second, I thought you were about to tell me something *awful* about him. How messed up is that?"

My throat tightened. "To be honest, with Connor... I've never felt safer. If I'm wrong about him, I don't think I could trust myself again."

Sam went still.

"What?"

His expression was unreadable. Then he exhaled, shaking his head. "Just... be careful, Luce. He's gone back to Amanda so many times. I don't want to see you get hurt."

I nodded, jaw tight. "I kind of hate hearing that, but—I appreciate you looking out for me." I straightened and gave him a tight hug, "Love you."

The corner of his mouth curved up, but it didn't quite reach his eyes.

"Love you too, bestie."

CHAPTER EIGHT

What We Never Said

LUCY

Laughter filled the dinner table, sparked by Sam's outrageous NYU party stories—each one wilder than the last. By the second round of drinks, I finally felt ready to face the daunting task of searching through my dad's office.

We divided the room, each taking a filing cabinet. Hours passed as we sifted through years of business documents, property blueprints, divorce papers, receipts, and proof of monthly child support payments. My exhaustion mounted with every drawer we closed.

Sam held up a bank statement, frowning. "I wonder whose name he kept striking out on these." He tilted it toward the light, squinting at the ink smudges.

I slumped into a chair with a weary sigh. "It's not here."

Sam exhaled, tapping the paper against his palm. "Must be in his room."

A hollow weight settled in my chest.

"Ugh, I need another drink." I pushed myself up and headed for the kitchen.

Sam was right behind me, already reaching for the bourbon.

Connor's hand grazed mine. The warmth of his touch sent a quiet shiver up my arm.

"How are you holding up?" His voice soft, threaded with concern.

I forced a breath, tucking my hands into my pockets. "I'm okay. Honestly, I don't think I'm ready to find this thing. It makes everything feel so... real. The idea of stepping into my dad's bedroom—I just can't. At least not tonight. Sam's here. I'd like to enjoy his first night without falling apart."

I sighed, then let out a small, sheepish chuckle. "Sorry... I don't even know why I just told you all that."

Connor's arms wrapped around me; his solid presence was everything. "I'm glad you did. And if that's the case, let's wait. There's no rush."

I let myself sink into him, absorbing the quiet reassurance in his voice. Then, Sam's earlier apprehension went off like an alarm bell inside me. I nodded, pulling away. "You're right."

Sam slid fresh drinks toward us as we took a seat at the dining room table. "So, Lucy," he mused. "What would you do if you suddenly owned this place?"

I took a sip before answering. "Honestly? No idea. The thought kind of freaks me out."

Connor's gaze seared my cheek from beside me. "How come?"

The words spilled out before I had time to process them. "If I inherit the ranch, what do I do? Drop out of RVC? I'm so close to finishing my undergrad."

Connor frowned. "That's right. Bob mentioned it's the top veterinary school in the world."

Sam grinned. "It is. And Lucy's specializing in equine medicine. The best of the best, folks!"

I shrugged, tempering his enthusiasm. "I always planned to move back and build my own practice here."

Connor nodded, thoughtful. "There's still time to figure it out."

"There is," I admitted, my voice softening. "Last week, I deferred a semester. I thought..." I paused, letting my new reality sink in a little further. "I thought I might need more time here with my dad before going back."

Grief sliced its unrelenting claws through me. I felt my shoulders slump under the weight of the harsh emotional drain.

Sam reached over, squeezing my shoulder. "I'm sorry things didn't go differently, Luce."

"Me too." I gulped down the rest of my drink, the burn of the bourbon keeping the ache at bay. "But... owning a successful ranch could be a solid future. Would I even need my degree anymore?"

Connor's voice was gentle but firm. "That's a decision only you can make. But your dad was so proud of everything you've achieved—I think your education is something worth holding onto."

I bit my lip, his words settling deeper than I expected. "Maybe. But we don't know if he left me the ranch anyway. No use worrying about it right now."

Sam rubbed the back of his neck. "Didn't mean to make things so heavy. Sorry, Luce." He clapped his hands together, forcing a smile. "Now, how about a game of pool? I'll even let you two fight over who loses to me first."

Connor stood. "Actually, I should probably let you two catch up."

I reached for his hand instinctively. "Before you go, I need to talk to you. Sam, do you mind? I promise you can have me for the rest of the night."

Sam winked. "Take your time." His voice dripped with suggestion.

I rolled my eyes. "You're impossible."

Connor shot him a warning look.

Sam giggled. "Sorry, not sorry!"

Connor exhaled, glancing at me. "Walk me out to the trailer?"

The night air carried a crisp, earthy scent, mingling with the faint tang of hay and cattle. A soft breeze rustled through the trees, the leaves whispering overhead. Gravel crunched beneath our feet, the rhythm matching the thoughts swirling in my mind.

I kept my hand wrapped around his, afraid to let go.

"Connor," I began carefully. "I need to know something."

"Anything."

I hesitated, then let the words tumble into the air between us. "Why didn't you ever reach out after I left?"

Connor's brow furrowed. "I could ask you the same."

Frustration tightened my throat. "*Seriously*? I wrote to you for two years after I moved. *Two. Years.* Letters, Christmas cards, emails. You were the only person I reached out to besides my dad and Sam. Yet—"

He froze mid-step.

His head snapped toward me, confusion darkening his gaze. "*What?*"

I stepped closer, searching his face. "Connor, I can get over it, but I need you to be honest—you believed the worst, didn't you?"

His face fell, as if I'd struck him. "No, Lucy. I didn't." His voice was rough, raw. "I swear, I never believed that rumor. That's why I asked about what happened. I've been wanting to know the truth for six years because I never once thought that was the real reason you left."

His gaze locked onto mine, fierce, unwavering. "Lucy, I—I would've written back if I'd known. I swear to you, I didn't get *anything*. Not a letter, not an email. And it killed me." His voice cracked. "I thought... you didn't want to hear from me."

My breathing faltered. "What? How is that even possible?"

"Maybe your emails went to spam, but letters? Those don't just disappear." His voice held a tinge of panic, his eyes searching mine. "I swear, Lucy. Seeing Sam get your letters, your calls—it nearly *destroyed* me. It was like I never meant anything to you."

My stomach plummeted.

Sam got my letters.

I sucked in a slow breath, fighting to keep my expression neutral.

I closed my eyes, bracing myself. "Promise me you're not lying."

His jaw clenched. "I never saw a single one."

My eyes shot open, searching. The tension in my muscles softened as my hands dropped to my sides.

Connor ran a hand through his hair, exhaling sharply. "I should have called anyway. I was young, and a complete idiot."

Tears pricked my eyes. "All this time, I thought you believed..."

Connor stepped closer, taking my hands. "*No,* Lucy. Not for a second."

The air between us crackled. He leaned in, resting his forehead on mine.

I whispered, "If you had feelings for me, how did you end up with *her*?"

He swallowed hard, jaw tightening. "The girl I loved left without saying goodbye. And Amanda was just... there. She made it seem like she was just as hurt as I was." His voice was almost bitter. "She became a distraction and then everything got so complicated..."

His eyes locked onto mine, the pull between us tightening like an invisible thread. An unspoken question hanging between us.

"And now?" I whispered, breath hitching. "Is there a chance you'll go back to her?"

His brows knitted. "No."

I inhaled shakily. "This is dangerous. If we..." I cleared my throat. "You know I have to go back to London."

"I know," he said, his voice rough as sandpaper..

"What do we do?"

He exhaled slowly. "I know what I *want* to do..."

The night air burned between us as his lips brushed mine—stealing my breath, my thoughts, my every last bit of my restraint.

Connor bent down, his breath warm against my skin, his lips grazing my jaw in a deliberate, agonizing tease. "I want *this*... want you," he said softly, the huskiness in his voice sending sparks coursing down my spine.

Without hesitation, my hands gripped his collar, pulling him in.

His touch ignited every nerve in my body. Connor's lips devoured me with a hunger that made the world around us disappear. His hands slid to my waist, pulling me flush against him as his mouth moved with desperate need over mine. My fingers threaded through his hair, holding him close as red-hot desire shot through me, overwhelming my senses. His lips trailed down to my neck, sending another shiver down my spine.

"Even after I left," I whispered breathlessly, "I imagined this. I imagined you... doing this to me."

He pulled back, his eyes widening in surprise. "You... did?"

I bit my lip, nodding. His gaze darkened. "I've had feelings for you for as long as I can remember."

Then his lips were on mine again, and the world around me ceased to exist. I gasped as his teeth raked against my lower lip. I thought I might burn alive.

I pulled back, my voice faltering. "We need to stop."

His hands dropped instantly, and he took a step back. I'd never seen anything like it—he'd respected my words the moment they left my lips. I swallowed down the raw emotion.

"Okay." He breathed. "We can move as fast or as slow as you want. I've been waiting for you for eight years. I can wait for as long as it takes."

"Thank you. That means a lot to me." I sighed, pinching the bridge of my nose, fighting back the emotions his words—and his actions—brought to the surface. I took a breath, looked back up at him, and grinned. "Well, your brother is waiting for me. But I promise we can resume this conversation later." I gave his hands a reassuring squeeze.

A deep rumble escaped his chest—half a laugh, half a sigh—his shoulders sagged under the weight of disappointment. "You're going to be the death of me, Lucy."

I smirked, rising onto my tiptoes to press one last kiss to his lips. "I might be."

Turning toward the house, I felt the heat of his touch still burning against my skin. A lingering smile tugged at my lips as I walked away, knowing sleep would not come easily tonight.

Just before stepping inside, I glanced back one last time. Connor stood there, his body taut with restraint, his gaze fixed on me with a longing that mirrored my own.

It took every ounce of my willpower to push forward, shutting the door behind me. My lips still tingled with the memory of his kiss, playing on a loop in my mind as my resolve began to fray.

CHAPTER NINE

Before Midnight

LUCY

After a late night of playing pool and several rounds of drinks, I went to bed dizzy with the haze of alcohol. Hot, wicked dreams, I hadn't experienced in years, spun a web of intoxicating scenes of touch, taste, and toe curling pleasure. Connor starred in every last, vivid moment. Sweet, breath-stealing need built inside me. His lips parted and trailed lower. My mind raced, begging and pleading with myself not to wake up.

Then I woke to the bed sinking down beside me, the heat of another body reaching my senses as an arm snaked around me.

I let out a sigh mixed with longing and desire. "I missed you."

"Ew! It's me." Sam smacked my arm.

I hissed at the sudden sharp sting. "Ouch! Hey! Sorry, I didn't realize..."

"Jesus, what kind of dreams were you having?" Sam chided, his tone a mix of mock disgust and curiosity.

"You don't want to know." I chuckled. "They may or may not have involved your brother."

"Okay, gross. What happened to you putting on the brakes with Connor?" Sam sat up, his narrowed gaze locking onto mine.

I sighed, running a hand through my hair. "After talking with him last night... something changed, Sam. He never got my letters. Not a single one."

His eyebrows shot up. "Wait—what?" His voice hitched with disbelief. "That's so weird."

"I know," I nodded, my stomach twisting just thinking about it. "But I believe him. Like you said, he's a good guy."

Sam frowned, tilting his head. "Yeah... you're right. And now that I think about it, I never saw any letters for him either."

I pushed myself up onto my elbows, my pulse quickening. "Is it crazy to think Amanda had something to do with it?"

Sam exhaled sharply, looking down at the blankets as he considered it. "It wouldn't be the craziest thing she's done, but how would she even pull that off?"

"Well, her dad's the mayor. Maybe there's someone at the post office she could manipulate into helping her?"

Sam scoffed, but didn't dismiss the idea outright. "Wouldn't put it past her," he admitted. "But that's a hell of a risk. Messing with the mail is a federal offense."

I frowned. "Like that would stop her?"

He hesitated, then shrugged. "Could be." But his voice didn't quite match his words—like he wasn't sure if he believed them himself.

Before I could press him, he threw off the covers and stood, stretching with a groan. "Listen, I'm gonna make breakfast. Then we need to get to work—we've got a lot to do for Papa Bob's celebration of life."

Before I could respond, Sam was already moving, slipping out the door and shutting it behind him.

I furrowed my brow, watching him go. It wasn't like Sam to sidestep juicy gossip, especially something *this* suspicious. But then, I hadn't considered how my dad's death was affecting him.

The realization sat heavy in my chest.

Frowning, I reached for my phone on the nightstand. The screen lit up with a new text notification.

Connor:

> I'd like to take you out tonight. A real date. Just you and me.

A slow smile spread across my lips, the weight in my chest lifting just enough to let in something lighter, something warm. I bit my lower lip as I typed my reply.

Me:

> *Pick me up at six. I know it's a long drive, but don't be late.*

Connor:

> *Haha! I'll do my best. See you tonight. Can't wait to have you all to myself...*

A slow, unmistakable heat curled low in my stomach.

I exhaled, shaking off the rush of anticipation, and forced myself out of bed.

Me:

> *Great. Now I need a cold shower.*

Connor's reply was a single winking emoji, and I couldn't help but giggle—an unfiltered, carefree sound I hadn't heard from myself in a long time.

He was bringing back parts of me I'd buried when I moved to London, pieces I thought had been lost to time and distance. And I wasn't upset about it.

By the time I made it to the kitchen, Sam had already set a plate out for me at the breakfast bar.

As I slid onto the stool, I tried—*really* tried—not to think about Connor lifting me onto that very countertop, his hands gripping my thighs, his body pressed between my legs.

Heat bloomed in my chest, spreading lower—traitorous, unbidden, and impossible to ignore.

Sam's voice snapped me out of it. "Do you have a list of what we need for Friday's celebration?"

"List?" I blinked.

Sam sighed. "Oh, bless your heart," he pouted, giving me a slow pat on the shoulder.

I narrowed my eyes at his hand in warning. Then, without missing a beat, he launched into planning mode, assembling a comprehensive list of everything we'd need for Friday's celebration of life.

Sam tapped his pen against his notebook, glancing up at me. "Alright, optional de-tails—do we want a chocolate fountain? Champagne toast?"

I wrinkled my nose. "No and no. Let's keep it simple."

He sighed. "You're really missing out on a golden opportunity for *class*, Luce. Just imagine: Papa Bob's face projected onto a giant ice sculpture, chocolate cascading like a damn waterfall—"

I shot him a look. "Sam."

"Fine, fine." He grinned, crossing something off his list. "So, what *do* we want?"

I leaned back against the counter, arms crossed. "Horseshoes, music, dancing. An open mic hour, so anyone can share their favorite stories about Dad with everyone."

Sam's expression softened. "Yeah. He'd love that."

A lump formed in my throat, but I swallowed it down, managing a small smile. "Yeah. He would."

We agreed a picture slideshow should play throughout the party—snapshots of my father's life, the things he loved, the moments that made him who he was.

Riding the high of finding such a perfect touch to the celebration, I sat forward, beaming, "Okay! Now what? Do we need decor or...?"

Sam leaned back in his chair, tossing his phone from one hand to the other with a frown. "Lucy, let's be real. You have no idea how to plan a good party."

I shot him a glare, but he held up a hand. "Hey, no offense. I just mean, now that I know what you want, I've got it from here." He caught his phone midair and pointed it at me. "Your job is the slideshow. It should be you picking the pictures. Besides, you were always the one making our class projects look like cinematic masterpieces. You'll make it great. Nay, perfection."

His confidence in me brought a flicker of warmth to my chest.

I swallowed, nodding. "Yeah, I think I'd like to make that for him. Feels like something I *can* do."

Satisfied, Sam turned his attention back to his phone. "Alright, let's see who in this town can feed a crowd without poisoning half of them..."

I huffed a quiet laugh, shaking my head. It was good to see Sam back to his usual self. It felt like a small piece of normal in the middle of all the chaos.

I got to work in the family room, sending out messages to my dad's friends and even Aunt Diane, asking for photos. Then, I pulled album after album from the built-in bookshelves, spreading them across the coffee table as I began sorting through years of memories.

The hours slipped by as I scanned my favorite pictures, arranging them into slides in chronological order on my laptop.

My breath caught when I came across the album from our trip to Glacier National Park. I flipped through its pages, each snapshot transporting me back to that perfect summer.

My dad, grinning in front of the towering mountain peaks, his arm slung casually around my mom's shoulders. Both of them were bundled in bright yellow life vests just before we went whitewater rafting. They looked so happy—so effortless together. Seeing them like this, their separation felt just as confusing now as it did back then.

A smile tugged at my lips as I lingered on a photo of me, arms outstretched for balance on a fallen tree over crystal-clear water. Dad stood just behind me, ready to catch me if I slipped.

Sam had come on that trip too. I chuckled, as my eyes caught on a picture of the two of us drenched from head to toe—the aftermath of an ill-fated rock-skipping contest that ended with both of us in the lake.

I turned the page. Tears pricked my eyes as I stared at the photo, frozen in time. My dad's arm slung around me as we sat by the campfire, marshmallows on sticks, his face lit with that easy, familiar smile that always made everything feel okay. The sting of losing him ran deep and fresh, tearing open a sudden, heavy longing inside me.

On instinct my eyes shut tight. My breathing went shallow.

I could still hear his deep, rumbling laughter from when I'd burned my first marshmallow. He'd plucked it off my stick, popped it in his mouth with a wink, and declared it "extra crispy gourmet."

Then—I could finally *breathe*.

A warmth spread through my chest as I turned the pages, the scent of old paper mixing with the soft hum of the house. The hikes, the late-night storytelling, the way Dad had challenged us to count how many stars we could see before our eyes gave up the fight.

That trip had been full of laughter, of easy happiness. I had never felt safer or more at peace than in those moments surrounded by nature, my parents, and my best friend sharing my tent.

Sam and I stayed up past bedtime, whispering scary stories until we spooked ourselves so badly we had to beg my parents to let us sleep in their tent for the night.

Now, going through these images, the memories felt both close and impossibly distant. The contrast made my throat tighten, but I clung to the warmth they brought.

Maybe, just maybe, those moments weren't gone.

Maybe they still lived here—in these pictures, in *me*.

By five o'clock, my hands ached from adjusting images and typing captions. My stomach growled, reminding me I hadn't eaten since breakfast.

I stretched and checked the time on my phone. I gasped and bolted for the shower.

After freshening up, I blow-dried my hair into a loose updo, curling soft waves at the front to frame my face.

As I finished my makeup, Sam knocked on the bathroom door. "Want me to pick out your outfit?"

"Actually, could you grab the sundress from my suitcase?"

"Only if it's not hideous," he teased.

I laughed. "If you think so, don't tell my mom. She designed it."

A moment later, he cracked open the door and handed me the dress—a sheer floral piece that tied at the neck. The plunging neckline and cinched waist flattered my figure, the fabric flowing effortlessly to my ankles.

When I stepped into the hall, Sam was waiting with my white strappy sandals.

"How did you know I wanted these?" I grinned.

He smirked. "I didn't have many options."

Sliding them on, I sat to tie the straps. A knock at the door sent butterflies swarming through my stomach. Warmth crept up the base of my neck.

Sam answered, greeting Connor with playful sternness as he stepped inside. "Here's the drill. First, you tap it, you wrap it. Safety first. Second, hurt her, I disown you. And finally, you better have her home by midnight." Connor raised his brow at his brother. Sam gave him a shrug, "What? I need to be awake enough to talk shit about your vanilla date choices."

Connor chuckled, but the laughter faded as his eyes met mine, sweeping over me...warm, appreciative. Heat crept up my neck.

"Ready to go?" I asked, injecting a brightness into my voice.

Connor grinned, his gaze unwavering. "Absolutely."

"You got rid of the plaid," I teased, taking in his dark gray dress shirt, polished sterling cufflinks, black slacks, and freshly shined leather boots.

"As requested by my oh-so-loving brother." He removed his black cowboy hat, bowing theatrically before placing it back atop his wavy hair.

I rolled my eyes, suppressing a smile. "I like a man who listens," I quipped.

"Lucky for you, I'm a fantastic listener," he shot back, his grin lazy, confident—the kind that made my pulse skip before I could stop it.

Taking his outstretched hand, I let him lead me to his freshly cleaned truck.

"You did all this for me?" I teased, grinning as I ran a hand over the spotless door.

Connor chuckled. "Impressed?"

"I am. I like that you cared enough to get all your yucky boy smell out before our date. It means a lot." Leaning in, I pressed a quick kiss to his cheek before climbing into the seat.

He shook his head, laughter rumbling in his chest. "Well, I think I'm glad you noticed... but also mildly embarrassed."

His laugh only made my smile widen. "Don't worry, no judgment. I like you whether your truck smells good or like a day of walking through cow patties."

Connor let out a full, unrestrained laugh as he shut the door behind me.

I leaned back against the seat, closing my eyes for a moment, letting myself *feel* it—the lightness, the joy, the anticipation humming beneath my skin.

This was going to be a great night.

A date with *Connor Lochland*?

A full-fledged, teenage dream come true.

Chapter Ten

He Remembered

Lucy

We pulled into the gravel parking lot of *The Wildflower Lounge*, a favorite local restaurant and bar nestled on the edge of town.

The exterior exuded rustic charm with its log cabin-style façade, and its warm amber lights glowed softly against the twilight sky. String lights looped around the porch railings, casting a cozy ambiance that hinted at the lively energy inside.

Through the large windows, I could see patrons mingling at the polished oak bar and couples swaying on the dance floor to the sounds of a live jazz band.

A wooden sign above the entrance bore the lounge's name, the letters skillfully burned into the surface, their dark edges contrasting beautifully against the rich, natural grain of the wood. Subtle carvings of wildflowers framed the text, lending an understated charm to its rugged elegance.

It was exactly as I had imagined it would be when I was younger—romantic, lively, and quintessentially *Montana*.

"Oh my gosh! I've never eaten here before," I gasped, childhood excitement bubbled up inside me.

Connor grinned. "I had a feeling."

The lounge had a strict age restriction, making it a favorite date night hotspot in town.

"You mentioned once you couldn't wait until you were old enough to come here when we were younger. Let's see if it holds up to your expectations," he said, opening his truck door.

He walked around and helped me down, his hand steady on my waist as I rebalanced myself in my heels.

"I can't believe you remember me saying that," I said, taking his arm as we made our way to the entrance.

Connor shrugged. "See? Good listener."

I let out a soft giggle. "*Apparently.*"

The restaurant was bustling, which surprised me since it was a Wednesday night. A singer's smoky vibrato darkened the atmosphere with layers of hidden seduction. I imagined Connor pulling me in, his hands slowly drifting down my sides, the heat of his breath on my neck.

"Lochland, party of two?"

I blinked, my cheeks heated as if everyone could hear my thoughts.

"Ready?" Connor stretched out his hand, offering a gentle grin.

My stomach fluttered and I nodded.

The young hostess led us to a polished wooden table in a separate room featuring a stunning chandelier adorned with elk antlers. The leather-lined booth had a small lantern lit on the table adding the right mix of rustic charm and romance.

"Oh my stars, Lucy Campbell, is that you?" Irene Waverly's voice carried across the room. Her bright red hair was pulled back into a tight ponytail, and a radiant smile lit up her porcelain features.

She hurried over to the table, her Wildflower Lounge uniform—a black button-up blouse tucked neatly into black dress pants with a matching apron tied snugly around her ample waist—presenting a polished, professional appearance.

"Irene!" I exclaimed, standing from the booth to give her a big hug.

She beamed at me with authentic, blinding joy. "I haven't seen you since high school. How have you been?"

"Okay," I said with a shrug and a forced smile, eager to steer the conversation away from myself before the sudden pang of grief became the focal point of the conversation. "My goodness, how have you been? It's been forever. Are you still writing?"

She shook her head with a light laugh. "My days of poetry are long over. But I'm doing great. I've got two little ones now. Jed and I are married. Life's *really* good."

"That's amazing! Wow, I'd love to stop by sometime and meet your sweet babies." I couldn't help but feel overwhelming happiness for her.

"We'll all be at your father's celebration this Friday," she said. Then she flinched, her hand flying to her mouth. "Oh God, forgive me. I got so excited to see you, I forgot myself. I'm so sorry for your loss, Lucy."

"It's okay, thank you," I said, waving it off.

Irene glanced at Connor, recognition lighting her face. "Connor *Lochland*! It's been a while. Haven't seen you here in a couple of months. How's Amanda?"

I swallowed hard as a knot formed in my throat. I wasn't sure if hearing Amanda's name would ever stop filling me with an instant, unyielding flash of hatred. God, I felt so childish.

Connor replied smoothly, "I'm not sure. We broke up a few weeks ago."

At that, I took my seat, offering him a tight smile.

"Oh my, I'm so sorry! I remember reading about that in *The White River Whisper*, now." Irene blushed, then her eyes flickered between Connor and me, widening with realization.

"Wait a minute—are you two on a *date*?!"

Connor took my hand, sending a thrilling flutter through me. "We are."

"Oh, I love this for you both!" she squealed. "What can I get for you to start for your drinks?"

"Could we please get some waters while we decide on a wine?" Connor asked, the picture-perfect gentleman.

Irene nodded. "Absolutely, I'll be right back with those."

My cheeks flushed as my eyes met Connor's apologetic stare.

His thumb brushed the top of my hand as he lowered his voice to apologize. "Sorry about that. Tonight was supposed to be just about us."

I shook my head, offering a small smile. "It's fine. It's a small town. Besides, you're allowed to have a past."

The words felt hollow even as I said them, but the logical part of my brain knew they were true.

"What's *The White River Whisper*?"

Connor cleared his throat, a small grimace tugging at the corner of his mouth. "It's an online gossip column the whole town reads obsessively. Unfortunately, I tend to end up on there... *a lot*."

"Oh," I chuckled, leaning in. "So I'm dating a local celebrity?"

Connor closed his eyes, shaking his head as his cheeks tinged with pink. "Not in my book."

"He's modest too," I teased, giving his hand a reassuring squeeze. "Don't worry, I don't read gossip articles. My mom's had her fair share of drama in the London spotlight. It's all just a bunch of fabricated tales with little basis in fact... more like speculation, just juicy enough to get clicks."

Connor shifted uncomfortably before clearing his throat. "Exactly. Well, anyway... I was thinking of ordering a bottle of wine. If you *like* wine, of course."

I grinned. "You're adorable. Yes, I love wine. I mean, I spent the last six years in high-society London—I kind of *had* to develop a taste for it."

He chuckled. "That's right. *I'm* dating a fancy socialite now."

I rolled my eyes. "Hardly."

He smirked, leaning in. "Okay, *London*, white or red?"

"Definitely red," I told him, scowling. "And you can call me *Lucy*, or Luce even."

"Not London, then?" He nodded, taking a deep breath, trying—and failing—to stifle his amusement.

"Nope. Not London."

His deep chuckle was contagious. "You got it, Lucy. Anyway, I have a favorite if you're okay with me picking."

I leaned back, a slow grin tugging at my lips. "Oh, I'm *very* interested in what *Connor Lochland* considers a good wine. Please *do*."

"Hopefully, I don't disappoint," he said with a grin, closing the wine list and setting it aside.

As I scanned the menu, my eyes widened at the descriptions.

"Well, look at that," I mused. "They've got local steak from *Campbell Ranch*—filet, ribeye, strip." A flicker of pride warmed my voice before I glanced at him with a teasing smile. "*And* there are tomahawks from *Lochland Farms*. Which is better?"

Connor flushed. "Entirely your choice. My cattle come from strong Campbell lines—your dad was generous when I started out. Quality-wise, there's no wrong option. The chef here knows how to do our beef justice."

"Nothing beats farm to table." I cringed. "Wow, that sounded basic!"

"Lucy Campbell, you are *anything* but basic..."

I cleared my throat as the rush of heat bloomed in my chest, "Thanks." I bit my lip for a moment before shifting topics. "Where *is* your ranch, anyway?"

Connor leaned back. "Actually... we're neighbors. My land borders your father's property."

My eyes widened. "Oh, wow. I didn't realize."

He shrugged. "It hadn't come up yet."

We ordered our wine and meals, settling into easy conversation. When the bottle of cabernet arrived, Connor took it and poured each of us a healthy glass.

He watched me with bated breath as I took a slow sip. "How is it?"

I grinned. "Not bad... for a rancher."

His hesitation was brief but noticeable. I softened, nudging his foot lightly under the table. "*Kidding.* It's *really* good. The perfect balance of smoky and fruity flavors. It's dry, but not bitter. It'll pair well with my ribeye. I love it."

He relaxed, that easy smile returning, making him somehow even more handsome. "I'm glad you like it."

When we finished our plates, Connor recommended the cheesecake brûlée.

The sugar cracked like thin glass as I dug into the first bite. The moment it hit my tongue I moaned. "Oh my God! This is the best thing I've ever eaten in my entire life."

Despite how nice the evening was going, my thoughts kept drifting— questions pressed in, intrusive and relentless, refusing to let me fully enjoy the moment.

I hesitated, then took a steadying breath. "Do you mind if I ask you something that isn't exactly *date-appropriate*?"

"Not at all. What's on your mind?"

I took another deep breath, and the words tumbled out in a rushed, jumbled mess.

"Thanks. I just can't stop thinking about how everything happened with my dad. I keep waking up from these weird dreams—like my mind is trying to piece together what happened, from the moment my dad got sick to... to him not coming home. Is that—*normal*?"

Connor set down his fork and leaned forward as a shadow of grief darkened his features. "After Alex... I had a *ton* of nightmares. He kept calling me, begging me to help him, and I could *never* get there in time." His words caught, cracking in his throat. He sipped some water then nodded, "But, after a few weeks they stopped."

I swallowed hard, the familiar lump rising in my throat. "Some of the nightmares are *really* awful. Maybe if I had clarity on what happened, they'd stop. But I don't know how much you know, or if you were even there—"

Connor stiffened. "No, Kyle was the one who brought him in. He needed to take time off after... everything."

Kyle.

He wasn't just another ranch hand, he was *the* head of operations, running the day-to-day alongside my dad. Kyle had gone to school with me and Sam, though he was a year ahead of us. Mostly, I remembered him as a rodeo guy—always polite, but never someone I'd known very well.

Connor continued, "I mean, I visited him in the hospital, but he wanted me at the ranch looking after the animals. So I did that. Sometimes the nurses would let me visit after hours. But I wasn't the one getting all the medical updates. *Diane* did, but Lord knows what she'd say happened."

I swallowed, my fingers tightening around the stem of my wine glass. "When I called, he said he felt like he was living in an episode of *The Twilight Zone*."

Connor shifted in his seat, his blue eyes growing distant as he nodded.

The memory had me gritting my teeth. "You know, I would have been here the day of his fistula surgery. I hate that I let Diane talk me into waiting to come out." I clenched my fists but, deep down, I knew I had no one to blame but myself.

"I'm so sorry, Luce. You couldn't have known what would happen." Connor reached across the table, placing a hand over mine.

I let out a bitter laugh. "Yeah, I don't know. My last conversation with him... he knew he wasn't okay. In my gut..." My voice faltered, my throat tightening as I glanced at Connor. "I just *knew* it would be the last time I spoke to him."

"Lucy..." He breathed, gently squeezing my hand.

"I told him how much I loved him. And when he told me he thought he was dying..." My voice wavered as unwanted tears swelled behind my eyes.

"I gave him *permission*, Connor." The words tumbled out, raw and aching. "I told him if something happened and he needed to let go, I'd be *okay*. But I'm *not*."

My breath hitched, my chest tightening as the weight of it pressed down. "It's *my* fault. He stopped fighting because of *me*."

The tears came in an unstoppable wave, spilling down my face. I grabbed the cloth napkin and buried my face in it, the fabric soaking up my quiet sobs as I struggled to pull myself together, my hands trembling.

"Luce, listen to me. This wasn't your fault." His thumb traced slow, soothing circles over my skin. "You didn't see how bad it was. I know it doesn't feel like it right now, but that conversation you had with him—it was a gift. It was *exactly* what he needed to hear."

I let out a shaky breath. "But I could've changed my flight," I argued, my voice trembling. "After I hung up, I told myself I was being paranoid. Two more days wouldn't make a difference, right?" My throat tightened. "I even asked the nurse if it seemed like..." I shook my head as my words trailed off. "He *insisted* my dad was okay, and I believed him. I convinced myself he'd still be there when I arrived. He was always there—he couldn't just... *not* be."

The words crumbled.

My head dropped as a silent sob shook through me.

Connor's grip on my hand was warm and steady, grounding me as it had so many times over the past few days.

"I know, Luce," Connor said, his voice raw, cracking under the weight of his own grief. He inhaled shakily. "He was larger than life. Someone who shined so bright, I thought nothing could ever take him down. Not *anything*. No matter how worried I was, I never once believed he wouldn't make it out of there."

I wiped my face with my free hand, comforted by the shared pain—knowing someone else understood the depth of my grief, the depth of my love for him.

Laughing softly through another sob, I nodded. "He really was the best. If I ever missed one of his calls, he'd leave these *ridiculously* long voicemails. At least two minutes long. Every single time."

Connor chuckled, a stray tear slipping down his cheek. "I can hear him now. *'Hi Lucy, it's your favorite dad...'*" His smile wavered before he continued. "He was so proud of you, you know. Talked about you constantly. I think the whole town knew when you got accepted into the Royal Veterinary College."

"I'm sure," I murmured, a small, bittersweet smile tugging at my lips.

Silence settled between us, thick with unspoken emotions.

The air around me became a little easier to take in. I felt myself calming, coming to terms with everything, yet I needed a moment to gather myself.

Forcing some steadiness into my voice, I broke the silence. "Hey, I'm just gonna run to the ladies' room real quick. I'll be right back."

I stood, moving through the restaurant in a daze. The buzzing conversations around me dissolved into meaningless static. I found myself at the bathroom sink, gripping the edges of the counter as I forced myself to take slow, deep breaths.

Suddenly, a voice cut through my thoughts.

"Lucy! It's *so* good to see you—and looking *so* good too, after becoming a teen mom."

Venom laced the syrupy sweet tone, false sincerity dripping from every word.

My stomach clenched.

No. Absolutely not. Not tonight.

CHAPTER ELEVEN

Smoke and Mirrors

LUCY

I turned to find a sleek figure standing beside me.

"Danika," I said coolly.

Her chocolate-brown hair fell into a sharp, blunt bob, every strand perfectly in place. Gold-flecked amber eyes narrowed slightly, and a forced smile tugged at her rouged lips—polished, poised, and calculating. A skill honed under the watchful eye of her best friend and mentor, Amanda Johnson.

Her smirk faltered, her saccharine tone slipping. "You do realize Connor's taken."

"Danika, no more games. We're not in high school anymore. You can drop the act. Stop doing everything Amanda tells you to do." I folded my arms, ready for this childish interaction to be over.

She tilted her head, voice dripping with condescension. "Oh, please. The only one playing games here is Connor. He lives to make Amanda jealous. At this point, he's gone through nearly every eligible woman in town just to get a rise out of her."

The words stung, but I forced myself to stay controlled. "That's nice. Anything else?"

"They love the chase," she continued, her voice lilting into mock concern. "It keeps them coming back to each other. Just thought I'd warn you. After everything you've been through, I'd hate to see you make a fool of yourself."

Anger curled in my chest, heat rising under my skin. "I'm sure you're just looking out for me," I said dryly, fighting the urge to say something I might regret.

Danika's smile sharpened, eyes gleaming with malice. "Listen, you can't just waltz back into town and take Amanda's man."

"I'm not taking anything. You know what? Never mind. This is ridiculous." I made to leave.

"Don't fool yourself—Connor brought you here because you're a convenient place-holder until she takes him back." Her eyes flickered to the doorway, so fast I almost didn't catch it.

I clenched my fists, my nails biting into my palms. "Danika, are you trying to stall me?"

"I'm looking out for my best friend." Her indifferent voice returned me to the present.

"No, Danika. Maybe if we were still teenagers. But not even then. Sam and I? We'd never corner and threaten people in bathrooms. Either grow up or move over, because this isn't cute anymore. It never was. Now, if you'll excuse me." I sidestepped around her, not giving her a second thought.

I stormed out of the restroom. My pulse pounded in my ears as I stalked back to the table, only to stop short.

Amanda was there.

And Connor stood beside our table *holding* her.

His arm wrapped around her shoulders, head dipped close as if whispering reassurances in her ear. She clung to him, her face buried in his chest, her body shaking like she'd been crying.

Deep breaths.

Connor's concerned gaze met mine as I approached. Amanda's glistening eyes flickered up and seemed to smile as she met my blank stare.

I closed my eyes, reminding myself to be the woman my dad expected me to be by swallowing the snide remark on the tip of my tongue. Instead, I masked my voice in kindness and asked, "Are you okay, Amanda?"

Her lower lip quivered. "No. It's a tough night. Sorry. Connor's the *only* person I can talk to about this..." Her eyes lit for a split second at the implication.

I wouldn't take the bait.

"If you needed to talk to Connor for a minute, all you had to do was ask. There was no reason to send Danika into the restroom to harass me." The exhaustion that filled my very bones wore into the strain dragging against each word.

Amanda's eyes went wide. "What are you talking about?"

"Lucy, please," Connor interjected. "I don't know what Danika did, but Amanda's actually having a rough night." He took a small step toward me, Amanda still clinging to his side.

"Please, don't tell her." Her glistening eyes batted up at Connor. "Not here. This is between us. Our past. Our relationship. Okay?"

My jaw clenched, hands curled into fists at my sides.

Connor's brow furrowed. "You okay?"

I let out a slow breath, forcing my voice to stay even, though my insides were burning. "I'm fine. Do you need a minute to finish your conversation?"

"I'm sorry, Amanda." Danika's voice sent goosebumps over my back.

Great. Now there's two of them. I stiffened.

Amanda gasped, her eyes filled with feigned horror. "Danika, did you ambush Lucy?" She shook her head as if distraught. "Her father just died. How could you? What were you thinking?"

Danika blanched. "I saw her here with Connor..." she began, her eyes searching Amanda's pouting gaze. "I just wanted to be a loyal friend to you... that's all."

Amanda's gaze narrowed. "Apologize to Lucy."

"Sorry," Danika said, with a little hair toss.

My eyes darted between them, my stomach twisting. "Connor, can we get back to our date?"

Connor's eyes clocked my fists tightening at my sides. A muscle feathered in his jaw. He opened his mouth to speak, but Danika beat him to the punch, placing a comforting hand on Amanda's shoulder. "Are you okay?"

Amanda's head fell into her hands, and she began to sob.

"This is bullshit." The hushed murmur came out before I could stop it.

Connor's head whipped up, then his eyes locked with mine. "Lucy. Maybe you should go cool off?"

"Right." I let out a sharp, humorless laugh.

Connor's forehead creased. "I'll be out in a minute..."

I scoffed, my patience snapping.

Beside my date, Amanda's lip quivered as she clung to his arm like her life depended on it. "I'm so sorry, Lucy. Thanks for giving us time to talk. It's just been a really awful night. Connor was just—"

"It's fine, Amanda. Talk to him. Hijack our date. I don't care." My voice turned to ice.

The corner of Amanda's mouth twitched, then she caught herself. Instead of smirking she burst into inconsolable sobs. My stomach dropped as Connor embraced her.

This bitch... I thought, shaking my head in disbelief.

"That's enough, Lucy." Connor's voice cut through the air. "I'll explain everything later. Just go. I'll meet you at the truck in a few minutes. Amanda needs me right now."

The sting of his words hit me like a slap to the face. I held back a fresh wave of frustration.

"Great. You do that. When you're done, take me *home*," I said, my voice like steel—cold, sharp, unyielding.

His head jerked back slightly, surprise flickering across his face. "Lucy, I swear I can explain—"

"No, Connor. I'm done." I gave a single nod to Amanda and Danika. "Goodnight."

"Lucy..." Connor started.

"Don't," I snapped. "You're right. I need a minute." I snatched my bag from the booth before turning and making my way out the front doors.

The crisp night air did nothing to temper the blazing anger. I paced the sidewalk outside the restaurant. Connor's defense of Amanda was almost too much to bear.

"Lucy! What happened?" Irene's voice cut through the stillness as she hurried out of the restaurant toward me.

"Nothing. I'm just an *idiot*," I said with a shrug.

"No, you definitely are not. You two were having such a nice time..."

My face soured. "You're right. But..."

Irene pressed her lips into a thin line. "I saw Amanda. What did she do now?"

"Nothing." My fingers curled into fists as my outrage flared, hot and unrelenting. "She's just got Connor wrapped around her little finger." I let out a sharp breath, my jaw tightening. "Damn it, Sam tried to warn me. I should have listened."

Irene let out an exasperated sigh. "Oh, Lucy, don't say that. Amanda makes Connor miserable. She still goes around screwing with people's lives. Did you know she had her dad pull funding from the elementary school to throw her twenty-first birthday party? Well, allegedly."

"Seriously? Must be nice having a corrupt mayor for a father," I scoffed. "Why doesn't Connor see her for what she is?"

"Nothing's ever that simple, Luce. Connor's a good man. He... I shouldn't say."

I quirked a brow at her.

"No really, you need to talk to him. He can't help wanting to be there for her," Irene frowned.

"And that's the problem. I love that he's so... him. But I don't have the strength to deal with Amanda just showing up all the time. You know how awful she was in high school."

"You're right." Irene's face fell slightly, regret slipping into her voice. "Lucy... I just wanted to say I'm sorry."

I raised my brow at her.

"For letting Amanda decide who I could and couldn't talk to," she explained.

I patted her arm, softening. "Seriously, don't worry about it. We're good. I don't even remember what you're talking about."

But I did remember.

There had been a full year where our entire grade acted like Sam and I didn't exist.

Amanda had spread some twisted lie, insisting we were contagious. That if anyone got too close, they'd catch AIDS and die.

All because, what? Sam had finally come out?

He was ready—ready to face whatever bigotry our small town might throw at him, ready to stop hiding who he was.

And she... she nearly *destroyed* him with her vicious lies.

My stomach twisted with fresh pain, the memory nearly unbearable. Much like Amanda's lingering presence in Connor's life.

She was a monster.

The things she'd said, the hatred she'd fueled—it was unthinkable.

I never knew why she started it. Or why she ended it. But those months were pure hell.

Tears pricked my eyes.

Irene's voice pulled me from my spiraling thoughts. "Thank you for that." Her shoulders sank with relief before her expression hardened. "And honey, just be patient with Connor. People like Amanda always get what's coming to them. True colors always shine through in time."

"Right." I let out a slow breath, offering her a sad half-smile. "I just hope he sees the truth before it's too late—for everyone's sake."

"Me too. With you, I don't think I've ever seen him so happy. I love that for him. I hope you two can work this out."

Her words were meant to comfort me, but they only added fuel to the storm of doubt roiling inside me. I'd been home for what, a few days? And the drama felt unending.

Between Aunt Diane and Amanda, I could only handle one toxic person in my life right now.

"Thanks for coming out here and checking on me," I said, forcing another small smile.

"Of course." She fidgeted with her pen a moment before adding, "And in case you're wondering how she knew you two were here... There was a tip on *The Whisper*."

"The gossip column?" I gaped at her. "That fast?!"

She nodded, then glanced toward the restaurant. "Listen, I'd better head back in and get back to work. My boss is probably wondering where I ran off to," she laughed. Then, her expression brightened. "But hey, I'd love to hang out sometime. I have this Saturday off, and it's karaoke night at *The Saloon*. If you're interested, it starts at nine."

I let out a quiet laugh, the first real moment of levity I'd felt since Danika cornered me. "That sounds fun. I'd love that." It'd be the perfect post-funeral distraction on Friday.

She perked up, bouncing slightly on her heels. "Great! See you then."

We hugged briefly before she turned back toward the restaurant, leaving me alone with my thoughts—and the weight of everything that had just happened.

I headed to Connor's truck, my frustration mounting again with every passing second. The cool night air did little to smother the fire burning beneath my skin.

My phone buzzed.

I pulled it out, expecting the worst, and groaned when I saw my mother's name flash across the screen. Without hesitation, I sent the call to voicemail.

Seconds later, a text popped up.

Lillian Sinclair:

Call me back.

I left it unread, then leaned against the passenger door, arms crossed, jaw tight.

Soft light poured out into the parking lot as Connor opened the door, stopping in his tracks when he locked eyes with me. His stare was dark, unreadable—something hidden just beneath the surface.

My stomach flipped.

My fists curled at my sides, tension winding through me like a coiled spring, ready to snap.

I pushed off the truck, bracing myself as he closed the distance between us.

CHAPTER TWELVE

Shattered Trust

LUCY

"Kyle just called."

Connor's statement stopped me cold.

"What? I mean, what did he say?" I blinked, disoriented.

"He's ready to come back—if you'll have him. He can take over management if you want me to take a few days off." His voice dropped, edged with something I couldn't quite place.

I hesitated, then nodded. "That's probably for the best. Send me his number."

Connor pulled out his phone and texted me Kyle's contact information. I saved it, knowing I'd have a ton to figure out before I officially put him back on the schedule. I had no clue how to pay him, no idea how to run a ranch without Connor. But I couldn't let that show.

Straightening my shoulders, I met Connor's stare, forcing myself to project confidence. His patient gaze made me falter.

I cleared my throat and lifted my chin. "Do you have anything to say before you unlock this door?"

Connor exhaled, his head dipping slightly. "I'm not sure what to say."

"Well, I can't help you with that." My crossed arms tightened over my chest as I glanced down at the gravel. "Can we go now?"

He sighed but unlocked the truck and opened my door. I climbed in, unable to look at him.

Betrayal still sat heavy in my chest.

"I'll stay at my place tonight," he said after a long silence.

I nodded. The fresh twist of pain made it hard to speak. "Fine."

"I'll still come by in the morning to handle chores, make sure the animals are taken care of until Kyle's up to speed." His kindness cut deeper than any argument could.

"You don't have to do that," I croaked, guilt clawing at me beneath my skin.

"I'm doing it. End of story." His tone left no room for debate.

A beat of silence stretched between us before he let out a slow, heavy breath. "What did I do wrong?"

I turned to him, my voice sharp with anger. "You *defended* Amanda. She had Danika harass me tonight. Then, you brushed it off like it was nothing. You're clueless to Amanda's manipulation. She's played God with people's lives, and it's always gotten her exactly what she wants. What did you *do*? You let her take over our date."

My voice trembled. "After seeing you two together..." I took a shaky breath, forcing back the tears threatening to spill. "If you want her back, go back to her. Just spare me the excuses. I have enough on my plate right now."

Connor's grip tightened on the wheel, his jaw clenching. "It's not what you think," he bit out, his voice low, strained.

I froze, his words hitting like a sudden gust of wind; a reminder of Irene's advice: *talk to him*. "Then explain it."

He let out another heavy sigh, his gaze fixed ahead, tension lining his face. "A year ago, I was in a really bad place. Alex had just died. You were..." He hesitated, rubbing the back of his neck. "You were dating some Oxford guy." A faint blush crept into his cheeks. "Not that it was any of my business. Your dad just mentioned it in passing, but... it *messed with my head*. I got wrecked one night at a gathering on my ranch, and the next thing I knew, I woke up next to Amanda."

I swallowed hard, a cold weight settling in my chest.

"We'd been broken up for several months," he continued. "I had no intention of getting back together with her... I still don't remember that night. But a few weeks later, she told me she was pregnant."

The words hit like a punch to the gut. My breath stalled.

His voice thickened. "I thought I had to do right by her. So, I asked her to be my girlfriend again, even though..." He shook his head. "I didn't love her. I *never* did. I tried, Lucy. I really did. And then... we lost the baby."

His confession hung between us, heavy and raw.

"I had a nursery set up. Walls painted, furniture built. I was ready to be a dad, even if it meant being tied to Amanda forever. But when we lost our little girl..." His throat bobbed as he swallowed hard. "I couldn't just *leave*. We were both grieving. Part of me needed her because she was the only one who understood. So, I stayed—until a few weeks ago. I finally realized I was only hurting her more by pretending." His voice cracked. "I couldn't keep lying to her, to myself."

My head spun. "Oh my God, Connor. I'm *so* sorry."

"No, I'm sorry." His voice was raw, breaking at the edges. "I didn't want to burden you with all of this. I know I ruined our date. But, Lucy, you have to believe me—you're the only one I've ever wanted."

His words chipped away at the wall I'd built around my heart, but I hesitated.

"If I'd been through something like that with her, I'd probably defend her too," I admitted. "But Connor, I can't handle any more interactions with Amanda right now. I just... can't."

He nodded slowly, determination deepening the crease in his brow. "I'll fix it. I'll talk to Amanda, to Danika—whoever I have to. I swear I'll make this right. I don't want to lose you. Not again."

My chest tightened. Everything in me wanted to throw caution aside. But...

"I don't think you can just *fix* this." My voice was barely above a whisper. "When it comes to Amanda, I don't think I can ever forgive her for what she's done to me or Sam."

Connor tossed his hat aside, raking a frustrated hand through his hair. "That was high school, Lucy. If she was that awful back then, she's changed. Today was the day she found out she was pregnant. Seeing me moving on tonight—it was just hard on her, you know? I didn't realize today was that day..."

"Connor, she saw we were at *The Lounge* on that gossip column you told me about. Then she sent Danika after me. She timed it so she could talk to you while I was stuck in the bathroom. You can see that, right?"

His face hardened. "No. She has every right to be upset. Danika was just being... Danika. Going through all that trouble just to keep you away? That'd be *insane*. What does she even have to gain?"

"Hurting me. Or maybe getting you back?" My voice was sharp, unwavering. "Listen, the last time she wanted to ruin my life, I ended up halfway across the world. That's not just petty drama, Connor. That's calculated destruction."

Connor's hands tightened on the wheel, knuckles white. "Wait. Amanda got you sent to London? Are you sure?"

I sighed, leaning back in my seat. "Well, not exactly. But no one did *anything* without her knowing. It's clear she either did it herself or gave someone else the green light."

Connor's jaw tensed, his voice riddled with disbelief. "Lucy, this sounds insane. I can't believe the woman I went through hell with could be capable of... that."

I clenched my fists.

Oh, if only he knew.

Connor's voice was cautious, hesitant. "Sam said she bullied you guys a little bit, but... this?"

My anger surged all over again. *A little bit?*

"Connor," I said, forcing my voice to stay strong, "she *tormented* me and Sam for years. She wasn't just some mean girl playing pranks—she made sure people feared being seen with us. She spread rumors, she isolated us, controlled the narrative, controlled everyone. And it worked." I let out a bitter laugh. "It's still working. I mean, you're *still* defending her."

He exhaled sharply, rubbing a hand over his face. "I'm *not* defending her, Lucy. I'm trying to *understand*."

"No, you're trying to justify her actions."

Connor's knuckles went white, his frustration palpable, but he remained silent.

I shook my head, the heat of my anger giving way to something heavier, something more painful. "This history between you and Amanda blinds you to who she really is. Part of you will always want to save her. That leaves no room for us."

His breath hitched like I'd landed a direct punch to the gut. He turned to me, expression raw, conflicted. "Only if you make it that way..."

I swallowed hard. "I'm done for tonight, Connor. I can't talk about this anymore."

The rest of the drive was in silence, thick with unspoken words. As we turned onto the long driveway leading to *Campbell Ranch*, my heart ached, cracking at the seams.

Connor threw the truck into park, then sighed heavily. "Lucy, please. Can we talk this through? We can't just leave things like this."

I twisted my fingers in my lap, unable to meet his eyes. "I don't know what else there is to say. Between my dad, Amanda, Diane... *everything*—it's just too much. If we're really being honest, we were always a bad idea."

He nodded slowly, his voice soft but firm. "Lucy, you can't mean that..."

I shook my head, unable to meet his eye. I squeezed out a response, each word tightening my throat. "I wish you the best, Connor."

I reached for the door handle again, but his hand caught my arm.

His piercing blue eyes locked onto me, raw and desperate. "Lucy, *please...*"

The lump in my throat nearly choked me. I breathed, my voice barely above a whisper. "Good night, Connor."

His grip loosened. He pulled back, nodding tightly.

I stepped out, my heart splintering as I glanced back one last time. His vulnerability was etched in the tight lines across his face. It took every ounce of strength not to cave, not to stay. The desire to comfort him tore at my insides.

He waited until I was safely inside before pulling away, his headlights disappearing into the night.

I leaned against the door, a storm of emotions churning inside me. Every part of me ached.

I swallowed down the ache in my chest and called weakly, "Sam?"

Footsteps shuffled from the living room, and then Sam appeared in his red silk pajamas, hands on his hips. "You're home early," he teased. But his face shifted to concern as he took in my expression. "Oh no. What happened?"

Tears welled in my eyes as I collapsed onto the couch. "That bitch won. Again."

Sam rushed over, taking my hands in his, his usual playful demeanor replaced with quiet patience. "Tell me *everything*."

I did. I spilled every last painful detail, my voice breaking as I relived it all.

"God, Lucy, I'm an asshole. I should have told Connor everything about Amanda. But I've lied to him for so long, it feels wrong to throw it all on him now." The sparkle dimmed in his midnight eyes.

I took the glass of wine Sam had poured me from the coffee table. "How did it start? Why didn't you say something right away?"

"Life was better, easier when she started dating Connor. You were gone, Luce. I had literally nobody. I was a fucking pariah until she made a deal with me."

I stiffened beside him. "Deal?"

"If I didn't say anything to Connor... she would call everyone off. I would be included. My life didn't have to be hell anymore. Fuck." He cringed. "Am I a sellout?"

"No! Absolutely not. I get it, Sam. I totally get it." I pulled him in and squeezed. "It's okay. I mean, it's not all okay. Connor's life would be so different if..."

Sam winced. "I know."

"Maybe you could fix it now? We're not in high school anymore."

"Luce, I can't. Connor will never forgive me. He hasn't been the same since..." His gaze went distant.

"Since the miscarriage?"

He nodded against my shoulder.

I shook my head. "Sam, the truth is going to come out eventually."

"But not right this second." Sam leaned back, putting me at arm's length. "Please don't say anything, Lucy. Let me figure it out on my own."

I hesitated.

"Okay," I finally agreed. It was his story to share.

"Now, let's turn this shitty night around."

He grabbed a bottle of wine and did what he did best: made me laugh.

"You know how to play *Never Have I Ever*?"

I nodded, a grin widening on my face.

"Let's play that, except it's called *If I Were a Total Bitch*, and instead of embarrassing confessions, we roast Amanda in all her delusional, dramatic glory."

By the end of the night, my cheeks hurt from smiling too much, and the tightness in my chest finally eased. As Sam poured me another glass, I leaned back against the couch, my thoughts drifting toward something resembling gratitude.

Through all the chaos, at least I still had Sam.

He was my rock. My family in every way that mattered.

CHAPTER THIRTEEN

Passing the Reins

LUCY

I woke just before sunrise, the urge to bury myself in work too strong to ignore. Keeping busy meant keeping my mind off *him*. Off last night. Off everything else that felt too raw to process.

But if I wanted to clean the stables and take care of the horses, I'd have to let Connor know where I'd be—to avoid running into him.

My fingers hovered over my phone, hesitation gnawing at me. The thought of reaching out made my stomach twist into knots, but I didn't have much choice.

I wasn't ready to face him again. *Not yet.*

Finally, I sent a quick message.

Me:

> I'm handling the horses this morning, then I'll be in the garden.

I swallowed. My heart pounded as I watched three dots appear, then vanish. I drew in slow breaths, but heat crept up my chest until my entire body burned like a furnace. I wanted to close my eyes, bracing for impact. I didn't. Instead, I held my breath, staring until—

Connor:

> *I'll let the guys know. I've already finished up what I needed to do and gave everyone their tasks for the day. I'm at Lochland Farms for the rest of the day. Don't worry about running into me.*

I stared at the screen, exhaling slowly.

Good. That's good. Right?

So then, why did it still hurt?

My heart sank, a painful echo of the feelings I had leaving White River all those years ago...a panging sense of *goodbye* rushing through me fresh and raw all over again.

I pulled on the only clean outfit I had—a stunning floral blouse and flared dress pants. Perfect for brunch in the city, absolutely *ridiculous* for ranch work. My only pair of jeans sat damp and forgotten in the washing machine. At least I still had my boots:the same ones I'd left behind along with my old life at the ranch.

I sighed at my reflection. I looked like an incapable city girl who would take one step outside and land right into cow manure.

From the couch, where he was watching cartoons, of all things, Sam let out a snort. "Where are you going dressed like *that*?"

"Don't start." I rolled my eyes, already exasperated. "I forgot to move my laundry to the dryer, so everything *stinks*. I only have nice outfits left. Not that I exactly packed for manual labor."

His smirk widened. "Ooh, Miss London is about to ruin a five-hundred-dollar outfit for the sake of farm work. This, I gotta see."

I grabbed my coffee, snorting. "You are more than welcome to join me in the stables."

He scoffed. "Hay, dirt, poop? Yeah, I'll pass." Lifting his bowl like a toast, he grinned. "By the way, I'm shocked you don't have a hangover. After last night, I half expected you to be dead to the world."

I shot him a smirk. "I'm building a tolerance."

He grinned. "So proud of you." Then his expression shifted, concern creeping in as he studied me. "But seriously... how are you after everything last night?"

I took a slow sip of coffee before setting the mug down with a little too much force. "Could be better. Hence, my designer outfit willingly heading toward its imminent doom. Don't worry, there's zero sentimental value here."

Sam swallowed, his frown deepening. "I'm sorry, Luce. Amanda's *psychotic*. Just... be careful around her, okay?"

"I will." Looking down, I swiped at imaginary lint on my pants just to give myself a moment. Then I changed the subject. "I'll be back later. My cell's on if you need anything. Love you."

"Love you, bitch! Enjoy scooping *giant turds*!" he called, waving as I headed for the door.

A breathy chuckle escaped as I waved back and shut the door behind me.

Outside, the sun's early rays stretched over the mountains. The towering peaks in the distance stood confident and unmoving, a stark contrast to the storm of emotions still churning inside me.

When I reached the stables, I focused on the rhythm of the work, hoping the physicality of it would quiet my racing thoughts.

The familiar scent of warm hay, leather, and horses wrapped around me, centering me in a way that nothing else could. Dust swirled in the morning light filtering through the open barn doors, and the gentle knickers of the horses filled the quiet space.

I ran a brush over Daisy's golden coat, the bristles moving in steady, familiar strokes. The repetitive motion soothed my frayed nerves, each pass of the brush a small act of control in a life that felt like it was slipping through my fingers.

I let out a slow breath, running my hand down the soft white stripe on Daisy's face, feeling the tension slowly leave my body.

Then, just as I finished combing through her mane, my phone buzzed in my pocket.

I sighed, pulling it out. My mood sank further when I saw the name flashing on the screen.

Aunt Diane.

The phone continued to vibrate, the name glaring up at me like a warning.

I stared at it, debating whether I had the energy to deal with whatever she wanted—or if I even *cared* to.

Forcing a cheerful tone, I answered, "Good morning!"

"Hi, honey. I hope I didn't wake you." Her overly sweet voice already had me on edge. "You can stop searching for the will." I froze, my stomach dropping. I'd completely forgotten about it. "James Duncan, your father's lawyer, reached out to me. Said he's been trying to reach you, but—get this—he didn't have your number."

My stomach clenched. "What? What does he want?"

"He wants to meet with us today. Eleven-thirty sharp."

"Yeah, I can be there. Where's his office?"

"I'll text you the address," she replied. "See you then, honey. Bye now."

"Bye," I murmured, ending the call. A quick swipe cleared the rest of my notifications—five more missed calls from Mom. I didn't hesitate. I still wasn't ready.

Dealing with Diane was already more than I could handle. The last thing I needed was to hear how much my mother supposedly loved my father... not after she left him, took me away, and stole six years of my life. Precious time I *could* have spent with my father.

I walked back toward the house, the white siding gleaming in the sunlight. My father had loved this place, from the dark-stained wraparound porch to the black-paneled windows. It was a sanctuary, and as the cool Montana air kissed my cheeks, I knew I wanted this to be my forever home. More than ever, I hoped the lawyer had good news.

"Great! You're back." Sam appeared beside me, as animated as ever.

I rubbed my temples. "Yeah, I need to get ready and meet Aunt Diane at the lawyer's office."

Sam groaned. "Oh my *God*. That woman is *unbearable!*"

"Please *don't* start."

He threw his hands up. "Fine, but she makes Amanda look like a saint."

I couldn't help but laugh. "I wouldn't go *that* far."

Sam smirked. "Close enough. She's a total drama llama."

I snorted. "Drama llama?"

He shrugged. "Yeah, just made it up."

We broke into a fit of childish giggles, and for a moment, the weight of everything else lifted. No matter how exhausting life felt, at least I had Sam.

The lawyer's office smelled of lemon polish and aged books, the scent both sterile and imposing. I sat stiffly in a leather chair across from James Duncan's massive mahogany desk, feeling small. The sheer weight of the moment pressed down on me, but the incessant sounds of Diane's sniffling and her over-the-top dabbing of her eyes grated on my nerves, making it impossible to fully process.

"So, James," she said, leaning forward, "can we skip to the part about what my brother left me?"

James remained calm and professional. "Mrs. Hayes, the official reading of the will occurs after the funeral, as per tradition. Today, we're here to discuss the management of the ranch. As I said on the phone, you really don't need to be here for this. I just need Lucy—"

My jaw clenched. *Of course she didn't need to be here.*

Diane's brow furrowed. "Management? I assumed that would fall under final dispersals."

James shook his head, folding his hands. "No. Your brother made prior arrangements. The ranch is currently in joint ownership between Lucy and himself."

"What?" Diane screeched, her tissue fluttering to the floor. "Joint ownership? Why would he do that?"

James remained unfazed. "Your brother wanted to ensure Lucy could immediately handle the ranch's operations, including payroll and bills. He trusted her to take over."

Diane scoffed. "She doesn't know the *first thing* about running a ranch."

I straightened in my seat, glowering at her. "Maybe not yet, but I can learn."

James cleared his throat. "To address that concern, Mr. Campbell arranged for Connor Lochland to assist Lucy during the transition. Connor has been managing the ranch for the past several months on his own and has worked closely with your father for years."

Diane's jaw dropped. "Connor? That *boy*? The one she used to follow around like a lost puppy?"

I clenched my fists. "Diane, let him speak."

James ignored the disruption, his tone even and unwavering. "Lucy, you are the rightful heir, but per the terms of the will, full legal ownership of the ranch will not transfer to you immediately. For the next year, Connor will remain on as manager and mentor to ensure a smooth transition. Only after that period will full ownership be legally yours."

Diane huffed, crossing her arms. "This is *ridiculous*. What about all the *time* and *money* I spent driving to the hospital, taking care of my brother's every need? Doesn't that count for *anything*?"

James turned his attention to her. "Mrs. Hayes, if you have any expenses related to the estate, you may request reimbursement with proper documentation. However, this may affect your inheritance."

Diane glared at him but said nothing further.

I, on the other hand, was still reeling from the shock of the terms my father had set forth. Connor was going to help me run the ranch? How was I supposed to face him after last night?

James handed me a folder. "Take this home and review it. If you have questions, feel free to reach out."

"Thank you," I said, my voice calm despite the turmoil clawing at my chest.

As we left, Diane muttered under her breath, her tone laced with warning. "Good luck, Lucy. You're in way over your head. And if you screw this up I'll be right here, ready to take what should've been mine in the first place."

Her words stung, but I refused to let her see it. Chin high, I walked past her without sparing her a second glance.

I climbed into my father's truck, fingers tightening around the wheel. My gaze lingered on the horizon for a moment, gathering myself before I threw it into drive.

Every instinct told me to turn back, to put this off just a little longer. But I couldn't. Not anymore.

Heart pounding, I gripped the wheel tighter and headed straight for Connor's ranch.

CHAPTER FOURTEEN

Fault Lines

LUCY

As I passed my childhood home—the cattle ranch I'd unknowingly co-owned for years—my mind reeled from the revelation.

As I neared the property line, a dense row of towering Douglas firs came into view, their deep green needles a stark contrast against the golden fields. Then, as the trees thinned, the land ahead opened up, revealing a wide gravel driveway beneath a sleek, metal sign:

Lochland Farms.

I turned in, my tires crunching over the pristine gravel as I took in the sight before me.

What had once been an empty stretch of land beside my home was now a masterpiece of precision and purpose. Where some ranches leaned into rugged charm, Connor's was a perfect balance of untamed Montana beauty and meticulous design.

His two-story home stood proudly on a gentle incline, its contemporary timber panels, sleek lines, and black steel framing exuding a touch of modern elegance. Floor-to-ceiling windows stretched across the front, reflecting the endless Montana sky, while a modern chandelier glowed faintly inside, barely visible against the glass.

The wraparound porch, furnished with smooth rocking chairs, small end tables, and a porch swing, invited quiet moments beneath the deep eaves. Lantern-style sconces flanked the walls—a subtle yet deliberate touch that reflected Connor's meticulous attention to detail.

The driveway curved past the house toward the barns and outbuildings, each structure clean-lined and purposeful. The barn, a striking slate gray with natural wood doors and black trim, was modern, functional, and immaculately maintained.

Beyond the barn, a series of paddocks stretched toward the rolling pastures, their fencing a flawless mix of steel and smooth wood. Quarter horses and a few roans roamed lazily, their coats gleaming in the late-afternoon sun. In the distance, black Angus cattle grazed against the jagged backdrop of the Highwood Mountains, their snow-capped peaks standing like silent sentinels.

Even the equipment area bore Connor's meticulous touch—trucks and trailers parked with precision, every tool and machine in perfect order. Where most ranches embraced a comfortable disorder, this was something else entirely.

This wasn't just a working ranch.

This was Connor's vision—his legacy.

I parked near the side of the house, unease creeping into my stomach. I couldn't believe I'd shown up here unannounced.

Before I could dwell on it, a chocolate Labrador retriever came bounding toward me as I shut the truck door, her round belly swaying with each enthusiastic step. Her tail wagged furiously, and the moment I crouched down, she placed her paws on my thighs, licking my cheeks with pure, unfiltered joy.

"Hey, sweetheart," I beamed, scratching behind her ears, a giggle escaping as she nuzzled closer. For a brief moment, all the tension inside me melted away.

"That's Willow," Connor's warm, familiar voice called from the porch.

I looked up, my heart stuttering at the sight of him.

"She's beautiful," I murmured, my fingers running gently over her soft fur. My gaze shifted to the roundness of her belly. "How far along is she...?"

Connor nodded, his expression unreadable. "Probably within the next week. Buddy's going to be a proud father."

A small smile tugged at my lips at the thought.

But then his tone shifted, turning measured. "What are you doing here, Lucy? I thought you made things pretty clear last night."

I hesitated, the words catching in my throat. Finally I managed, "Were you aware of any stipulations in my father's will?"

He shook his head, a slow, confused furrow deepening on his brow.

"Okay." I sighed. "Can we talk?"

Connor studied me, his gaze searching, before finally gesturing toward the porch.
"Come on."

I made my way up the smooth steps to join him on the porch. He gestured for me to
sit, and I carefully lowered myself onto a handcrafted rocking chair, leaning forward to
keep from moving, tension knotting every fiber of my being.

I hadn't been invited inside.

I couldn't blame him.

Still, it stung like hell.

Being near him was overwhelming. The hurt from last night tangled with the undeniable pull between us had my emotions teetering on the edge of overload.

Connor exhaled, setting his coffee down. "Well, what's going on, Lucy?"

I hesitated, my fingers tightening against the arms of the chair. *Just get through this.*

Before dropping the news that he was stuck with me for the next year—*if* he agreed to
help—I figured I should at least try to smooth things over.

"Connor, I just want to start by saying… I'm sorry for coming here after how last night
ended."

Connor's expression darkened. "Lucy, just say what you need to say." His rough tone
edged with disappointment.

I swallowed hard. "Sorry, okay." I braced myself, pushing through the lump in my
throat. "My father secretly added me as co-owner of the ranch a few years before he…"
Passed away. Died. Left this world. The words stuck, thick and suffocating, before I could
settle on one.

Connor's head tilted slightly, his hand coming to rest lightly on my forearm. "It's okay,"
he said quietly. "I understand. Keep going."

I inhaled sharply, forcing myself to stay in the present. "In order for me to gain full
ownership of the ranch, there's a catch." My throat tightened as I finally forced out the
words. "And that's where you come in."

Connor's eyes widened, snapping to mine.

I flushed but pressed on. "For the next year, my dad wanted you to be my manager…
and my mentor. I'm guessing he expected you to teach me everything outside of animal
care—like managing finances, payroll, taxes, contracts, ordering feed. I know how to cull
cattle and mend fences, but I've never hired ranch hands, tracked inventory, or even seen
a full breakdown of what we sell."

My breath picked up as the sheer weight of it all came crashing down.

Connor raised a hand, his voice calm. "It's okay. I've got it. I can mentor you, teach you like your dad taught me." He hesitated, then added, "There are some things I've been meaning to tell you about."

I looked up, suspicion creeping in. "Like what?"

"It's important for us to be on the same page from here on out," he said evenly. "I've been managing *Campbell Ranch* for a couple of years now while running my own ranch here. And after your father helped me build *Lochland Farms*, we set up joint business ventures and contracts—like you saw at *The Wildflower Lounge*."

"Wait... you're *actually* still on staff?" My stomach tightened at the realization. I'd assumed everything Connor had been doing around the ranch was just him *helping me* until I could figure out how to keep the business running.

"It's unorthodox, but technically, I don't take a paycheck. My salary pays off the loan your father gave me to start my business. He gave me a shot when I was broke, living in a trailer on his property."

I blinked, the pieces falling into place.

My father hadn't just *believed* in Connor—he had *invested* in him. And Connor, in turn, had been repaying that debt with sweat, sacrifice, and something else entirely.

Loyalty.

I exhaled, shaking my head. I'd always known my dad cared about Connor, but I hadn't realized just *how much*. "He treated you like family."

For a brief second, Connor's expression softened, something unreadable flickering behind his eyes. Then, just as quickly, his tone shifted back to cool professionalism. "Yeah. He did."

I drew in a smooth breath, matching his energy. "When can we start?"

Connor leaned forward, resting his elbows on his knees. "You're caught up on bills, payroll, and orders. I've stayed on top of everything, so nothing's behind. Like I said before, I think getting you up to speed should wait until after Friday."

Friday.

The funeral.

The celebration of life.

The last official goodbye.

I stiffened. "Fine. But why didn't you tell me you were the ranch manager? I felt *guilty* having you do all the work this week—then you stayed in that tiny trailer when your house is right next door? I don't get it."

Connor's jaw ticked. "There were bigger things to focus on, Lucy." His voice dropped lower, steady, unwavering. "And I stayed in the trailer because I wanted to be close. In case you needed me."

My stomach twisted. *Of course that's why he stayed.*

Connor was just that kind of guy.

Even as kids, he was always there: loyal, reliable, like he *just knew* when I needed someone. And now, whether I wanted to admit it or not, his presence had been my anchor this past week, the only thing keeping me from completely unraveling under the weight of my grief.

I frowned, words failing me for a moment. "That—" I sighed, releasing a fraction of the stress bundled tight in my chest. My voice softened. "Thank you."

"Of course. It's just what friends do."

Friends.

The word sliced like a dagger straight to my gut.

Hadn't that been what I *wanted*?

After last night—

After his blind trust, his unwavering misplaced loyalty to Amanda—

After watching him *defend* her while I stood there feeling like an idiot—

"*Right,*" I breathed, barely above a whisper.

Connor reached for my hand, his blue eyes burning with something unreadable. "Lucy, please, can we just pretend last night never happened? Everything was going *really* well before..."

"Connor, this has been the worst week of my life. I can't think straight..." I swallowed hard, searching for the right words.

"I know that the hold Amanda has on you isn't something I can compete with. And right now? I don't have the mental or emotional energy to even try."

His hand tightened slightly around mine, like he was afraid to let go. But I already had one foot out the door.

Connor's expression tightened with determination. "She reached out to me." He hesitated, then stiffened, like he was bracing for impact. "Actually... she's here."

The blood drained from my face.

"She's *here*?" I blinked, scanning the area. "I didn't see her car."

"She parked on the other side." He sighed, rubbing the back of his neck. "I was going to tell you. I just—I wasn't expecting you to come over."

"Why is she *here*?" My voice came out sharp, my pulse spiking. "Like, *physically* here?"

"She messaged me this morning. Said she wanted to talk in person, it was a tough night."

I let out a sharp breath, my stomach twisting.

"It's not like that. We're not..." His jaw tightened.

I shook my head, trying to process.

He would *always* rescue her.

The front door creaked open, and Amanda stepped out, looking... *guilty*.

I rolled my eyes, unable to stop myself.

"Hey, can I interrupt?"

Bile rose in my throat. "Were you *eavesdropping*?"

Amanda took a careful step forward, her voice soft, almost hesitant. "Lucy," she said with a sickeningly sweet smile, "I just wanted to say—you have my blessing to be with Connor."

I huffed out a laugh. "How *generous* of you."

Amanda winced, and Connor stepped in. "Lucy, please—"

"No, Connor, I get it." Amanda cut him off, her voice dripping with honeyed sweetness. She turned to me, her expression carefully measured. "Lucy and I have a lot of history. But I mean it. I want to make things right... if I can."

She hesitated, and her level eyes twitched, the wheels spinning beneath her calculated stare. "Listen, I told Danika to back off. And Lucy, I really hope we can talk—just the two of us. Maybe we can finally put the past behind us?"

Connor placed a reassuring hand on her back.

My eyes flicked to his gentle, reassuring touch—*the same touch he'd always offered me*—and something inside me snapped.

"Put the past *behind* us?" My laugh cut through the air as I turned to Connor. "Did she tell you everything she's done? To Sam? To *me*?" My voice thinned, the weight of years pressing forward. "Did she tell you that after Sam came out, she told everyone we both had AIDS? No one would come near us for an entire year." I clasped a hand over my mouth realizing I was breaking my promise to Sam.

Connor's face blanched. "Amanda... is that true?"

Her eyes filled with perfectly timed regret. "It was awful of me, I know. But I *swear*, Sam and I became friends later. I'd never do something like that now."

Friends?

Shock slammed into me. "Sam... and *you*?"

She nodded. "He didn't tell you?"

I stared at her, then at Connor.

My whole world tilted.

Screw promises. The truth needed to come out.

"He told me everything, Amanda. What you two share, isn't friendship."

Amanda froze, then her voice melded into the perfect blend of sympathy and conde-scension. "Maybe he was just waiting for the right time to tell you."

Her syrupy demeanor made my skin crawl. She was baiting me, trying to manipulate the situation. But I had *years* of experience with her tactics. I shoved down the fire building inside me, forcing myself to stay composed.

"Sam became your friend because *you* left him no choice." I shook my head. "Should we take a little walk down memory lane?"

Amanda stiffened. "Lucy—"

I raised a hand, feigning reassurance. "No, it's okay because all is forgiven, *right*?" My voice dropped to something sharper, colder. "Let's see... remember when you had me sit in red paint in class? *What did you call me after pointing it out to everyone?*"

Amanda's mouth worked, but no words came.

I smirked. "That's right—*Bloody Mary.* You made sure *everyone* called me that for years." I let out a humorless chuckle. "Fun times. What else? Oh, right—you *locked me in a janitor's closet* and left me there until after *six o'clock.* No food, no water, no bathroom. I actually thought I was going to *die* in there."

Amanda shifted uncomfortably. "Lucy, you don't have to do this."

But I did.

And so, I unleashed all the remaining pieces of my suppressed resentment. "You're right. Because it's *okay* now since you're a *good person.*" My cheeks ran red and I clenched my fists to keep my voice level. "I don't know *how* you managed to turn our entire class into homophobic monsters—but you did. Oh yeah, and you told everyone I was *pregnant*, including my parents. For *what*? So that when you finally got me *shipped off* to London, you could suddenly be *best friends* with Sam?"

My jaw clicked as I rocked it side to side, trying to release the tightness.

Amanda folded her arms. "I'm *sorry*, but everyone thought it was *funny*. I get why you think I was bullying you or whatever—"

"That wasn't *bullying*, Amanda." My voice was low and sharp, laced with years of swallowed fury. "You created a *hateful, toxic environment* that made every single day unbearable. And Sam? If he became your friend after I left, it was because he had *no one else*. He had to become friends with you just to *survive* his last two years of high school. You made sure of that, too."

I exhaled, steadying the tremble in my hands. "What I don't get is *why*. What did I do to make you *hate me* so much?"

Amanda's expression darkened, her fragile, wounded act slipping away.

Finally.

"Are you *kidding*?!" she shrieked, her voice cracking. "First, everyone *skipped my party* to go to *yours* in fifth grade. Then everyone thought you were *so cool* competing in those *stupid* horseback riding competitions. My dad *paid* for my straight A's, yet *you* still had a higher GPA. In high school I thought, *finally*, people would get *over* you. But *no*, you had the *hottest guy in school* wrapped around your little finger and you didn't even know it. Enough was *enough!*"

The confession hit like a slap, but not in the way she intended.

I took a slow breath, centering myself as the tremor in my hands disappeared.

"So," I murmured, tilting my head. "You *admit* you lied to Connor about missing me. That you were *never* devastated when I was sent away. Meaning your entire relationship with him started on a *lie*." My voice hardened. "Did you *ever* actually have feelings for him? He's a real life human being, Amanda. You can't treat people like property!"

Amanda's jaw clenched, her fists tightening at her sides.

I met her gaze head-on, unwavering. "Do me a favor, Amanda. Take your *fake guilt* and get the *hell* out of my life."

Her expression faltered.

I took a slow breath, squared my shoulders, and lifted my chin. "So if you could kindly leave, I'd very much appreciate it."

Connor stood beside me, tense and unmoving.

Amanda's face reddened, her hands balled into fists. Pure hatred burned in her eyes.

"I will *ruin* you, Lucy Campbell," she seethed, her voice dripping with venom. "I will *ruin* you, and I will take your *gutless father's* precious ranch down with you."

Connor's voice was low, sharp, and final.

"*Get out.*"

Amanda blanched.

Connor's tone hardened, unrelenting. "Get your fucking purse and *leave. Now.*"

Her face twisted in desperation. "Connor... I'm *sorry.* I just got so *angry.* You know how I get when I'm upset." Her wide eyes locked onto his—searching, pleading. But whatever warmth or understanding she expected to find there was gone.

Connor's stare was ice-cold. Unforgiving.

"Connor, *please*—"

His teeth clenched, his entire body coiled with barely restrained fury. "I don't know who the hell you are, Amanda. And now? I don't know if anything—*anything*—you've ever said to me was real." He let out a sharp breath, shaking his head. "You told people my *brother* had AIDS. *Fucking AIDS,* Amanda." His voice turned rough, guttural, a deep, shaking anger unlike anything I'd ever heard from him.

"You admitted it. Do you have any fucking *clue* how hurtful, how *dangerous* a lie like that actually *is?!*" His hands curled into fists at his sides, his voice trembling with barely contained rage. "And Lucy's right—you *manipulated* me into dating you. I see that now. I *see you* now." He took a sharp step forward, his fury crackling like a live wire between them. "So if you don't get off my property *right now,* I'll call the sheriff and have you escorted off."

Amanda stood frozen, her chest rising and falling in rapid bursts before she scoffed, spun on her heel, and stormed toward her car.

The engine roared to life, tires skidding as she tore out of the driveway, gravel spraying in her wake.

A sharp curse left Connor's lips as he ripped his hat off and threw it to the porch floor. His breath was heavy, his jaw locked so tight it looked painful. He turned away, hands braced on his hips as he paced, chest heaving.

I'd seen Connor angry before.

But *not like this.*

Not this kind of raw, seething fury.

I hesitated, watching Connor pace, his hands braced on his hips, shoulders tight as he worked his jaw.

A vindicated part of me wanted to say, *I told you so.* Wanted him to sit in it a little longer—to feel what it was like to be blindsided, to have someone you trusted shatter your perception of them.

But another part of me, the part that had known Connor my whole life—just felt... *tired.* And so incredibly *sad.*

I took a slow breath, my voice softer than I expected. "Connor, I'm sorry."

His shoulders tensed. "How could I have been so *stupid*?" His voice was rough, hoarse.

I shook my head. "You didn't know—"

"But I *should* have. You kept trying to tell me..."

"I did."

He turned sharply, stormy blue eyes locking onto mine, something raw and unraveling beneath the surface.

"Why didn't Sam ever say anything?"

I swallowed hard. "Survival? Fear?"

Because he was embarrassed.

Because you were too close to see it.

Because part of you probably did know.

I didn't say any of those things.

Those thoughts belonged to me—to my own hurt, my own years of trauma. And right now, *giving voice to them* wouldn't change anything.

Instead, I stepped closer, searching his face. "This isn't your fault, Connor."

His jaw clenched, but he didn't pull away when I lifted my hands to his face, my thumbs brushing lightly over the tension there.

For a second—just a second—his expression crumpled. Then he exhaled sharply, his body going rigid beneath my touch.

Something in my chest tightened.

I *should* have pulled away. Should have let the moment breathe instead of letting my emotions tip it into something else.

But I didn't.

Instead, my fingers traced along his cheekbone, brushing away the single tear that ran down his stubbled cheek.

Connor swallowed hard. "I should have believed you," he murmured, voice tight with regret.

I sighed, trying to let go of the last of my anger with one long exhale. "Connor, you see the best in people. And that's one of things I... like most about you." I hesitated. "But sometimes... it means you don't see the worst in them until it's too late."

His throat bobbed, and he nodded reluctantly.

Then his arms wrapped around me, solid and sure, his heartbeat hammering against mine. "I'm *so* sorry, Lucy."

I stiffened for a fraction of a second. Because I hadn't *fully* forgiven him. There was still *so much* left unspoken.

But then... I melted.

I let myself sink into the warmth of his embrace, let myself breathe him in, let the weight of everything settle between us.

Connor was overwhelming in every way: his presence, his strength, his touch. A *dangerous* kind of comfort.

One I could drown in if I let myself. And God help me, I wanted to. But I no longer trusted myself. *Especially* when it came to men.

I squeezed my eyes tight. Begging myself not to remember them. To remember *Callum*.

"Lucy? You okay?" Connor tensed around me.

"I'm fine." God, I hated being *that* girl. The one whose abusive relationships shifted her entire outlook on men.

My faith in something good had all but been lost until Connor showed up for me at that stupid airport.

My head spun and my stomach roiled. So instead of letting my thoughts take me under, I pulled back.

The loss of his warmth sent a shiver over my skin.

Connor dragged a hand through his hair, his lips twisting into a wry, self-deprecating smirk. "Well," he exhaled, voice rough, "guess I've learned my lesson: always trust a Campbell."

"Yeah." I grinned, allowing my mental spiral to fade into the background. "Don't forget it."

A chuckle rumbled through his chest, and my fingers twitched at my sides, aching to press against him again.

Get it together, Lucy.

My emotions had been all over the place this week. But one thing hadn't changed. My feelings for Connor hadn't faded. Not even a little.

Even when he shattered my confidence in him—in *us*—by defending Amanda.

But now?

Now, I knew couldn't let those feelings dictate my next steps.

My guard went back up, slipping all too easily back into place, closing off the most vulnerable parts of me.

I inhaled shakily, gathering myself. "I should probably head home."

Connor looked up at me. "How about we go inside for a little bit? We still have a lot to discuss. And, honestly?" He exhaled, rubbing the back of his neck. "I need a second to recover from all that. How are you?"

I let out a breathy laugh. "Still a little shaken up."

His head tilted, a flicker of his usual playfulness creeping back in. "Just a *little*?"

I nudged him. "Just a little."

The tension between us eased—just a sliver—as we laughed, everything settling into an uneasy truce.

For whatever reason, despite the walls I'd thrown up, I said, "Okay, let's see where Connor Lochland lives now."

CHAPTER FIFTEEN

At Least Friends

LUCY

The moment I stepped through the threshold to Connor's home, I froze.

The house was *gorgeous*. All my intrusive thoughts slid back into a dark box, hidden under lock and key, as I took it all in.

It had the warmth of a Montana ranch home but none of the cluttered, rustic disarray I usually saw in places like this. Everything was intentional; from the sleek lines of the furniture to the natural wood elements that made the space feel inviting. It was modern rustic—clean, polished, but still full of character.

He shrugged off his jacket, tossing it over the back of a chair. "Built it myself."

I turned sharply to face him. "Wait, *what*?"

Connor smirked, leaning a shoulder against the entryway wall. "Designed the whole thing. Drew up the plans, made a few changes along the way, but yeah." He rubbed the back of his neck like it was no big deal.

"You designed this?" I turned in a slow circle, my breath catching as I took it all in. "Connor, this is... unbelievable."

His mouth pulled into a lopsided grin, clearly pleased but too modest to say anything. Instead, he tipped his head toward the kitchen. "Come on, I'll give you the tour."

I followed him past the entryway, my boots tapping softly against the dark-stained hardwood floors.

The kitchen was massive—bright and open, with an oversized island topped with polished butcher block. The rest of the countertops gleamed with quartz. A deep farmhouse sink sat beneath a wide window, framing the endless Montana sky. The appliances were top-of-the-line—double ovens, a six-burner gas stove, and an enormous fridge that looked like it could fit half a cow inside. *It probably did*, I thought with a soft laugh. The sleek matte-black cabinets contrasted beautifully with the warm wood tones, tying everything together in effortless perfection.

"This is *amazing*," I breathed, running my fingers over the island's smooth surface. "I mean, my dad's kitchen is nice, but this is..." I trailed off, shaking my head.

Connor chuckled. "Figured if I was gonna build my dream house, I'd do it right. I love cooking, and I hate feeling cramped in a kitchen."

I raised a brow at him. "You love cooking?"

He shot me a look. "Why do you think I keep making us meals?"

"Obligation?" I drawled with an apologetic wince.

He lowered his gaze. "Seriously?"

"I knew you could cook, but *this*? This kitchen is next level," I laughed, shaking my head. "It all makes sense now, the epic breakfast, the fajitas. You really *love* to cook. Who would have thunk?"

Connor smirked, giving a small, almost sheepish shrug.

He led me into the living room next, and I nearly stopped in my tracks.

The ceiling vaulted impossibly high, raw wood beams stretching upward where they met at sharp angles, giving the space a dramatic, open feel. A wall of windows spanned the entire height, framing an absolutely breathtaking view.

Rolling grasslands stretched endlessly, dotted with clusters of pine and fir trees. In the distance, the lake nestled between our properties shimmered beneath the late afternoon sun, its glassy surface reflecting the sky in rippling hues of gold and blue. And beyond that, the jagged peaks of the mountains loomed, their snow-capped tops cutting against the sky.

I exhaled slowly, taking it all in.

"*Wow.*"

Connor crossed his arms, gaze fixed on the view. "Best part of the house."

"No kidding." I turned to him, eyes still wide. "How do you ever get anything done? I'd just sit here and stare all day."

He huffed a quiet laugh. "Trust me, it's not easy."

"Oh, I feel it. This whole place has already been a needed distraction," I mused.

Connor's expression shifted, the weight of our unresolved discussion flickering in his eyes. "Last thing is the upstairs. Want to see?"

I nodded, tension creeping back into my jaw as I followed him upstairs, my fingers gliding along the sturdy wood railing. The second floor was just as impressive, with an open loft overlooking the living room.

As we moved down the hall, Connor slowed in front of a closed door. His hand lifted, pressing flat against the smooth wood, fingers splaying just slightly as if grounding himself.

I caught the subtle clench of his jaw, the way his chest rose and fell with a quiet inhale.

"This would've been my daughter's room," he murmured, voice barely above a whisper.

My breath caught.

I didn't move, didn't speak—just waited.

After a long pause, Connor let his hand fall away and stepped back, his expression carefully unreadable.

"Come on," he said, his voice back to its usual steady calm.

I followed, my throat tight, the weight of that closed door lingering in my mind.

I resisted the urge to reach for the handle, to ask the questions forming on the tip of my tongue. *Some things weren't meant to be pried open before their time.*

Connor moved ahead, his posture stiff but composed, and I took his unspoken cue to follow.

When he opened the door at the end of the hall, the heaviness of the moment faded into the background as bright light spilled from the master bedroom, unveiling the grand finale.

The space was expansive but not excessive, carrying the same modern-rustic elegance as the rest of the house. Exposed wood beams stretched across the ceiling, adding warmth to the sleek finishes. At the far end, sliding glass doors opened onto a second-story deck, framing an unfiltered view of the land.

Beyond the railing, cattle grazed lazily in the fields, the land rolling gently toward the distant tree line, where the late afternoon sun cast long shadows over the golden grass.

"This is incredible," I murmured, walking toward the doors. "You wake up to *this* view every morning?"

Connor leaned against the frame, arms crossed. "Not bad, huh?"

I huffed a laugh. "'*Not bad*' is an understatement."

I turned back to him, but he was watching *me*, not the view.

For a long moment, neither of us spoke.

Then he cleared his throat. "You should see the bathroom."

I followed him inside, and...okay, *this* was ridiculous.

The oversized walk-in shower was lined with sleek charcoal tile, the kind that looked like polished stone, with multiple showerheads, including one of those massive rainfall ones mounted in the ceiling.

"This is bigger than my bedroom," I joked.

Connor smirked. "Figured I might as well go all out." He gestured around the space. "There's another bathroom and a guest room with a private balcony up here, but it's more of the same." He chuckled. "I didn't show you the powder room or my office downstairs, but you'll see those soon enough once we start working together."

"That's fine. It feels like you've already shown me the best of the best." I hesitated, nerves tightening in my stomach. "Should we go back downstairs and talk?"

Connor's smile faded slightly, replaced by something quieter, more thoughtful.

"Yeah. Let's do it."

We made our way back to the kitchen, the tension from earlier settling into something calmer, easier.

Connor grabbed a bottle of whiskey from a cabinet and poured two glasses, sliding one across the counter to me. "You drink whiskey during the day, or is that too cowboy for you?"

I rolled my eyes but took a sip, the smooth burn settling warm in my stomach.

Connor leaned against the counter, studying me. "You ready to start working together?"

I exhaled heavily. "I think so. You really had no idea my dad wanted you to do this with me for a year?"

He exhaled, shaking his head as he stared down at the counter, deep in thought. "He'd made me promise, if anything happened—but I didn't know he'd stuck it in writing."

My throat knotted. "What did you promise him?"

"That I'd help you learn the ropes, make sure the ranch ran smoothly if—"

I nodded, not needing further explanation. "But a year of mentoring me wasn't what you had in mind."

"Not exactly. I don't think you'll need a full year, maybe a month or two. But what would have happened if I'd said no?"

"I guess someone else gets the other half of the business? I don't know. I hadn't thought to ask," I shrugged.

He frowned, his throat bobbing as he hesitated. "Lucy... I'm sorry. About last night—"

"Connor," I started carefully, setting my glass down. "I get why you needed to believe Amanda. I do. But..." My voice wavered, and I swallowed hard against the ache rising in my throat. "It really hurt when you didn't believe me."

His head dipped, exhaustion pulling at his features as he gave a small nod. "I'm really sorry Lucy. You have every reason to be mad at me." He huffed, his shoulders sinking. "I got lost in my own grief and couldn't see what was actually happening. The fact is we almost had a child together." He picked up the glass of whiskey and knocked it back before pouring another. "And the crazy part? Even now, I'd give anything to make that a reality again. I should feel like I dodged a goddamn bullet, but... I built this home hoping to start a family someday." He let out a heavy breath, lifting his glass to his lips. "I knew I'd never *love* Amanda. Hell, my parents, your father, couldn't stand her and I... I guess I'm the idiot who wanted to think I saw the *real* her. A side no one else got to see. And now I know that was all a lie. But my little girl... she was innocent in all of it."

His voice cracked, and he took another long, slow sip, swallowing more than just whiskey.

I felt the weight of his grief settle between us. I understood what it was like to lose my father. The raw, endless void of pain. But losing a child? I couldn't fathom what he must have gone through, *still* be going through.

"I don't expect you to understand," he admitted, shaking his head. "Hell, I barely understand it. But last year, I thought I lost everything. And I went through it with *one* person. Unfortunately, that person was Amanda. That's always going to tie us together. Knowing it was built on lies doesn't change that."

A lump tightened in my throat. "I hear you." I hesitated, my pulse drumming in my ears. "Does that mean Amanda will always be part of your life?"

He didn't hesitate. "No. I'm done with her." His voice was firm, absolute. "I can't get pulled back into her twisted web again. But..." He sighed, rubbing a hand over his face. "She'll always be part of my past. She'll always have that piece of me that broke the day we lost her."

I inhaled shakily. I closed my eyes for a beat, forcing myself to strip my own history with Amanda from the equation. I knew what it was like to have a toxic ex. I'd made the choice, same as Connor. I'd made excuses. Excuses I couldn't touch or even look at right now.

I took a deep sip of my whiskey, bracing myself for the naked truth I was about to lay bare.

"Connor, I've dated some... *really* awful guys." My voice was quiet, but the words felt like a confession. "Those experiences... they'll always be with me. I know what it's like to carry the scars of things that happened during a relationship, to accept that you may never fully heal from them."

Connor's gaze sharpened, his fingers curling tighter around his glass.

I exhaled. "I could never hold your past against you. All you did was try to defend someone you thought was a good person, someone who shared such a traumatic loss with you. And honestly? Your loyalty and need to protect the people in your life? I was wrong before. That's not a flaw, Connor. It's incredible." I locked eyes with him. "Maybe my issue is that it's hard for me to accept because of *my* past with her. At least, that's probably what Dr. Fenwick would say."

"Dr. Fenwick?"

"My therapist back home." I rubbed my palms along my jeans, trying to ease the nervous energy building inside me. "Anyway, I know I can eventually let that go when it comes to *us*. I just..." My voice cracked slightly, and I pushed through it. "I don't know how long it'll take for that hurt to go away. Once my walls go up—"

Connor didn't move, but I saw the way his body tensed. "What happened, Lucy? You didn't have this guard up when you left."

My heart stopped.

Breathe in.

Breathe out.

"You don't know how bad my previous dating experiences have been. That duke was nothing compared to..." I felt every muscle in my body go rigid.

Connor went to my side placing a gentle hand at my back. "Lucy..."

I shook my head. "It's fine. Unfortunately, that's shaped who I am now. Trust doesn't come easy anymore. But I've known you for so long, Connor. When you comforted Amanda, sent me to that fucking parking lot it..." I slammed my eyes shut.

"Wish I could go back and fix this." His voice cracked.

"Don't. You've already apologized. More than once. This is my issue now, and I'll do my best to get back there with you. Just be patient with me. I promise we're at least friends again, and that might be all I have in me."

His expression faltered—a flinch that barely lasted a second but hit like a blow to my chest.

"Friends," he repeated, his voice almost unreadable. Then softer, "That's fine. Whatever you need. Lucy, if you ever need to talk, I'm here. Always."

He ran a hand through his hair, exhaling hard. "I hate that I wasn't there for you after you left." His jaw tightened, something breaking in his expression. "That—" He swallowed hard. "That kills me."

His eyes met mine, raw and unguarded.

"I promise you," he said, voice thick with emotion. "Each day from here forward, I'll show you—you *can* trust me again. I've got your back, Lucy. I need you to know that."

He hesitated, something warring behind his gaze.

"I..." His lips parted, but he stopped himself, face crumpling with an emotion I couldn't quite name.

Then finally, a quiet, tortured confession—

"I care about you. More than you could ever know."

I nodded, a soft, sad smile pulling at my lips.

I stood from the chair and pulled him into me. We stayed like that, just holding each other for what felt like an eternity.

Connor's arms wrapped around me, and I felt the pain, the distrust—the walls I'd built so high around myself—begin to loosen.

Each slow exhale eased the weight pressing against my ribs.

It felt like we'd hit reset.

Like we'd cleared the wreckage and found something *solid* beneath it.

And for now, that was enough.

CHAPTER SIXTEEN

The Mess We Carry

LUCY

The sun had dipped low behind the barn, casting long shadows across the porch as I climbed the steps up to my father's home. My boots scuffed against the wood, the sound stark against the quiet evening hum. Connor followed not too far behind. He'd come back with me to grab a tool he'd left inside.

"Thanks for helping me with learning the ropes around here." I said as Connor reached for the door handle.

"Didn't we already establish you don't need to thank me anymore?" His brows knitted before he gave me a playful grin.

I chuckled. "Yes, we did."

Inside, Sam's laughter rang out from the kitchen. The lighthearted sound sent a pang through me—a sharp contrast to the weight of guilt pressing against my ribs. I'd told Connor everything, even after Sam asked me not to.

"We're back!" I called.

Sam's voice carried into the entryway as he turned to us, grinning. "Oh good! You're both here. Does this mean Mom and Dad are back together?"

Connor walked in and grabbed his multi-tool off the kitchen table. His tension thickened the air around us.

Sam frowned. "You okay? Sorry I made that joke..."

Connor exhaled sharply. "Sam. I know everything."

The color drained from Sam's face. "What do you mean?"

Panic flared in my chest as I blurted, "I'm sorry, Sam. I let Amanda get to me. I went off, and then she admitted to everything she did to us. To you." My throat tightened. "It's kind of a good thing right? Connor knows..."

"Lucy, how could you do that?" Sam glared at me before forcing a false smile back into place. "I'm sorry, Connor. I—"

Connor stepped forward. "No. *I'm* sorry." I let out the breath I'd been holding as he embraced his brother. "I'm so sorry you went through that shit. I'm sorry you didn't feel like you could talk to me. I would have been there. I would have stuck up for you."

Sam's throat bobbed as he pulled back. "It's fine, Connor. Really."

Connor shook his head. "No. That wasn't just bullying, Sam. That was bigotry."

Sam's jaw tensed. "Please don't go there, Connor."

"I'm serious. That kind of rumor is dangerous in a small town. I mean, if the wrong person believed it..." He shook his head, exhaling sharply.

"Yes. I know," Sam bit back. "Please don't straight-splain how hate crimes happen to gay men in small towns, Connor. You think you get it because we're brothers and you've watched more musicals than your buddies, but you don't. You *can't* get it."

Connor's disappointment settled into the furrow of his brow. "Fine. Then let's talk about why didn't you at least tell me after Amanda and I broke up the first, second... even the third time? At what point were you going to let me know she was an absolute monster to you? Our wedding?"

"Of course not, Connor. I wouldn't have let you marry her... I don't think."

"You don't think?" he scoffed. "You're my best friend, Sam. I tell you everything. Why didn't you talk to me long before I was with Amanda?"

"I just couldn't, okay? You're always so *perfect* all the time. I can't live up to that. Being Connor Lochland's brother isn't easy. I didn't want you to think... I couldn't take care of myself."

Connor ran a hand through his thick, dark hair. "Sam. I'm not perfect. You can't always use that as an excuse when you—"

"See?! This is what I'm talking about. You always have the moral high ground. I can't win."

"Stop." Connor growled. "Just be real for a second. We're brothers. You should have told me."

Sam flinched. His fingers tapped against the countertop, his gaze darting between us. "I'm sorry! It was just survival. That's it."

"Fine." Connor's lips pressed into a thin line.

Sam let out a strained breath, running a hand down his face. "I can't believe you told him, Lucy."

My mouth fell open a moment as I stammered, "You weren't there. Amanda was—"

"Amanda is always Amanda," Sam shot back. "You promised."

"Hey, don't blame Lucy," Connor's voice rose.

"Are you kidding me?" Sam gaped at him. "After Lucy and I talked the other night, I decided I was going to tell you... in my own time."

"And when was that exactly?" Connor clipped.

I took a step forward. "No. You're right, Sam. I did promise you I wouldn't say anything. You should have been the one to speak your truth. But enough is enough. I've been gone for six years because of that narcissistic bitch. I'm not the same person who left. Thanks to several months of therapy, I can finally stand up for myself. This was me trying to get closure." I began to pace, throwing my hands up in unrestrained frustration. "I've been surrounded by drama since I landed. Jesus, I just lost my fucking dad! And believe it or not, I'm a mess. So forgive me if I'm not dealing with Amanda's or my aunt's bullshit anymore!" The words left me lighter, like I'd finally let something go.

Everything stilled.

Silence pressed into the corners of the room.

Sam shifted on his feet. He cleared his throat. "Sorry, Luce."

Connor's eyes burned holes into me. I met his gaze as he said, "Do you want to go for a walk? With me, I mean. I can show you the property. A lot has changed since you left."

I worked my jaw, taking a moment to breathe. I couldn't tell if he suddenly wanted to *fix* me or just wanted to be *there* for me.

I closed my eyes and reminded myself: *This is Connor. He's the guy that shows up for you. The one who comes to the airport to make sure you're not alone when...*

His deep baritone broke me from my thoughts. "It'll help me start that mentorship."

"Mentorship?" Sam's brow raised, his eyes darting between us.

"Ugh. My dad put a stipulation in his will. Long story, but Connor's my mentor now."

"Wow. Okay." Sam's frown tightened as he held back a grin. "That should be fun."

"It will be," Connor agreed, giving me his famous lopsided grin.

I sighed. "Alright then. Let's go on this tour, shall we?"

Sam held up a hand. "Hang on. Before you two head out, Connor, are we good?"

"Yeah. We can talk more later. But we're good." He did that quick, single nod men always give each other after an argument. Then he leaned forward and the two engaged in their secret handshake.

Sam stepped back and added, "I also have some updates on the celebration of life."

"Oh yeah?" I said, brightening.

"So, number one, I've secured floral arrangements donated by the amazing Miss Jenna. Number two, Michael, the zaddy chef at *The Wildflower Lounge*, is catering. He also insisted on donating to the event. He's bringing Papa Bob's favorites—loaded mashed potatoes, cornbread casserole, ribs, the works. But don't worry, I still have a table for the potluck. The party supply store that's an hour out of town has our tables and chairs reserved. I'm working on getting volunteers to go pick them up."

"Sam, thank you. For everything you're doing. For my dad. For me."

"Of course, lover."

I chuckled. "You're ridiculous. Did you want to come with us?"

Sam shook his head. "I promised my parents I'd come stay with them tonight. I'm leaving shortly to have dinner at their place, and then I'm spending the night. If that's okay with you. I don't want you to feel like you have to be alone..."

"No, of course that's fine. Enjoy your family. I give anything to..." A pang raked against my heart and I suppressed the rush of emotions that hit me all at once. Fanning my face to dry my eyes, I walked over, closing the gap between us, and gave him a hug. "Never mind. I'll see you when I see you?"

"Absolutely. I'd much rather be here with you than with my parents and their five bloodhounds," he teased.

I laughed again, grateful we were able to move past all this so quickly. "Have fun. Love you."

"Love ya," Sam waved. "You two have fun!" He paused, then studied us. "Also, what *is* going on with you two now?"

Connor looked to me and shrugged.

I shook my head. "Don't worry about it. We'll catch up later. Okay?"

Sam gave me a slow, pensive nod. "Alright..."

"Tell Mom and Dad 'hi' for me," Connor added with a little wave as he made his way to the back sliding doors that faced the pastures.

Sam scoffed. "You tell them. You're the one who lives here."

I snorted. "That's very true, Connor..."

"Fair point." He chuckled.

We said another round of goodbyes before going our separate ways.

As Sam headed to the bathroom, Connor slid open the backdoor for me. "You okay?"

I chewed my lip before shrugging and stepping out onto the porch deck. "Yeah. As good as I can be. I feel so messy right now, but... that's normal, right?"

He followed behind me and shut the door. "That's okay. I can handle messy."

"Good, 'cause that's all I got in me today." I exhaled, straightening with a humorless chuckle. "Are you ready to show me around the ranch? I've been curious about those new structures over there." I pointed. "I should probably learn what they're actually for—especially now that this all is my responsibility."

"Well, it's not *all* your responsibility. I'm still here to help. I mean, I *am* the manager, after all." Connor's lips tugged into a soft smile—not forced, not wary. Just... easy.

"You know what I meant." I rolled my eyes. "Anyway, let's do this."

"Sure thing, boss." Then he tipped his hat and gave me a wink that left my knees weak.

I shook my head, refusing to become a cliche.

I had a ranch to run.

CHAPTER SEVENTEEN

His Favorite Place

LUCY

The land sat cast in a golden glow as a streak of red highlighted the sky. We had maybe an hour or two of light left to complete the tour. Connor led me toward the ATV shed behind the barn.

"When did this get built?" I asked as we approached.

"A couple years ago," Connor said, casually tossing me a helmet.

I raised an eyebrow, spinning it in my hands. "What's this for?"

"We could still *walk*, but where's the fun in that?" He smirked.

A slow grin spread across my face. "True."

I glanced over the lineup of four-wheelers, side-by-sides, and dirt bikes, all ready for action.

Amusement danced in his gaze. "Pick your poison—just not this one. I'm driving this bad boy." He patted a dark blue side-by-side. "Think you can keep up, *London*?"

Oh, it was on.

I swung a leg over a red four-wheeler, revving the engine. "Try me."

We tore off across the gravel path, kicking up dust as we sped toward the back half of the ranch. Wind whipped through my helmet, stinging the back of my neck.

The thrill of speed was a desperately needed escape from the crushing weight of grief, the tangled mess of conflict, and the suffocating pressure of a legacy I wasn't sure I could uphold.

In that moment, I could leave it all behind.

The main barn and stables came into view first, their deep red paint vibrant against the Montana sky. "Did my dad paint these recently?" I asked, shouting over the wind and rumbling engines.

"Yeah, probably within the last two years!" Connor called back.

The wood was well maintained, standing strong despite the elements. The stables housed my show horse, Daisy, alongside the working horses—a mix of Quarter Horses and Mustangs.

Though four-wheelers made the job faster, they couldn't replace the instincts and agility of a good horse. My dad had always preferred to be on horseback. I could picture him in the saddle, hat low over his salt-and-pepper hair, guiding the herd with quiet confidence. The memory warmed me in a way I hadn't felt since he passed.

We rode past the pasture fenced off for the horses to graze and stretch their legs. A few lifted their heads at the sound of our engines, ears twitching before they resumed lazily swishing their tails.

Ahead, near the tree line, sat the bunkhouse where the ranch hands stayed—far enough from the main house to give them privacy, but close enough to the animals that their walk to work was easy.

Further down, past the split-rail fencing, stood the calving barn—a newer structure, built after a brutal winter storm wiped out half a herd of calves.

I slowed my ATV. "I remember when Dad had this built. He wanted the breeding stock to have a safe place to give birth without risking exposure to the elements."

Connor nodded. "It's a good practice."

We continued down the dirt path, approaching the sorting pens. Sections for breeding, vaccinations, disease control. It was a lot. Seeing it all laid out made the sheer scale of what I'd inherited finally start to sink in.

"You took it easy on me my first day back," I noted, scrunching my face at him.

Connor smirked. "Didn't want to overwhelm you."

"I'm not some helpless city girl, Connor."

He held up his hands. "Never said you were. But it was your first day."

"Whatever." I sighed, then scanned the pens, a frown forming. "What are we prepping for right now?"

"Breeding season. Your dad ran a tight operation. Only the best bulls are used for genetic improvements. They're divided by age, weight, and purpose," Connor explained, pulling up beside me. "Breeding heifers stay in one section, steers in another, and bulls have their own paddocks to prevent any, uh, unplanned family reunions."

I snorted. "You mean so they don't get busy whenever the mood strikes?"

He grinned. "Exactly." He gestured toward a distant pasture. "See that pen over there? That's where the breeding bulls stay when they're not with the herd."

I followed his gaze, spotting the thick-necked bulls, their massive frames powerful. They were intimidating, even from a distance. "How many head of cattle do we even have?"

Connor's brows lifted slightly. "You don't know?"

I pressed my lips together, shaking my head. "Not yet. But I will when you tell me."

He smirked. "Between all the pastures, feedlots, and sale cattle? About fifteen hundred."

I blinked. "Fifteen hundred?"

Connor's lips quirked into a lopsided grin at my wide-eyed expression. "Multi-million-dollar operation, Lucy. Your dad was as much a businessman as he was a rancher."

"Geez. I didn't realize he was making that much." I shook my head, staring out over the land. "Did he always have this much property?"

"Actually, Bob bought up the empty land behind and around your original property. That's how I ended up with the land next door—he sold it to me when I couldn't find the right place within a decent commuting distance to here and town."

I exhaled, letting it sink in. I was standing in the middle of an empire. And now, it was mine.

"Come on. Let me show you the processing facility." He waved me forward as he slowly rolled ahead on his vehicle.

As we drove up, my stomach twisted. Growing up, I'd treated so many of these animals like pets. It was the part of the business my father wanted me to understand, but never made me watch.

"Here's where the final stages happen," Connor explained. "Some are sold live, but others are processed here on-site. Our meat is USDA-certified, so we handle our own butchering. Cuts transport costs, ensures quality."

"I hate this part," I admitted, trying not to frown. "But I do appreciate this setup. On-site means less stress for the animals. And at least they get to live a good life before... you know."

Connor shot me a look, failing to hide his amusement at my clear discomfort. "Exactly." He revved his engine. "Think you're up for a little fun?"

I narrowed my eyes. "Depends. What kind of fun?"

"Race you to the south pasture."

Before I could react, he took off in a cloud of dust.

"Oh, hell no!" I yelled, gunning it after him.

The wind roared as I pushed the four-wheeler to its limit. Connor had the lead, but I saw my chance to cut ahead. Veering right, I cut through a shallow creek bed, kicking up water as I powered forward.

I glanced back to see Connor laughing, shaking his head as he tried to catch up. The rush of adrenaline, the speed—it was the most alive I'd felt in days.

Skidding to a stop at the pasture gate, I threw my hands up. "Winner!"

Connor pulled up seconds later, shaking his head. "Cheater."

I grinned. "Smart. There's a difference."

His lips quirked. "We'll see about that."

I arched a brow. "What do you mean?"

"Race you to the lake." He barely finished the sentence before gunning it, kicking up dirt again as he tore off down the path.

"Seriously?!" I shouted, flooring it after him. "You're the cheater!"

The terrain changed as we neared the lake, the air shifting from hay and earth to crisp pine and water. I veered right, then jumped a small hill, cutting in front of him once again. Connor pushed his side-by-side harder, but I was already in the lead when I reached the shoreline and skidded to a triumphant stop.

Connor pulled up beside me, shaking his head. "I'm starting to think you have an unfair advantage. Maybe a hidden rabbit's foot somewhere?"

I smirked as we climbed off the ATVs. "Maybe you just need to be faster."

His laughter rumbled low and warm, and suddenly, I was acutely aware of how close we were standing. I shifted a step to the right, hoping he wouldn't notice how much his closeness affected me.

The lake shimmered in the fading sunlight, casting golden ripples across the surface. The world felt quieter here, more intimate.

Connor's voice was softer now. "You know, this was your dad's favorite spot."

I swallowed hard, nodding. "It's mine too."

He glanced at the water, then at me. "It's beautiful."

He wasn't looking at the lake anymore. My stomach fluttered under his heated gaze.

Keeping my eyes ahead, I whispered, "It really is."

The silence stretched between us, neither of us quite willing to break it.

The sun dipped lower, the sky streaked with amber and violet, the soft rush of water against the shore the only sound between us.

For a moment, I thought he might reach for me.

I tensed. I wasn't ready.

Not yet.

But then the air shifted. Something unspoken slipped between us, and reality settled back in.

"Tomorrow's Friday." I let the words fill the space between us. Leaving their meaning in the subtext as a knot formed in my throat because I couldn't say it. I couldn't bear the thought. *Tomorrow we'd finally lay my dad to rest.*

"You want to talk about it?" Connor offered, his features hardening under the pressure of his own grief.

I shook my head. "But I do need to get back and read over my eulogy one more time. Make sure it's perfect."

"Lucy, it doesn't need to be perfect. Just say what's in your heart and on your mind." Connor's advice didn't touch me.

"No. It's my last gift to him. I can't screw this up," I rasped as my mouth went dry.

Connor turned to face me, his eyes darkening. He hesitated, then took my hands. "Lucy, you are the greatest gift that man ever had."

My face twisted as silent tears drifted down my cheeks. My lip trembled as I swiped away each new droplet as if that would stop them.

Connor pulled me in and held me.

My shoulders shook as I let every ounce of heartache out.

And when the last tears fell into the damp spot on Connor's shirt, I released him without a word. Then, we turned back to our ATVs, threw on our helmets, and made our way toward the house.

My mind went numb as we drove. I focused on the wind lapping over my cheeks. I didn't remember parking, only how heavy each step felt as we walked back to the house.

Connor watched as I ascended the porch steps. "Goodnight, Lucy. See you in the morning."

I looked back over my shoulder, my hand reaching for the door handle. "Night."

I peeked out the window as he started the walk back to his property, disappearing into the darkness.

The weight of tomorrow settled over me again, heavy and unavoidable.

I wasn't prepared.

I never would be.

Buddy brushed against my leg. I patted his head absently, his tail wagging in proud little thumps.

"Come on, boy," I murmured, my voice distant to my own ears. "Let's get you some dinner and then off to bed for both of us."

I lay awake for hours, my mind a storm of thoughts—the funeral, Connor, the ranch, Amanda—my father, Diane.

The funeral.

The funeral.

The funeral.

When sleep finally came, it wasn't peaceful.

But at least it came.

CHAPTER EIGHTEEN

My Father's Daughter

LUCY

I was vaguely aware of the soft knocks in the distance when Buddy launched off the bed, bolting for the door, barking and bouncing on his front paws.

Groggy and irritated, I threw on my robe and shuffled toward the front door. As I reached for the handle and cracked it open to peer outside, my jaw nearly hit the floor.

"*Mom*?" I blinked, taking in the sleek, poised figure of Lillian Sinclair—the woman who had, *technically*, raised me.

Her chestnut-brown hair was meticulously pinned back, her hazel-green eyes—identical to my own—framed with elegant eyeshadow. A small, netted veil swooped over one eye, perfectly matching the custom black gown she'd no doubt designed herself. It hugged her figure snugly: a perfect blend of high society and Southern grace, with buttons that ran down the fitted bodice.

"Hi, honey. And please, call me *Mother*." Her lips pouted as she spoke, her British accent as impeccable as ever. "May I come in?"

I gritted my teeth. *How dare she show up here today?*

Being the well-mannered woman my father raised me to be, I stepped aside and let her in. "What are you doing here?" I asked, keeping my tone neutral.

She sighed. "Well, if you'd answered my calls, you'd know I was invited to today's events... as well as requested to be here for the reading of the will."

I gaped. "Wait. Really?"

She nodded, her elegant composure etched into every precise movement. "Darling, how are you holding up? I know how much you loved your father."

Here we go again, I thought bitterly.

"I'm okay," I said, voice flat.

She pressed her lips together before producing a sleek garment bag. "I brought you a dress for the funeral. I thought you'd want something special."

"Mom, when *everything* you own is 'special,' so none of it's special," I muttered.

She frowned, her perfectly manicured brows knitting together. "Lucy, please. I'm waving the white flag here. I just want to be there for you, my darling. Can't you stop pushing me away—just this once—and let me in?"

I sighed. I wanted to resist. I wanted to push back, but rejecting her kindness now felt cruel. "Fine, *Mother*."

Her face lit up. "Oh, wonderful!" She turned and called toward the door, "Eric, bring in the items!"

I groaned. "Mom, you brought your assistant?"

"*Mother*," she corrected, as though I'd forgotten, "and yes, of course. How *else* would I be able to do my best to help you today?"

Her sincere confusion softened me, but I still wanted to roll my eyes.

"Fine. I appreciate you wanting to be here and... *mother* me," I ground out. "Can you just give me a moment to shower?"

"Absolutely." She beamed, stepping forward to plant two air kisses on either side of my face.

I hurried off, letting the warm water clear my thoughts.

By the time I dried off, a deep chuckle echoed from the living room, sending a flutter through my stomach. I tightened the towel around me and peeked out.

"Connor?" My curiosity slipped into relief. He'd come, as promised.

Again.

His eyes sparkled with amusement when he caught me peeking. "Good morning."

"Lucy!" My mother's voice went shrill. "You're indecent! Go get dressed this instant!"

I arched a brow at her. "I need the dress you brought, don't I?"

Connor smothered a smirk behind his calloused hand, his blue eyes dancing with silent laughter.

With an exasperated huff, my mother shoved the garment bag into my arms. I sighed, turning on my heel and walking off.

Every movement felt excruciating as I slipped into the dress. I hadn't even taken in the design—I already hated it, if only for what it symbolized.

When I stepped out, I felt myself go pale. The world tilted and my legs weakened. Connor's brow furrowed as his eyes swept over me, filled with quiet concern. He was at my side in an instant, an arm wrapping around me, lifting and helping me walk to the breakfast bar.

"You look beautiful," he murmured.

I nodded, my voice hollow. "I hate that I look beautiful today."

His chest rumbled with a quiet chuckle. "As opposed to ugly?"

A weak grin found me. "I guess that *would* be worse."

Connor guided me to the breakfast bar, settling beside me. "Are you up for this guy to do your makeup?"

I shrugged. "Better than me having to do it."

Connor bent close, his breath warm against my ear as he whispered, "Just say the word, and I'll escort them out, okay?"

I nodded, unable to speak past the lump in my throat.

I was silent, but my gratitude ran deep. From the moment I set foot back in White River, Connor had made sure I was never truly alone. And that was something I'd *never* forget.

As Eric dusted, blended, and powdered my face into perfection, Connor kept hold of my hand. Or maybe I was the one holding on. Clinging to him as if he were the only thing keeping me from falling apart.

"So, you two are courting now?" my mother asked, her tone as composed as ever, though a slight edge of curiosity slipped beneath it.

I rolled my eyes—earning a sharp look from Eric, who signaled for me to stay still. "No, Mother. And I don't think people call it that anymore."

My mother hummed, clearly unimpressed, but didn't press further.

That, thankfully, ended the conversation.

Then, reality set in.

I was going to my father's funeral.

There was no escaping it.

No waking up from this.

It was *real*.

My breaths came quick and shallow, my chest tightening with each inhale. My grip on Connor's hand tightened—my only tether to solid ground—as the room tilted again, my head going light.

That familiar sensation crept in. The slow unraveling. The quiet pull of detachment, like slipping beneath the surface of deep, unending water.

Somewhere, distant and fading, Connor's voice broke through the fog.

"Lucy, are you okay?"

Then—nothing.

I blinked awake, already buckled into the passenger seat of Connor's truck, my fingers curled around a small purse that—somehow—I knew matched my dress perfectly.

Awareness sharpened with each passing second, dragging me back into the moment.

I gasped. "My eulogy!"

Connor squeezed my hand. "It's here. You had me grab it. I folded it and put it in your purse."

I pressed my fingers to my temples. "Connor, I'm not okay. Something's wrong with me. I—I think I need to go to the hospital or—"

He held my hand tighter. "Lucy, it's stress. You'll get through this."

"What's happening to me?" I whispered, gripping his fingers.

He traced slow, soothing circles over my knuckles that had gone completely white. "You're strong, Lucy. Stronger than you realize."

I nodded, but everything felt like moving through thick, suffocating mud: heavy, sluggish, as if even the air around me resisted.

Still, I endured.

The excruciating drive stretched on, silence wrapping around me like a weighted blanket. I rested my head against the window, watching the world blur past in muted colors, the road stretching endlessly beneath us.

The truck rocked gently as we rolled into the church parking lot. I lifted my head, blinking away the haze of exhaustion.

Empty.

The lot stretched before us, eerily still, the absence of cars unsettling.

"Where is everyone?" I breathed.

Connor's frown deepened. "Diane didn't... of course she didn't tell you." His jaw tensed as he muttered a quiet curse. "This is the private hour. Close family and friends get to say goodbye first."

My breath caught.

The air felt too thick, my chest too tight.

"Wait... is he—" My voice faltered. "Is he *in* there?"

Connor's grip on my hand tightened. "You don't have to go in."

Before I could fully process, the truck door yanked open, the rush of cool air startling me.

"Lucy, honey, come on," Aunt Diane urged. "This hour goes by faster than you'd think."

I shook my head furiously, my limbs heavier than bricks, incapable of movement.

"Lucy, he looks wonderful. So handsome, so at peace."

I glared at her. "*No.*"

Diane hesitated. "It'll help you feel better."

I clenched my jaw. "I *don't* want my last memory of him to be seeing his *corpse.*" My voice wavered, but I forced the words out. "No one told me there was a viewing."

My chest tightened, anger and grief tangling into something sharp and uncontrollable. My voice climbed. "No one said he'd be on *display* for the entire town!"

Diane's eyes widened. "I—I thought you'd want an open casket. I told Todd—"

"You *chose* this?" My breath hitched. "It wasn't *his* request?"

Diane flinched, then doubled down. "I've lost so much, just like you. But I keep going. That's what we do, Lucy. We push through—like family."

I exhaled sharply, my voice dropping into something low, something dangerous. "Get. *Away.* From. Me."

Diane hesitated, then took an uneasy step back.

My fingers curled into fists as I wrenched my gaze to the dashboard, jaw locked tight.

Footsteps crunched against the gravel.

A hushed whisper passed between her and Connor.

Seconds, minutes, or maybe an eternity later, Connor's hand squeezed mine.

"Lucy, it's almost time. They're closing the casket now." His warm voice was gentle, careful. "Do you want to greet guests as they come in, or sit by the podium before your speech?"

The weight of everything—the responsibility, the *finality*—suffocated me. My breaths turned rapid, shallow, erratic. Panic clawed at my ribs, tightening like a vice, threatening to pull me under again.

"How could he do this to me?" I gasped, my voice splintering under the weight of grief. "I'm not *ready*!"

A sob tore through me, raw and ragged. My body shook, trembling beneath the force of it.

Vision blurred, darkening at the edges.

Then... warmth.

Strong arms wrapped around me, steady and unyielding. A voice—deep, familiar, anchoring me to the moment.

"Breathe, Lucy. Breathe."

Connor.

His presence brought me to awareness as I drifted somewhere between now and nothing.

The last thing I remembered was cold water spilling over my fingers, the sharp bite of it against my trembling skin. My mother's murmured pleas. The weight of a blanket cocooning around me.

Sunlight.

Warmth spread across my face, the scent of pine and earth grounding me. A steaming cup of tea rested between my hands, its heat seeping into my palms. My breaths came easier now, though my chest still ached—raw, heavy with everything unspoken.

I turned to Connor, my voice hoarse. "Where am I?"

"The remembrance garden." His voice was smooth, full of admiration. "Your dad donated it—to honor our loved ones who have passed."

I blinked.

Of course he had.

But this time, grief didn't hollow me out. Instead, tender warmth filled the spaces where sorrow had settled. My father's presence surrounded me, rebuilding me piece by broken piece. I could feel his love for me within the love I still held for him, and my strength returned—slow, resolute, with each passing second in the sun.

I nodded, exhaling slowly. "I have to go in there."

Connor stood with me, his fingers wrapping around mine: solid, unwavering.

One step. Then another. My heels clicked softly against the stone pathway, a rhythmic echo swallowed by the hush that had settled over the gathering. Each step carried me forward, toward the church.

Toward my father's funeral.

Inside, the air was thick, heavy with the mingling scents of antique wood, polished pews, and the overwhelming perfume of lilies. Too many lilies. Their cloying sweetness curled in my throat, nearly suffocating. The body heat from the sheer number of attendees only thickened the oppressive atmosphere, making my dress feel suddenly too tight.

The choir's voices rose, filling the vaulted space with a powerful hymn that trembled in the air, vibrating through the wooden beams and stone walls. It was a song of faith, of mourning, of farewell. Each note felt like a tightrope, pulling me forward as I took slow, measured steps toward the altar.

Rows upon rows of pews were filled, creaking beneath the shifting weight of those gathered. Eyes followed me: some soft with sympathy, others assessing, expectant.

Beyond the pews, people lined the walls, pressed into every available space at the back of the church. They were the real heroes, the ones who had come not out of duty or social obligation, but because my father had mattered to them. They stood in quiet reverence, enduring the discomfort of an overcrowded church simply to pay their respects. Stained glass windows cast fractured beams of colored light over them, as if Heaven itself acknowledged their presence.

I wanted to look at them—to draw strength from them—but my gaze strayed, almost landing on the casket that loomed ahead. A sharp, aching tremor ran through me, and I cast my eyes downward, unwilling—*unable*—to face it just yet.

Beside me, my mother and Connor walked in quiet step, their grips firm on either side, silent anchors against the tide of my grief.

The sheer finality of this day pressed against my ribs, threatening to drag me under once again. But I forced my feet to keep moving. I had to. My father had given so much to so many.

Now, I had to do this for him.

The pastor's calm, reverent voice drifted over me, warm, steadfast, yet the words slipped through my grasp, distant and blurred.

I focused on the stretch of red carpet beneath my feet, tracing each thread as if counting them could somehow stitch together the pieces of me that had shattered the day I didn't get to say goodbye.

Then, it was time.

Connor gave my hand one final squeeze before I rose, my legs unsteady as I made my way toward the podium. My fingers trembled as I unfolded the paper, smoothing it against the polished wood.

I lifted my head.

The sea of faces blurred for a moment, but then I saw them—the ranch hands, my father's friends, our neighbors. People who had known him for decades. People who had loved him.

People who had *lost* him.

A deep breath. A balancing inhale.

I gripped the edges of the podium, drawing strength from the faces before me, from the love that filled the room.

I swallowed, then began, "My father loved so many things in this life.

"He loved fishing, hunting, and gathering with friends. He loved sitting around a fire, telling stories, and sharing laughter over a good meal. He loved *helping* people—not because he *had* to, but because he genuinely cared. And maybe, he even helped some of you here today.

"He loved this town like family, and looking around this room, I see that love reflected in all of you. The sheer number of faces here today is proof of the bonds he built, the lives he touched.

"I believe he forged those connections because he understood struggle—because he never forgot where he came from. And that's why he worked so hard to pay his blessings forward. His success was never just his own; he saw it as something to be shared, something to be given freely to those who needed it most. That was the kind of man he was.

"And because of this, he meant so many things to so many people.

"For some of you, he was the guy you talked sports with. Maybe you also loved classic movies and shared an in-depth review of the latest blockbuster because, man, could he talk about films... for *hours*."

A soft rumble of laughter spread through the church.

"Maybe you shared a drink, bowled a few rounds, played golf, or spent a quiet afternoon fishing together. Maybe you bonded over your love of collecting sports memorabilia, or maybe you were just someone who confided in him, because he treasured privacy and the need to have a trusted person to talk to.

"And maybe some of you here shared his love of The Carpenters. Who here enjoyed talking to him about their music?"

A few hands went up—hesitant but amused.

I sighed dramatically. "You? Ugh. Why did you encourage him? Do you have any idea how much every single person in this room knows about Karen Carpenter, now? Do you

think we *wanted* to know that much? I mean, she's amazing, beautiful, insanely talented...
but come on. There's love, and then there's *obsession*."

Laughter rippled through the crowd. And for just a moment, the suffocating weight
of grief eased.

"But more than anything, my dad loved God. That's where he found his strength,
his perseverance, his unshakable kindness. He carried his faith in everything he did—his
work, his friendships, even in the way he loved me.

"I haven't set foot in a church in six years. But somehow, I know... he's glad I'm here
today."

A lump tightened in my throat as I unfolded the paper, my father's last message to me
lingering in my mind.

"A month ago, he sent me a text. Short, simple, but it stayed with me. He told me this
was one of his favorite verses... Thessalonians 5:16-18:

" *'Rejoice always, pray continually, give thanks in all circumstances; for this is God's will
for you in Christ Jesus.'*

"These are the words my dad would want us to live by. This is how he tried to live, no
matter what life threw at him. See, sometimes life will pile things onto you—heartache,
loss, hardships—but those things cannot be our focus. My dad would tell us to think
about what we still have to rejoice over, the things to find gratitude in, even if it's the small
things.

"So today, I will take my father's advice and choose to be thankful. I'm thankful for
the years I had with him, for the lessons he taught me, for the love he poured into my life.
I'm thankful for every single person here who knew and loved him.

"And I'm thankful—so thankful—that I have the honor of calling Robert Campbell
my dad."

Silence.

A sniffle.

Another.

A deep, shuddering breath from somewhere in the crowd.

I picked up my paper, turned to take those awful steps away from the podium.

Then—*applause*.

A slow build, hesitant at first, until the entire room was on its feet, clapping. Not
because this was a performance, not because my words had been grand or poetic, but
because at the end, they had been *his* words.

I gripped the podium one final time, gathering every worn fragment of myself.

I had done it.

I had given my father one final gift.

I turned to step down—legs weak, breath shaky—when Connor caught me, his arms wrapped around my waist before I could stumble.

"You were perfect," he murmured, voice thick with emotion.

I pressed my face into his chest, letting the steady rise and fall of his breath tether me. "I don't feel perfect."

"You were." He pressed a kiss to my temple, his grip firm, unwavering. "You *are.*"

I swallowed hard, nodding against him. "I just need to get through the rest of today."

"You will," he promised. "And I'll be right beside you."

The rest of the service blurred.

People came up to offer their condolences—hugs, kind words, stories about my dad. Some made me laugh, some made me cry, but all of them left me feeling the weight of just how much he had meant to this town.

I shook hands, exchanged pleasantries, thanked everyone for coming. My mother floated around, greeting people like she was hosting a gala instead of her ex-husband's funeral. Diane kept herself busy directing guests, while Sam—

Where was Sam?

I realized I hadn't seen him *once* today.

Then he was at my side.

"Sorry," he murmured a whisper in my ear. "I ran late and was stuck at the back."

Relief flooded me. I had everyone I needed by my side.

By the time the service ended and we made our way to the cemetery, I was drained.

The burial was simple. Quiet. Prayers were spoken, hands laid on shoulders, murmured condolences exchanged. Flowers fell, one by one, against polished wood.

Then—just like that—it was over.

A final goodbye.

A chapter closed.

CHAPTER NINETEEN

The Weight and the Light

LUCY

Preparations for the celebration of life were underway. When Connor dropped me off at home, we spotted Sam, who'd left the burial early to get here before anyone else. He moved like a man on a mission. A fire seemed to be lit beneath him as he fluttered around the yard, everywhere at once—giving orders, adjusting decorations, double-checking every last detail for the evening's event.

I made my way over to him. "Hey, Sam. How's everything going?"

He barely glanced up as he rearranged a floral arrangement on one of the tables. "Hey, Luce. It's coming along!"

"Do you need any help?"

Sam straightened and looked around. "Everything's taken care of here. How are you?"

The gravity of the day pressed down on me. "I'm exhausted. But I'm okay."

Sam came around the table and pulled me in for a hug. "Why don't you get some rest? Or a coffee? Something."

I shook my head. "No, I need something to do."

"Why didn't you meet the rest of your family at Diane's thing?"

My brows rose as I eyed him. "Really?"

He chuckled. "Sorry. Why did I ask? I can't believe your mom made it out."

"Yeah... I'm surprised, too."

"Did you go to the reading of the will?" Sam asked, fiddling with the placement of the floral arrangement on another nearby table, unable to stay still.

I frowned. "No. I don't need to be there. James will send me a copy."

"That's probably for the best." Sam's eyes flickered up and he grinned. "Looks like you have a visitor."

But before I could say anything else, he nodded behind me then took off, weaving through the tables and volunteers.

Then a familiar, deep voice came. "Hey, Lucy." Connor's hand settled on my back. "You doing okay?"

I let out a heavy breath. "Yeah."

He raised an eyebrow. That quiet, patient look that told me he wasn't buying it.

The weight in my chest pressed harder. "Fine. I skipped the signing of the will to avoid my mother and Diane. Now they're all at her house like we're all one big happy family." I scoffed. "You'd think she never shipped me off to a whole other continent during the divorce.

"Hey, you get to feel whatever you want to feel today. Besides, you couldn't pay me to be at a brunch hosted by Diane." His brow titled up, giving me a level gaze."

A grin split across my face. "Not even for a million dollars?"

"Not even for a billion." He lowered his voice, emphasizing the seriousness of the situation, and we burst into shared laughter.

After catching my breath I placed a hand to my chest. "I feel bad. My cousins are in town and I've left them alone with their mother."

"And *your* mother." He added, his eyes lit with mischief.

I gasped. "Oh my God. You're right!" Then I shrugged. "Shame for them. They'll forgive me later. At least Tanya and Taylor have each other."

"That's true," he mused. as a truck with *The Wildflower Lounge*'s logo pulled in. "Everything's set here. Looks like Michael's about to pull out the smoker and start the meat. Do you want to grab the dogs and go for a walk before guests arrive?"

I hesitated. More alone time with Connor sent blood rushing to my head. Even now the pull between us was palpable. I knew I needed to keep my distance—for my own sake. But somehow, everything felt easier around him. Better.

I nodded. "Sure. You're right, they need to go out before everyone gets here."His lopsided grin sent warmth through my chest, soothing the ache of the day. "Great. Let's grab Buddy."

I put up a hand to stop him. "I've got him. I'll meet you at your truck."

He nodded and turned to leave.

As I reached the top of the porch steps I looked out at the quiet hive of activity—tables being set, chairs arranged—and my heart filled with pride. My dad would have loved this. The community coming together to celebrate instead of mourn. I could hear him now: *Lucy, don't focus on what you've lost. Remember the good times we had.* A hint of a smile whispered against my lips, then I headed inside where I was immediately greeted by a bouncing Buddy. His paws tapped with electric joy against the hardwood floors.

"Wanna go for a walk?" I asked, my tone high pitched babying.

His tail revved up to top speed in reply.

"Alright. Let's go." I opened the door and told him, "Go! Go get Connor!" Buddy sprinted across the yard and leapt into Connor's arms as if they hadn't seen each other just this morning.

I couldn't help it. I melted a little... okay, my insides turned to complete mush.

Connor opened the door to the backseat of the truck, and Buddy hopped in, tail smacking him in the face before he spun and sat in the back seat. Connor shut the door and opened the passenger side for me.

"Such a gentleman," I said, climbing in.

He grinned, bright and effortless. "My pleasure."

"Are my eyes puffy? They feel so dry. I don't think I've ever cried so much in my entire life," I worried.

Connor's crystal blue eyes studied mine, reviewing every nook and cranny. "They're perfect. You look beautiful as always."

I flushed under his intensity. "Thanks."

"Any time." He said, closing the door before walking around to the driver's side.

We drove in the kind of quiet that felt comfortable. Healing.

As I climbed out of the truck, my black dress billowed around me, and Connor's gaze tracked every movement. Heat crept into my cheeks as his eyes locked onto mine.

Clearing his throat, he called, "Willow, come here, girl."

Willow stirred, struggling to push herself upright from where she lay sprawled on the porch. Her belly stretched taut, sides rising and falling in heavy pants.

Seeing her, I felt myself shift gears, slipping with practiced ease into veterinary-student mode. "Let's see how mama-to-be is feeling before we go."

I climbed the steps and knelt beside her, gently palpating her belly, feeling for movement and the positioning of her pups. I gave her a thorough once-over, checking for signs of dilation or distress.

"Are you up for a walk, girl?" I asked softly.

Willow's tail thumped against the porch, slow but steady.

Connor crouched beside me, rubbing her head. "How's she looking, doc?"

"I'm not a doc yet," I reminded him with a small smile. "She should be fine for a short walk. We'll let her decide how far she wants to go." Then, I glanced up at him, brow raised. "Have you been monitoring her temperature?"

Connor's face fell slightly. "Not yet."

I gave him a pointed look. "Start today. Now, actually. Can you grab a thermometer?"

Connor nodded. "Absolutely, I'll be right back."

As he disappeared inside, Buddy joined me, greeting Willow with an enthusiastic wag of his tail before flopping down beside her and licking the side of her face. I grinned, warmth spreading through me at the sight of their easy companionship.

When Connor returned, he asked, "I need to watch for a drop in temperature, right? If she's between 98 and 99 degrees, she'll go into labor within a day."

"Exactly." I smiled, a hint of pride playing at my lips as I took the thermometer from him. "And... looks like she's good. Willow, do you want to lead the way?'

As I stood, I glanced over at Connor, who was watching his dog with so much love my toes curled in my sandals. He was a good man. One of the few.

After such a heavy day, our fight about Amanda felt like nothing. Trivial. Distant. What mattered was the man he was when things fell apart. The kind of man who is there for you in the best and worst of times.

My walls crumbled, just a little more.

I watched as he bent down, stroking Willow's fur, smiling as she greeted him with fervent kisses. He murmured something into her ear, and her entire body wriggled with excitement.

Then he stood, and the moment shifted.

My breath caught as I realized how close I'd moved toward him. His blue eyes locked onto mine, piercing straight through me.

"Ready?" he breathed.

My lips parted, then closed.

I swallowed, gathering myself. "Yeah."

We set off side by side, keeping a slow, relaxed pace across Connor's property. As we neared the barn, Buddy and Willow playfully nipped at each other.

"They really love one another," Connor mused, watching them with open affection.

"It's really sweet," I said, my heart swelling.

Connor stopped abruptly. "I hope you know how much I care about you, Lucy."

His words stole my breath.

My heart pounded against my ribs.

"I don't care where you are in the world. I swear to you, whenever you need me, I'll be there. Day or night."

I took a shaky breath and nodded. "I know."

And I did.

I reached out, rubbing the side of his arm. He stiffened slightly, then shifted, stepping closer. His hands found my arms—gentle but firm—like he needed to feel me, to bind himself to this moment.

His intense blue eyes searching mine as if looking for something only I could give him.

When I didn't say anything—couldn't say anything—his hands fell away.

"Okay," he murmured.

We continued our gentle walk, the warmth of the sun's rays soothing something inside me with each passing second.

After a while, I exhaled slowly. "You know... I've never experienced anything like what I did this morning. I don't even remember half the day."

Connor nodded, his gaze soft. "Stress and grief will do that to you. I get it—I've been there. I think it's just our body's way of protecting us from the sheer... weight of it all."

I inhaled deeply, letting his words settle. "Yeah, apparently. But I do remember you. You were there every moment, every step of the way. You pulled me out of wherever I'd gone in my mind and gave me the strength to go into that church today and honor my father... Connor," I whispered, closing my eyes for a brief moment. "I can never thank you enough for that. And I promise, I'll never forget it."

"Lucy, you don't need to thank me. It was nothing."

I frowned at him, nudging his arm lightly. "It was *not* nothing, Connor."

He shrugged, rubbing the back of his neck, unsure what to say.

Heat rushed to my cheeks. He affected me more than I cared to admit.

I felt safe. Adored. Cared for. Loved.

He didn't need to say it. I just knew.

After a beat, Connor broke the silence.

"Lucy..." Connor's voice was low, almost hesitant. "After Alex died... after we lost the baby, I didn't think happiness was in the cards for me anymore. I told myself that kind of life—the kind I'd dreamed of—was over."

He exhaled, shaking his head. "But then, you came back."

"Connor..."

He shook his head. "It's okay. You don't have to say anything. I just need to thank you, because now I have hope. No matter what happens between us, there's light at the end of the tunnel again. And I have *you* to thank for that."

The words settled between us, heavy with meaning, shaping everything from this moment on.

And in that, I also found hope.

Hope that my grief wouldn't consume me forever. Hope that the future—*our* future—was waiting, just ahead, ready for us to step into it.

All I had to do was be brave enough to trust not just him, but myself.

CHAPTER TWENTY

A Father's Choice

LUCY

By the time we got back to the ranch, the celebration was in full swing. The band tested their mics outside the ATV shed, and tendrils of smoked meat curled through the air. Cars lined both sides of the long driveway, while people walked up in droves carrying dishes or games to share, their laughter and easy chatter weaving into the evening. A warmth of appreciation settled in my chest. No matter how much had changed, the town's generosity hadn't.

"*Shoot!* I'll be right back." I gave Connor a quick apologetic glance and darted inside, grabbing my laptop, hooking it up to the projector, and setting the slideshow to play on a loop throughout the night.

I could hear Diane's shrill voice as I got closer. "Oh, I just assumed Lucy would sell. I mean, she's been gone so long, poor thing."

My jaw tightened, the words landing like a slap. But before the frustration could fully settle, my gaze caught on Tanya and Taylor—my cousins, my safe place. Seeing them here felt like a missing piece of home clicking back into place.

Tanya, a couple of years older than Taylor, had dirty blond hair streaked with natural highlights from being outdoors. She kept it cropped short, full of fun, choppy layers texturized for extra flair.

Taylor's light blonde hair, by contrast, was long and silky, cascading past her shoulders with simple, flowing layers at the ends.

Both had the same striking green eyes, but their features set them apart—Tanya's high cheekbones and button nose gave her a playful sharpness, while Taylor's face was more oblong, her longer, more distinctive nose a near match to my own.

"Hey, guys!" I called, my excitement bubbling over as I waved.

The two sisters pulled me into a tight group hug, their warmth overwhelming. Nearby, Connor casually steered my mother and aunt away, giving us a moment to catch up.

"Lucy, I know we spoke at the funeral, but Taylor and I just wanted to say it again—we're here for you," Tanya said with a smile that didn't quite reach her eyes. "Uncle Robert was the absolute best."

I swallowed against the lump in my throat and forced a smile. "I know. Thank you guys."

"You've done such a great job setting up this party, little cousin. Everything is arranged so perfectly—it's so sweet. I love it," Taylor cooed.

"Actually, this was all Sam. I just made the slideshow and did what I was told," I explained with self-deprecating laughter.

"Well, it's perfect. I love how the games are on the other side with the firepits, and the 'fancy' area is here, where you can see the food and dancing as you drive in. Uncle Bob would have *adored* this party," Taylor beamed.

I nodded, taking in the celebration unfolding around me. "I wanted paper napkins and plates, but we compromised—hard plastic plates that look real and embroidered paper napkins. You can take the Sam out of New York, but you can't take the New York out of Sam."

Just then, I spotted Sam surrounded by a group of former high school football players, Danika clinging to the arm of one of the guys. She swatted Sam's arm as if he needed to stop being so *funny*.

"Sam's popular now," I murmured, my voice tight with lingering resentment.

Tanya had graduated before we started high school, but Taylor had been in the same class as Connor when I left. She nodded appreciatively. "Yeah, he really spread his wings after you left White River High."

A cold knot twisted in my stomach. "Yeah, I heard."

"Becoming Amanda's lackey will do that." Taylor frowned, then added with her usual bright cheer, "But it seemed to be the right move because clearly everyone loves him."

"Actually, that's what happens when the enemy dates your older brother," I growled.

Taylor's furrow deepened. "I never understood her power over them."

I scoffed. "Me neither."

Tanya jumped in, lightening the mood. "Well, that was a fun walk down memory lane. I'm *starving*—let's grab food before my mom and stepdad eat everything."

We fell into easy giggles and took a quick spin around the buffet table.

As night fell, people filled every inch of the space surrounding my home. The air was thick with the scent of smoked barbecue and sweet summer air, laughter humming over the property like a gentle current. String lights glowed overhead, casting everything in a gentle glow, as if the world had softened, just for tonight.

The music started, and before I could even process what was happening, Connor's hand found mine, his touch firm but careful.

"Dance with me?" His voice lowered and became rough at the edges, sending a thrill down my spine.

I met his gaze, heat creeping into my cheeks, and nodded just enough for him to pull me onto the dance floor.

The band began playing a cover of Lonestar's *Amazed*, the familiar melody sinking into my skin, curling deep in my chest. Connor's arms slid around me, pulling me close, his hands settling at the small of my back.

Slowly, we began to sway.

The world blurred, narrowing down to the quiet between us, the steady rhythm of the music, the rise and fall of his chest beneath my fingertips.

He was solid. Warm. Familiar.

I pressed my face into the crook of his neck, inhaling the grounding, unmistakable scent of him... cedar, leather, and something entirely *Connor*. His breath hitched as I exhaled against his skin.

His fingers flexed against my back, tightening his hold just enough that I felt it *everywhere*.

"You're pretty good at this," he murmured, his lips brushing the shell of my ear.

A slow, delicious heat unfurled inside me, settling low in my stomach.

I pulled back just enough to meet his eyes—those bright blue eyes that had always felt like home.

"Yeah?" I whispered, my voice breathless.

Connor swallowed, his gaze dipping to my lips before returning to my eyes, his expression unreadable, a storm of emotions swirling behind them.

"Yeah," he rasped.

The air between us crackled, thick with everything I'd been trying to avoid.

The rest of the world faded—the laughter, the voices, the music—all of it dimmed until there was only him.

Only us.

His thumb brushed over the small of my back, a subtle touch that sent a trail of fire up my spine. I didn't think—I just moved, my hand sliding up to the nape of his neck, fingers threading through the soft thick waves there.

His eyes darkened, and for a second, I swore he was going to close the distance between us, to claim the moment, to claim *me*.

But instead, he exhaled shakily, pressing his forehead to mine, as if savoring the tension, letting it build, letting it consume us both.

"Lucy..."

My name barely more than a whisper, a prayer on his lips.

I swallowed, my heart hammering against my ribs.

I could kiss him.

God, I *wanted* to kiss him.

But I wasn't sure if I was ready to step over that edge, to let go of the last slivers of hesitation still holding me back.

So I didn't move, my heart racing, thundering—caught somewhere between anticipation and uncertainty.

We just stood there, locked in something deeper than a dance, something that felt like the moment before it had all fallen apart.

The song slowed, the last lingering notes settling around us like an unspoken promise.

Connor pulled back just enough to look at me, his thumb tracing the curve of my spine.

The song ended, but we didn't move.

We just stood there, locked together, eyes unbreaking.

And then, in an instant, the spell shattered.

Over Connor's shoulder, I caught movement—someone's hands cutting through the air, animated, frantic.

Amanda.

She stood locked in a heated conversation with Sam. His arms flailed, his expression twisting with quiet anger.

My brows furrowed, and Connor must have felt my body tense because he turned slightly, glancing back.

"What the hell does she think she's doing?" he murmured.

"I don't know," I said, my voice suddenly tight. "But it can't be good."

"Yeah," Connor agreed. "Let's break this up."

We stepped off the dance floor and made our way toward them. As soon as we neared, Amanda clammed up, her expression unreadable.

Connor greeted them with a raised brow. "Everything okay over here?"

Amanda's sharp gaze flicked to where Connor and I stood, our hands clasped in an unabashed show of unity. Something unreadable flashed across her expression before she answered.

"We're fine," she said coolly. "Just clarifying a few things."

My eye twitched. "There's nothing left you have to say to him." I turned to Sam, my voice softer. "Are you alright?"

Sam shook his head, jaw tightening. "I'm fine."

My stomach churned at the rising tension in the air. "Okay, good."

"I'm going to go check on Chef Michael. See how everything's going," Sam said, excusing himself.

Amanda's eyes narrowed into a smug gaze. "I'll go. But this isn't over." She warned before stalking off towards the parked cars.

Connor chuckled dryly. "Great. Can't wait."

I exhaled, rubbing a hand over my face. "I was having a perfectly nice time and now I'm waiting for the other shoe to drop."

Just then a familiar voice cut through the noise beside me, low and urgent.

"Lucy, can I speak with you?"

I heaved a sigh and turned to find my mother standing there, her expression tight and hands clasped together.

I flicked a glance at Connor, who gave me a questioning look.

"I'll be back," I murmured before following her inside the house.

The moment I shut the door behind us, she started.

"Lucy," she said urgently, her voice trembling slightly. "All these people... so many of them *hate* me. They think I lied to steal your father's money. It's absolutely absurd. It's not like I even *wanted* a divorce, and why would I lie?"

I tensed, my breath catching at her admission. "I... Mom, do we have to do this *now*?" I asked hesitantly, my heart hammering in my chest at the years of unspoken resentment that had built there, waiting to unleash on her.

She pressed forward. "Yes. Because after all these years, the only opinion that matters to me is yours. Do you believe *I* made up those rumors just to leave your father and get a *paycheck*? I asked that man for nothing. He insisted on enough funds to start my fashion line. I was ready to tear up that stupid check when..."

I blinked, thrown off by the sheer desperation in her voice. "When what?"

"I looked at you and I wanted to show you what a woman can do. I wanted to create something for *you*." Her eyes glistened.

I swallowed, unsure what to say.

"I know you hate the fashion world. But at the time... I wanted you to have a strong woman in your life, showing you exactly what you're capable of. "

My shoulders sagged and I walked over to the couch and sat down. "Well, you did do that."

She exhaled sharply as she joined me. "Today has been the worst day of my life, Lucy."

"Mother, please don't."

She swallowed hard. "I don't know why you don't believe me. Your father was..."

"Why I don't believe you?" My lip quivered. "You've never once believed me! I told you I was a virgin. That I couldn't be pregnant and Amanda lied to you. But you never once believed me! You took me away from my home, my friends, and dad. I'm not angry anymore, but it still hurts. So, no. I don't believe anything you have to say. You lost that trust the day you chose not to believe me."

"For the last time, Lucy. It wasn't Amanda."

"Okay, fine. Danika, or some other person doing it for her instead," I snapped.

Her face fell, confusion flickering in her eyes. "Lucy... are you really telling me the truth?"

A sick, twisting feeling coiled in my stomach. "Yes. But this is the last time I say. I don't care if you believe me anymore."

She nodded, guilt swimming in her eyes. "I do, darling. I really do."

"Well, maybe it's too late." Fresh tears stung my eyes, six years of defending myself. Six years of pleading with my mother to hear. And she waited until now to believe me? Today of all days.

"Honey, please forgive me," she whispered. "I truly thought it was best to take you back to London. Your father agreed."

The couch dropped out from beneath me, until the shock swallowed me whole.

"Dad... *agreed*?" My voice was barely above a whisper.

She nodded slowly. "He never believed the rumor. But he thought... maybe there was something else going on that you weren't *telling* us. And if..." she paused, thinking hard on her next words. "He just thought that maybe it was for the best. It was a difficult decision, but we came to it together."

A sharp, aching pressure settled in my chest.

"Of course you can say that now," I said through clenched teeth. "Dad isn't here to defend himself."

My mother frowned but reached for my hand and I jerked it back. "I'm not lying, darling."

I stood up, my pulse roaring in my ears. "I have to go."

Outside, the speeches had started. The soft hum of people talking, laughing, remembering my father should have been comforting, but my thoughts were in a spiral.

Connor found me at once, his expression dark with concern. "What's wrong?"

I shook my head. "Nothing."

"Do you want me to get you out of here?" Connor asked, brow furrowing.

I exhaled sharply. "No. It's fine. My mother just said my dad agreed that I should go to London."

I felt Connor's gaze on my cheeks. "Why would he do that?"

"I don't know," I hissed. "It's fine. She's probably lying to make herself look better. Let's just enjoy the rest of the night."

Connor pulled me in for a side hug and I let his scent overwhelm all my thoughts, the pain, the unnecessary drama.

The night carried on, but my mind remained elsewhere. I plastered on a smile, let my cousins pull me into a dance, played some rounds of cornhole and horseshoes; guys versus girls, but the weight of my mother's words refused to leave me.

CHAPTER TWENTY-ONE

Then He Sang

LUCY

My eyes felt heavy, pressure building behind them from mental and physical exhaustion as I rode in the passenger's seat of Taylor's rental. Lately, my life felt like a bad reality show, with enough emotional whiplash to make my head spin. And after Amanda's threat and the five missed texts from my mother, I knew it wasn't over.

I kept reminding myself that this was *real life*. That I had to stay *present*. I had to face the pain to move through it. At least, that's what Dr. Fenwick's recent email informed me, along with a list of suggested virtual appointment dates and times. Apparently, the loss of my father meant my therapist was happy to work outside her normal hours to check in. And to be honest, it felt good to know she was there for me.

I chugged down the remainder of my now-lukewarm to-go coffee as Tanya, Jenna, and Irene argued in the back over whether we were starting our karaoke night off with Spice Girls or Taylor Swift. Their voices overlapped in playful chaos, each passionately defending their picks while skimming their phones for more ideas.

Taylor suddenly turned up the radio, eyes lighting up as she squealed, "I *love* this song!"

I gave her a weak smile and blinked myself into further awareness as I registered the music—"The Sign", an old Ace of Base '90s hit. The car erupted in off-key singing and convulsive dance moves.

Giving in and letting go, I counted to four and inhaled, *hold 2, 3, 4... out 2, 3, 4, 5, 6....* A simple reset and I felt more ready to enjoy the night.

After the song ended, Jenna turned to my cousins. "When do you two head back home?"

"I go back Tuesday morning," Tanya answered, nodding toward her younger sister. "I think Taylor leaves Monday."

Taylor sighed. "Yup. *Super* early Monday morning."

I frowned. "That stinks. Maybe we can do lunch or dinner tomorrow?"

Taylor perked up. "My mom's doing a family dinner tomorrow night. I *think* you're invited... but knowing my mom, who knows? She's nuts."

I chuckled. "I'm good on a family dinner at Aunt Diane's. Thanks, but no thanks. Let's do lunch. Maybe we can check out *The Rustic Roast*? I haven't been there yet."

"Oh yeah!" Tanya said. "We should go. I've been really wanting to try it."

With our plans locked in, we rolled into the roped-off parking lot of *The Saloon*, a squat building crouched low against the gravel-speckled dirt. Orange and yellow neon flickered against the weathered wood siding mimicking firelight. A row of Harley-Davidsons stood guard out front, their chrome flashing under the buzzing sign.

"Oh my gosh! A real girls' night! This is so exciting." I beamed, determined to wring every drop of fun from the evening.

Taylor raised her brow out at me. "Don't get out much?"

I shrugged. "Veterinary school. My life is classes, homework, and take-out."

Irene led us up the porch stairs, and we shoved through the front door. Deafening jukebox music blasted us in the face the moment we stepped inside. The scent of beer, cigarettes, and sweat permeated the air. My boots peeled off the sticky laminate floor with each step as I moved deeper inside.

In the back left corner, two retired cowboys—thin, nearly identical in their snake-skinned boots, jeans, and frilled rodeo tops—leaned over a pool table. Their chunky rings and gold chains caught the light, flashing under the overhead lamp.

"Guys, help me with these," Irene called, tugging a round metal table toward its twin.

We scattered, yanking folding chairs into place until we had enough for our little group. I dropped into a seat with my back to the bar, facing the scuffed dance floor and the small stage where Nora, the karaoke DJ, adjusted her gear.

Taylor plopped a thick songbook onto our tables. "What's first?" she asked, passing out slips of paper and stubby pencils.

Irene chimed in, "You don't *have* to use the book. Nora can pull up almost anything, just ask her. The book helps if you don't know what to pick."

Jenna eyed us. "Come on. We have to start with Ace of Base now... Am I right?"

"How about Shania Twain's 'Man! I Feel Like a Woman?'" Tanya suggested with a shrug.

I sighed. "There are *way* too many options."

Irene nodded. "True. But, just an idea, we could do *all* of them. Give them to Nora and let her mix them into the rotation randomly?"

We glanced around at each other, nodding in agreement.

Taylor grinned. "Sounds good to me."

My mind drifted to the last time I did karaoke: Sam and I locking ourselves in his room, belting songs for hours. On weekends when I stayed over, we sang and practiced like we were going on tour. I always imagined my first real karaoke performance would be with him.

A sharp pang tightened my chest. Sam should have been here for this. He would've loved it. But he'd needed to stay back and help his mom with some wardrobe emergency.

I rubbed at the crease in my brow as more memories flooded in. "You're My Best Friend" by Queen had been a favorite of ours. Sam's dad would eventually come into the room around midnight, his voice calm but firm. "Alright, you two. We can hear you on the other side of the house. Time to keep it down."

For whatever reason, his request always sent us into a fit of giggles the moment he closed the door, followed up by Connor yelling through the wall, "Stop!"

"Lucy, what song are you picking?" Jenna nudged me, pulling me back to the present.

I blinked. "Umm..." A lightbulb went off. "It's a surprise."

I carefully wrote my choice, folded the slip, and handed it to Irene, before she walked off to drop them with Nora.

Jenna got our drink order and headed to the bar. Nora's voice boomed through the mic.

"Goooooooood evening, party people! I'm your karaoke host, DJ Sing-It-To-Me Nora! We're about to kick things off, but first... it's karaoke night! That means half-off wells and on-tap beer until midnight! If you'd like to sing, grab a slip and join the fun!"

Then, in full rhinestone-clad glory, she launched into "9 to 5" by Dolly Parton.

And just like that, I knew tonight was going to be *exactly* what I needed.

I began clapping and singing along, swaying in my seat, which got everyone at the table to join in. Belting at the top of my lungs felt cathartic, loosening the physical stress stiffening my body.

Jenna returned with the bartender and helped set our drinks down on the table.

I lifted my rum and coke. "To Girls' Night?"

Everyone joined, shouting over the music, "To Girls' Night!"

The song ended and Nora came over the speakers. "Okay, first up, kicking off the night—we have The White River Belles!"

"That's us!" Irene squealed, clapping her hands together with untamed excitement.

"Oh *shit*!" Jenna half-shrieked, then downed her entire whiskey sour and slammed the empty glass onto the table.

I took a large swig of my own drink before following Tanya, Taylor, and Irene onto the stage. Behind me, Jenna leaned over my shoulder squealing, "I'm so nervous."

I giggled, butterflies flaring in my stomach. "Good thing no one expects us to be good," I teased over my shoulder.

Nora handed out microphones. "One of you will have to share. I only have four mics."

"Jenna and I will share," I said, taking the last mic.

Irene bent over to peer at all of us at the far end of the tiny stage. "I wonder which song it'll be!"

The words flashed across the screen.

"The Stroke" – Billy Squier.

My stomach dropped, then I burst into a fit of laughter.

It was *my* song choice.

We all sang at once, an absurd mix of tone-deaf, off-key, and surprisingly decent voices melding together through the speakers. What we lacked in vocal talent, we made up for with ridiculous dance moves and suggestive gestures that had everyone in the bar cracking up.

I left the stage breathless, adrenaline buzzing through my veins—the good kind, for once. I couldn't stop laughing as we took our seats again, reaching for our drinks in between gasps of air.

A round of tequila shots appeared before us. "We heard this is someone's first time at *The Saloon*. These are on the house. Have fun ladies!" The female bartender winked before heading back behind the busy bar.

Irene's eyes lit. "Oh, hell ya!"

We cheersed and downed the smooth liquid courage, feeling the burn before biting into a slice of lime, the sour tange offsetting the liquor.

I leaned back, warmth blooming under my skin as the alcohol kicked in. The doors to the saloon swung open, and my heart skipped a beat.

Connor led the way, flanked by Kyle, Johnny, Chuck, and Noah—boots polished to a shine, silver belt buckles catching the low bar lights, cowboy hats tilted just right. They were all part of the Campbell Ranch family, the same crew who had gone up against us in last night's games during the celebration of life.

Connor wore a royal blue plaid shirt, his sleeves rolled to the elbows, exposing the taut muscles of his forearms. His dark gaze locked onto mine, a slow, deliberate pull that sent a shiver of awareness down my spine.

Then, with that signature confidence, he tipped his hat toward me before following the guys to the bar.

A fresh wave of heat surged through me, low and deep, stealing my breath.

Irene groaned. "They better not be here to crash our girls' night."

Jenna smirked. "Oh, they *totally* are. After how we dominated last night in horseshoes, I bet they're looking for redemption."

I chuckled, not particularly caring either way. Connor had me locked in place, that connection between us crackling with electricity. Maybe it was the drinks, or maybe it was just *him*, but a slow, simmering inferno unfurled inside me, making my skin feel too tight.

Taylor shrugged. "I wouldn't mind another friendly competition."

I forced my attention away from Connor and glanced at her, only to notice her gaze focused on Kyle.

I teased, "Yeah? I think someone wants to get a little *extra* friendly with a certain special cowboy?"

Taylor's cat-like smirk widened. "That doesn't sound so bad."

Irene rolled her eyes. "Ugh. If I'd known tonight was gonna be about getting laid, I would've gotten a sitter and made Jed come too."

Tanya sighed. "My husband is several states away. I'll be your man tonight, Irene. Us married girls have to stick together."

Irene grinned. "Okay, you're my new favorite."

"Don't worry, we're not splitting up," I assured Irene, convincing myself as much as her. "This is my first girls' night. I'm not letting those guys crash it. Everyone agrees to stick together until it's time to head out?"

Jenna, Taylor, Irene, and Tanya nodded their approval as Kyle approached.

"Nope! This is *our* table, buddy," Irene quipped, crossing her arms with a playful edge. "No boys allowed."

Kyle raised his hands in surrender. "Don't worry, we'll stay at our own table." A slow grin spread across his face, his brown eyes alight with mischief. "I'm here to propose a rematch... a battle of the sexes, if you will."

When his gaze landed on Taylor, something unspoken flickered between them. I grinned, watching the sparks fly.

"You're on," Taylor fired back, her words a flirtatious dare.

Kyle's grin widened, his deep brown eyes gleaming. The disco lights flickered over his dark skin, shifting in shades of blue and gold like a city skyline at night. "Let's settle this with a two-round battle: groups first, then duets. Audience decides the winner."

Irene extended her hand. "Deal."

With that, it was *on*.

The Saloon came alive, the atmosphere thrumming with that classic dive bar energy: tables packed, drinks flowing, the dance floor buzzing with anticipation.

Nora took to the mic, grinning as she surveyed the room. "Alright, people, we've got ourselves a friendly competition tonight! It's The White River Belles versus The Reckless Cowboys! Your job is simple—cheer nice and loud for the team you think wins each round. The group with the biggest crowd reaction takes the point! Got it?"

A roar of excitement filled the air, and Nora laughed. "That's what I like to hear! Buckle up ladies, it's about to get *hot* in here! First up, we have The Reckless Cowboys performing 'Save a Horse (Ride a Cowboy)' by Big & Rich!"

The guys took the stage, strutting with purpose. Kyle gave a playful smack to his ass, then the music dropped. Chuck jumped off the stage, dipping down with the most erotic moves the town had ever seen. My jaw dropped as Connor ripped open his shirt, swung it over his head, and slowly rolled his hips to the chorus. His eyes locked onto mine, never wavering for the remainder of the performance.

Women around the bar shrieked in delight, phones raised high as they snapped photos and frantically posted the performance.

Tanya shouted, "You guys are cheating!" but her protests were drowned out by the roar of the crowd.

As if in direct response, each man held onto their cowboy hats, thrusting out their hips sending a rippling roar through the small bar. My mouth went dry as Connor bit his lip. Every nerve in my body lit up. I thought I might burn alive under his hooded gaze.

Irene smacked the table grabbing everyone's attention. "New plan! Lucy, you're our secret weapon. Ladies, if they want to fight dirty, we fight *dirtier*."

Each of us took in our assigned roles, nodding in agreement.

She rushed up to Nora to give her our new song choice, then hurried back to our table, clapping with giddy enthusiasm.

As the song ended, Nora cheered, "Let's give it up for The Reckless Cowboys! I don't know about you, but I'd love to save a horse to-*night*!"

Laughter and whistles filled the room as I downed a glass of ice water, steadying myself just as we were called up to the stage.

As I passed Connor, his fingers grazed down my arm, slow and deliberate. My breath caught at the unexpected contact. Shocked, in the best way, by this new, flirtatious side of him, I forced myself to shake off the red-hot sensation still sizzling under my skin. I managed to refocus just as the first notes of "Don't Cha" by The Pussycat Dolls blared through the speakers.

One of my well-kept secrets was that I could *really* sing. I slowly slunk down and brought myself back up in a seductive tease. My ladies fanned out around the stage, dancing, twirling, and teasing the audience, singing backup as I strutted straight toward Connor. Running my hand down his chest, I threw my head back, crooning out each lyric, swaying my hips before him. Flipping my hair, I pushed away from him and sashayed off, sending the entire bar into a frenzy of cheers as I ended the song back on the stage.

"Wow! What an incredible performance! Choosing a winner for round one is going to be tough," Nora said, her voice buzzing with excitement. "Alright, let's hear it! Cheer as loud as you can for your favorite performance! Who thinks The Reckless Cowboys took this round?"

The women in the bar lost their minds—a few men cheered as well, clapping their hands.

"Who thinks The White River Belles have it?"

Deafening cheers and thunderous applause erupted.

"Alright, it's a close one, but the audience has spoken. This win goes to... *The White River Belles*!"

We broke into shrill screams, jumping and hugging each other over the win.

Kyle called out, "It's not over yet!"

Connor continued to watch me. I flicked my gaze to him. His intense stare burned into me, heavy with promise, stealing the breath from my lungs once again. Heart pounding,

I rushed back to our table, dropping my eyes to the ground trying to shake how much he affected me.

After a few more performances, the moment everyone had been waiting for arrived—the first duet battle between Taylor and Kyle.

The tension between them crackled like a live wire, unspoken but impossible to ignore.

My jaw dropped as my cousin belted out the first few notes. *Damn*, she could actually *sing*. And together? They were electric. Their voices melded together effortlessly, thick with emotion, their chemistry undeniable as they performed "Need You Now" by Lady A. Every lingering glance, every brush of their hands sent a ripple of energy through the crowd.

In the end, to my *utmost* pleasure, another point went to the ladies.

Next up: Jenna and Chuck. They failed spectacularly at their rendition of "Love Shack" by The B-52's, but made up for it with their outrageous dance moves. Chuck won the first point for the guys, which prompted a chorus of *boos* from our table.

Johnny turned to us from the guy's table. "Hey! We never did that when you guys won *twice in a row!*"

I threw my head back in laughter before taking another free shot.

A few singers later, Tanya and Johnny took the stage. Tanya did her best, but Johnny turned out to be an incredible singer, putting us in a tie.

Then, Irene went up against sweet, shy Noah, whose nerves got the best of him. His voice shook for the duration of their song. Even with Irene going off key several times, we still managed to pull ahead.

And then, the final round began.

Nora called Connor and me up to the stage.

"You sure you know this song?" I asked in a low whisper.

"Absolutely," he said with adorable confidence. "Sam forced me to watch the movie so many times I have every single lyric memorized."

The opening notes of "Rewrite the Stars" from *The Greatest Showman* filled the room.

Connor had to start us off. After hearing him in the barn, I knew he'd need every ounce of his charisma to win this.

But then—he *sang*.

His voice was a mix of rich baritone and liquid honey, smooth and utterly intoxicating. My heart stopped, along with my breath.

He stepped toward me, pressing his forehead to mine, his hand gliding down my arm before taking my hand and spinning me—perfectly timed with Zendaya and Zac Efron's dance in the film.

I closed my eyes as he pulled me close, my back molding against his chest, his heat seeping into me. His breath skimmed my ear, sending shivers down my spine. We swayed in time with the music, our voices weaving together, effortless and unspoken, as if we were the only two people in the packed room.

Our harmonies blended—soft and yearning, a perfect fusion of warmth and longing—as we drifted down the stage and across the empty dance floor, lost in the moment.

The final note lingered in the air, trembling between us.

Then—Connor dipped me, his grip strong, unshakable.

And his lips were on mine.

A soft gasp escaped me before I pulled him in. The world blurred at the edges, the noise of the crowd fading into nothing. There was no music, no audience. Only him. Only *us*, in this perfect moment.

The entire bar erupted into screams of applause, snapping us back into reality. My eyes shot open in surprise, my breath still caught between us.

Connor pulled back, his gaze sweeping over my stunned expression before settling on my lips. A slow, knowing grin tugged at the corners of his mouth, his eyes alight with mischief. A low chuckle rumbled from his chest as he steadied me on my feet, his touch lingering just long enough to send my pulse racing.

Hope now danced in his eyes, and I—

I was in deep.

Nora's voice boomed through the mic. "*Wow!* I don't think *The Saloon* has *ever* seen a performance like *that*. Who knew our very own Connor Lochland was hiding the voice of an angel behind those charming good looks? Let's give it up for Lucy and Connor!"

I slid my tongue against my cheek, nodding at him. "Yeah. *Who knew?*"

"You did the same thing! Your voice was god-awful in the barn," Connor teased.

I rolled my eyes. "Yeah, because it would've been weird to sing really well when you were so *bad*."

He shrugged, his eyes wide with innocence. "Well, I wanted to make you laugh."

The crowd erupted into cheers as Nora took the mic. "Looks like that's another point for The Reckless Cowboys, ending tonight in a *tie*! That means one last group performance to settle this once and for all."

I sighed. "I can't believe you beat me."

He shrugged, a teasing glint in his eyes. "You never stood a chance, sweetheart."

I swatted his arm, but it only made his grin widen.

"You're the worst," I chided, though amusement tugged at my lips.

Irene cut in. "If you two are done flirting—we still have a competition to settle."

Fueled by sheer grit and our undeniable need to win, *The White River Belles* delivered one final performance of "The Sign" by Ace of Base, ending the night victorious.

The perfect girls' night was complete, and best of all... I had yet another win over Connor I'd never let him forget. But as I touched my lips, still tingling from his kiss, I realized...

Maybe he was the one who really won tonight.

CHAPTER TWENTY-TWO

Not a Doc

LUCY

Taylor waved as she hopped into Kyle's truck, shooting a wink over her shoulder.

"I guess I'm in charge of the rental," Tanya grumbled.

Irene sighed wistfully. "Ah, to be young and in love."

Jenna chuckled. "Aren't you younger than her?"

Irene shrugged. "Yeah, but married people get to say things like that."

I beamed at my friends, still buzzing from the alcohol and the kiss that still lingered on my lips. "Tonight was so much fun. Thank you for the invite, Irene."

"Of course," she said, but her expression shifted, her lips curling into a wicked grin as she looked behind me.

I *felt* him before I even saw him—the familiar warmth at my side, the quiet energy that stole my breath. My eyes fluttered shut for a second as I savored his closeness.

His deep voice sent a shiver down my spine. "Can I give you a ride home?"

I reigned in my smile in an attempt to keep things cool. "Sure. That would save Tanya the extra stop."

Tanya gave him a grateful nod. "I would appreciate that."

"Alright, it's settled then."

Connor's polite smile shifted into something undeniably teasing as his eyes locked onto mine.

I gulped, and my cheeks flared red.

Shaking myself, I turned to say goodbye to my friends before walking the torturous distance to Connor's truck.

The idea of being alone with him set my skin on fire.

Settled inside, we turned toward each other at the same time, both of us starting to speak at once. A soft chuckle passed between us.

"You go first," Connor offered, his voice low, inviting.

I shook my head, my pulse thrumming. "That's okay, you go."

He sighed, unable to hide the smile pulling at his lips. "Lucy, that kiss..."

"It was incredible," I breathed, finishing his thought.

His Adam's apple bobbed as he swallowed, nodding. "It was."

The air grew thick, humming with that undeniable pull. His gaze darkened, sending a rush of adrenaline through my chest as my heart pounded.

I placed a hesitant hand over his. "If you don't think it's a terrible idea... I'd like to do that again."

I barely got the words out before his lips crashed onto mine.

Desperate, needy, relentless.

I met his hunger with my own, gripping his shirt and pulling him closer. His fingers dug into my thigh before pulling me toward him as if he couldn't get me close enough.

And then—everything faded.

There was only him, his touch, the way he consumed me.

His hands explored my lower back, then slid upward until they framed my face. My own fingers roamed over the hard ridges of his chest, my entire body coiling with need.

I gasped as he sucked my lower lip into his mouth, raking his teeth along the sensitive skin, his tongue flicking over it—a tease that sent a sharp pulse of pleasure shooting through me.

"Take me back to your place. *Now*," I whispered, breathless.

Connor pulled back just enough to meet my gaze. His eyes went molten, dark with want.

He didn't hesitate. I hopped off him, buckling in as he threw the truck into drive.

The tension between us simmered during the twenty-minute drive to his ranch, Connor's palm sliding over my inner thigh, stoking the fire that blazed between us.

Buzz. Buzz. Buzz.

Connor's fingers flexed on the wheel, jaw tightening as he glanced at the screen. A second later, his expression shifted from heat to alarm.

Incoming call: Paula.

"Hello?" Connor answered, his voice suddenly thick with concern.

"Sorry I didn't call sooner. Willow's in labor—I think she's in trouble. One of the puppies must be stuck." The woman's voice was tight with worry.

My brain snapped into focus, sobering instantly. I straightened in my seat. "Hi, Paula, this is Lucy Campbell. We haven't met, but I can help. How long has she been in labor?"

"About an hour."

"Has she delivered any puppies yet?"

She cleared her throat. "Yeah, two."

"Are they nursing?"

"Yes."

"How long has she been actively pushing with no progress?"

Her voice wavered. "Almost thirty minutes."

A pang of urgency tightened in my chest. *That's too long.* "Can you see the puppy?"

A pause. "No."

"Is she still contracting?"

"Yeah, but they're weak."

"Okay, listen to me," I said, keeping my voice calm and authoritative. "Gently massage her belly. That should help stimulate contractions. Keep her comfortable, and make sure she's staying warm. We'll be there in just a few minutes."

"Okay," she breathed and ended the call.

Connor tightened his grip on the steering wheel. "Lucy, is she going to be okay?" His voice caught at the end, a raw vulnerability that made my chest ache.

I exhaled, already running through possible complications in my mind. "Let's see what's going on once we get there. I'm sure she'll be okay."

Connor swallowed. "Paula's a great ranch hand. She volunteered to stay with Willow when I told the guys I wasn't going to be able to make it to karaoke tonight. Actually, she insisted. Apparently I don't do anything fun anymore." He frowned.

I nodded, offering him a reassuring smile. "It sounds like Willow's in great hands. We're already at the turnoff for our road—almost there."

Connor didn't slow down as we reached the driveway. Instead, he kicked the truck into full gear, speeding toward the house before skidding to a halt. He killed the engine and jumped out. "Follow me."

I didn't hesitate, trailing behind him as he took the stairs two at a time.

Inside, Paula was kneeling beside Willow in a well-prepared whelping box: blankets, towels, and a heat lamp glowing in the corner. A whelping kit sat open beside her.

Despite his best efforts, panic flickered across Connor's face.

I crouched next to Willow, immediately noting her rapid panting and the thick strands of drool pooling from her jowls. My stomach tightened. *Not good.*

I spoke aloud as I assessed her, keeping my voice controlled. "I'm just checking her vitals."

Connor nodded, then turned to the ranch hand. "Thanks, Paula. We've got it from here."

She hesitated before giving him a quick hug. "Let me know how everything turns out."

"You got it." He called back as she disappeared down the stairs.

I placed my hand gently on Willow's side. Her heart was racing.

I pressed my fingers against her gums, watching how slowly the color returned. *Too slow.* "Her gums are pale. This isn't just labor fatigue," I said, pressing my thumb against her leg, checking for stiffness.

The muscles were trembling, weak.

My stomach sank.

"She's crashing. Low calcium."

I grabbed the calcium gel from the whelping kit and quickly applied it to her gums, rubbing it in so it would absorb faster.

"She won't be able to push without this."

Connor swallowed hard. "Is it eclampsia?"

"Yes, but it's not severe yet. Thankfully we got here when we did, she's going to be okay." I squeezed his arm briefly before focusing back on Willow. "Once this kicks in, her contractions should strengthen."

Connor stroked Willow's fur, his voice soothing. "Good girl, Willow. You're doing great."

"Stay on that side, keep petting her. Help her feel as calm as possible." I snapped on gloves, lubricated my fingers, and carefully inserted one into Willow's birth canal. "Okay, the puppy is stuck at a bad angle. I'm going to reposition it."

With slow, careful movements, I maneuvered the puppy into a better position.

The next contraction hit, and relief flooded through me as the puppy slid out.

Willow turned, licking the newborn clean. But something was wrong.

Its breaths came out shallow and weak.

Thinking fast, I grabbed the glucose solution from the kit and rubbed a drop onto the tiny pup's gums. *Come on, baby.*

After a few heartbeats, the pup twitched, then let out a tiny, high-pitched squeak. I exhaled the breath I hadn't known I was holding and placed him at Willow's belly.

"The nursing will help release oxytocin and stimulate more contractions," I explained.

As Willow licked her baby, I massaged her abdomen, encouraging her body to keep going.

One by one, the rest of the puppies came, easier and without further complications.

By the time the last pup was born, Willow was alert, nursing, and much more stable. I kept a close eye on her for any signs of excessive bleeding or distress, but everything looked perfectly normal.

I checked each puppy, rubbing my hands over their tiny bodies. "They're all doing great, Connor. Good temperature, good breathing, and they're all nursing well."

Connor let out a slow breath, tension melting from his shoulders.

"You just saved her life."

I nodded, my eyes crinkled as I grinned. "Not bad for a London girl, huh?"

A flicker of amusement danced in his heavy blue eyes. "Not bad at all."

"Well, she still needs close monitoring for the next few hours. If she crashes again, we'll need more calcium, and she'll need high-energy food to recover."

Connor nodded. "Got it. And, Lucy..." He swallowed. "Thank you again. I don't know what I would've done without you. The nearest vet open at this hour is over an hour away."

I glanced at Willow and her squirming, healthy puppies, a smile tugging at my lips. "I'm glad I could help."

I glanced at the clock—3 a.m. The weight of exhaustion hit me like a freight train. I yawned and stretched.

"You should get some sleep," Connor murmured.

I shook my head. "Absolutely not."

"Lucy, you've been up all night—just lay down in my bed. I'll wake you if anything changes."

I gave him a pointed look. "If you're not going to sleep, make me coffee."

Connor sighed, rubbing a hand over his face, then relented with a tired smirk. "Fine. Sure thing, doc."

I called after him as he walked out, "Not a doc!"

By 7 a.m., I still sat watching the whelping box in the chair Connor had brought in for me.

He leaned forward in his own seat, watching me with amusement glinting in his eyes. "If you're done staring them down like a mother hen, I think you can finally get some sleep."

"Fine," I finally relented. "But Buddy needs breakfast. Can you go over and feed him before I crash?"

Connor's lips twitched. "You don't trust me to handle them yet?"

I sighed, then leaned across the arm of my chair and kissed him on the cheek. "I trust you," I said without hesitation. "But Willow had a complicated birth, and I don't want to be far if anything changes."

Connor sighed. "Fine. I'll take care of Buddy. But on one condition."

I raised an eyebrow. "Oh?"

"When I get back, I'm cuddling you."

I scoffed, but grinned despite myself. "No funny business?"

"Nope. Just sleep." He winked.

"Okay," I murmured, my voice thick with exhaustion. "Deal."

As soon as he left, I grabbed a clean shirt and gym shorts from his closet. I froze, the meaning of our last exchange hitting me. I trusted him. I kissed him, *several* times. And it felt... right. I crawled into bed, deciding to consider the ramifications of the night at a later time. The moment my head hit the pillow, sleep pulled me under.

CHAPTER TWENTY-THREE

What Love Looks Like

LUCY

When I woke a few hours later to my pre-set alarm, I felt Connor's warm body pressed against me. His arms encased me as if he feared I'd disappear while he slept. I carefully wriggled out of his arms and checked on all my new patients.

I knelt beside the whelping box, running my hands gently over Willow's fur. She looked up at me sleepily but content, her body curled protectively around her nursing puppies. I carefully checked each pup, feeling their bellies for fullness and warmth, making sure they were all latching properly.

Satisfied, I smiled down at the new mom. "You're doing such a great job, Mama."

A low, grumbling voice from the bed filled my chest with intoxicating ease. "I love how good you are at this. It's probably the sexiest thing I've ever seen."

I grinned, unable to help myself. "Well, you, in nothing but boxers, lying in that bed, is probably the sexiest thing *I've* ever seen."

"Then you should definitely join me." He placed a hand on the mattress and patted the blankets beside him.

I rolled my eyes. "Not in here with the dogs, you weirdo."

A low rumble of laughter escaped him. "No funny business is still in effect. *Promise.*"

"Let me finish up, and I'll be right there," I said. Then I went to work refilling Willow's water bowl, making sure she had plenty to drink after nursing all night. I double-checked the heat lamp and bedding, ensuring the whelping area stayed warm and clean. Once I was sure everything was set, I stood and stretched, glancing back at Connor, who was watching me with amused patience.

"I'm coming!" I insisted with playful indignation before trotting over to the bed.

I jumped in and snuggled up to him, his warmth seeping into my skin as his scent enveloped me.

Propping himself up on his arm, he smirked. "Do you think this could count as a second date?"

I let out a giggle. "Absolutely *not*."

"Why not?"

"Connor!" I scolded, swatting his chest as I turned to face him.

His head fell back as a deep laugh escaped him, the smile stretching across his face transforming his rugged features, somehow making him even more attractive. "What? The miracle of birth doesn't do it for ya?"

A snort escaped me before I could stop it, and I immediately slapped a hand over my face in horror. "Oh no. What have you done?!"

His grin widened. "Wait. What was that?" he teased, gripping my wrists, trying to pull them away from my blushing face. "Did you just *snort*?"

A full-on belly laugh rumbled from him, making my cheeks burn even hotter. I groaned, laughing despite myself as he gently pried my hands away.

Then our eyes met.

And just like that—everything seemed to stop.

I reached up, framing his face in my hands, and he leaned down over me, pressing a slow, soft kiss to my lips. Anticipation buzzed across my skin as his body hovered above mine. My breath quickened, and need hummed deep within me.

Connor's hand moved slowly, hesitantly, beneath the shirt I'd stolen from his closet. I gasped at his touch, my legs instinctively wrapping around his waist, pulling him down to me. Our lips and tongues tangled in a dark, intoxicating symphony of touch and taste as desire crashed over me. My hands roamed the hard contours of his chest, reveling in the once-forbidden pleasure of him

"I need you, Connor," I whispered my plea as he pressed against me.

His hand trailed lower, teasing. My eyes fluttered shut, electricity crackling through me.

Connor's fingers dipped beneath the waistband of my shorts, moving with slow, tantalizing ease. A shiver ran through me as he slid them off, his dark gaze roaming over my bare skin. Gently, he placed his hands on my knees and spread them open, his eyes burning with hunger.

"Lucy," he murmured, his voice thick with reverence.

A rush of heat pooled inside me at his raw intensity, my insecurities fading under his appreciative gaze. Then he dipped his head, pressing slow, teasing kisses down my thigh, each one leaving a trail of fire in their wake.

"Connor..."

His lips moved lower, his warm breath sending a wicked pulse through my core. And then—he kissed me, his tongue gliding over me with exquisite precision. My back arched as a moan tore from my lips, my fingers clawing at the sheets.

The sensation overwhelmed me, pleasure curling as his mouth moved with delicious purpose. I glanced down, my breath stuttering at the sight of him watching me beneath hooded eyes, his hunger evident in every flick of his tongue.

"Oh God," I gasped, biting my lip as another moan escaped me.

Connor hummed against me, the vibrations sending shockwaves up my spine as his fingers joined his mouth, pressing inside, beginning a slow, deliberate rhythm.

Pressure built, need coiling tighter. "Please," I begged, my hips lifting to meet him.

A dark, satisfied sound rumbled in his chest. He quickened his pace, his name tumbling from my lips as my body went rigid—then unraveled, pleasure surging through me in wave after wave. I trembled beneath him, breathless, my body went limp from release.

Connor's lips traced a slow, tortuous path up my body, each kiss leaving a spark in its wake. His rough hands gripped the hem of my shirt, sliding it up inch by inch, fingertips skimming my skin, igniting a trail of molten desire along their path. My breath caught as he pulled the fabric over my head, and his eyes darkened as he took me in.

"You're perfect," he murmured, low and husky.

Goosebumps prickled across my skin—not from the cool air, but from the way he devoured me with his gaze, his touch, his presence. His palms smoothed over my bare skin, tracing, teasing, as his mouth followed, lips grazing sensitive flesh.

A shiver ran through me, my body arching instinctively toward him, craving more—more of his hands, his mouth, the way he made me feel like I was the only thing in the world that mattered.

"You are so beautiful," he groaned, his lips trailing across my jaw.

A flush crept up my neck at the sincerity in his voice, but I had no time to dwell on it because his mouth was on my breast, his tongue circling the sensitive peak as his hand cupped the other. His thumb ran over my nipple, sending a shockwave of fresh primal desire coursing through my entire body.

"Connor," I gasped, my fingers raking down his back. "I need you inside me."

He growled against my skin, his breathing ragged as he pushed himself up. Then he paused, his bright eyes wild with his own need. "Are you sure?"

"Yes." I exhaled, knowing that once we crossed this line, there was no going back.

I didn't care.

I reached for him, my fingers slipping beneath the waistband of his sweatpants, pushing them down along with his boxers. My breathing stopped at the sight of him—taut, hard, and pulsing.

"Please," I whispered, desperation threading my voice.

His jaw clenched, his control unraveling as he positioned himself between my legs. With practiced ease, he rolled a condom over his length, his gaze never leaving me. Then his mouth devoured mine, claiming me. He pulled back and gritted his teeth, sucking in a sharp breath as he slowly pushed inside, stretching me, filling me.

A cry escaped me at the overwhelming sensation. Connor stilled.

"Are you hurt?" His voice was rough, restrained.

I shook my head, panting. "Don't stop!"

That was all he needed to hear. The last thread of hesitation came undone, replaced by pure, unrestrained passion. He let out a short gasp as he sank deeper, pressing against me, fitting like we were made for each other.

His deliberate rhythm teased, tormented, a promise in every thrust. His arms caged me in, muscles flexing as he held himself steady, his heavy-lidded gaze sending a rush through me. He leaned down, nipping at my ear.

"Lucy..." My name a rough whisper, worshipful and full of longing.

Every measured movement sent waves of heat curling through me, tension building with each electric, wicked push. My hands dug into the rippled muscles of his back, desperate for more, for everything, for him.

"*Connor*," I cried.

Connor let out a strangled groan, sitting up slightly, his fingers gripping my hips, lifting me, as he increased his pace, hitting the spot that sent fireworks exploding through my body. A scream tore from my lips as I shattered around him. Connor arched back, crying out until his forehead dropped to mine as our heavy breaths tangled in the space between us.

He collapsed beside me, pulling me into his arms, holding me tight against his chest.

We lay there, tangled together, our skin still flushed, our breaths uneven. Connor pressed delicate, lingering kisses into my hair, my cheek, my jaw.

I took slow, measured breaths, letting my body recover, my mind still catching up to what had just happened.

Connor groaned with pure, heartfelt satisfaction. "That was incredible, Lucy."

A slow smile spread across my face—honest, unguarded, real. "Yeah... it really was."

A moment of comfortable silence stretched between us.

"Connor?"

His hand traced lazy, absent-minded patterns along my spine. "Yeah?"

I hesitated, my pulse thrumming in my ears. "Can we make a promise to each other?"

His fingers stilled for half a second before continuing their slow, deliberate path across my skin. "What kind of promise?"

I swallowed, the words spilling out, firm with resolve. "No lies. No secrets. No drama. Not between us."

Connor shifted slightly, his chin brushing the top of my head. His voice was rough as if ready for sleep, low, unguarded. "I like that." A slow breath, then, "I promise not to keep anything from you, Luce. Not ever. No secrets. No lies. And definitely no drama."

A sharp, aching squeeze wrapped around my heart.But here, wrapped in Connor's arms, I chose to believe in him, in us.

I let out a slow breath, my chest tightening before finally loosening. "Same."

His arms tightened around me, pulling me impossibly closer, sealing the promise between us.

Connor murmured against my temple. "You are so perfect."

My stomach twisted.

"Please don't say that." I cringed, turning to face him. "I'm not perfect. I can promise you that."

He chuckled, tilting his head. "I know. But... you're perfect for me."

My lips parted slightly, but no words came.

I bit my lip, trying to suppress the urge to argue with him. "Aren't men supposed to be bad at expressing their feelings?"

Connor's blue eyes darkened, the teasing edge fading into something deeper. "You really have no idea, do you?"

I blinked. "What?"

His fingers brushed down my arm soft, reverent. "You are so, so beautiful, Lucy."

His words landed like a weight in my chest.

My face scrunched up at him. "Why do you keep saying that?"

Connor's gaze never wavered. "Because you keep trying to hide from me. But you're absolutely stunning." His voice remained quiet, steady. "I've imagined this moment longer than I care to admit, and... You're even more incredible than I ever dreamed."

Tension built in my jaw. I didn't know how to accept that. "Thank you."

Flat. My voice was flat.

Connor frowned, tucking a stray strand of hair behind my ear. "What's wrong?"

I shook my head, forcing a smile. "I'm fine."

But I wasn't.

Memories hit like a tidal wave, unbidden, unwanted. They unleashed their fury, dragging me under before I could fight them off.

Connor propped himself up on his elbow, concern sinking into his brow. "Lucy. You're *not* fine."

I bit my lip, trying to shove it down, to put them back into that *goddamn box* I'd kept them hidden inside. "Being with you is all I want to focus on right now," I managed.

His thumb brushed against my cheek. "Nothing you say will ruin tonight."

His tenderness undid me.

A tear slipped free, trailing down my cheek bone.

A knot formed in my throat. "It's fine," I insisted before meeting Connor's incredulous gaze. "It's just... no one has ever treated me the way you just did. That's all. Not a big deal."

Connor's body tensed. "What do you mean?"

My pulse hammered.

Uncertainty tightened in my chest.

Then—

The words fell from my lips, feeling foreign on my tongue. "After I moved to London, everything just... fell apart. My mother didn't believe me. You weren't talking to me. Sam barely called those first few months..." I swallowed hard, pushing through the lump in my throat. "I felt so alone. And part of me just... *gave up*."

Connor's fingers gripped my waist, but he stayed quiet, letting me speak.

"If people already thought the worst of me, what was the point in fighting it?" I let out a bitter laugh, the sound hollow. "I started acting out just to piss off my mother. Wearing shorter dresses, pretending to be *that* girl."

My throat clenched. The anger I had buried for years clawed its way to the surface. I forced a breath, trying to recover.

"But... I didn't want the attention that came with it." My stomach churned. A raw ache settled in my ribs, pressing down, suffocating. "I was so stupid. So naïve."

The words felt small.

Empty.

Because the truth was, I had never wanted *any* of it.

Connor's entire body tensed beside me, but he stayed silent, giving me the space to press on. He rested an uncertain hand on my arm, then gently stroked my skin in a slow, soothing rhythm.

"One night, while my mother was out, an old business associate of hers stopped by." The words came out mechanically. "He was charming at first, acted like he was just there to drop something off. But then... he wouldn't *stop*."

Connor inhaled sharply. His hands paused—but he didn't pull away. Didn't let his anger take up the space I needed. Instead, he exhaled slowly, grounding himself, and let me continue without breaking in with his own storm of thoughts.

I gripped the sheets, anchoring myself in their familiar smooth texture. "After he...*touched* me," my voice wavered, the words barely escaping. "I just stopped caring. I let myself disappear." The admission cracked something inside me, fragile and worn. "And for a long time..." I closed my eyes, hating to admit this to anyone, including myself. "I blamed Amanda."

His grip on me stiffened. "Amanda?"

"She's the reason I got sent away. And I blamed her for *everything* that happened after." I scoffed. "Which I know is ridiculous. Saying it out loud, I *hear* how crazy that sounds. But I needed *someone* to blame. If it wasn't her fault, then it had to be *me*. I'm the problem. *I'm* the reason..."

Connor squeezed his eyes shut, his face reddening. When he opened them again, his voice was low, barely controlled. "Lucy. This *wasn't* your fault. It was *his fault*. The only person responsible is the motherfucker who *did that* to you."

I let out a shaky breath. "I know."

He raised his brows at me.

"I mean I know that's how I'm supposed to feel. It's hard, Connor. It's so easy to believe *everything* he told me that night... I let it consume me." My voice faltered, a knot tied itself around my chest, constricting my airways. "I believed I was *worthless*. I'd *asked* for it..."

My pulse hammered in my ears. "I kept telling myself that because he didn't *rape* me, it wasn't *that bad*. I should just *move on*. Shit happens to everyone. Get *over* it."

I exhaled sharply, my thoughts jumping, tangled in the jumbled mess of memories.

"My ex... he was so much worse." My voice shook.

"The duke?" Connor darkened, the question coming out like gravel.

"No. Before him." A sick feeling twisted in my stomach. "He was the first guy I dated in college. *Callum*."

Connor gave me a reassuring squeeze. "What happened?"

"We'd been dating for a couple weeks and one night... he was so angry. *Furious* with me. Like an idiot, I followed him back to his apartment, begging him to believe me—that I hadn't *cheated* on him."

The words stuck in my throat, rage and agony crashing over me in waves.

The raw, *endless* pain.

I wanted to scream.

I swallowed hard. "He convinced himself I was sleeping with a guy in my fucking study group at RVC." I stiffened, knots forming along the length of my back. "I guess the fact I hadn't slept with him yet made him think..."

The memory hit like a wrecking ball, sudden and suffocating.

Flashes of that night tore through me like lightning, sharp and violent.

A mask.

His hands around my neck.

The pure, unrelenting *fear*.

My lips trembled as I choked out, "He took *everything* from me that night."

Connor's jaw tightened, his grip on me firm but gentle. He exhaled slowly, his forehead pressing against mine. "Lucy..." My name came out rough, strained.

For a long moment, he just held me, breathing me in, as if trying to absorb the weight of my words. Then, finally, he whispered, "I hate that you went through that. That I wasn't there. That *no one* was."

His hands skimmed down the length of my spine. "You deserved someone who would protect you. Who saw you. Cared for you." His breath hitched, and I felt the tremor in his muscles as his voice dipped lower, tight with controlled rage. "And if I ever find out who he is—"

I placed a hand on his chest, shaking my head. "Connor... no. It's over. I need it to be over."

His throat bobbed, eyes searching mine. After a long pause, he nodded. "Okay." He exhaled, pressing a soft kiss to my forehead. "I won't push, but just know—no matter what, I'm always here for you. *Always.*"

I squeezed his arm tighter, fighting back the tears that ran unchecked down my cheeks, spilling over my shivering jaw.

I closed my eyes, needing to release the last pieces of my past—the hidden parts of me no one else had seen. Not my mother. Not even Sam.

Swallowing, I spoke into the silence stretching between us. "Maybe I really did ruin myself."

"Don't ever say that." Connor's grip on me was firm, but gentle. "You didn't ruin anything. You're *not* ruined."

Tears still pricked my eyes. "Sorry, I didn't think any of this would come up right now. But the way you look at me, the way you just... *treat* me..."

I sucked in a deep breath. "My entire relationship with sex has been guys using me, tossing me aside. And then there's you."

Connor softened behind me, stroking his fingertips through my hair.

"I know I'm not supposed to thank you anymore..." A small grin tugged at my lips. "But thank you for making sure I enjoyed every second. For showing me how much you care. For asking for consent. You truly *saw* me, and that means everything to me. More than you could ever know."

I lowered my voice, my heart pounding as I admitted, "I know I can trust you with every part of me... I—I've *never* had that before."

He exhaled, his tension easing slightly. "Lucy..."

I let out a weak laugh. "You probably wish you hadn't asked now, huh?"

He cupped my face in his hands, his thumbs tracing slow circles on my cheeks. "Not for a second. I just—I can't imagine what you've been through." His voice thickened. "And I hate to think how different things would've been if you'd stayed. But you wouldn't be *this* Lucy. Everything you've been through... it doesn't define you. But it's made you into the strongest, bravest, most incredible woman I've ever known."

His hand slid up my arm, slow and worshipful, tracing the path to my jaw. A touch that said: I see you. I feel you. I *understand* you.

"I love you, Lucy."

A tremor ran through me, my chest tightening at the sheer sincerity in his voice.

"You... *love* me?"

Connor's thumb brushed along my cheekbone, his gaze never wavering. "God, Lucy. I really do."

Warmth blanketed me. My chest swelled with something deep, something right.

A small smile reached my lips. "I love you, too."

I closed my eyes, letting the words settle inside me.

Connor held me tighter, whispering against my skin, "I will *always* love you, Lucy."

I melted into him, letting go of the past. Not erasing it, but refusing to let it define me. For the first time in years, I felt *free*.

The burden I'd been carrying with me these last four years wasn't just mine anymore. And he *loved* me.

CHAPTER TWENTY-FOUR

Kissed, Caffeinated, and Caught

LUCY

I stretched in bed, waking to the sound of running water. My fingertips grazed cool, empty sheets. I reached for my phone as a reminder flashed across the screen: *Lunch with Tanya and Taylor at The Rustic Roast in forty-five minutes.*

"Shit," I breathed.

The bathroom door swung open and Connor walked out in all his chiseled glory, a towel slung low around his hips. His damp skin glistened as he dried his hair in a hand towel.

"Everything okay?" He flashed me a wicked grin.

I snapped my jaw shut, realizing I'd been gaping at him. "Yes. And no. I'm running late—I need to be at *The Rustic Roast* in less than an hour."

He strode closer to the bed. His fingers trailed slowly up my arm. "That's plenty of time for me to show you how much I appreciate you, once...or *twice*."

My cheeks burned. "I don't have clothes or my truck here. I really need to go home and get ready."

Connor eyed me thoughtfully before grabbing my hand and pulling me up from the bed. The moment our bodies pressed together, I became painfully aware of my nakedness.

His skin was still warm and slick from his shower, his arms wrapping around me with deliberate slowness. His breath ghosted over my ear. "Would being late really be so bad?"

I bit my lip, my smile widening as I hid my face in the crook of his chest. "Maybe not. But my cousins *are* leaving soon. It's probably my last chance to see them before they head home."

Connor pouted, and I kissed the frown off his lips. I meant it to be a quick, chaste press of affection.

But he had other ideas.

The moment he deepened the kiss, I was gone.

Everything else—my cousins, my plans, even time itself—faded into nothing. There was only his heat, his hands, the way he guided me back onto the bed with effortless ease.

"Tell me to stop, and I will," he murmured against my lips.

I didn't.

He let the towel drop and I wrapped my legs around his waist. His lips scorched my skin, igniting every nerve. He laid me back then, lifted my legs into the crooks of his elbows before he breathed, "I love you, Lucy." Before he thrust into me, his eyes locked onto mine.

I cried out, pleasure crashing into me with relentless force.

He froze. "Did I hurt you?"

"No! Don't stop," I ordered.

He grinned.

Then he was moving and my body responded to him in ways I didn't know were possible. He loved me. And somehow everything felt... *different*. Better.

His pace quickened, his grip tightening as his heated gaze devoured every movement, every gasp, as I writhed beneath him.

I lost all sense of what was up or down, only knowing that I never wanted this feeling to end. His name was on my lips. "I love you."

My words unraveled him, and he collapsed on top of me. My limbs were heavy, useless, completely spent.

My eyelids fluttered as I basked in the thorough, glorious job Connor had just done.

And damn me if I didn't want more—even if I couldn't move, walk, or talk.

I swallowed, my mouth dry, then patted his back weakly. He rolled onto his side, sweat beading along his forehead as he caught his breath.

"Sorry, I couldn't help myself," he rasped.

I gave a breathless laugh. "Yeah. I know the feeling..."

Then, the reality of time hit me like a freight train.

I forced myself upright.

"Don't you have work today?" I teased as I made my way to the bathroom.

"Took the day off," Connor called after me. "Told them I was up late with Willow."

I turned the shower on, shaking my head. That wasn't a lie—but it sure as hell wasn't the *whole* truth. I stepped into the warm cascading water.

Then a low, heated voice rumbled behind me. "May I join you?"

I smirked over my shoulder. "Didn't you already shower?"

Connor said nothing, just opened the glass door and stepped in.

Before I could protest, he crowded me beneath the warm cascade, stealing my breath with a deep kiss.

The hot water caressed our bodies, the steam curling around our tangled limbs. I was a goner as he took me again and again.

I slumped against him, heart pounding, head spinning, only one thought formed:

"*My cousins are going to kill me.*"

Connor's deep laughter rumbled through his chest.

I grinned, still breathless, as he slowly set me down. "Did I say that out loud?"

"I guess I'll have to apologize for keeping you," he mused.

I rolled my eyes and quickly soaped up. "*Or* you could let me handle it."

Five minutes later, I dried off in record time, pulled on my previous night's outfit, and picked up my phone then dialed Tanya.

"Hey, Lucy! We just parked and are about to walk in."

"I'm so sorry," I said, "Willow went into labor last night. Things got complicated. I'm running late, but I'll be there as soon as I can."

Across the room, Connor's jaw dropped.

You blamed the dog? he mouthed, eyes wide.

I bit my lip to keep from laughing as Tanya gasped. "Oh my gosh! Are all the puppies okay?"

"They're happy and healthy. Mom's doing great."

Tanya sighed in relief. "Oh, good! Well, don't worry, we'll be here when you arrive."

"Thanks! See you soon." I hung up and turned to glare at Connor. "You almost blew my cover."

His chest shook with laughter. "Not my fault! Also, you can't blame poor Willow."

I smirked. "Don't even, you used the same excuse to get out of going to work today."

"That's different," he insisted, the rumble in his chest distracting me.

I laughed, "Okay, fine. But, I'm not telling my cousin I'm late because I was too busy having sex with my new boyfriend."

"Boyfriend?" Connor echoed, raising an eyebrow.

My eyes glimmered as I smirked back at him, "Yes. My *secret* boyfriend."

Connor folded his arms, grin widening. "Really?"

"You technically work for me." I huffed a laugh, "Maybe we don't tell everyone just yet?"

He chuckled, "Fair enough. But I wouldn't label what we did as just sex."

I pursed my lips, trying and failing to suppress my smile. "*Fine*. It was mind-blowing, *life-altering*, stop everything—"

He plopped onto the bed. "Ooo, life-altering? I like that."

I grabbed my purse and kissed his cheek. "See you later. I need to hurry up, my truck's all the way next door."

"This conversation's not over, London!" He called.

With a final smirk, I rushed out the door.

The coffee shop was bustling with the post-church crowd, the low hum of conversation blending with the clatter of cups and the rich scent of espresso.

It took me a moment to spot my cousins near the window, sitting in a cozy corner booth. I waved and made my way over.

"Isn't that what you were wearing last night?" Tanya eyed me knowingly.

My cheeks flushed. "I had to stay the night to help with the dogs."

"Sure." She drawled.

Taylor bit her lip as she took me in, eyes sparkling. "I love this for you. Why don't you grab a coffee, and then tell us *everything*?"

I glanced at the long, winding line near the counter and groaned. "I really need caffeine, but I don't want to waste time standing in line when I could be spending time with you guys."

Tanya waved me off. "Go get your coffee. The line's moving fast—we'll save your seat."

I hesitated for a second, then nodded. "Okay. Be right back."

Turning on my heel, I made my way toward the back of the line, weaving through the bustling café.

Just as I reached my spot, the bell above the door jingled, signaling another customer's arrival.

Then came the voice.

Smooth. Saccharine. Laced with venom.

"Fancy seeing *you* here this afternoon."

I stiffened, then turned, my expression souring. "Amanda. Always a pleasure."

Her smirk was knowing, sharp. "Likewise. Have you talked to *Sam* lately?"

"If you have something to say, say it," I shot back.

Amanda scoffed, her judgmental gaze dragging over my outfit like hot coals. "I'll take that as a no." A cat-like grin spread over her wicked features. "So, what's it like knowing the whole town knows you've taken my leftovers?"

My hands curled into fists. "How can you reduce Connor to 'leftovers' after everything you two went through?"

For a fleeting second, Amanda's smirk faltered. Her eyes widened slightly, a flicker of uncertainty crossing her face. "Went through?" she repeated, before slipping her mask back into place. "You're right, I guess I let my feelings about you cloud my judgment."

I exhaled through my nose, forcing down the irritation clawing up my throat. "Right... Let's *try* and be civil for his sake."

Amanda's lips pressed into a thin line. "Fine."

I reached out my hand to shake on it. "Truce?"

She rolled her eyes, crossing her arms over her chest. "I'm not *touching* you."

I let my arm fall to my side. "That's fine with me."

Her eyes widened briefly before she scoffed. I sighed and turned my back to her, making my way to the counter.

I returned to Tanya and Taylor with a frilly, blended coffee drink in hand—whipped cream, chocolate drizzle, more dessert than coffee.

Taylor raised a brow. "What did you get?"

I took a sip, savoring the sweetness. "Caramel Mocha Freeze. I had them add an extra shot of cold brew, so hopefully it actually wakes me up and doesn't just make me crash from all the sugar."

Tanya's gaze lingered over my shoulder, her expression furrowed in suspicion. "What did Amanda want?"

I sighed, leaning back into my seat. "Nothing crazy. We called a truce."

Tanya raised a wary brow. "If you heard half of what she's done to anyone who's tried dating Connor in the past... Let's just say I *doubt* that truce will last."

My stomach twisted. "I'd ask what you've heard, but honestly, I don't think I can handle it right now. I've pretty much hit my drama limit."

Taylor grinned, leaning in conspiratorially. "I heard one girl went to the beauty salon and left bald because the chemicals made her hair fall out."

I grimaced. "Okay, *wow*. That's insane. There's no way that's true," I insisted, getting immediately sucked in.

Taylor shrugged. "I don't know... I mean..."

I shook my head. "I can believe she started a rumor that it was her, but I doubt it actually *happened*. Anyway, can we talk about something else? Literally *anything* else."

Tanya smirked. "Alright. How about you and Connor? That little performance at *The Saloon* is the talk of the town. Even my mom knew this morning."

My eyes widened. "*What?!*"

Taylor pulled out her phone, turning it towards me. "It made it on *The White River Whisper*."

I gaped at the headline: *White River's Bad Boy Gets Down and Dirty at Karaoke*. My heart sank further with each photo: Connor and me dancing. Kissing. Even worse—speculation about my past: "*Why did Lucy leave all those years ago?*"

"Who writes this garbage?" I seethed.

Taylor shrugged, "It's anonymous. But the whole town reads it."

I exhaled sharply, suddenly feeling the weight of the entire café's stare.

Judging.

Whispering.

I clenched my jaw. "I have to fix this."

Tanya leaned forward. "How? You don't even know who wrote it."

I sighed. "Maybe I should do an interview, set the record straight?"

Taylor frowned. "No one reads the actual town paper anymore."

I groaned. "I'll figure something out."

Taylor pursed her lips, then tapped her phone. "There's an anonymous tip submission. Maybe you could try sending your side of the story there?"

I rubbed my temples. "Maybe."

Tanya shrugged. "Or you could just *ignore* it. Everyone will be onto the next scandal soon enough."

I huffed out a breath. "You're probably right—*anyway*, how's dear old Aunt Diane?"

Tanya rolled her eyes. "Mom's mom. I swear, half the time I can't tell if she's actually upset or just putting on a show."

Taylor snorted. "Classic narcissist."

I took another sip of my drink and flicked my gaze out the window. "I'm not saying a *word*."

They both laughed as we eased back into our usual topic: our insane family members.

After lunch, we hugged goodbye, agreeing that *The Rustic Roast* was officially our new favorite spot.

I smiled the whole walk back to my truck. Despite the gossip, excitement for the future warmed my steps.

Then, my phone rang. Connor was calling.

I answered, beaming. "Hey! How are you?"

His deep voice was taut with stress. "Lucy, can you come over right now?"

My stomach dropped. "I was about to head home. What's wrong? Is Willow okay? The puppies..."

"They're fine."

"Are you upset about the article in *The Whisper*? I saw—"

"It's not that." He cut me off. "I'll explain in person."

A knot tightened in my chest. "Connor, you're freaking me out. What's going on?"

His voice softened. "I'm sorry. I wish I could say more. Just... come over, please?"

I swallowed hard. "Yeah. I'm on my way."

CHAPTER TWENTY-FIVE

No More Lies

LUCY

I let myself into Connor's house, my mind still spiraling with what he could need to tell me that couldn't be done over the phone.

Connor called from the kitchen. "We're in here!"

We? I paused, setting my things down on the entry table before making my way toward the kitchen.

Connor stood hunched over the island, his hands gripping the butcher block counter like it was the only thing keeping him upright. Beside him, a nervous Sam fidgeted with the hem of his cashmere sweater.

I stiffened.

Then my eyes followed Connor's glare to the pile of unopened letters spread out between his tense arms.

I stepped closer, recognition striking me with a harsh slap. My breath caught. "Those are the letters I sent. The *cards*. How did you guys find these?"

Sam's face turned beet red as he stared at the floor, unable to meet my gaze. His silence suddenly spoke volumes as the sharp sting of betrayal stabbed through my chest.

No. No way.

"It was *you*?" I accused, my voice rising. "Sam, you *stole* Connor's letters?"

Sam flinched, shifting backward. "I—I came here to explain."

"How could you possibly explain *this*?" My voice cracked, fury blazing under my skin. "What *else* have you done, Sam? Did you delete the emails, too?!"

"I had no choice!" he shot back, his face crumbling with pain.

I gaped at him, my pulse hammering in my ears. "There's always a choice, Sam. How could you..." My words fell away as his shoulders slumped.

When he spoke again, his voice was small. "I was protecting someone."

The air grew thick.

Anger simmered beneath my skin, still burning but no longer unchecked.

I sighed and sank onto a barstool. "Who?"

Sam's jaw tightened, a deep-set sadness threading through his tone. "My ex-boyfriend."

I blinked. "Boyfriend?" I asked, shaking my head. "You didn't *have* a boyfriend until college..."

Sam's gaze dropped to the floor as he let out a long breath. "I'm so sorry, Luce. I couldn't tell you. He was... *is* in the closet, and his father's a complete asshole."

I clasped my hands together to stop them from trembling. "Just start at the beginning. Tell me everything."

I noticed now that his cheeks were blotchy and the rims of his eyes red as he continued, "I guess it's important to first know that my ex was on the football team. His father used to beat him after he'd lose a game... I need you to understand, we *had* to keep our relationship a secret. He didn't want me to tell anyone just in case it accidentally slipped..." He squeezed his eyes shut, shaking his head. "One day we were in the boys' locker room. Everyone had gone home and... things were getting steamy. Then, Amanda walked in on us." Sam's lip quivered. "Lucy, I had to protect him. Protect *us*." His voice went hollow, distant. "She threatened to *out* him. So, I begged her to keep it quiet. I promised I'd do *anything* if she swore to keep quiet."

Connor stiffened beside me. "Sam..."

He shook his head. "I swear, Connor, I didn't know what she was going to ask me to do." His eyes glistened, heavy with regret. "She wanted to know *everything* about Connor. His favorite things. If he liked anyone at school." Sam met his brother's gaze. "I told her you wanted to take Lucy to homecoming, and suddenly... my job became getting you to change your mind. I told her there was *no way* you'd ever—"

My inhale hissed inward as my voice cracked. "You... you didn't."

Sam's face twisted with years of guilt. "I swear, I never meant to hurt either of you. Amanda came up with the whole plan—what I had to say, who I had to talk to. I wasn't going to go through with it, but then she threatened to out my ex again, and I panicked. I made the call to your mom. After that... I knew I could *never* tell either of you the truth. That I was the reason you were gone. I knew if I did...you'd *both* hate me."

Tears welled in his midnight-blue eyes. His shoulders shook as he sobbed.

I wanted to collapse under the weight of it all, but I forced myself to sit upright.

Connor's voice lowered, tight with something between anger and disbelief. "You were Homecoming King senior year because of your friendship with Amanda. You got close to her. Closer than either Lucy or I ever did. And in the end, no matter what your reasons, you *benefited* from lying to us. Did you ever stop to think that maybe she wasn't using you, but *you* were using us?"

Sam winced. "I hate that I benefited from your pain. I feel sick about it. *All the time.* And if I could undo how it happened, I would." His gaze dropped, voice barely audible. "But I wouldn't undo loving him or protecting him. That's the truth, even if it makes me a terrible person."

"Fine," I exhaled shakily. "But the letters. Why hide them? I was already gone."

"My job was to make sure nothing got in the way of Amanda's relationship with Connor." His eyes were distant. "If she ever found out you two were writing to each other, she would've lost it, and my ex would've paid the price."

Connor's hands curled into fists. "When Amanda first started talking to me, she knew *all* the right things to say..."

Sam closed his eyes and whispered, "That was me."

Connor's expression cracked—a mixture of pain, confusion, devastation. I placed my hand over his, but he barely reacted. "Connor..." I tried.

He shook his head at me. "I should've reached out to you myself. Asked if you were okay. Tried to understand *why* you hadn't called. But I didn't. Instead, I let Amanda—someone I barely even knew—manipulate me. I never told you this, but I thought you chose to leave without saying goodbye. That's what I was led to believe," Connor's eyes narrowed at Sam, "that you had a choice to stay and didn't. Then rumors went around and I thought nothing of it, just small town gossip. But I let myself believe you wanted to leave White River. That you didn't care that you left *me*."

I squeezed his fingers. "Connor, it's okay. We've talked about this. We were kids. You couldn't have known."

His jaw tightened. "I still did what I did, and I'm so sorry for what that did to you, Lucy. God, if I'd called you. Let you know how I felt..."

I couldn't speak.

The self-blame, the guilt—it was all there, carved into his pained expression, tightening his features like a wound he refused to let heal. But it wasn't just about not calling me. He was blaming himself for what *happened* to me in London, as if a phone call could have changed everything. As if his voice on the other end of the line could have stopped it.

I shook my head, searching for the words to free him from this needless, self-inflicted punishment.

But before I could find them, his expression hardened. He turned back to Sam. "Is there anything else you need to tell us? Now's the time to say it."

Sam swallowed hard again, his face paling. "It gets worse."

A stone dropped into the pit of my stomach.

I squeezed Connor's hand, bracing myself for the worst.

"The threats never stopped," Sam said, his voice raw. "Once I broke things off with my ex, Amanda had even more leverage—what I'd done to you both. Every time you broke up with her, Connor, I had to figure out a way to fix it..."

Something in Sam's eyes told me everything.

And then... it all *clicked*.

Amanda's reaction at The Rustic Roast—like she'd forgotten their history entirely. Like none of it was real, as if it had never *touched* her. The way Connor had never actually remembered that night or how she'd conveniently wound up in bed with him.

The pieces snapped together, forming a picture I didn't want to see—but one I could no longer ignore.

Oh. My. God.

My breath halted. I couldn't just say it. If I was wrong, I'd be opening a wound that didn't need to be touched.

I forced myself to look Sam in the eyes. He was already watching me, like he knew what I was about to ask. His eyes held something I didn't want to see... regret.

My pulse hammered.

I forced the words out, barely more than a whisper. "Was she ever pregnant?"

Sam's face crumbled.

He shut his eyes and shook his head. "*No.*" His answer was barely audible.

A sharp inhale sounded beside me.

Connor's head snapped toward Sam, his expression flickering from confusion to sheer disbelief. "*What*? No. That's impossible. Lucy, you can't think that—"

I paused, the weight of the moment crushing down on me. "Amanda isn't the most creative person. She had Sam tell a lie about a pregnancy scare to get me sent away. What if she used the same lie to trap you in a relationship with her?"

He shook his head. "No. That can't... who could lie about something like that?"

I needed him to see it, but I tensed, knowing how much this would break him.

"Connor... did you ever see a sonogram?"

His body went still. "Yes. Amanda texted me pictures."

I clenched my jaw. "Just on your phone? Nothing printed?"

His brow furrowed, and the first sliver of doubt crept in. "The printer at the office was always broken..."

I pressed forward carefully. "Did you ever go to any of her appointments?"

"She always scheduled them when I couldn't leave work."

A beat of silence stretched between us.

His breaths grew unsteady, the weight of realization sinking into his bones.

"No..." The word fell from his lips, barely a sound. His bright blue eyes locked onto mine, darkening with panic as his mind worked through the truth he no longer could ignore. "No, no, no... No."

Then, suddenly, he snapped.

He turned on Sam with an intensity that made my heart seize. "How could you?!"

Before I could stop him, Connor lunged forward, grabbing Sam by the collar and slamming him into the wall.

"Did you tell her to trick me that night?! Did we even have *sex*, or did she just crawl into my bed and let me believe we had?!"

Sam gasped as Connor's grip tightened, his face twisted with raw fury.

Sam's hands shook as he grabbed Connor's wrists, struggling against the sheer strength of his rage. "Connor, I—I never thought she'd *actually* go through with it! I made one comment, one joke and she..." he choked out.

Connor froze.

His eyes widened with something even worse than anger: betrayal.

Then, as if the air had been sucked out of his lungs, his grip loosened. He let go so abruptly that Sam crumpled to the floor, coughing as he caught his breath.

Before I could say anything, Connor grabbed his hat and stormed out, slamming the door behind him.

"Connor, wait!" I chased after him, my pulse roaring in my ears.

When I reached him, he was trembling, his breath coming in ragged gasps. His fingers flexed and curled into fists at his sides, his entire body fighting against itself.

Without hesitating, I wrapped my arms around him.

He stood rigid for a heartbeat—then broke.

His shoulders shook as he collapsed into me, silent tears spilling free.

I held him, saying nothing, just anchoring him to me. His hands gripped the back of my shirt like he was afraid to let go.

Slowly, his breathing evened out, the tension in his shoulders easing little by little.

The sound of the door creaking open made my head snap up. Sam stepped hesitantly onto the porch, his face wrecked with guilt.

I shot him a narrow glare. "You need to go."

Sam's shoulder sank, nodding before turning and disappearing down the steps.

Connor spoke, the roughness in his voice tearing at my soul. "I'm sorry, Luce, do you mind giving me some space? I need a minute to process everything." He went rigid with unspeakable pain.

My heart broke.

Then I saw red.

"That's fine. I need to go do something anyway."

I stepped back, giving Connor the space he needed. I ducked inside to grab my purse, then stormed out to my truck, tunnel vision consuming me.

Yanking my phone from my pocket, I pressed call.

"Amanda, we need to talk. *Now*." My voice went ice-cold, steady, *dangerous*.

A pause. Then, irritation. "Seriously?" she spat. "I'm not *talking* to you. *Bye*."

Before she could hang up, I said the magic words.

"Sam told me everything."

Her breathing halted.

Silence.

Then, her tone sharpened. "Meet me at *The Rustic Roast* in twenty."

"I'll be there."

I hung up and gripped the steering wheel so tightly my skin stung.

Amanda was done with the lies and the reckless way she toyed with people's lives.

I'd make sure of it.

CHAPTER TWENTY-SIX

Checkmate

LUCY

I sat in the corner of *The Rustic Roast*, seething. My fingers drummed against the worn wooden armrest of the chair, my patience thinning with every passing minute.

A young barista hesitated near my table, tucking a stray piece of hair behind her ear. "Uh, sorry to bother you, but... are you the girl from *The Whisper*? The one who kissed Connor Lochland?"

I sighed, my jaw tightening. "Unfortunately."

Her eyes widened with excitement. "Oh my God, you're like, *famous* around here! Did you really have his baby and give it up for adoption?"

I snapped my gaze to her. "What?"

She clasped her hands together, practically vibrating with anticipation. "Yeah! Everyone's talking about—"

I cut her off. "No. I've never been pregnant. Amanda Johnson started that rumor because she—" I caught myself, pressing my lips together. *No. Sam started that rumor. Sure, Amanda told him what to say, but he did it.*

The barista's mouth fell open. "Whoa. So she *is* that crazy?"

I inhaled through my nose, forcing a tight smile. "Could you bring me a menu, please?"

"Right! Of course." She nodded quickly and hurried back toward the counter.

The bell over the door jingled, and Amanda strutted in, looking like she'd walked straight off a movie set. Flawless makeup, pristine white romper, sunglasses perched atop her sleek blonde waves. She slid them off in one smooth motion, tucking them into her designer purse as she made a beeline for me, a smirk playing at her glossy lips.

Amanda sank into the chair across from me, crossing her long legs leisurely. I leveled her with a glare. "Took you long enough."

"I had a last-minute detail to wrap up. But what does it matter? You're here to try and blackmail me, so let's not pretend you're the morally superior one," she countered, folding her hands in her lap as if sitting for a Vogue interview.

I searched her face for any sign of weakness, but her expression remained a perfectly controlled mask. So I cut straight to it. "I don't want to blackmail you. I'm here because you're going to apologize to Connor."

"Excuse me?"

"You faked a pregnancy to trap him in a relationship he didn't want. You blackmailed his brother. You told him you had a fucking miscarriage. How far were you willing to go to keep him, Amanda?"

Her left eye twitched—so fast, I might have missed it if I wasn't looking. Then, just as quickly, her lips curled back into a self-satisfied smile. "It wasn't my idea." She leaned forward slightly, her voice silk and venom. "Sam said if I were pregnant, Connor would do anything for me. And he was right. Connor did... *everything* for me. That little thing he does with his tongue? *I* taught him that." She baited me, and for a split second, heat rushed through me before I remembered who I was dealing with.

My voice went low, lethal. "Who the hell *lies* about being pregnant?"

A shadow passed over her face, but she masked it with a sigh. "Ugh. Don't be so dramatic. So, what's your deal? You must *want* something in return for not telling Connor."

"I told you what I want. It's over Amanda. Connor already knows." A slow grin of satisfaction crossed my face "He's never going to believe anything you say again, and it's not because of me or anyone else. It's because of the constant string of lies you've spun since we were kids."

The young barista hesitated as she set the menu between us, her eyes darting between Amanda and me like she'd stumbled into a reality show she wasn't supposed to be watching.

Amanda gave her a saccharine smile. "Thank you, Abby. We'll let you know if we need anything else."

Abby turned, pulling out her phone, typing furiously.

I leaned in, voice sharp. "Do you have any *idea* what you've done? Connor's been carrying the weight of a loss that never even existed. And for what?"

"Because I love him," she growled.

"That's not love, Amanda. You're not *capable* of love."

Amanda rolled her eyes. "Oh, please. He's *fine*."

"He is *not* fine, you selfish bitch." My grip tightened on the armrests, white-hot rage curling in my chest.

And then, she smiled.

A slow, pleased, feline grin.

"Wow," she mused. "I didn't realize what a *powerful* hold I still have over him."

My vision slowly tunneled as blood rushed to my ears.

"You think this is *funny*?" My voice rose, raw and unsteady. "It's not *you* he cares about, Amanda—it's the *baby* he *thought* he was going to have. Don't you understand that?"

She *laughed*.

That was it.

My chair scraped against the floor as I shot to my feet, glaring down at her. "You're telling the truth to the town about *everything* you've done. *Today*. Don't you want to repent? Take responsibility for your actions? Prove you're not this awful person you've turned yourself into over childhood jealousy. Be the better woman."

Amanda shifted, feigning boredom. "Here's how this is going to go." She pulled her phone from her purse, flipping it toward me.

The air in my lungs turned to ice.

A video played on her screen—grainy footage of me and my ex.

Callum.

In that twisted Halloween mask.

A shaky, hidden-camera angle.

Me, getting shoved onto a bed.

His hand closed around my throat.

My hands clawed at him.

Terror in my eyes.

My vision blurred, throat closing around a sob.

I gasped, choking on air, unable to look away.

Amanda's voice was a sickening purr. "I had no idea you were so... *kinky*, Lucy."

My stomach churned.

I trembled, barely able to force the words past the solid-brick lump in my throat. "What are you going to do with that?"

She leaned in, her expression eerily calm. "Oh, I'm posting it *everywhere*. By tonight, Connor will see exactly who you really are—disgusting, damaged, *worthless* goods."

My fingers curled into fists.

She smirked. "Your father's *legacy* will be ruined. And Connor? He'll *never* look at you the same. Unless..."

Rage flooded my veins.

Before I could stop myself—before reason could surface—that primal urge took control. My fist collided with her cheekbone.

The crack was sickeningly satisfying.

Amanda tumbled from her chair, dazed.

I grabbed her phone, my fingers trembling as I hovered over the screen. For a split second, I wanted to delete the video—to erase the horror. But I stopped myself.

My breathing came in ragged gasps as I pocketed the phone instead.

Evidence.

Amanda gasped, then let out a piercing shriek. "Someone call 911! She attacked me!"

The entire coffee shop went still. The barista froze mid-pour, customers stared, and the weight of my actions pressed into my chest like a steel beam.

I crouched beside Amanda as she cradled her swelling face. "Do you have any idea how *illegal* it is to distribute non-consensual porn?" I hissed, my voice shaking. "This isn't a sex tape, Amanda. It's evidence that I was *raped*."

Amanda's lips parted, her breath hitching in what could have been shock—or maybe just the realization that she'd finally lost control.

"How did you even get this?" I seethed. "Who sent this to you? Where did you find it?!"

Then... sirens.

The wail of approaching police cars shattered the stunned silence.

I rose to my feet, exhaling sharply as the flashing red and blue lights washed over the coffee shop windows.

Outside, the patrol cars skidded to a stop.

I walked out of the café on my own, hands already lifted. I didn't resist. Didn't argue.

The weight of what I'd done settled over me.

But I didn't regret it.

Not one damn bit.

Deputy Foster stood by his patrol car, arms crossed, watching me approach.

His sharp brown eyes swept over me before flicking toward the café, where Amanda was still inside, crying into the hands of a stunned onlooker. He shook his head with a quiet sigh before turning to me.

"You really went after the mayor's daughter?" he muttered. "What the hell were you thinking?"

I exhaled slowly, my pulse still pounding. "I was thinking I'd had enough of her bullshit."

Foster let out a dry chuckle before glancing toward Amanda, then back to me.

"Well, she's definitely pressing charges for assault. So, before I cuff you, I need to check your person for a phone you allegedly stole."

I nodded, my throat tightening. "It's in my back right pocket."

He pulled it out, flipping it over in his hands before giving me a sharp look. "Why'd you take it?"

I swallowed hard, my voice barely above a whisper. "To give to you. She has a video on there. Of me."

Foster's expression darkened.

I forced myself to continue, though my stomach churned. "She threatened to release it. I think she thought it was just a sex tape—but nothing on that video was consensual."

Silence hung between us, thick and heavy.

I clenched my fists, trying to hold back the shame creeping up my throat.

Don't cry. Don't let this break you.

Foster's voice was softer now. "Lucy, are you alright?"

I shook my head, my lip trembling despite myself.

He nodded, understanding. "You were coerced, blackmailed, and harassed by Miss Johnson, is that correct?"

I gave a shaky nod.

His jaw tightened. "Is there anything else I need to know? Why did you meet with her today?"

My breath shuddered out of me. "I wanted her to own up to everything she's done. To stop lying to everyone. To take ownership for her actions."

Foster tilted his head slightly, listening.

I swallowed, forcing the words out. "We just found out she lied to Connor about being pregnant, blackmailed my best friend into lying about me so I'd get sent away to London. And now that we know, I just... I needed her to know she didn't have a hold on anyone anymore."

My voice cracked, but I pushed on.

"I needed her to finally stop. To *apologize*."

Foster studied me, something unreadable flickering across his face.

Then, he turned toward the café.

"Amanda Johnson," he called, his tone clipped and professional.

She stepped out onto the sidewalk, her expression shifting from fake tears to calculated charm.

"Deputy, I need to press charges," she sniffled. "That woman—"

Foster held up a finger, silencing her. "I'll get to that."

Amanda blinked, taken aback. "Excuse me?"

He raised the phone. "This was reported stolen. Mind unlocking it for me so we can confirm it's yours?"

Her lips parted. A flicker of panic danced in her eyes before she quickly masked it.

"I—I don't have my passcode memorized. I, um, use Face ID," she said, too fast.

Foster smirked. "That so?" He turned the phone toward her.

Amanda hesitated. Then, the screen unlocked.

Foster clicked on the video file. A second later, his expression went completely stone-cold.

"Amanda Johnson," he said, his voice dangerously quiet. "Turn around and place your hands behind your back."

Amanda's face drained of color.

"What?" she shrieked. "No—she *hit* me! She stole my phone! You can't do this! Do you know who my father is?!"

"Yeah," Foster said flatly, snapping the handcuffs over her wrists. "And I don't give a damn."

Amanda struggled, twisting in his grip, but he held firm. "You can't arrest me! That video wasn't—"

"You're under arrest for distribution and possession of illicit materials, blackmail, and harassment. You have the right to remain silent, and I highly suggest you use it."

Amanda froze.

I let out a breath I hadn't realized I was holding.

Foster turned back to me. "Technically, what you did could be considered assault." His voice softened, understanding clear in his eyes. "But under these circumstances, it sounds a hell of a lot like self-defense. You did what you needed to do."

I nodded quickly, still in shock.

Foster gestured toward one of the officers. "Book her."

Amanda screamed in protest as they loaded her into the back of the patrol car.

I stood there, stunned, shaking, but victorious.

It was over.

She was finally done.

CHAPTER TWENTY-SEVEN

Broken Lullabies

CONNOR

I stared at the floor, whiskey burning down my throat, thoughts spiraling with every bitter swallow. Grief shadowed my days—always lurking, patient.

After Alex, I thought pain couldn't dig deeper.

But it had.

The old wound had torn wide open, letting something darker seep in.

I took another swig, then slammed the glass onto the counter, breathing hard. Anger coiled tight in my chest, with nowhere to go.

I had to do something.

Anything to fix this gaping hole opening up beneath me, ready to swallow me whole.

My pulse roared as I lifted my gaze to the staircase.

The nursery. A room frozen in time. A cruel fucking lie.

Breaths ragged, I gripped the whiskey bottle and stormed up the stairs, each step heavier as grief and resentment knotted my muscles. I forced myself forward. The staircase seemed to stretch before me, the task to reach the top like a hike up a steep mountain. By the time I reached the door, my hands trembled violently.

For months, I hadn't been able to open it.

Now, I *kicked it in*.

The door crashed open, echoing through the empty house. Blood thundered in my ears as my gaze fell upon the nursery, setting the bottle of whiskey on the floor against the wall

A sick memorial to something that never was.

I worked my hands. Open. Closed. Open. Closed. A muscle clicked in my jaw, then... I tore the crib apart, wood splintering beneath my hands just like the lies that had splintered my world. The changing table followed, crashing violently, scattering tiny clothes I'd carefully folded—clothes that I'd painstakingly picked out, yet had never been meant for anyone real. Bitter laughter escaped me, harsh and hollow.

"Why?!" I let out a guttural roar.

My fists tore through the rocking chair next, the one I'd painstakingly crafted, sanded, and stained until it was perfect. It splintered against the far wall, which cracked under the brunt of my rage. Hands empty, they curled into tight fists, striking the walls relentlessly until my knuckles split raw and red.

I staggered back, panting, my strength drained.

The nursery—wrecked.

Just like me.

Collapsing onto the floor, I reached over and yanked the whiskey to my lips, drinking straight from the bottle, desperate for numbness that wouldn't come. My head sank into the shallow dent in the wall. I closed my eyes—not from fatigue, but because I couldn't stand the sight of the disheveled room, the blood-smeared holes, the fractured chaos that threatened to reveal memories I wasn't ready to face.

I inhaled, drawing in the courage I needed to face the demons crowding the room. I clenched my jaw, teeth grinding as I opened my eyes and let it all in.

Amid the wreckage lay a tiny stuffed bear—the first gift I'd chosen for a daughter I'd been so happy to bring into this world. My blood stained its soft fur as I reached over and clutched it, praying this was all a bad dream.

My head dropped back against the wall.

Exhaustion dragged against my bones.

I barely registered soft footsteps approaching, hesitant and careful.

"Connor?" My name echoed in the distance.

Then, fingertips gently touched my face.

Warm. Tender. Familiar.

Lucy.

I blinked, my vision hazy with alcohol. Her face slowly came into focus, those hazel eyes filled with tenderness only she possessed. Her dark, auburn hair fell forward as she crouched before me. She cupped my face, thumbs grazing my cheekbones, holding my gaze until I couldn't look away.

"Connor," she whispered.

Why was she here? Why wasn't she running from this disaster I'd become?

I braced myself. Waiting for her to take in the destruction, finally see the damage that lived inside me, then run.

Instead, she reached for my hand—the one still gripping the bloodied bear.

"Let go," she murmured.

I couldn't.

She leaned closer, her eyes shining with compassion and pain. "You loved me through my grief. Let me love you through yours."

Gently, patiently, she pried my fingers open. The bear tumbled from my grip, landing with a soft bounce at my side.

Lucy lifted my battered hands into hers placing feather-light kisses over my fingers. Her gaze careful, filled with understanding, she pulled me into her, her touch free of pity or judgment. She just held me.

For the first time since the lie shattered, I felt myself breathe again.

I took in her scent. Lavender and honey. My body relaxed into hers.

"Come on," she coaxed, guiding me to sit upright, her gentleness a balm to the rawness inside me. "Let me take care of you."

Part of me wanted to push her away. But I didn't.

I couldn't.

She guided me to the bathroom, sat me down on the edge of the soaking tub, and began tending my wounds. I watched her, confusion mingling with awe.

"Lucy," I rasped, the question barely forming on my lips. "Why?"

"Why?" She furrowed her brow, her nose scrunching up in that adorable way it tended to do when she was confused.

I tried again, hissing as she cleaned the cuts over my knuckles. "You're still here. Why?"

Her gaze softened, warmth pouring from those almond-shaped eyes I loved so damn much. "Because you don't have to face this alone."

My throat tightened. Lucy believed *she* was broken—but until this moment, she hadn't truly seen the depths of my own baggage. She didn't know I'd spent so long pushing everyone away, determined never to rely on *anyone* again. Not after she'd left. Not after Alex. Not after the idea of *her*. Now Bob...

My chest filled with a heavy sorrow, a boulder sized burden that I kept trying to ignore.

"Let me in." She whispered. "I'm here."

My head dropped, and soothing fingernails scratched along my scalp. I closed my eyes, warring with who I was without Lucy and the man I wanted to be for her here and now.

When I was with Amanda, it'd been out of guilt and obligation. I never let her in. But with Lucy, everything was different. She made it easy, made me believe I could survive even this.

My voice cracked, but the words spilled out, raw and honest. "Stay."

She nodded, tugging me up and guiding me to the bed before lying beside me. I wrapped an arm around her, pulling her against me as I buried my face in her hair. Her fingers intertwined gently with mine beneath the blankets and gratitude filled me. I wasn't alone. Thank God I wasn't alone.

I released a shaky breath.

Maybe—just maybe—I'd survive this after all.

Because she was here.

Because she loved me.

Chapter Twenty-Eight

Spin, Truth, and Fire

Lucy

I lay awake, staring at the ceiling, unable to stop thinking about last night.

Connor. The nursery. A lost gaze. A man unraveling before my eyes..

Even in sleep, his grip on me remained firm. His arm locked around my waist, body curled protectively against mine.

My fingers twitched over his forearm, uncertainty creeping in. I wanted to be his anchor. But how? I wasn't like him. I didn't always know the right thing to do.

I turned to face him, taking him in. He ground his teeth, his face twisting in the remnants of whatever nightmares followed him.

I should have said something last night.

But what do you say to someone who'd already lost too much?

My phone buzzed.

I startled, blinking myself back to the present.

Connor stirred beside me, his grip tightening, pulling me closer as if his body knew I might slip away.

Carefully, I reached for my phone, squinting against the glare of the screen.

James Duncan.

A pit formed in my stomach.

I shot upright, answering before my mind could process the weight of an early-morning call from my attorney.

"Hello?"

James sighed—never a good sign. "Good morning, Ms. Campbell. It's James. I wanted to inform you that Amanda Johnson has been released on bail."

The bedspread bunched in my fists.

"What?" The word barely escaped my lips.

"As your attorney, I strongly advise you to avoid any direct contact with her. If she reaches out to you or continues making threats, we'll move forward with filing a restraining order."

I exhaled slowly, but it did nothing to ease the tension in my chest. "Okay. Thank you for letting me know. If she contacts me, I'll call you, and we'll go from there."

"That's the best course of action," he agreed. A pause. Then, his tone shifted. "I wanted to inform you that a formal investigation has been launched into Callum Prescott."

Everything inside me went still.

James proceeded carefully with practiced professionalism. "Unfortunately, the video Amanda had in her possession was obtained through an untraceable source. The aggressor in question is masked in the footage and operates outside U.S. jurisdiction."

A cold wave swept through me, draining all the color from my skin.

"You're saying there's nothing you can do," I murmured, my voice detached, distant.

James hesitated. "We can't prosecute him at this time, no. Without verifiable evidence tying Callum directly to the crime, law enforcement cannot pursue charges internationally."

I squeezed my eyes shut. Fresh pain sliced through wounds that had never fully healed.

"But," James continued, his tone shifting, "the video does serve as direct evidence of extortion against Miss Johnson. The case against her is getting stronger by the day. In fact, after your encounter at *The Rustic Roast*, several people have come forward, willing to testify against her."

Relief crashed into me so suddenly that my entire body sagged.

"That's... that's good."

"It is. As long as you avoid further confrontation with her, everything will continue to run smoothly."

I rubbed my temple, the emotional whiplash leaving me drained. "Thanks, James. I'm sure we'll talk soon."

"Yes. If anything changes, I'll be in touch. Have a good rest of your day."

"You too."

I hung up, staring blankly at the blankets.

Connor shifted beside me, his voice rough with exhaustion. "What was that about?"

His warm, solid presence pressed against my side.

I winced. "There's a lot you missed yesterday."

His eyes sharpened, sleep fading as he propped himself up. "Tell me."

Something inside me recoiled. I hesitated, wanting to protect him. But he needed to know.

"I went to confront Amanda yesterday."

Tension bled into the room.

Connor's entire body stiffened, his gaze narrowing into something lethal.

"She..." I couldn't say it.

"What?" he growled.

I lay back down, staring at the ceiling, suddenly unable to meet his eyes. "Instead of taking ownership for everything she's done, she tried blackmailing me with a video."

Silence.

Suffocating, deafening *silence*.

Finally, Connor croaked, "What kind of video?"

My stomach twisted. *Disgusting*. That's what Amanda had called me.

And right now?

I felt like it.

"Connor, maybe we should talk about this later," I whispered.

His hands clenched into fists. "No. Tell me everything."

I shook my head. If I told him, it would only break him further.

"Lucy." His voice was low, dangerous. "No secrets. Remember?"

I closed my eyes. "Right. No secrets."

I let out a shaky breath. Then I told him.

Connor tried and failed to look calm, the muscle in his jaw ticking violently.

"I'm so fucking sorry, Lucy."

Sorry.

I was so *sick* of everyone telling me they were sorry. Sorry for my father's passing. Sorry for lying. Sorry for not believing me. Sorry. Sorry. *Sorry.*

"It's fine," I clipped.

"It's not. I'm going to fix this." Connor clenched his jaw, then stood from the bed, shoving a hand through his hair.

"Connor, don't…"

He didn't say a word as he grabbed his phone off the nightstand and strode toward the sliding door that led to his porch.

The second he stepped outside, I exhaled shakily and finally glanced at my phone screen.

News alerts. DMs. Everything was there for the entire world to see. The entire show-down at *The Rustic Roast* on every online platform.

My hands clenched around my phone, my pulse hammering against my ribs. *How did this get out?*

Through the sliding door, Connor's voice carried—low, short, barely restrained. His fingers flexed at his sides, his free hand clenching and unclenching like he was fighting the urge to hit something.

A cold shiver crawled up my spine.

Who the hell is he talking to?

I stared at my phone, then back at the porch door where Connor paced like a caged animal.

Everything was falling apart. And everyone knew. My past. My present. The lack of a case against a masked attacker. It was all laid bare for all to see.

I couldn't think.

I couldn't breathe.

More notifications. Each one a gruesome car wreck I couldn't look away from.

Curiosity, twisted with dread, led me to a trending thread.

"Did you read about Lucy Campbell? She was pregnant at 16! Where's the baby now???"

"Always thought the Campbells were the epitome of grace. Guess everyone has skeletons."

"Feels like a smear campaign. Why dig into her past now?"

Each comment sliced through me. Some sharp, others dull, but the onslaught was relentless.

I've done it.

I've ruined my father's legacy.

And for what?

So I could finally stand up to Amanda?

Aunt Diane was right. I'm not worthy of this responsibility…

More notifications rolled in. This was spiraling out of control, becoming the kind of story that followed you for a lifetime.

Then...

I read another comment that sent ice through my veins:

"Looks like another case of someone trying to play the victim card. Not buying it."

My lungs ceased moving. The words blurred.

"Victim card?" I whispered, my voice shaking. "Screw you."

The faint sound of the sliding door opening and closing, then movement as Connor sank the bed down beside me. One look and his hands grasped mine. "Breathe, Luce. It's going to be okay. Just breathe."

I gasped, the air stinging as panic lodged itself in my chest, constricting, suffocating.

"What the hell am I going to do?" I choked out.

Connor's hand slid over mine, steady, grounding. "It's going to be okay. We're going to fight back, Lucy."

"How? Who were you talking to?"

Connor's eyes flitted down, unable to meet my face. "Amanda's father."

"What did he say?" I bit out.

His throat bobbed. "He wants me to convince you to drop the charges against Amanda."

I stiffened, then shot him a narrowed stare.

"Don't worry, that's not happening," he assured me, his tone firm, unwavering. "But it's clear, his team is already working on a counterattack."

"Counterattack? Against what? I didn't attack anyone," I spat.

Connor shrugged. "Well... there's a viral video of you punching Amanda all over the internet."

"I know," I grumbled.

"Unfortunately most of the initial articles make Amanda look terrible, which puts Tom's reelection in jeopardy." He ran his fingers through his hair. "Lucy, I've spent enough time around the Johnsons to know how they play this game. They'll try to discredit you, launch their own articles, twist the narrative.

"They've already started. It's so bad, Connor."

"Is there anyone you know who can help do some damage control?" he suggested.

"My mother can help." My head throbbed. "She's dealt with PR nightmares for years. She'll know what to do."

He looked at me, his blue eyes full of quiet determination. "I'll be here every step of the way, Luce. We'll figure this out. Together."

I met his gaze, comfort swelled in my chest.

"I'll call her," I whispered.

Connor pulled me closer, pressing an easy kiss to my forehead.

I reached for my phone and dialed.

"Lucy, darling." Her voice smooth, controlled, but I heard the strain beneath it. "Are you alright?"

My voice cracked, fragile as glass. "Not great. You're on speaker with Connor. I need some advice."

A distant thought echoed in my mind, I hadn't asked my mother for advice in... I didn't think I *had* ever asked her for advice.

Her tone immediately shifted into something ready, sure, prepared—like she'd been waiting her entire life for this moment. "Of course. What can I do?"

I hesitated, then forced the words out. "How do we stop these articles from hurting the ranch?"

A pause. Then, her British accent clipped, "Lucy, I need complete honesty. What else will be said? What's true, what's not? I can't help if you hold back."

I closed my eyes and stiffened. Connor's hands massaged the length of my arms, gentle and reassuring. His support gave me strength, courage. I straightened my spine. Lifted my chin as I told her everything.

Through every painful detail—Amanda's lies, the string of awful men in my life... Connor never let go of my hand.

Silence stretched before my mother exhaled.

"Oh, Lucy." Her voice wavered, just for a second. "I cannot believe you've carried all this alone for so many years."

A lump rose in my throat.

"Thank you for trusting me, darling." Then, her tone hardened. "And that brute of an ex of yours will *not* get away with this." She exhaled, her elegance cracking with anger.

A muscle feathered in Connor's jaw.

Then, sadness crept into my bones at their reactions.

"I don't know what to do," I admitted with quiet reluctance.

She didn't hesitate. "Well, darling, the first rule of damage control: you can't fight what you don't understand. What's being published? A scandal? A smear campaign? A passing headline?"

My eyes widened. "I don't know."

"That's fine. The second rule: never let someone else tell your story first." Her voice turned sharp, authoritative. "Amanda must answer for her crimes. If you let this die down she'll always believe she can get away with it."

My throat tightened. "What do we do?"

"Get ahead of it. Release a statement to the press before the Johnsons further spin their own version. If you're not comfortable with cameras, issue a written statement, but have James review it first to ensure nothing you say can hurt your case."

I frowned. "I don't use social media. I never have."

"Like it or not, Campbell Ranch is a brand, and you are now part of that brand. I'm sorry to say you can't avoid the rest of the world anymore, Lucy."

I hadn't even thought of it like that.

"Your father had a small marketing team. Contact Myka. She knows your brand inside and out. I'll send you her contact information. But Lucy, you must handle this carefully. Start considering what you want people to think when they hear 'Campbell Ranch?'"

My chest clenched. "Integrity. Generosity. The things my dad stood for..."

"Then we'll start with a charity event. Something that embodies the ranch's values. Reach out to your allies in the industry, especially in White River. We're going to control the narrative before the bad press does."

I hesitated. "We?"

Her voice softened. "Yes, we."

Connor shifted beside me. "We could do something with the 4-H kids. Or a fundraiser for the local FFA chapter. Something real, something the town can rally behind."

A smile tugged at my lips. "I love those ideas. The Future Farmers of America chapter here in White River is such an important program for our local teens."

"I love it, too," my mother added with sincerity.

A lump formed in my throat. "Thanks, Mother. I really appreciate you staying and helping. I know how much you're needed back in London."

The walls between us began to crumble.

Her tone softened further. "Lucy, my sweet, darling girl, I am not abandoning you now. Not when you need me. I can help. And if you don't have a public relations expert, I have one for you. They're based in the U.S. and have never let me down."

"Mother, I really do appreciate it."

A pause. Then, softer this time, almost hesitant:

"You can call me Mom, if you'd like."

Warmth unfurled in my chest. "Thanks, Mom."

Her voice softened even more, filled with something I hadn't heard in a long time—true emotion, not just practiced politeness. "My pleasure. *Truly*." She paused a moment before she continued, "People admire strength in the face of adversity. Not theatrics. You have Sinclair in your blood as much as Campbell. You can do this."

She was right.

I had spent *years* misjudging her, thinking she was cold, distant. Maybe in reality she'd simply never let emotions overpower her when it came to business. And now I needed to do the same.

Her voice dropped low with warning. "Amanda is reckless, Lucy. She won't go down quietly and neither should you."

A flicker of fire sparked within me. Not fear. Not doubt. Just strength. *Mine.*

I lifted my chin, resolve settling into my bones as her words filled me with a newfound confidence. "You're right."

"Good girl. Now, call James after we hang up and run everything by him before you release a statement. Understood?"

"Yes. I'll make sure I do that."

She let out a breath. "Good. And Lucy?"

I swallowed hard. "Yeah?"

"I'm always here. Thank you for trusting me."

Another unexpected lump formed in my throat. "Yeah. I'm glad I called." I gave an appreciative smile to Connor. Then I frowned as one last question came to mind. "So, you think I shouldn't take the mayor's deal and drop the charges?"

"No, darling. As your father would have said... 'we don't negotiate with terrorists.'"

A small, unexpected laugh escaped me. "That's *exactly* what he would say."

And, with one crisis down, I felt more than ready to take control of the rest. "And Mom?"

"Yes, darling?"

"Sam told me it was him." I frowned. "I can understand why you'd believe him, but why didn't you ever tell me?"

She sighed. "You were losing enough. I didn't want you to feel like you'd lost your best friend, too."

My eyes widened. Every emotion roiled through me: grief, exhaustion, regret. My jaw trembled before I gently cried, "Thank you. I love you, Mom... I'm sorry for being so awful to you..."

"Oh, Lucy! I love you so much. There's nothing to forgive. I hope I can earn your forgiveness for not believing you. I should have listened..." Her voice wavered with her own tears.

I shook my head, sniffling. "Can we just start over?"

"That... that would be truly wonderful, darling. I would love that."

After an emotional goodbye I hung up the call, gripping the phone tight in my hand. I stared blankly at the wall, unable to process all the feelings and thoughts churning inside me.

Without a word, Connor pried my phone from my grip, holding the power button until the screen went black.

"That's enough for now," he said firmly.

"I have to fix this. You heard my mom..."

"Later." His blue eyes softened. "Come on, Luce. You need real food, not more stress. We both do."

I hesitated. But Connor pressed a soft kiss to my temple and pulled the blanket away, tugging at me.

"Up," he teased. "Before I throw you over my shoulder."

Despite everything, a small breath of amusement escaped me. "You wouldn't."

His smirk deepened. "Want to find out?"

He took my hand and led me downstairs. His hand stayed firm at the small of my back, keeping me aware of his presence. Keeping me from spiraling. And with that, I knew that with him... I was safe.

CHAPTER TWENTY-NINE

More Than a Meme

LUCY

By the next day through the following week, I had an entire team working to ensure nothing in the press jeopardized what we were building. The legal statement was finalized and sent to news outlets alongside a carefully crafted press release. Myka had an entire social media campaign ready to launch, with a newly hired photographer on her way to shadow me any day. Soon enough, this entire situation would be buried beneath a narrative of strength and resilience—not scandal and tragedy.

I read over the laundry list of strategic moves and damage control my PR guy, Vincent, had planned. I'd already completed several interviews, with more lined up throughout the week—including one with a national magazine and several podcasts with highly respected voices in the ranching community.

This was my chance to show the world I was more.

More than whispers of inheritance, grief, and drama.

More than a viral video.

More than a meme.

Unfortunately, my little indiscretion was still *everywhere*.

For every video my team managed to take down, five more popped up in its place. The internet latched onto the moment like wildfire, turning my loss of control into a spectacle.

As I sat at the computer in my father's office... *my* office... my phone rang.

"Hello?"

"Hi, darling. I canceled my flight and was able to extend my stay at the hotel." My mother had thrown herself into planning our charity gala for the local Future Farmers of America program.

"Oh, perfect. Thank you so much!" I smiled.

"Eric's coming over later to overhaul your wardrobe from London fashion icon to badass cattle rancher."

"Mom!" I gasped. I'd never heard her say so much as a "crap" or "damn it" in my entire life.

She chuckled, "Oh Lucy, I was married to your father. You can't truly think I've never cursed before."

My eyes popped from their sockets. "I can and I certainly do."

"Well, I apologize for never acting human around you. I'm remedying that now." I could hear the smile in her voice.

"Well thank you for calling. I need to get back to work. And I really love everything you sent me on the plans for the charity event." I said, trying to exude every ounce of gratitude I felt. This gala wasn't just about optics. It was about values. About what Campbell Ranch stood for. What *I* stood for.

"No problem, darling. Have a good rest of your day."

We hung up and I returned to my spreadsheets. I didn't stop to drink. I didn't stop to eat. I worked through lunch with stubborn determination to prove something: that I was worthy.

By mid-afternoon I moved onto updating orders, but my heart wasn't in it. Mentally I prepared for the most important call of my new career: convincing our most prominent buyer, Weston Calloway, to keep us on as his beef distributor. As I mouthed some key reasons Campbell ranch is the best choice to do business with, a text lit up my screen.

Kayla:

> Hi Lucy! This is Kayla Schultz, the photographer Myka hired to shadow you over the next week. I'll be arriving at the ranch tomorrow at 7 AM. I was told I could stay in the trailer beside your house for the week. Let me know if that works—I look forward to meeting you!

I typed out a polite confirmation and got back to work.

Minutes later, Kyle entered the office, quiet but purposeful.

"Lucy, I have those reports done—should be in your email now."

I glanced up. "Thanks, Kyle." I pulled up the report and scanned the numbers.

Kyle lingered in the doorway.

I looked up, the words coming with ease. "If we allocate more land to rotational grazing, we'll improve soil health and maximize pasture use. Let's start small—test it with one herd and monitor the results."

Kyle nodded approvingly. "Smart move, boss."

I hesitated before he turned to leave. "Kyle."

He glanced back. "What's up?"

I leaned back in my chair, brow furrowed. "The guys all live in the bunkhouse, but you're head of operations. Were you supposed to have your own cabin, or... *wait*. Is that trailer yours?"

Kyle chuckled, his dark eyes bright with amusement. "Don't worry about it, Luce. Yeah, the trailer's mine. But I offered it to Connor while I was on leave so he could be onsite while..."

His smile faltered. A flicker of pain and grief crossed his face before he swallowed hard, his throat bobbing. His gaze drifted, lost in a memory.

I sat up, concern tightening in my chest. "Kyle, you okay?"

He exhaled sharply, shaking his head like he could dispel the weight of it.

"I was there when it all happened," he murmured. "I should have gotten your dad to a doctor sooner—" His voice caught, his jaw clenching tight.

I stood abruptly, my arms wrapping around him before I could think better of it.

"No." My voice firm but gentle. "It wasn't your fault, Kyle. You didn't know how sick he was. Nobody did."

His shoulders shook beneath my grip. "Lucy... I am so sorry."

I felt like I could fall apart with him. But for his sake, I couldn't.

I pulled back just enough to meet his eyes. "Kyle, you gave him more time. Time to call me. Time I wouldn't have had if you hadn't gotten him to the hospital when you did. My dad was so stubborn—he never went to the doctor. You *couldn't* have gotten him to go sooner. I swear to you, there's nothing you could have done differently."

Kyle's eyes glistened, and his chest rose with a deep, shuddering breath. "Thank you." His voice was barely above a whisper. "I don't deserve your kindness."

I let out a heavy sigh. "Yes, you do. My father loved you. He respected you. He wouldn't blame you, and neither will I." I gave him a small, knowing smile. "Like he always said, shit happens."

Kyle let out a wet chuckle, shaking his head. "Yeah... that sounds like him."

The tension eased just a little.

"Now," I said, straightening. "I totally just gave your trailer away to my photographer. I'm going to fix that right now."

Kyle shook his head, a real smile breaking through. "She can use it. It's only temporary. Then I'll move it back beside the bunkhouse so you can have more privacy.

I tilted my head. "I appreciate that. But I can have Kayla stay in my guest room instead."

Kyle arched a brow. "You want a stranger in your house?"

I hesitated. "...That does sound a little weird."

He smirked. "Let her take my trailer, and when she's gone, we'll stop letting people borrow it. Deal?"

I huffed a laugh. "Deal."

Kyle nodded. "I'll loop Connor in on the grazing plan and get the guys on board."

"Perfect."

"Hey, boss?"

"Hmm?"

"What's actually going on between you and Connor? Was that kiss at *The Saloon* really just a performance?" Kyle asked, before stepping back his face falling. "I'm sorry. It's none of my business."

"No. I get it..." My stomach knotted at the idea of lying about my relationship once again. "Does it matter?"

Kyle shrugged. "I care about you both. I just want to see you two happy. And..."

I frowned. "And?"

"Forgive me, Lucy. But I don't want to see Connor hurt again. So, *if* you two are together... Please be careful with him. That's all." Not waiting for a response, he turned and left.

I sat stunned and blinking.

The office landline rang.

I straightened, shaking off the conversation. Then, I pressed the receiver to my ear. "Campbell Ranch, this is Lucy."

A deep, authoritative voice responded. "Ms. Campbell, this is Weston Calloway. I'm returning your call. Though I must say, I was expecting to speak with Connor. What can I help you with today?"

Weston was a major buyer. Connor had encouraged me to handle this myself. If I could prove my competence to him, we'd be set—our other buyers would likely follow his lead.

This was the most important phone call of my new life as owner of Campbell Ranch.

I steadied my voice. "Yes. I wanted to personally assure you that despite the rumors, Campbell Ranch is running as smoothly as ever. I was hoping to confirm your next order, as I know you were undecided."

Weston sighed. "Lucy, one thing you need to know about me—I don't like drama. What's stopping me from going elsewhere? Like next door to Lochland Farms?"

I resisted the urge to roll my eyes. "Lochland Farms is fantastic, but they're a smaller operation. With the quantity and frequency of your orders, Connor's ranch wouldn't be able to keep up with demand. But I think you already knew that."

A pause.

Then, a low chuckle. "I like you already, Miss Campbell. And you're on schedule?"

"Absolutely. Quality is guaranteed."

Weston hummed. "I've been a buyer for years—I know when someone's struggling with the media and how that impacts business. Bad press shakes confidence. So tell me, Lucy... are you offering discounts to retain your current buyers?"

A test.

Connor warned me about this.

I smiled. "Campbell Ranch produces some of the highest-quality beef in Montana. That level of quality doesn't come cheap. If cost is your priority, I'd suggest looking elsewhere."

Another pause.

Then, a satisfied chuckle. "Alright, you have a deal. We'll stick with Campbell Ranch for now. Your father never let us down, and it sounds like you're just as shrewd. I respect that. If our next order meets expectations, we'll continue doing business."

Pride swelled in my chest.

I wasn't just surviving in this role. I was thriving.

I could do this.

I *was* doing this.

CHAPTER THIRTY

Where the Stars Bear Witness

LUCY

I sat on the back porch taking in the evening sun as it melted into the horizon. The rolling pastures breathed in the glow of dusk. Tall grasses swayed in the evening breeze, carrying the crisp scent of pine and sun-warmed earth. The expanse of my land stretched before me, endless and untamed, each acre a testament to the legacy I was still learning how to hold onto.

As the last rays of sunlight dipped below the jagged peaks in the distance, I settled into the chair my father built with his own two hands, tucked into the quiet corner where the deck met the back of the house.

My fingers idly strummed the rough, sun-bleached wood of the table. My laptop sat open and fully charged in front of me, waiting for Connor to arrive for our first end-of-day meeting. I decided I couldn't let my schooling go to waste. With Connor's support and encouragement we made tentative plans on how to make a remote ownership work, so I could still fulfill my dream of becoming a veterinarian. The first step: weekly recorded meetings.

A slow smile spread across my face as I spotted Connor riding up on his dark brown Quarter Horse, Blaze.

He tied him off at the porch post and joined me—but not before bending down and kissing me long and deep.

I nearly fell off my chair.

When he pulled away, I blinked in a daze.

"Ready to get this meeting started?" His deep voice teased, mischief twinkling in his blue eyes.

I exhaled, steadying myself. "First off, no fair. I'm completely distracted now."

Connor grinned, clearly satisfied with his work.

"Second, what if someone saw you?" I crossed my arms, trying for clear displeasure, but the warmth in my voice betrayed me.

His brows furrowed, his voice clipped, defensive. "I checked to make sure no one was around."

I cleared my throat. "I'm so sorry, Connor.. I know this isn't ideal…"

"Lucy, it's okay. This is your future in the balance. I don't want to ever do anything to jeopardize that." He assured me, reaching out and running a soothing hand over my arm. "Sorry I got frustrated. It's just been tough these last two weeks."

"I know… and thank you. Honestly, I've been wanting to kiss you all day. I really… enjoyed that." I gave him a slow, over-the-top wink and a wag of my brow.

Connor's smirk broadened as he leaned back against the railing, watching me with that damned self-satisfied expression.

I pressed on, feeling my cheeks go scarlet. "Since this is our first official meeting, I wanted to set the standard for how they will go—both now and when I'm away. I've shared a document with our meeting minutes via email. You can review it later or pull it up now. I'll be updating it every time we meet so we have a clear record of everything we go over."

Connor's warm gaze was laced with pride. "Look at you. You're a natural."

"And *you're* still distracting."

His grin deepened as we took our seats at the table.

I powered through. "First order of business—how do we ensure I stay involved in day-to-day operations while I'm at school?"

Connor leaned forward, his expression serious now. "I'll give you daily reports, and we can schedule a standing video meeting each week. Do Fridays work? You can send me anything outside that via email. Also, I was thinking of setting up security cameras so you can check on the animals anytime. The vet's already agreed to email you reports."

"Fridays are perfect, and I love the idea of cameras."

"Anything else?"

"Just that you can call me anytime—day or night—if something urgent comes up."

Connor nodded. "Can do."

"Second order of business—managing my time in person. I'll fly back for every holiday and break. And I've made a decision about when I'm moving back." I paused, flicking my eyes up to meet his. "Since my undergrad has to be in person, I'm stuck studying there until I've finished with it, but after that, I can do postgrad online which means... I'll be moving back here in a year!"

Connor's bright eyes glimmered. "That's the best news I've heard all day."

"Good," I smiled, letting the news settle between us before pressing on with the agenda.

"For legal purposes, James advised that we document all meetings, mentorship moments, and major decisions. It'll make it easier for me to officially take full ownership and prove we met all the requirements of my father's will."

Connor nodded. "Makes sense."

"At the bottom of the minutes, I added a section where you can list everything you've taught me so far."

Connor frowned, leaning back in his chair. "Can I just say how much I hate this stipulation? I don't think I have much more to teach you. Your idea about allocating more land? Spot on. You're capable, smart, you *grew up* here..."

A pleased smile tugged at my lips. "Thanks, Connor. But it's what my dad wanted. He never mentored me, but he *did* mentor you. There are things he was able to teach you that—"

He swallowed, his jaw tightening. "That he can't teach you now."

The weight of it sat thick and heavy between us. My eyes burned, but I forced myself to nod.

"Well," Connor cleared his throat, "you're still the boss."

I huffed a small laugh. "Hopefully, everyone else sees it that way. I'm basically a stranger who has very little time to prove herself over this next year . Which is going to be hard to do, because I'll be in another country putting my studies above this place." I frowned, the truth of my words sinking in.

Connor held my gaze. "No one is going to think that. They already see your father in you, Lucy." He reached across the table, his hand settling over mine.

A lump rose in my throat. "Really? You're not just saying that?"

"No." His grip tightened slightly, reassuring. "They were talking about it after you left today. They all felt like a part of him was still here—because of you. You have nothing to worry about. The ranch hands already like and respect you."

My stomach fluttered, warmth spreading through my chest.

Connor's voice softened. "I promised I'd never lie to you, Lucy. No secrets, no drama. Not between us."

I exhaled slowly, letting his words sink in. "Thank you. I... *really* needed to hear that."

Connor nodded, then leaned back, his familiar smirk returning. "You should join us tonight. Every week the workers from both ranches get together for drinks, food, maybe some music. This week everyone's meeting outside the bunkhouse here at Campbell Ranch. Next week it's at my place."

I hesitated, but his easy confidence made it hard to say no. "Yeah, I could stop by for a bit."

Connor's grin widened. "Great. They'll be happy to see you."

I bit my lip, a flicker of uncertainty passing through me, then nodded. "What time does it start?"

The smell of charred burgers and burning mesquite drifted through the cool night air, mingling with the low hum of conversation and bursts of laughter from the gathering.

The fire pit behind the bunkhouse crackled, sending orange embers drifting into the dark Montana sky.

Connor sat on a log beside the fire pit as I approached, the warmth from the flames wrapping around me like a welcome embrace.

"Well, look who we finally get to steal for a night!" Johnny grinned, tipping his beer in my direction.

A few of the other guys cheered and whistled playfully.

I smirked. "Well, I'm happy to be here," I chuckled. "You know, I used to sneak out when I was a kid to come to these Friday night get-togethers, hanging around until someone finally told me to get to bed."

"I didn't realize you were so rebellious," Connor teased.

I rolled my eyes. "Yup, that's me. Such a rebel."

"Hey lady! 'Bout time we had another woman around here." Paula nudged my arm with a wide grin.

"Agreed. I was starting to feel outnumbered," I teased.

Paula snorted. "Honey, you don't know the half of it." She tipped her drink toward the crowd. "These guys don't know how to take advice unless it's shouted at 'em or you hit 'em over the head with it."

I grinned. "Good thing I can do both."

"That's what I like to hear," Paula smirked.

Kyle handed me a cold beer. "Here, Lucy. You're officially one of us now."

I took the bottle, clinking it against his. "Appreciate it."

I settled onto one of the wooden logs, pulling my jacket closer as the chill from the night air nipped at my skin. Across from me, Johnny leaned forward, gesturing toward the sky.

"You ever see anything like that back in London?" he asked, tilting his head toward the stars scattered across the night sky.

"Definitely not," I mused, inhaling the crisp night air, enjoying the sting as it filled my lungs.

Johnny smacked his lips. "Now's the time where they really light up. Just look at 'em. Imagine how long it's taken for their light to reach us from however many light-years away."

I followed his gaze, my breath catching as the vastness of the Montana twilight stretched endlessly above us. "It's beautiful."

"Generation after generation, men... *and* women," he corrected, flinching away from Paula's glare. "Well, people like us have been working these lands, staring up at this very same sky, for how many thousands of years?" he continued, voice softer now. "This land was once rough, wild. This untamed thing until our ancestors settled here. It has history. If only this land could talk. What memories could it share? You know?"

"You're starting to lose us, Johnny," Kyle jabbed playfully.

Johnny swatted the air. "What I'm trying to say is that once your dad chose this place, made roots on this land, he began a new story. Over the last several decades, the men and women who've worked here put their blood, sweat, and tears into shaping this place into what you see today. And now? It's yours, Lucy. Part of your story, too."

Something deep inside me settled.

His words were a reminder.

This place, these people—they weren't just employees. They were family.

"Thank you, Johnny," I breathed.

Connor's hand brushed my shoulder as he walked past, slow heat radiated beneath his touch.

Paula took a slow sip of her beer, joining me on the log, the fire crackling as embers popped, floating effortlessly towards the night sky before their orange light dimmed and turned to wisps of ash. "You're good for him, you know."

I glanced at her, surprised. "Who?"

She nodded to Connor who joined a group of guys gathered around the grill, her hard gaze steady. "Never liked Amanda. Wasn't right for him. Never really *saw* him. Not like you do."

I swallowed down how honored, how touched her words made me feel, giving her a soft smile. "Thank you, Paula. But we're not—"

Before I could say more, someone handed Connor a guitar.

"Oh, hell no," he muttered, trying to pass it off.

"C'mon, boss!" Chuck urged. "Just one song!"

Everyone echoed their agreement, clapping and stomping playfully.

Connor's ears turned pink. "You're all so needy."

I smirked. "Come on Lochland, let's hear one."

His blue eyes locked onto mine, something dangerous and teasing flickering there.

"Fine. But only *one*."

Everyone cheered as he returned to the fire pit, guitar in hand. He settled back down and strummed the first few chords.

The moment he started singing, I forgot how to breathe.

The rich, gritty warmth of his voice wrapped around me, pulling me into something deeper than the song itself. He wasn't just playing for them.

He was playing for *me*.

My chest tightened, my entire body attuned to every note, every subtle shift in his expression.

I was falling. *Hard.*

For him.

For this place.

For these people.

And as the fire burned brighter as Kyle tossed in a fresh piece of firewood, the stars stretched above us, and Connor's voice filled the night...

I never wanted to leave. Yet, being surrounded by people who weren't just coworkers but family, one absence gnawed at me.

Sam.

The thought hit fast, sharp. My best friend should have been here—but he wasn't. Because of his *own* awful choices, the wounds still too raw for me to touch.

I shoved the thoughts back into their box, and reached for another beer from the open cooler.

As the night stretched on, the buzz of alcohol loosened my tongue and softened the edges of my control. I laughed more freely, more often. It felt good. Safe. But at some point, I caught myself leaning too easily into it.

Paula nudged my arm, then handed me another beer. "So, you and Connor aren't...?"

I hesitated. "Aren't what?"

She gave me a knowing look. "C'mon, Lucy. The pictures on *The Whisper*... the way he looks at you."

I flushed, heat crawling up my neck. "Paula... between you and me, we're working on making all of that go away. We have to keep things professional. At least for now."

Paula tilted her head, brow lifting in curiosity. "Because...?"

I sighed, lowering my voice. "You know what it's like. I have to prove myself. An owner of a company romantically involved with an employee, especially being a woman... It'd ruin my reputation, my father's legacy..."

Before I could say something I wasn't ready to share, I grabbed a red Solo cup and filled it with water.

Paula exhaled, watching me. "I get it. But none of us here would care. Hell, I for one am *rooting* for you two."

A lump formed in my throat. The words hovered—dangerous, tempting, ready to spill. But once I let them out, I couldn't take them back.

I forced a small smile. "I need some air."

She frowned, but didn't push. "Alright. Yeah."

I wandered across the property and found myself heading toward the barn. The crisp scent of fresh hay mixed with the lingering musk of cattle as I stepped inside. The calving barn stood mostly empty, save for a few heifers Kyle had brought in for routine checks.

The quiet felt almost unnatural. Soon enough, this space would be filled with the restless shifting of laboring cows, the sharp cries of newborn calves.

I walked through each section, running my hands along the fencing, pressing against the wood, absently testing for weak spots.

The barn door creaked behind me.

Boots scuffed against the floor. A warmth—*his* warmth—settled behind me before I even turned.

"Lucy..." Connor's rough voice, barely above a breath, overwhelmed my senses.

My pulse skittered. I swallowed hard and turned to face him. His blue eyes burned into mine, raw, intent.

"Connor... I think everyone already knows we're—"

I didn't get the chance to finish.

He stepped forward, his closeness radiating against my skin, stealing the rest of my words. His fingers brushed my cheek, trailed beneath my chin, tilting my face toward his.

His grip tightened. His voice was low, firm. Unshakable.

"I don't care."

A sharp inhale. My heart quickened.

His gaze burned into mine— certain, unwavering. "I've been waiting too long for a moment alone with you."

I stopped breathing.

"I can't stop thinking about you." His voice turned hoarse, rough with emotion. "Your lips. The smoothness of your skin. How perfectly we fit together..."

Each word crashed into me, one after the other.

I couldn't breathe.

He stepped closer, fingers curling around my hands. "But before I take you right here in the barn, I need you to understand... I am madly, deeply, head over heels in love with you. There's no force on this earth that could stop it. Not the distance between us. Not the time we'll spend apart this next year."

The raw urgency in his voice hit me like a freight train.

I turned and slid my hands up behind his neck, threading my fingers through his hair. "Not bad," I teased.

His dark brow lifted.

A slow grin. "You continue to express yourself so well... for a cowboy."

His low chuckle vibrated against me. He opened his mouth to speak, but I pulled him in. Our lips melded together, and everything else burned away. The waiting, the forced professionalism, the long hours of pretending we weren't desperate for each other.

His kiss became ravenous—not just a declaration, but a need. A need to show me. A need to make me feel how much he loved me.

I drew back, breathless, my fingers still tangled in his hair. "And I need you to know, I love you, too, Connor. Always. One year a part won't change that."

A sharp exhale. Something shifted in his expression.

Then, in one swift motion, he had me.

His arms crushed me against him, hands gripping my hips, lifting me like I weighed nothing. Before I could register it, my back hit a hay bale and my legs wrapped instinctively around his waist.

His hands roamed—tracing, gripping, claiming. I fisted his shirt, yanking him closer, needing more, needing everything.

Connor growled low in his throat. His lips left mine, blazing a trail down my throat—hot, frantic, unrelenting.

I arched into him, letting go of everything but this.

The way he felt. The way he consumed me.

His shirt? Gone. I barely registered the sound of buttons scattering. Mine? Ripped. Torn away like he couldn't stand the space between us.

I gasped as the cool air kissed my skin, but then—his mouth was on me. Hot, demanding, teeth grazing, tongue soothing.

"Connor," I breathed, my voice wrecked.

His fingers found the button of my jeans. Yanked. Then the slow slide of the zipper sent a shiver through me, before he pushed them down and the cool night air set goosebumps prickling over my skin.

I reached for his belt, but he beat me to it—tearing it loose, shoving his own jeans down just enough.

And then—

He was inside me.

A sharp cry escaped my lips as he filled me, stretched me, branded me.

Connor let out a ragged groan, burying his face in my neck. His body was heat and muscle and need, pushing me higher, harder.

I clung to him, nails biting into his back as he drove into me—fierce and unrelenting.

No holding back.

No careful restraint.

Just raw, desperate, blinding need.

Pleasure crackled through me, fast and unforgiving. I shattered around him, my body convulsing as I gasped, "Connor—"

His pace stuttered. A low, guttural groan tore from his throat as he followed, his body shuddering as he lost himself completely.

For a long moment, we remained there, tangled together, breathless, undone.

His forehead pressed against mine, our heartbeats still frantic but in sync.

I let out a shaky breath, sated and spent. "That was…"

Connor let out a husky chuckle, his arms tightening around me. "Yeah. It was."

I exhaled, sinking into him.

Here, with him, in this moment—

I wasn't just happy.

I wasn't just satisfied.

I was completely, utterly his.

CHAPTER THIRTY-ONE

No Filter

LUCY

"Okay, now lean up against that post right there. Yes. Tilt your chin up just a bit. Perfect!" Kayla snapped photo after photo in rapid succession.

I fought the urge to fidget, stomach churning with the distinct feeling that I could be doing literally anything more useful than posing for pictures. She gave me new directions, trying different angles, snapping what felt like hundreds of photos.

Then, Kayla's camera lowered, her brown eyes widening as she tucked a stray strand of her black pixie-cut hair behind her heavily pierced ear. Her expression shifted—like she'd just spotted something far more interesting than me.

I didn't have to turn my head to know...

It was Connor.

She bit her lip, waving her finely tattooed arm at him. "Hey! I'm Kayla, the photographer shadowing Lucy this week."

Connor tipped his hat. "Connor Lochland, ranch manager." His gaze found mine, sending a shiver of awareness through me. "Could you check on Willow and the pups for me? I need to run into town for supplies."

"Absolutely," I assured him. "See you later," I added, forcing a casual smile and an overly tight wave, too aware of Kayla's presence.

Connor nodded once. "Thanks, Luce." His gaze lingered for half a second longer than it should have before he turned and strode toward his truck.

Kayla immediately raised her camera, snapping a few candid shots of him.

I exhaled through my nose, keeping my voice light. "Can I see what we've gotten so far?"

Kayla shifted as she scrolled through the camera screen. "Yeah, absolutely."

My eyes widened. I never liked photos of myself, but what she'd captured here... I looked strong. Capable. Confident.

Everything I wanted the world to see when they thought of me.

Kayla's brown eyes were distant. As if in a dream she asked,. "So, he's single, hot, and has puppies?" She practically swooned.

I forced a neutral expression. "Yup, apparently." My stomach knotted at the lie and jealousy reared its ugly head with a flash of heat beneath my skin.

She hesitated, her gaze flicking between me and the direction Connor had disappeared. "You two aren't a thing anymore, right?"

I stiffened. "Right."

It didn't even sound convincing to my own ears.

"Oh, good," she sighed, all too relieved.

I cut her off, eager to change the subject. "Come on, I'll show you the calving barn. It's one of my favorite places on the ranch."

Kayla began snapping pictures as we walked, but I forced myself to focus on work. It was important to capture real moments, and to her credit, she didn't slack. By the end of the day, we had enough social media content to last a year—maybe more.

She even took photos while I checked on the puppies. They were happy and healthy. I felt better for seeing them.

But the day felt longer with Kayla shadowing me. I became hyper-aware of every move I made, every interaction.

And as much as I tried to focus, darkness followed me as my mind wandered to why we had to do this in the first place. Then to Amanda's promise at the celebration of life. I kept catching myself glancing toward the road, scanning for a flash of headlights that didn't belong. It was ridiculous, I knew that. But knowing Amanda was out there, I couldn't let my guard down.

The work day ended. Kayla joined the ranch hands for dinner while I headed back to the house, Buddy trotting beside me.

As I sat down to some leftovers, Connor knocked lightly before letting himself in. "Hey, how was your day?"

I let out a long breath. "Could have been better. You have a not-so-secret admirer," I teased.

He raised his brow. "What do you mean?"

"Kayla." I stiffened before forcing a smile. "I kind of can't wait for her to leave."

He wrapped his broad arms around me, placing a gentle kiss to the top of my head. "How come?"

"Because I keep dodging conversations about you. I'm ready to scream, Connor. She thinks you're single and is very, *very* interested in you." I frowned, suddenly losing my appetite.

"You could've told her the truth," he said, though we both knew that wasn't really an option.

I eyed him. "Seriously? And what happens when Kayla tells the wrong person? And worse, what if it gets back to Amanda? We've seen how she gets leverage on people—how she twists things to try to get to us. At this point her only goal would be to ruin our lives." My stomach tightened. The paranoia took hold of me.

He exhaled hard through his nose holding back his own frustration. "Lucy, she'll only have leverage if we keep lying about our relationship."

I froze, then scrunched up my face before shaking my head. "I thought you supported this. What about the other ranchers or our buyers?"

"I get it, I know you're right," he cut in gently.

"That *we're* right. We decided this was the right choice together..." I stood from the table and crossed my arms over my chest.

His lips pressed together, jaw tightening. "Yes, but that was before everyone started asking. Lucy, I hate lying and I know you do too."

"I do. I'm legitimately sick over it." I place a hand on my churning stomach. "I just don't see any way around it. Diane is actively looking for reasons to make me seem incompetent."

"I know..." A beat passed before he sighed and nudged me lightly. "Don't worry—I'll let Kayla down easy."

I rolled my eyes and couldn't help but grin. "Thank you."

"Besides that, how was the rest of your day?" He asked, pulling me into his arms and starting to sway us back and forth.

"Well, I feel like a fraud," I stated, matter-of-factly.

His brow creased. "How...?"

I retreated from his grasp and walked the short distance to the living room, dropping onto the couch. I gestured to my still-perfect hair. "I'm too... pretty."

His abrupt laughter filled the room. "What on earth are you talking about, Luce?"

I huffed. "I put on two outfits today. Eric did my makeup and hair in the morning and then did a touch-up in the afternoon." I huffed a sigh before explaining, "Women don't wear a full face of makeup to work outside all day. If we know we're getting sweaty and dirty, there's no makeup going on our faces. But I've been poked, prodded, wiped down, and brushed off so much. Just *look*," I gestured. "I don't have a speck of dust on me. I get why some shots need to be polished, but *all* of them?" I let out a sharp scoff. "I want people to see the real me—working the land, getting dirty, no makeup, hair in a messy ponytail. *That's* authentic. It's real and what other women like me *want* to see. Not a model playing country girl for a day."

Connor gave me a warm, reassuring smile. "Then tell Eric and your mom you're going without hair and makeup tomorrow. They're in fashion, not ranching. Looking perfect is important to their world. Not ours. Maybe offer a compromise? You could alternate days to get both types of shots for our marketing efforts."

I nodded, already reaching for my phone. "Yeah, I like that. I'll text them now."

Before I could hit send, a sharp knock at the door made me freeze.

Connor frowned. "I'll get it."

I was still typing when I heard a shrill voice that made every muscle in my body tighten.

"Hi, Connor. Is Lucy home?"

My eyes shot up, and I stood, squaring my shoulders, bracing myself. "Aunt Diane, what are you doing here?"

Her resting scowl deepened as she spat. "Is that any way to greet your aunt?"

I crossed my arms. "What do you want?"

Her tone sharpened. "Lucy, I loved your father. He was *my* brother, after all. I just dropped by to say you're not doing too bad of a job. If I came across as harsh, well, I'm a big sister—I'm protective." She leaned forward through the doorway and began shooting her head around, looking at every inch of the home within view.

"I think that was supposed to be an apology. So, thanks," I said flatly. "Anything else?"

She huffed and shook her head. "I guess not." Then she turned to Connor, pulling an envelope from her purse, making a point to hand it to him. "Here's my RSVP for the fundraiser. My husband Earl and I will be there. Hopefully, it's not as much of a disaster as the state of my brother's house."

Her gaze flickered over me, assessing, judging.

I clenched my jaw, swallowing the sharp retort rising in my throat.

Connor didn't let the moment linger. "Thanks. I'll update the head count. Have a good night." He stepped forward slightly, his presence calming, solid, protective, blocking her from entering further inside.

Diane's lips pursed and with one last narrowed glare at me, she spun on her heel and strode toward her brand-new car—one she'd bought with her recent inheritance from my father.

The moment the door shut behind her, I let out a long, slow breath.

"She's too much," I muttered, rubbing my brow, completely drained.

Connor leaned against the counter, crossing his arms over his broad chest. "I guess the one nice thing was that she was complimentary? Sort of? At least the first part…"

I let out a dry laugh. "Yeah, after threatening to steal my company if I showed any signs of weakness."

His jaw tensed, joining me on the couch. "Well, she's crazy—and I've been meaning to say that can't happen. Even if she did make you look incompetent, this isn't 'Wolf of Wall Street'—she can't waltz into a boardroom and have you voted out. You're the sole owner. No one can take this ranch from you. Not Diane. Not Amanda. Not anyone."

I nodded, pressing my cheek against his chest, letting the steady rhythm of his breathing soothe me.

"Let's grab Buddy and head back to your place," I murmured. "We can check on the dogs, get you something to eat. I'm too tired to think about anything else today."

Connor kissed my temple. "Alright." Then a slow smirk raised on his lips. "Could you maybe be dessert?"

A high-pitched giggle escaped me as he nipped at my ear.

"Stop!" I squealed as he tickled my side.

The rumbling laughter that filled the room put all earlier tension at ease.

I jumped off the couch, crouching into attack mode. "Don't get closer!"

"Or what?" He smirked.

"I'll tickle you back!" I chuckled, bracing myself. Yet somehow I was fully unprepared when he lunged forward and slung me over his shoulder. "Put me down!" I shrieked in a fit of endless giggles.

He smacked my ass. "Not until you admit I win."

"Win?!"

"Yeah. You've got three wins on me. This tickle war... it's my win."

I pouted. "Don't you mean four wins?"

He paused. "How is it four?"

"I beat you in both races. That makes two..."

He grumbled. "I guess that's true. Horseshoes make three, and karaoke night is four..."

"Yep. Even right now I'm winning."

He plopped me back down on the couch. "How's that?"

"Because I just tricked you into putting me down." In a flash I took off from the couch, but he was right behind me scooping me into his arms.

"Oh no don't!"

My legs kicked into the air. "Okay! You win!"

"Thank you!" He sighed, his satisfied grin meeting me as I spun around. "You going to let me drive you tonight?"

"Nope. I'm not letting anyone catch us driving in from your place in the morning. Everyone's already suspicious enough."

"And you driving across our properties on that ATV *isn't* suspicious?" He raised a brow at me.

I shrugged. "I'm Batman. No one will ever catch me."

Spit flew everywhere as Connor tried and failed to hold back his laughter. "Okay, 'Batman.' Let's go... You hear that, Buddy? Your mom thinks she's a superhero."

Buddy jumped up, excited to now be acknowledged.

I rolled my eyes at the two of them. "Ha. Ha."

Connor's bright smile made me melt. "Come on, Buddy. We'd better get in the truck before she throws something at me."

CHAPTER THIRTY-TWO

What She Built

LUCY

The summer was coming dangerously to an end.

As I lay beside Connor, his calloused hand ran the length of my bare thigh, his touch sending a shiver through me. I gasped, eyes fluttering closed as a soft groan escaped my lips. Rolling over to face him, I cupped his jaw, his grown-out beard scratching gently against my skin. I pulled him closer, drinking him in.

"Good morning," he murmured over my jaw, his breath a welcome heat brushing over my skin.

"Morning," I yawned.

Connor propped himself, studying me. "What are you thinking about?"

"I can't believe I go back to London next week," I pouted.

"I know. These last few months have gone by so fast. You ready for the fundraiser tonight?" He asked, his voice husky, still thick with sleep.

I nodded, catching my breath. "Yeah. My speech is done. I'm nervous, but excited."

"Well, I've got some of the guys working security. No one's getting in unless they're on the list." He ran his fingertips the length of my arm in slow, soothing strokes.

I smiled, but my stomach still twisted at the idea that we even *needed* security. "At least that's *one* thing I don't have to worry about. Though I can't imagine Chuck and Noah being much of a deterrent."

"Don't forget Johnny," he said, tucking a strand of hair behind my ear. "What else are you worried about?"

"What happens if no one shows or we don't meet our fundraising goal? What if everyone thinks I can't hack it or..."

"Shh, there's no use stressing. It's going to be a fantastic night. You've more than proven yourself, Lucy. Besides, whatever happens, you're going to look stunning doing it," he teased.

"My outfit *is* going to be incredible," I smirked.

Connor's grin widened. "Yeah, I guess when your mother is Lillian Sinclair, that's never a concern."

"Facts." I breathed. "But I have to admit, she really outdid herself this time."

In all her wisdom, my mother had designed something truly special: a custom black pantsuit that was both elegant and commanding. The blazer had just the right amount of sheer fabric, subtly feminine yet undeniably powerful. The fitted vest hugged my torso perfectly; its large, striking buttons adding a bold touch. And the sleek, flared pants? Absolute perfection.

"I'm so glad I'll have you by my side tonight." I pressed a kiss to his shoulder.

A deep, satisfied hum rumbled in his chest at the touch of my lips. "I'll always be by your side." Then he paused before adding, "Too bad it'll be as your manager tonight."

Sadness cracked through me. "I know. You hate it. I hate it." Frustration built inside me, and my body tensed.

Connor's jaw ticked, but he quickly schooled his features, trailing his hand up my side. "But that's later. Right now, I'm here as your boyfriend. And as your boyfriend, I'd love to take a shower with you before we start getting ready."

I bit my lip as a grin spread across my face. "I think that sounds like the perfect way to start our day."

Connor jumped up then and scooped me into his arms. I let out a sharp yelp of surprise, laughter bubbling out as I wrapped my arms around his neck, squealing as he planted scruffy kisses along my neck.

He set me down as he threw on the hot water. "Prepare for the world's longest shower." His voice dropped low with such promise.

I gasped as he pulled me in for a long, luxurious kiss before I could think of a response. Then—the rest of my worries, my thoughts, my concerns melted away until there was only us in this moment.

I headed back to my house to finish getting ready. Eric and my mother were already there, waiting to help me look my best for the *Future Farmers of America* charity gala. Eric gave me a knowing once-over, my hair still wet from the thorough cleaning I'd received at Connor's strong, careful hands. I shuddered at the memory, then flushed as I caught Eric's gaze again.

My mother, ignoring or oblivious to the exchange—I wasn't sure which—sighed. "Well, let's get to work, shall we? Eric, start with a quick blow dry and style before makeup, please."

He immediately got to work, and a mere two and half hours later, I was ready to show myself to the rest of the world.

I turned, checking myself in the mirror.

My shag cut was expertly texturized and voluminous, framing my face flawlessly, the longest layers brushing just below my shoulders. My makeup was precisely applied, but the dark red lip was the real statement. The deep crimson stood out against the sleek black of my suit.

My mother stepped forward, finishing the look with a white pearl necklace, and handed me a golden belt buckle to break up the darkness with just the right touch of warmth.

"Look at you, my darling. Montana strong. A female business owner. You're not just stepping into your father's boots, as they say—you're making them your own."

I beamed at my reflection, giving a small twirl. "You know, I feel like the princess of cattle right now." I let out a short chuckle.

My mother held a gentle hand over her mouth. "You're too funny, Lucy."

"Thanks." I gave a self-satisfied grin. "I mean it, Mom. I look perfect. The event decorations you picked are stunning. Thank you for making tonight go as smoothly as possible."

"My pleasure, dearest. I only want tonight to be absolute perfection for you." She squeezed my shoulders, giving me a reassuring smile from the mirror.

My stomach dropped and balled up tight.

"What's the matter, Lucy?" Her soft voice cooed beside me.

I sighed. "It's nothing, just... Sam. I wish he were here." The ache was almost unbearable.

My mother rubbed her hands over my arms, then turned me to face her. "He hasn't reached out? Not once?"

I shook my head, holding back the tears that threatened to fall. "No, but I haven't either. I still can't believe he kept so much from me. That he'd help Amanda for so long. I get his reasons, but it hurts so much."

"I know, darling." My mother hesitated, then took a wary step forward before opening up her arms in invitation.

A small half-smile crack on the corner of my mouth. I nodded and closed the gap, embracing my mom. "You know we haven't done this in..."

"Too long," she finished, squeezing me tighter.

I gently pulled back. "Well, there's no use dwelling on Sam right now. Tonight's about our FFA kids."

"And showing everyone once and for all you're the rightful leader here at Campbell Ranch." she added, beaming with pride.

A swarm of nervous butterflies jolted my stomach into nausea. "I just want everyone to know I'm going to continue to build on the legacy Dad started." I shoved down the pain and forced a bright smile.

"Lucy, you are," she sighed. "You know... you can't make everyone happy. I know what I just said... But what actually matters is that you prove to yourself you belong here. It is clear you're the right person to take over your father's ranch. I think it's about time to stop caring what anyone else thinks and start believing in yourself, darling."

I bit my lip, overwhelmed and tight with anxiety. "Okay."

"Shall we head down?"

"Yeah." I exhaled, straightening my shoulders.

"Wonderful." She beamed, pride glittering in her gaze. Then, with a slight tilt of her head, she asked, "Are we waiting for Connor to walk down with us?"

I cleared my throat and any lingering unresolved emotions. "He's meeting us there."

She linked her arm through mine, her smile warm. "Good. I'm happy I get to escort you down. It's probably the only time I'll have you all to myself tonight."

A small smile touched my lips. "True..." I paused, searching her hazel eyes. "Mom, can I ask you something?"

She patted my hand gently. "Anything."

I hesitated as I led her to the front door.

Once we stepped outside, I took a deep breath and asked, "Why did you and Dad separate?" I furrowed my brow. "I mean, he must not have had hard feelings. He left you more money than his own sister in the will."

"Oh my. I suppose that *is* true." My mother's lips curved into a wistful smile. "Well, he never really *did* like his sister. Loved her, of course, because family is family. But like her?" She let out a soft chuckle. "No, not ever."

I laughed, shaking my head. "That checks out."

She sighed, a distant look in her eyes. "Your father was my one great love, and I was his. But he saw that I was struggling, living here in Montana. There were parts of it I loved, but after years of being away from home, it... ate at me. I wish I had talked to him about it more, or he'd talked to me before making up his mind on what would be best for me, for *us*. Maybe we could have worked things out instead of..."

She paused for a moment before continuing, "I suppose it's true. I couldn't pursue my dreams of being a fashion designer here. And being so far from my parents, my sisters, and brother... it wore me down. But Robert never really told me *why* he wanted me to go back—why he thought we should separate. At least, not until this year, when he was in the hospital."

A shadow of heartbreak crossed her expression, and my chest tightened.

"He wanted me to be happy," she whispered, "but I was never truly happy after leaving because I'd lost him. Our family was broken apart. And in the process, I thought I lost you, too."

Pain twisted in my stomach. All those years I resented her. All those times I thought she was selfish, a gold digger...

I had been so completely, *unbelievably* wrong.

"Mom, I'm so sorry."

I wrapped my arms around her, the weight of every misunderstanding, every cruel word, pressing down on me.

She held me tight, smoothing a hand over my hair. "Oh, Lucy. There is nothing to forgive."

Her voice was soft, filled with unshaken love.

Then she kissed my cheek. "I love you so much. Your father and I are *both* so incredibly proud of you."

And just like that, the dam broke.

But this time, the tears felt different.

They weren't born from loss, but from love.

I let them fall, let them cleanse every doubt, every insecurity. Because I felt it.

A warmth, a presence, like he was here, standing beside me.

I closed my eyes, a slow smile lifting at the corners of my lips. A scent enveloped my senses, worn leather, bourbon, wet soil—it was him, my dad's fragrance wafting in the air surrounding me, unmoving even in the gentle breeze. In my heart, I spoke to him. *Thank you, Dad. I miss you so much.*

I swallowed thickly, blinking away the tears.

My mother laughed softly as she dabbed my eyes, protecting my makeup. "Now, now," she teased, "no need for theatrics."

I let out a short, huffed laugh, one that felt lighter than anything I had let myself feel in a long time. "Ah yes, I do have Sinclair in me after all."

We walked arm-in-arm toward the old equipment barn, original to the property. It was now transformed into something truly breathtaking.

The massive barn doors stood wide open, the space was draped in warm, golden string lights. A soft glow cast a dreamy, intimate ambiance.

Elegant wildflower and eucalyptus centerpieces adorned the tables, their delicate fragrance mingling with the scent of aged wood and fresh hay. Candlelight flickered across polished table settings, casting a warm glow over the room. The air hummed with conversation. Laughter weaved through the clinking of glasses and the soft, lilting melodies of a live string quartet.

Waitstaff in crisp black-and-white uniforms moved seamlessly through the crowd, carrying trays of gourmet hors d'oeuvres—mini filet mignon bites, seared scallops, smoked salmon crostini.

The polished wooden counter of the bar at the far end of the barn was lined with bottles of top-shelf whiskey and wine, offering guests handcrafted cocktails and aged bourbon served in crystal tumblers.

A banner hung high above the stage, elegant yet bold:

"FFA Charity Gala Hosted by Campbell Ranch"

This wasn't just an event—it was a game changer. The funds raised tonight would bring newer generations into the farming and ranching community, something we desperately needed now, more than ever before. The decline of young adults entering the world of agriculture was a threat to the production and sustainability of American-raised and grown food. Facts about the average age of farmers in America and projections for the future of the industry were framed in glass picture frames above the silent auction table.

I smiled as more and more people wrote down their bids, knowing that each donated item laid out on the long tables lining the side of the barn opposite the bar was helping a worthy cause. I allowed myself a slow exhale of relief.

This was how I would honor my father's legacy.

This was how I would make sure his values lived on.

Tonight truly was a new beginning.

A large man with a groomed silver mustache and beard walked over and clapped a broad hand on my shoulder. "Lucy Campbell?" He boomed with a broad grin, his skin bright red as his glass of bourbon sloshed around in his other hand. "Weston Calloway. Pleasure to meet your acquaintance, in person that is."

"Mr. Calloway! It's great to officially meet you." I beamed. "I hope you're enjoying yourself."

He gave a gruff nod. "You've done a fabulous job. Bob would be so proud."

I nodded, glancing around the room. "I think so, too."

Weston chortled. "He'd never be caught dead in a black tie event, but damn it, he'd love seeing the work you're doing to encourage young people into the industry. Great work, young lady. Great work." He patted my shoulder, then walked off as he was called over to another group. "Talk later, Ms. Campbell."

The dance floor suddenly came alive, the smooth melodies of the string quartet gave way to a livelier tune that had couples swaying beneath the warm glow of the string lights. Men in well-tailored suits, many wearing their best cowboy hats, spun their partners in elegant gowns, the skirts of their dresses catching the candlelight as they twirled. Boots and polished dress shoes tapped against the wooden floor in time with the music, the occasional burst of laughter ringing out as guests lost themselves in the moment.

I moved through the crowd, shaking hands, accepting warm congratulations, exchanging smiles with familiar faces.

"This is the best gala I've attended in years," one woman gushed, her diamond earrings catching the light. "Everything is *flawless*, Lucy."

"Your father would love everything you're doing here," a longtime business associate added, his grip firm as he shook my hand. "You've stepped into this role with grace and strength. The industry is lucky to have you."

"Thank you," I managed, my heart swelling with pride.

"You know, I wasn't sure what to expect when Robert's daughter took over," another guest admitted, not unkindly. "But you've more than proven yourself. You're a force to be reckoned with. And you're so young to boot. We've all been talking about how impressed we are, Ms. Campbell. Keep up the good work. And please be sure to host more events like this, we're having the best time."

I smiled, holding my head a little higher. "That means the world to me."

As I continued through the barn, the compliments kept coming.

"Exceptional planning."

"A brilliant cause."

"Your leadership is inspiring."

I had fought so hard to prove myself these last few weeks, to be seen as more than just Robert Campbell's scandalous daughter. And tonight? Tonight, I felt it. The respect, the admiration. It wasn't just about what my father had built—it was about what I was building here and now.

I glanced toward the open barn doors, my breath catching as I saw Connor standing there, scanning the room. The moment his eyes found mine, everything else faded away.

I excused myself from the small group I'd been speaking with, then began sifting through the crowd as I glided toward him. I was filled with love, appreciation, and a warmth so deep it softened every jagged edge inside me.

"What do you think?" I gestured toward the dazzling room.

Connor's gaze filled with something that sent my stomach flipping, and he grinned. "It's fantastic. I saw the bids at the silent auction. Lucy, you're raising above and beyond the set goal. That's incredible. *You're* incredible."

I bit my lip and attempted to extinguish the squeal of excitement that bubbled up my throat. "I can't believe it's going so well!" I radiated pride, my cheeks aching behind the smile that wouldn't go away. Then my eyes locked back on Connor, and that never-ending grin vanished.

A shadow crossed his expression, turning his features hard as he looked somewhere behind me.

The microphone crackled to life.

A sickeningly sweet voice rang out. My stomach roiled, churning with nausea.

"Hello, everyone! I hope you're all having a wonderful night. Let's give a round of applause to our beautiful host, Lucy Campbell!"

My blood ran cold.

I knew that voice.

The applause was polite but hesitant, uncertain.

Amanda Johnson. She was here. *But how?*

I turned slowly to face the enemy I'd been dreading since the day she made bail. And then everything fell into place.

She stood on stage, dressed in a caterer's uniform, microphone in hand, grinning like she *owned* the room.

Oh. Hell. No.

I spun on my heel, scanning the crowd until I found James. He was already on his phone.

Our eyes met.

He gave me a small thumbs-up and mouthed *911* at me.

A wave of relief crashed over me.

But Amanda?

She wasn't finished.

Dread raked its heavy, suffocating claws over me.

"Yes, yes," she cooed, milking the moment. "Isn't she just great?"

I spotted her father at the base of the stage, his expression tight, pleading with her in hushed tones. His usually calm features were turning shades of purple and red.

Amanda barely acknowledged him.

She twisted back to the crowd.

"Some of you may have heard about Lucy's recent legal issues." She tilted her head, her voice thick with mock sympathy. "For those of you who haven't, well... let's just say I'm standing here tonight to tell you the truth. Because the person you're all supporting? She's a liar."

A murmur swept through the crowd. A few hands clamped over wide-struck mouths. Heads turned toward me, brows furrowed, questioning.

Connor went rigid beside me.

Before I could move, he was already pushing through the crowd, making his way toward the stage.

Amanda's voice dripped with venom.

"And here's the man of the hour—*Connor Lochland*." Her smile was bright and fake. "You see, Lucy was so jealous of my past relationship with Connor that she made up this whole blackmail story just to ruin my life. *Crazy*, right? I mean, the woman punched me in the face and somehow escaped assault charges!"

Connor's voice came faintly over the speakers.

"Amanda, stop this." His deep tone was calm, controlled—but laced with warning.

"I don't think I will," she sneered. "Now that she's rich and powerful, she thinks she can—"

A new voice cut through the room.

One that sent a shock of disbelief through my system.

"*Enough.*"

The microphone was yanked from Amanda's hands.

I gasped.

Sam.

Sam?!

He strode onto the stage, expression unreadable.

"I'm sorry for this interruption, folks." His voice held a mature confidence and strength I hadn't heard before.

Connor seized the moment, grabbing Amanda's arm and leading her offstage. She thrashed violently, making a last, desperate attempt to wrench free, to snatch the mic back from Sam.

"Get off me," she spat, twisting against Connor's grip. "You're all making a huge mistake! *She did this*!"

She struggled, but a swarm of familiar faces closed in—my ranch hands. *No*, my new family.

I smiled as I watched them close ranks around her.

Mr. Johnson rushed forward, shouting at them. "Let go of my daughter! I'll take it from here!"

Sam turned to the stunned crowd. "Well, that was fun!"

A soft rumble of uncomfortable laughter filled the room.

"I'm sure many of you don't know me, I'm the younger, gayer Lochland brother." A few more chuckles lifted across the barn. Then Sam cleared his throat as his brows knitted together in visible discomfort. "All joking aside, I never planned to do this here, not like this. But after that display, I don't think I have a choice." He took a breath. "Everyone here deserves the truth, and unfortunately, I'm one of the few people who can say I know all sides of the story." He swallowed, drifting his heavy gaze to me. "Amanda Johnson has built her life on lies. And I know this, because I helped her."

Gasps rippled through the room.

He let the weight of his words settle before continuing.

"The reason she did it? She's been jealous of my best friend, Lucy, since we were kids. It started with simple bullying, and became something so much worse as we got older. Amanda, despite her gorgeous demeanor, is insecure—just like the rest of us. But unlike regular people, she's rich. Entitled since the day she was born. And when her lies became too big—too dangerous—she became desperate to keep them buried. She would say and do anything to protect her image. Including blackmailing me, Lucy, and anyone else she had to, in order to get her way. But the apple doesn't fall far from the tree."

The barn was silent as Sam pulled out his phone and held it up to the microphone.

Mr. Johnson's voice crackled over the speakers.

"Hi, Sam. Amanda tells me you're thinking about testifying against her in court. I'd like to remind you of a certain ex-boyfriend who hasn't come out of the closet and would like to keep it that way. I'm not asking you to lie, per se. I'm asking you to keep your mouth shut, and no harm will come to your friend's reputation. Everything will remain as it should be."

The silence that followed was deafening.

A fresh wave of murmurs swept through the crowd.

After a weighted pause, Sam's voice rang out, clear and unwavering.

"As you can see, *blackmail* runs in the family."

The tension in the room was thick, suffocating.

Then, Sam turned to face me.

"This is nothing compared to the threats I've gotten over the years. It's nothing to what Amanda put tonight's hostess through. I won't go into all the details because some things should remain private. But, all you need to know is that Lucy Campbell has handled this nightmare with more maturity and grace than *anyone* else could have. She saved this ranch from a PR disaster orchestrated by Amanda's father. She built this event. And she stood strong... even when people *like me* failed her."

He let out a hard, shaking breath.

"I let Amanda control me for years. I was too much of a coward to stand up to her. But not anymore."

Emotion clogged my throat. The weight of it all crashed over me.

Then, Sam's gaze swept over the crowd.

"If you judge Lucy by her actions—by what she's built, by what she's fought for—you'll see the truth." His voice was firm, unwavering. "She's proven, time and again, that she's strong. Honest. The kind of leader this industry needs. And this event? It's proof of who she really is."

The barn was silent. Then—

One slow, deliberate round of applause rang out.

Then another.

And another.

It spread through the room, building, growing louder.

I felt my lungs expand, releasing a breath I hadn't realized I was holding.

The tension in the air shifted.

Amanda was gone.

Sam had set the record straight.

And the night was ours again.

An older woman placed a cool hand on my shoulder.

She smiled. "Don't worry, Lucy. Everyone loves a little drama at these things." Her voice lilted. "It's the only reason to attend."

I let out a rough, unexpected laugh.

And just like that, the weight in my chest began to ease.

Despite everything, the night was still, by some miracle, *mine*.

CHAPTER THIRTY-THREE

No More Hiding

LUCY

"Sam!" I called after him, spotting him outside the gala, heading toward his truck. "*Wait*."

He turned, surprise flickering across his face as I approached. "Lucy."

"Hey," I said, searching for the right words. "I just wanted to say thank you for what you did in there. You saved my entire event. Actually, you saved *me*. Without you stepping in, I wouldn't have stood a chance against her lies. *Thank you*."

His head dropped, and he rubbed the back of his neck, a shy smile tugging at his lips. "It was nothing, Luce. Least I could do after everything I did…"

I swallowed past the lump in my throat. "It wasn't *nothing*. I'm so grateful for what you just did. More than you'll ever know."

He huffed a small laugh, then glanced toward the barn. "My ex wrote a statement for the courts confirming his involvement—the blackmail, everything. I sent it to James a few hours ago. She's facing multiple charges of blackmail."

"That's huge." I let out a breath. "Thank you, Sam."

His grin turned sheepish. "I'd say 'least I could do' again, but that'd be redundant. And you know how much I *hate* that."

I chuckled, and something inside me loosened. I had my best friend back.

"I've really missed you," I admitted.

His expression softened. "Same. And I know it'll take time, but I promise I'm going to do everything I can to earn your forgiveness and trust back."

Before I could respond, Connor's voice rumbled beside me. "Well, I can't speak for Lucy, but I forgive you, brother."

Sam's head snapped toward him, his face shifting from hopeful to stunned.

Connor stepped forward, placing a hand on Sam's shoulder. "After what you did in there, I'm so damn proud of you."

Tears filled Sam's eyes, and the two brothers embraced.

A small, warm smile tugged at my lips.

When they pulled away, I smirked. "Well, if he can forgive you, I guess I can too," I teased. "After all, if things don't work out between Connor and me, you're getting me in the divorce, right?"

A bright, beaming smile spread across Sam's face. He scooped me into his arms, spinning me around as I squealed in protest.

"Sam, put me down! I'm the hostess of a sophisticated event, remember?" I scolded, laughing.

He did as I asked, but his expression sobered. "I just... I never thought you guys would forgive me."

Connor squeezed his shoulder. "Of course we would... eventually. Sam, you're our family."

"Exactly. And besides, BFF means *best friends forever*," I added, crossing my arms playfully. "I take that title very seriously."

Sam exhaled a laugh, then pulled both of us into a tight group hug.

This night was finally perfect.

Kyle clapped Sam on the back as he passed. "Hell of a thing you did tonight, Sam."

Sam's cheeks reddened. "Thanks."

The distant wail of sirens carried through the night as a patrol car pulled up the driveway.

Red and blue lights cast eerie flashes against the warm glow of the barn.

Amanda thrashed against the officer's grip, manicured nails curling into restrained fists as she spat venom at anyone who dared meet her gaze.

"This is a mistake!" she screeched, heels digging into the dirt as they dragged her toward the cruiser. "Do you know who my father is? I'll have your badge for this! You're all going to regret this!"

Her mother stood off to the side, perfectly composed, adjusting the expensive silk scarf around her neck. She wasn't even looking at her daughter—like she'd already decided Amanda was a lost cause.

Amanda tried again, her voice dripping with manufactured pain. "Deputy Foster, you don't understand. Please... don't do this." Her eyes welled up with tears. "Lucy, she isn't as innocent as she seems. She stole *everything* from me."

Amanda's wild gaze darted around the crowd, searching for a sympathetic face. For literally *anyone*.

No one stepped forward.

Amanda's eye caught on her best friend, Danika. "Danika! Tell them! I'm innocent."

Danika crossed her thin arms over her chest and turned to her date, quietly asking him to escort her inside.

"Traitor!" Amanda screeched. "I'll *ruin* you for this. I know *all* of your secrets."

Danika froze, her small frame stiffening for a moment before continuing back into the barn.

With that one simple action, everyone who had once fawned over Amanda—the so-called friends who gossiped with her over champagne—took a step back.

Her plum-faced father still wouldn't look at her.

"Daddy," she sobbed, voice cracking. "Help me."

His jaw tightened. But he said nothing.

For the first time, Amanda Johnson had no one left to manipulate.

Then Mr. Johnson froze, his face draining of color, eyes darting frantically between the uniformed officers who began to surround him.

The recording of his voice still echoed in my mind: *"I'm not asking you to lie, per se. I'm asking you to keep your mouth shut, and no harm will come to your friend's reputation."*

But it wasn't just in my head.

It had played over the speakers for *everyone* to hear.

A second officer approached Mr. Johnson, his expression unreadable. "Mayor Thomas Johnson, you're under arrest for blackmail and witness intimidation. Please turn around and place your hands behind your back."

Gasps rippled through the crowd for the second time that night.

He stiffened, sweat glistening along his receding hairline.

"You—you can't be serious," he stammered. "This is absurd! You have no right—"

The officer didn't hesitate. "We have the right, sir. And a whole barn full of witnesses."

Murmurs spread like wildfire.

Powerful investors. Ranching elites. People Mr. Johnson had undoubtedly schmoozed for years.

Now?

They were watching his downfall unfold in real time.

He searched the crowd for support. His dark brown eyes flicked to his wife.

She didn't move. Didn't say a word. Didn't *care*.

The officer seized his wrist, yanked it behind his back, and snapped the cold metal of the handcuffs into place.

"You're making a grave mistake!" he roared. "Do you have any idea who I am?" He struggled against the cuffs. "I'll have your whole department shut down for this!"

The officer remained unfazed, rattling off his Miranda rights with practiced detachment.

Amanda, who had fallen eerily silent, snapped back to life.

"Daddy!" she shrieked, eyes wild. "*Do something!*"

But he couldn't.

Not this time.

The officer shoved Amanda forward, cutting off her threats as the patrol car door was yanked open.

The click of the door slamming shut sent a pulse of finality through me.

It was over.

The Johnsons were finished.

My eyes met Deputy Foster's. He gave me a slow, loaded smile as he tapped the body camera attached to his chest, and I gave him a bright, grateful grin in return.

And then—

The entire barn erupted.

Cheers. A collective exhale of relief as the Johnsons' reign over the town collapsed under the weight of their own corruption.

Connor's hand pressed against the small of my back.

"You did it," he murmured.

I swallowed, my throat tight. "We did it."

And this time, there was no one left to save them.

Connor, remembering the prying eyes around us, let his hand fall from my waist. A chill ran over my skin where his reassuring warmth had been, and my heart sank. His expression hardened, his voice resolute. "Hopefully, this is the last we'll be hearing from them."

I exhaled slowly, the adrenaline still thrumming beneath my skin. "At least until the hearings."

James strode up beside us, his expression sharp with satisfaction. "That restraining order paperwork is already in motion. Amanda sealed her own fate the second she crashed this event." He nodded toward the flashing police lights. "And judging by the fallout? We're going to need a new mayor."

"No kidding," Sam muttered, shaking his head. A humorless chuckle escaped him, but there was an unmistakable weight behind it.

I should've felt triumphant. This was what she deserved. But all I felt was... tired. Tired of fighting ghosts. Tired of her voice echoing in my head like she still held any power over me. She didn't. Not anymore.

I took a calming breath, my skittering pulse finally beginning to slow. "We should get the gala back on track. The FFA deserves a proper charity event, not..." I gestured toward the commotion beyond the barn doors. "That."

Connor's gaze flicked to mine, warm with admiration. "Agreed."

I squared my shoulders, pushing away the lingering tension. "I do believe I still have a speech to give."

The applause still rang in my ears as I stepped back inside the barn. A hum of chatter filled the air—guests murmuring about the arrests, the downfall of the Johnsons, the sheer drama of the evening. But the night wasn't over.

Not for me.

I took a steadying breath and approached the stage. The microphone stood waiting, the gentle glow of the overhead lights casting a soft halo over the podium.

Connor gave my hand a reassuring squeeze before stepping back into the crowd. My mother met my gaze from across the room, standing beside Eric, her hands clasped in silent encouragement. Kayla was already back to snapping photos, her sharp, observant eye capturing every second of the night's turning tide.

I exhaled, smoothing my hands over the sleek fabric of my suit before stepping up to the microphone.

The barn slowly quieted.

Hundreds of eyes turned to me.

I swallowed, finding my voice.

"Tonight didn't go exactly as planned." A few chuckles rippled through the audience, cutting through the lingering tension. I let a small smile tug at my lips. "But if my father taught me anything, it's that you don't quit just because things get hard. You face the challenge head-on, adapt, and keep pushing forward."

I glanced around the room, taking in the faces of the people who had supported me, stood by me, *believed* in me.

"This event—this cause—isn't about me or tonight's unexpected entertainment." A few chuckles scattered through the room. "It's about the *Future Farmers of America*. About investing in the next generation of ranchers, farmers, and agricultural leaders across our country. My father believed in that mission wholeheartedly. He built Campbell Ranch not just as a business, but as a community, as a place that lifted others up."

A lump formed in my throat, but I pushed through it.

"And I hope, wherever he is, my father is looking down tonight and knows... I'm exactly where I'm meant to be."

I let out a soft, shuddering breath.

"I want to thank everyone who helped make this night possible. We've gone above and beyond our fundraising goal, and thanks to everyone in this room, we're going to be able to support our local FFA in a huge way. This is a life-changing amount of money for these kids and this wonderful program. So a big thank you to our generous donors, our esteemed guests, the ranchers who took time out of their busy lives to be here tonight to support this important event. To my mother, Lillian Sinclair, who—despite our differences—has shown up for me in ways I never expected. To the hardworking men and women who make Campbell Ranch what it is. You are the backbone of this operation, and I couldn't do this without you."

I let my gaze drift to Connor, who stood near the front, watching me with quiet pride.

"And to the family I've found at both Campbell Ranch and Lochland Farms," I continued, my voice thick. "For years, I thought family was just about blood. But I've learned that family is about the people who stand beside you, the people who fight for you, the people who love you... even when you don't always deserve it."

My eyes found Sam's.

"Sam, you once told me that I was the most honest person you knew." My voice wavered, but I kept going. "Honesty is something I've always valued. It's how my father raised me. It's how I want to lead this ranch. And tonight, I need to be honest with all of you about something that has been weighing on me because there is something I've been lying to all of you about."

A hush fell over the room.

I felt my pulse hammer in my throat, but I squared my shoulders, lifted my chin, and met Kayla's camera lens head-on.

"Ever since I took over my father's business, I wanted to keep my personal life separate from my role as the head of Campbell Ranch. I've been afraid of how everyone in this room would view me after they learned what I've been keeping from each of you and outright denying. I did all of this to maintain the perfect image of professionalism and strong leadership. But the truth is, I'm done pretending. So, here it goes..."

I turned, finding the one person who mattered most, and took a deep breath.

"I am madly, deeply, head-over-heels in love with Connor Lochland, and have been since we were kids."

A murmur rippled through the audience. A few raised eyebrows, a few stunned expressions—but also understanding ones. Encouraging ones.

I pressed on.

"He isn't just someone I care about—he's someone I can't imagine my life without. And I know that for some of you, this might be a conflict of interest. Some of you may think it's unprofessional, and I understand that completely.

"But I can't spend any more time pretending that the person who means everything to me is just an employee, just my ranch manager, just some name on payroll. He is so much *more* than that. He is my partner, my confidant, my best friend."

Connor's face was unreadable, but I saw the flicker of something in his blue eyes—something deep, something overwhelming.

"So if that changes how you see me, that's okay." I continued, lifting my chin. "But I refuse to lead this ranch, my father's legacy, without full honesty. And the truth is—I love Connor Lochland. And I'm not afraid to say it."

For a moment, the room was silent.

Then—

Applause.

Loud, resounding applause filled the barn, genuine and full of approval.

Over the roar, Paula's voice cut through, crystal clear: *"HELL YES! GET IT, GIRL!"*

Laughter rippled through the crowd, a lightness cutting through the weight of the moment. I shook my head, smiling.

Connor was already moving, weaving through the sea of people with purpose.

And then—right there, in front of *all* of White River, in front of the skeptics, the supporters, and everyone in between—

He pulled me into his arms and kissed me.

The whole barn *exploded*. Cheers. Whoops. Hollers. Even a few whistles.

I melted into him, the weight of secrecy dissolving, lightening the load from our shoulders.

Connor's lips brushed against my ear as he whispered, "I love you too, Lucy Campbell." His breathing was slow and smooth. "No more hiding."

I relaxed into him, taking in his rich, soothing scent. Allowing the moment to solidify in my memory for all time.

The cheering faded into the background as his lips found mine once more. Endless joy and adoration filled my being. I felt like I belonged. Here. With him. In this place.

This was my home.

This was my truth.

And tonight?

Tonight was all I'd hoped for and so much more.

CHAPTER THIRTY-FOUR

All In

LUCY

Connor's ATV cut smoothly through our properties in the Montana night, headlights casting long beams of light over the empty road. My fingers played idly with the fabric of my pants, nerves still buzzing under my skin as everything replayed in my mind.

The gala. The speech. The arrests. My confession.

I glanced over at him, taking in his sharp profile. His hands gripped the steering wheel, his calloused fingers flexing every so often, something burning in his gaze as he looked ahead.

I reached for his hand, threading my fingers through his. He brought them to his lips, pressing a kiss against my knuckles before resting them on the center console. His grip sent a jolt of electricity up my arm.

"What a night," I commented, biting my lip as I took a moment to memorize every line and curve of his profile.

His lips quirked up, but his gaze stayed on the road. "How are you feeling about everything?"

I sighed, leaning back against the headrest. "I should be exhausted, but I'm wired."

Connor hummed low in his throat. "Not surprising. You just had the most dramatic charity gala White River has ever seen." His thumb traced small circles on my skin. "And you stood up in front of damn near everyone and told them you love me."

A small, breathy laugh escaped me. "Yeah. Guess I did."

"Wasn't expecting that." He cast me a sideways glance, eyes glinting under the glow of the dashboard lights. "Not that I'm complaining."

I smirked. "Good."

His jaw ticked, and then, without warning, he pulled off onto the dirt path. My pulse kicked up. He didn't say anything as he drove a short way to a wooded section of his property, then parked. He killed the engine, plunging us into silence except for the sound of our breaths.

Connor turned in his seat, eyes dark, intense. "Say it again."

The air between us crackled.

I swallowed. "I love you."

His restraint snapped.

In an instant, he was on me—unbuckling my seatbelt, pulling me into his lap. My hands found his face, his hair, desperate to be as close as possible. His lips crashed into mine, hot and urgent. I gasped as he tilted my head, deepening the kiss, his hands roaming, gripping, claiming.

I pressed against him, the firm lines of his body igniting something deep inside me.

"I want you," I breathed against his lips.

A rough exhale left him. "Not here." His voice was tight, strained. "I need you in my bed."

I shivered at the promise in his words.

He wasted no time starting the ATV again, peeling out onto the road, his grip on my thigh enough to set my entire body on fire.

We barely made it through the front door before Connor had me pressed against the wooden surface, his mouth claiming mine, his hands seeking, possessive. My hands worked at the buttons of his dress shirt, sliding it off his shoulders before tossing it aside. He was all heat and muscle, and I drank him in—every inch of his six-foot frame.

His hands found the zipper at the back of my suit, and with a slow, torturous pull, the fabric slipped from my body. I gasped as the cool air met my skin, but Connor was already there, pressing kisses along my jaw, my neck, my shoulder.

"You looked so damn good tonight," he murmured, voice thick. "Had to stop myself from pulling you into a dark corner and kissing you senseless."

I grinned against his lips. "Nothing's stopping you now."

A growl rumbled in his chest, then he lifted me effortlessly, carrying me down the hall.

We collapsed onto his bed in a tangle of limbs, laughter mingling with gasps as we made up for lost time. His hands, his mouth—he knew exactly how to unravel me. And I let him, surrendering completely.

He slid inside of me, stretching, filling me, familiar and yet this time it felt *different*, somehow better. My heart was open, light. Nothing constricted my chest, and for the first time in several weeks, I could breathe freely. And *God,* did I bask in the sensations that flooded me in waves, relentless, unbidden.

Connor thrust deeper, and I let out a sharp, carefree cry of pleasure. He cursed under his breath as I trembled beneath him.

"Connor," I nearly sobbed, "Make me yours."

The words were a desperate plea. A dark need I couldn't name—only feel, sharp and consuming.

His speed quickened. "Fuck, Lucy. You're mine. *Only* mine. Now and always. And I'm yours."

"Yes," I cried out as I shuddered around him.

We stayed like that for a blissful eternity, neither of us willing to break the connection.

Sometime later, tangled in the sheets and each other, I traced my fingers along the strong planes of his chest, my cheek resting against the crook of his shoulder. His arm was draped over my waist, fingertips drawing lazy patterns along my hip.

The adrenaline from the night had finally burned out, leaving behind bone-deep contentment.

For a while, we lay there, our breathing syncing together as one.

Then, softly, Connor said, "How are you feeling after everything?"

A slow smirk rose across my face. "That was earth-shattering." I chuckled as I snuggled closer into him, wrapping my leg over his waist.

A low rumble of laughter vibrated from his chest through my entire body. "That's nice to hear. I meant about tonight, Amanda, the gala. Everything."

I let out a slow breath, considering my answer. "Relieved. A little overwhelmed. But mostly... happy."

He pressed a kiss to my temple. "Good."

I propped myself up on my elbow, looking down at him. "What about you?"

His expression turned thoughtful. "God, I was so pissed when Amanda grabbed that mic. I couldn't believe she went to such lengths to sneak in, and the rage I felt seeing her again..." He swallowed. "But then, Sam," he shook his head. "I don't think I've ever been prouder of him."

I smiled. "Me too."

Connor's fingers tucked a loose strand of hair behind my ear. "And you. What you said up there." His eyes softened. "You didn't have to do that."

"Yes, I did." I brushed my thumb over his cheekbone. "I don't want to lie anymore. I could tell it was bothering you, and it was starting to wear down on me. I think it was slowly slipping into breaking our 'no drama' promise. And besides, the women around here need to know you're not single. I think there were a lot of hearts broken tonight," I teased.

"Oh geez, Lucy." He chuckled. "I don't know about all that, but that was definitely the most romantic thing anyone's ever done for me."

I pressed a gentle kiss to his jaw. "That... is heartbreaking. I was just fixing the mess I made."

"By declaring to the world you're madly, deeply... 'head-over-heels,' was it?" His grin widened, the smile reaching his eyes.

"Oh God." I groaned, feeling laughter bubbling up in my chest. "I can't believe I said that. It's true, but ugh, so cheesy!"

We lay there laughing together for a moment.

Then—

A long, heavy pause stretched between us.

Connor shifted, rolling onto his side, his expression suddenly guarded.

I knew that look.

The moment of peace was about to break.

Sadness crept into the small lines creasing the corners of his sky blue eyes.

"I don't want to talk about it yet," I whispered.

His lips pressed together. "Luce—"

I closed my eyes. "I just want to stay here, in this moment. With you."

His chest rose and fell beneath my hand. "Me too." He exhaled slowly. "But we need to talk about it. We've avoided it long enough. One business meeting and a handful of brief mentions doesn't count as discussing this as a couple."

I sighed, knowing he was right.

I was leaving.

Again.

My stomach knotted as reality set in.

"The idea of leaving you, leaving home again, it's a whole other kind of grief I don't know what to do with. Connor... how can I do this? As much as this is important, part of me would rather quit school than go finish. After everything that's happened. After everything I've established here. After we've solidified our relationship. This is going to be so hard, in so many ways." I admitted, my voice barely above a whisper.

Connor's hand found mine. "It's only a year. We'll figure it out."

Tears burned at the backs of my eyes. "I don't want to lose this." I squeezed his hand. "I don't want to lose *us*."

"You won't." His grip tightened. "Long-distance isn't ideal, but it's temporary, and you can't quit when you're so close to finishing your undergrad. You'd regret it the rest of your life."

I blinked up at him. "What if it's harder than we think?"

Connor's expression softened. "Then we work through it. One day at a time."

I bit my lip. "I've never done this before."

"Neither have I," he admitted. "But, I'm pretty sure we've both been through worse."

I nodded, fighting back the emotion rising in my throat. I didn't know if I should laugh or cry.

Connor cupped my face, his thumb sweeping over my cheek. "Luce, I love you. And I know you're scared. But nothing about that changes just because you're in London, and I'm here. If anyone can do this, it's us. I never stopped loving you when you left the first time. And now that you're mine, there's no way in hell I'm going to let anything get in the way of us." He ran his hand over my cheek, forcing our eyes to lock, and it was like he could see into my soul. "I swear, Lucy, every day I fall more in love with you. I believe that means we're going to be okay. No matter what."

A tear slipped down my cheek. "You're really all in on this, aren't you?"

"Hell yes, I am." His lips curved into a small, reassuring smile. "You're it for me, Lucy Campbell. There's no one else. No one I'd rather wait for."

My breath hitched.

"Say it again," I whispered.

His gaze darkened, and his voice dropped to a husky murmur. "I love you."

I swallowed thickly. "I love you too."

He brushed his lips against mine, slow and sweet. "We can get through anything together."

I clung to him, letting his warmth, *his love*, wrap around me.

And in that moment, I believed him.

I believed in us.

CHAPTER THIRTY-FIVE

Your Favorite Dad

LUCY

I walked the pastures with an easy, unhurried peace, letting the crisp Montana air fill my lungs. In just two days, I'd have to head back to London.

But it no longer felt like home.

Connor did.

With Amanda denied bail and her father released on house arrest after posting his, the world seemed just a little bit brighter.

The morning after the gala, Connor and I woke up grinning at the article in *The White River Whisper* detailing the demise of the Johnson Family, along with another article announcing White River's "Most Eligible Bachelor" was taken. That one *still* brought a soft smile to my lips.

In the distance, Connor spotted me from horseback and rode up to meet me.

I bit my lip, letting my eyes roam. "Do you have any idea how unfairly attractive you are?"

He smirked. "Well, I do have a title to uphold—'Hottest Man in White River,' or so I've heard. Should I pull up the article to double-check?"

I rolled my eyes, swatting at the air between us. "Ugh. Don't believe everything you read."

He chuckled, then dismounted, stepping toward me. "Oh, I don't. I just take *your* word for it."

I rolled my eyes, and then it all hit me at once.

"I'm going to miss it here," I admitted, the familiar ache settling in my chest.

Connor's hands found my waist, pulling me flush against him. "I'm gonna miss you so much," he murmured. He lifted his cowboy hat off his head, using it to shield us from prying eyes. "So, I'm going to take advantage of the fact that you're still here... and kiss you right now. *During working hours.*"

I grinned as his lips met mine, slow and sweet.

"You should get going," I teased, stepping back. "Those cattle aren't going to cull themselves."

I turned, walking away with all the confidence in the world, throwing a glance over my shoulder. "Oh, and Connor?"

"Yeah?" He paused, adjusting his reins.

"You *are* the hottest man in White River."

His smile could have lit up the whole sky.

And with a tip of his hat, he rode off. His figure blending into the landscape of the ranch.

Unable to stop smiling, I turned and headed back up to the house.

There was one last item on my to-do list before I left for London.

It had taken me weeks to build up the courage. And now I was finally ready.

I walked into my father's bedroom, taking in the space. The solid wood bed frame and matching furniture. The dusty boots collapsed beside the bed. Simple, rustic, *him*.

I wanted to sort through his things, to decide what to keep, what to donate... It was the last piece of closure I needed.

My eyes caught on a white plastic bag lying on the bed. The name **Robert Campbell** was scrawled in black Sharpie.

I froze.

There it was.

The hospital bag.

My father's last belongings, untouched, waiting for me.

I swallowed and allowed myself to sit on the edge of the bed, carefully taking the thick, smooth plastic into my hands. I took a slow, steadying breath, then opened it.

Inside was his last outfit. Dust-ridden and well-worn. The scent of leather, dirt, bourbon, and sweat wafted out of the bag, wrapping around me like a ghost of a hug.

I pulled out each item, one by one.

His phone. His wallet. A Sudoku puzzle book. A pencil.

Then—

A carefully folded piece of paper.

My brow furrowed as I opened it.

My breath stopped.

It was a letter.

My name, in my father's familiar handwriting, scrawled at the top.

Heart pounding, I began to read.

Dearest Lucy—My favorite daughter,

If you're reading this, it means I never made it out of this damn hospital. And for that, sweetheart, I am so very sorry.

I need you to know something—I love you. More than I could ever put into words. And I am so damn proud of the woman you're becoming.

By now, I imagine you've got some questions. Probably a few choice words for me, too. And I suppose I owe you an explanation.

Let's start with the ranch.

You're probably wondering why I never told you I made you part owner of the ranch. I should have. And I'm sorry. When I visited you in London, that was the paperwork you were signing. I don't know why I went about it that way, but I had this feeling it was necessary, and I think I was scared to admit what it all meant. Still am if I'm being honest. I really thought we'd have more time together, but then again, maybe part of me didn't.

Anyway, I know you'll take good care of the ranch, Luce. You've got a good head on your shoulders, and you care about this land and the animals as much—if not more—than I do. If something happens to me, I don't want you wading through probate just to buy a sack of feed or make payroll. The work doesn't stop just because a Campbell kicks the bucket. This way, the ranch can keep running, no questions asked.

Which brings me to my next apology.

I may or may not have meddled a little when it comes to you and Connor... Alright, a lot.

I know I put you in an impossible situation with the stipulation in the will, and for that, I am sorry. But I have my reasons. And I figure by now, you've probably started to figure those out for yourself.

See, I saw the way you two looked at each other when you were kids, and I sure as hell saw how torn up he was after you left. That boy never stopped loving you, Lucy. Not for a second. And I know he's been through hell with that Amanda girl—(by the way, I never could stand her).

But Connor? He's a good man, Luce. One of the best I've ever known. And if you give him a chance, I think he'll prove that to you a hundred times over.

Laying it on thick, aren't I? But I bet it's working.

Now, for my last apology.

I'm sorry I let you leave home all those years ago.

I know it must've hurt, me not stopping you. But something was off back then, Luce. You'd come home from school quiet, you'd lost that Campbell spark in your eyes, like you were carrying something too heavy to put into words. I didn't know what it was, and I didn't push—maybe I should have.

I thought London might be good for you. Give you space. A fresh start. Maybe some new people to lean on.

And look at you now. Top of your class. Accepted to RVC. You took on the world and came out swinging. You're incredible.

All I've ever wanted was for you to be happy. And if my meddling ways weren't well received, I suppose I'll have to apologize for that, too.

Since I can't be there to tell you, whoever you choose to spend your life with, you have my blessing.

Especially if it's Connor. He's been like a son to me. And damn it, if I had my way, one day he'd be my son-in-law, too. It doesn't have to be him. But that sure would be something.

I love you, Lucy. Know that I'm always with you. I hope that even when I'm gone, you'll just feel it—know it deep down in your bones I'm still there, still rooting for you.

Love always,

Your favorite dad

Each word hit me like tiny raindrops, soft at first—until they built into a full-on downpour. By the time I reached the end, his message, his love, had soaked into me completely.

I cried. I laughed. And, for a moment, I had heard his voice as if he were right there beside me.

I pressed the letter to my heart. His words weren't just ink on a page.

They were *him*.

Tears blurred my vision as I whispered, "I do feel you, Dad. I love you so much. *Thank you.*"

I sat for a moment, shaking with a sob I hadn't even realized I'd been holding in.

Then, carefully, I folded the letter and tucked it into the breast pocket of my shirt. It felt good to keep it close.

And then, I got to work.

With each item, I made piles—keep, toss, donate, gift.

The work was draining—but also healing.

By the time the sun dipped below the horizon, his room was done.

I stood in the doorway, taking it all in. The space was still his. It always would be. While I technically owned the house now, this room... it didn't belong to me. Not yet.

But that was a matter for another day.

CHAPTER THIRTY-SIX

Exactly as It Should Be

LUCY

The small airport was quiet as Connor walked me to check my bags. My heart clenched as I turned to him, boarding pass safely saved to my phone.

I took one last, long look into his deep blue eyes.

"Promise me you'll take good care of Buddy."

"I will."

"And find those pups good homes?"

"Of course." He exhaled softly, tucking a loose strand of hair behind my ear with gentle fingers. "I know I've said it a million times, but we're all going to miss you. *Especially me.*"

Then he pulled me in, holding me against him.

Memories of my first night back flashed through my mind—the plane landing, the crushing weight of grief pressing down on me, losing it at baggage claim. *And then him.* Connor. His warmth. His steady hands. He'd made sure I wasn't *alone*.

I was crying in his arms again, just as I had then.

But this time, for completely different reasons.

He smiled, pressing his forehead to mine. "This is all just for now. You'll finish up school, and then you'll come home—to *our* home. Right?"

I took a deep breath. "Right."

I pulled him in for one last kiss, savoring the moment—the feel of him. *One last time.*

"See you soon."

"See you soon," he murmured. "I love you."

"Love you more."

He chuckled, that deep, familiar rumble. "We'll argue about that later."

I laughed through my tears and turned toward security.

I wasn't the same Lucy I was when I'd left London all those weeks ago.

I was someone stronger. More capable. Ready.

The next year would be nothing compared to the hell I'd survived already—losing my dad, facing Amanda, confronting my past, stepping into my role as a business owner.

An undergraduate degree and a long-distance relationship?

Those struggles would be a breeze by comparison.

And with that—

I stepped into the next chapter of my life.

No secrets.

No drama.

Everything was exactly as it should be.

Epilogue

The soft hum of the city wrapped around me as I leaned against the window of my London flat, watching the early evening bustle below. Lights flickered on in the neighboring buildings, and car horns punctuated the drizzling rain.

It was familiar now, the rhythm of London. But it still didn't feel like home.

Not like White River.

I felt like I was floating through my days, waiting to return to my real life.

My laptop screen glowed in the dim light, and Connor's face filled the frame. He was sitting on the oversized couch at his house, Buddy sprawled out beside him, his tail thumping lazily against the cushions. The warmth of the scene, the golden hue of the light behind him, made my heart ache.

"Hey, gorgeous," Connor's voice was smooth and steady, the hint of a smile tugging at his lips. "Buddy and I have been missing you something fierce."

I chuckled, my chest tightening. "I miss you guys too."

Connor smirked. "Yeah? How much have you missed us?" He leaned forward, resting his elbows on his knees.

"So much," I teased.

"No coffee yet, I take it?"

"Nope." I sighed, shaking my head. "Did you have a good lunch?"

"Leftover steak sandwich and fries." His warm voice blanketed me with comfort. "How's school? How's my favorite future vet holding up?"

I exhaled, pushing a hand through my hair. "Still not a vet yet..." I eyed him, and he gave me a knowing smirk as he took pleasure in irritating me. "I'm busy, *exhausted*. But good." And it was true. My courses at the Royal Veterinary College were demanding; however, I was thriving. I spent my days between lectures, labs, and clinical rotations, and my nights buried in textbooks. And somehow, in between, I managed to keep up with the ranch—weekly video calls, business meetings, reading reports, sending emails.

Whenever I could, I'd check the security cameras Connor installed to see how the animals were fairing. It was a delicate balance, but I was making it work. Thankfully, Connor held down the fort—more than capable of running the ranch without me—but he still kept me thoroughly involved as planned.

Connor's brow furrowed slightly. "You sleeping enough?"

I shot him a look.

"Lucy..."

I sighed. "What? I'm sleeping as much as I can."

"Uh-huh." He didn't look convinced. "And eating?"

"Connor, I swear—"

"Hey, I'm just making sure you're not wasting away over there," he teased, though his eyes softened. "You've got a lot on your plate, Luce. I just don't want you to forget to take care of yourself."

I nodded, swallowing past the lump in my throat. "I'm doing my best, Connor. I study, work, eat when I can, and sleep when I can. I'm not going out or socializing. I'm tired, but I'm *okay*."

"Well, maybe going out and having fun for a change wouldn't be a bad thing," he suggested, and though the screen became pixelated for a second, I could still see the deepening furrow of his brows.

I groaned. "There's not enough time in the day for fun."

"Fine." He sighed, then grinned, changing the subject. "So, when am I seeing you again?"

I smiled. "After exams. A couple more months, and then I'm home for a few weeks."

"Damn right, you are." His voice dropped, something deeper, more serious threading through it. "I can't wait to hold you again."

Heat bloomed in my chest. "Same."

Buddy let out a soft whine, as if sensing the moment, and I laughed. "Tell him I love him."

Connor rubbed Buddy's ears. "She loves you, boy." Then he glanced back at me. "And I do too, Luce."

"Love you more." My face split into a wide grin.

He scoffed, shaking his head. "Nope. Not possible."

I chuckled, biting my lip. "I should go. I'm meeting my study group at a coffee shop in a bit."

We had a standing late evening study group at seven thirty on Wednesdays. And ever the perfectionist, I always took advantage.

Connor nodded, his gaze lingering. "Call me later?"

"Always."

With one last smile, I blew a kiss and ended the call.

For a moment, I just sat there, staring at the blank screen, the quiet settling around me like a weight. *This was the hardest part of being here—hanging up.* Knowing that thousands of miles stretched between us.

Shaking off the melancholy, I grabbed my bag and my books and headed out into the cool London night.

The small café was bustling, the scent of espresso and fresh pastries. I spotted my study group in the corner, already deep into their notes, and made my way over, sliding into a chair with a tired sigh.

"Long day?" Olivia, one of my classmates, asked with a smirk.

"Always," I muttered, flipping open my notebook.

Olivia teased, "With a fit American cowboy ringing me at all hours, I wouldn't get a wink of sleep either."

I took a sip of my coffee, letting the warmth seep into my chest. I closed my eyes and gave myself a small, much-needed moment of reprieve.

The café was cozy. The hum of conversation, the scent of freshly brewed espresso—it was almost like home.

The conversation shifted to exams, case studies, and upcoming rotations, but I found my attention drifting. Maybe it was the exhaustion, or maybe it was just the city pressing in around me, but my gut felt... unsettled.

A prickle of awareness ran down my spine.

I lifted my gaze toward the counter—and saw him.

Callum.

He was standing near the register, waiting for his drink, his profile unmistakable.

That same confident stance. That perfectly tailored coat. That smug air that clung to him like a second skin.

My blood ran cold.

For a second, I thought I was imagining things.

But then—he turned.

And our eyes met.

A slow, knowing smile curved his lips.

Dread coiled in my stomach, thick and heavy.

He was *here*.

In London.

What was he doing back?

He was supposed to be studying in Cambridge.

Yet, here he was.

I couldn't breathe. My pulse pounded in my ears.

I hadn't seen him in years, but nothing had changed. The same easy arrogance. The same cold calculation in his dark eyes.

I gripped the edge of the table, forcing myself to stay composed.

He had no power over me.

Not anymore.

And yet—

As he lifted his cup in a mock toast, tilting it just slightly in my direction, a taunting reminder of a secret only *he* knew—

That awful feeling settled in my bones.

I closed my eyes and I saw it again.

The video.

His mask.

Pushing me down.

Holding me in place.

His hands gripping my neck.

My jaw clenched. Panic and fear pulsed through me, then was replaced with something else.

Pure. Unfiltered. *Rage.*

He'd been untouchable.

But maybe...

Just maybe—

I could make him face justice.

Take him down a notch and show him what it feels like to be helpless.

My hands tightened around my seat as I remembered to breathe.

And in that moment, I realized—this next year in London wasn't going to be as easy as I'd once so foolishly thought.

Afterword

Dear Reader,

Thank you for joining me on this journey. Writing *Love Me Through the Grief* has been one of the most meaningful and transformative experiences of my life. Through Lucy's story, I was able to explore my own grief—something deeply personal and, in many ways, healing.

I hope her story moved you as much as it moved me. Falling in love with Connor, watching Amanda finally get what she deserved, witnessing Sam's redemption—it was all incredibly satisfying. While I started with a clear outline, something beautiful happened along the way: the characters took on lives of their own. The dialogue, the emotions, the quiet moments—they began to shape the story in ways I didn't always anticipate, and that made writing this book an unforgettable ride.

This story began as a reimagining of how I lost my own father in 2020. I made Lucy younger, gave her a fictional hometown to return to, and built a world around her that echoed pieces of my own. Like Lucy, I faced toxic people during the hardest moments of grief—but I also had my people. My support system. My lifelines. That duality—grief and support, pain and love—is what I knew I needed to explore, and what I hope resonated with you.

Lucy's story continues in *Love Me Through the Storm*, which is currently in the works as of June 2025. Familiar faces will return, new journeys will begin, and—spoiler alert—yes, I believe Sam deserves a happy ending. His story may or may not be the focus of Book 3.

If you connected with this story, I'd be so grateful if you left a quick review on Amazon, Goodreads, Barnes & Noble, or shared it with your friends online. Reviews and reader support mean the world to indie authors like me—they help new readers find this book and keep these stories alive.

Finally, please remember: you deserve to be loved through all your grief, trauma, and humanness. You've got this. And I'm so honored you chose to be here with me.

With love,

J.S. Tazwell

www.jstazwell.com

Follow me:

Instagram, Threads, Facebook: @j.s.tazwell

TikTok, Lemon8: @authorj.s.tazwell

X (Twitter): @JSTazwell

Acknowledgements

Bringing *Love Me Through the Grief* into the world has been a journey of healing, heartache, and hope—and I could not have done it without you.

To everyone who believed in this book enough to back it on Kickstarter: thank you. Your support, encouragement, and trust gave this story the wings it needed. Every single pledge, comment, and share helped turn a deeply personal dream into a published reality.

You didn't just help fund a book, you helped me believe in myself as a writer.

A special thank you to my early backers and ARC readers who saw this story in its rawest form and offered their feedback and love without hesitation. Your words mattered more than you know.

To my husband, your love and support held me steady through every moment of doubt and overwhelm. I could never have done this without you.

To my editor, Derek Moreland, thank you for being both a brilliant editor and a loyal friend. Your unwavering belief in me, your thoughtful insight, and your fierce cheerleading helped shape this book into its best form.

To my friends, you encouraged me when I doubted myself, talked me down when I spiraled, and encouraged me through every draft, deadline, and late-night writing session. Thank you for showing up.

To Liz Bullard, thank you for allowing me to feature your generous review on the back of the cover. Your kind words captured the heart of this story so beautifully, and I'm deeply grateful.

And with heartfelt gratitude, I want to recognize the following backers for their generous support: Robin Barrett, Lacy, Kate Jolly, Dee Hausner, Leo, Myka, Etaine Raphael,

Silha Bess, Amanda Schmitt, Liz Bullard Writes, Tonya LeBlanc, Renée Elosgé Cólindres, Danielle Steimel, Sue Mills, and Selina Barrett . Your belief in this story means more than words can say.

To my friends, family, and readers who continue to champion *Love Me Through the Grief*—thank you for being part of this chapter. You are forever part of this book's story.

With love and gratitude,

J.S. Tazwell